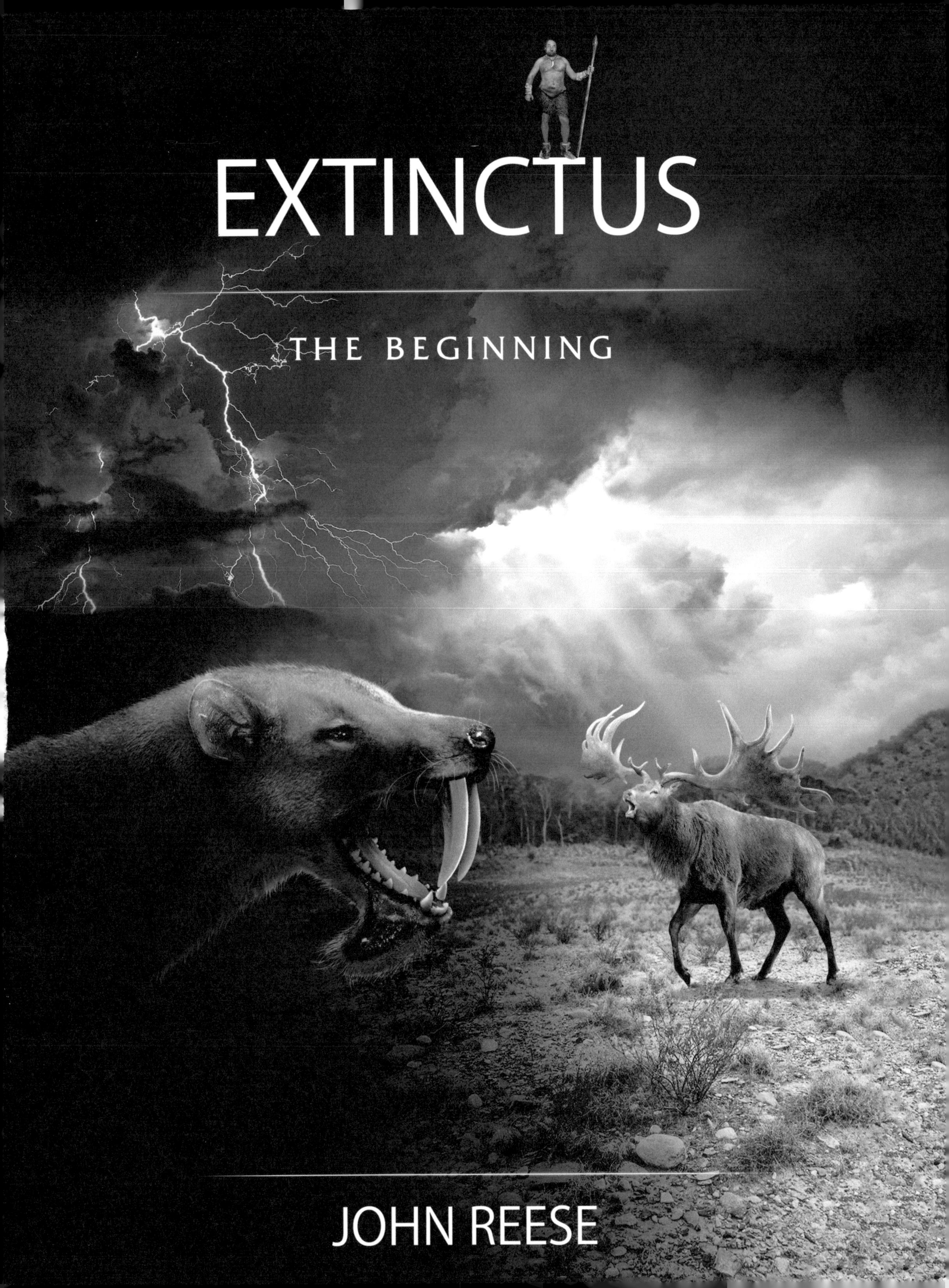
EXTINCTUS
THE BEGINNING
JOHN REESE

AuthorHouse™
1663 Liberty Drive
Bloomington, IN 47403
www.authorhouse.com
Phone: 833-262-8899

Interior Image Credit: Roman Uchytel

This book is printed on acid-free paper.

ISBN: 978-1-6655-0448-5 (sc)
ISBN: 978-1-6655-0449-2 (e)

Library of Congress Control Number: 2020920285

Print information available on the last page.

Published by AuthorHouse 07/14/2021

authorHOUSE®

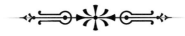

Table of Contents

Chapter 1

Curious Medicine

The heavy condensation from an early morning rainfall, clung tenaciously to the lush green foliage of the surrounding sub-tropical jungle, like the inside of a massive terrarium. The mist from the nearby waterfall added to the gloomy, foggy morning. The early light of day slowly penetrated the tree top canopy, gently filtering its life-giving rays to the dense forest floor below. The lone random song of an early bird announced the break of dawn. Small, warm blooded mammals scampered beneath the rotting vegetation, vegetation amassed from the leaves of giant trees, trees reluctant to give up their foliage. This scene, normal to this lush environment, played out for millennium: only the species, both plant and animal, changed over time.

Millions of species slowly evolved over millions of years, as Earth metamorphosed. The seas raged, claiming new territories, until they eventually receded as land masses reclaimed ancient sea-beds. Land masses violently collided, resulting in severe continental upheaval, upheavals that caused mountains to lift to the heavens. In other situations, entire land masses became isolated, causing divergence of species both plant and animal. Life forms exploded, evolving to fit every niche in the environment. Only a few of these life forms, in correlation to the scope of species, were successful. Most genera ventured down evolutionary dead ends. They were either unable to adapt to the changing environment, or they became too specialized as their prey species evolved to run faster and think smarter. Some species were lucky; most were unlucky.

Millions of species have evolved on Earth, 99% of them have gone extinct. The greater part of this 99% naturally died out, but many species were decimated by the hand of one species—Homo sapiens, and they fell into extinction. Humans, in only a brief span in geological time, have altered the course for millions of species. The human conquest to dominate all other species through domestication or domination, has led to the extinction of millions of species. If a species was stronger, humans wiped it out. If a species was weaker, they exploited it. Such was the evolution of the hominid. This tale is the story of what can happen when humans go too far. My name is Fire Eagle, a native Lakota Sioux. My twin brother, Takoda, bears witness to the unbelievable story that follows. At first, I was unaware that my brother had any part in this tale, but as I read from various journal entries and countless notes, his involvement became quite clear to me.

It was early summer in the year 2010 when I ventured into the South Dakota wilderness to live off the land for the summer. I went alone, to gather my thoughts and enjoy the isolation nature gives for those who seek it. Some may call it a quest, but I prefer to look at it as a spiritual retreat. The elders of my tribe selected me to train and learn the ways of the medicine man, the man responsible for the inner sanctum and spiritual vigor of the tribe. This was no small task and carried great responsibility.

Why chosen for such a role, I often wondered, but such are the ways of the unexplainable— the elders saw some hidden potential in my being. So, with great purpose I entered the badlands to seek spiritual guidance. The spiritual future of my tribe rested on my shoulders.

Towards the end of the long summer, as I contemplated what it meant to be a medicine man, I became rejuvenated by my journey to return to nature, so I decided to pack up camp the next day and return to civilization. I spent the evening sitting peacefully by a large campfire, occasionally moving away from the fire light to gaze up at the nighttime sky, a sky filled with millions of tiny, varying illuminations of refracted light. The moon revealed itself to me sometime around midnight. Its luminescence further lit up the surrounding landscape. At peace with myself, with nature, and with the world, I realized it was time to return home.

I retired to my tepee shortly after the moon appeared in the nighttime sky and fell into a deep, restive sleep, the kind that induces dreams; the type of dreams one remembers without much difficulty and can deeply affect the unconscious dreamer when they awake. I became completely absorbed in this dreaming state, impervious to the outside world, until a strange light filtered into the tepee causing me to lose contact with my sub-conscious reality dream.

The strange light moved into the tepee accompanied by a dense fog, a fog which magnified the intensity of the bluish light. Now fully awake, I sat up and gazed at the approaching blue light, which manifested itself in the form of a bluish orb that was two feet in diameter. Stunned by the magnificent display of energy, I quickly moved closer to the edge of the tepee to escape under the canvas if necessary.

The blue orb started to oscillate, creating a loud buzzing sound, as it increased in rotational velocity. This increase in speed frightened me, causing me to lift the outer edge of the tepee and slip one leg under the side wall so I could escape the strange ball of spinning energy if I felt threatened.

Before I could get my second leg under the heavy wall, the blue orb disintegrated into thousands of tiny particles, which flew around the interior of the tepee until colliding in the center of the room. The particles miraculously transformed into a white, hairless, human-like form.

After several minutes, the shape completed its amazing transformation, which culminated when the hairless humanoid spoke.

"Don't be afraid," the strange creature said as it looked around my primitive shelter. "I'm not here to harm you. I've come to tell you an astonishing story, so it is recorded."

Calmed by the soft-spoken words of the life form, I pulled myself back into the tepee, stood up and walked closer to the white, human-like creature. The intruder motioned for me to follow him outside by pointing to the flap which covered the opening to the tepee.

I followed the odd being outside and asked, "What do you want with me? Where did you come from?"

Once outside the tepee, the humanoid bent down, picked up a large leather pouch filled with various notes and wrinkled manuscripts, and handed it to me.

"These are the only written records of the events that have happened so far," the white hominid explained, as he gazed at my physical appearance with a bewildered look on his face.

"You look very familiar."

Well...I can assure you; I haven't seen anything like you before."

The white, hairless human replied, "I need you to be witness to this story, in case the unimaginable happens. I have come from a world called Extinctus, a world were all extinct species still exist as they did when they roamed your planet. Extinctus is as ancient as the planet Earth, full of millions of species living as they did in their own time, struggling to survive day in and day out. On Earth, 99% of all species have gone extinct; some by natural selection, others by failed evolutionary experimentation, some by not changing as the climate and environment evolved, and many by the hand of the human species. It is this latter one, extinction by the hand of your species, which brings me to your world. Occasionally, under the rarest of conditions, our two worlds become intertwined, overlapping for brief periods of time. One of these rare events is recorded in the notes and manuscripts I just handed you."

The human-like creature pointed again to the leather pouch in my hands, then continued, "I know this is unbelievable for you, but I reassure you it's very real. I'm not here to scare or harm you in any way, I'm merely doing as instructed. Someone in your world needs to know the truth and be available to help us, if needed, when the time comes."

"But why me?"

The humanoid stared at me through extremely large orbital sockets and said, "You are somehow linked to our world, but I do not have that answer for you. If needed someday, you will get the answer you wish, but now I must get ready to leave. I cannot sustain my energy long in this world."

The white, hairless human bid me farewell, bent down and picked up a beautiful ivory object still lying on the ground where the leather pouch once laid. The unusual human walked a few feet from me, muttered a series of numbers and words, then vanished.

I watched in disbelief as the strange human-like creature disappeared as quickly as it had appeared. Shaking my head, briefly stunned by the bizarre encounter, I slowly walked back into the tepee.

I was unable to sleep, so I turned on a battery-operated light hanging from one of the tepee poles and opened the leather pouch. I removed from the weathered pouch a thick, makeshift binder holding many documents, along with drawings of strange creatures, and territorial maps rich in detailed specifics.

I spent months studying the material from the leather pouch in detail. The material outlined a curious tale, one more peculiar than any I had heard or read about and portrayed realistic drawings of beasts never seen by the human eye. Creature's horrendously hideous, stupendously strange, breathtakingly beautiful and marvelously magnificent, enriched the precious documents. The pages chronicled a myriad of rare species, ones that roamed the Earth long before the evolution of humans, others alongside the various stages of human development, and some without humans even realizing they existed at all.

Some stories are true, some are fiction, and others fall somewhere in between; I will let you decide this one. I will try to re-create the tale as best as possible from the materials given to me by the white, hairless humanoid. At times I will rely entirely on the manuscripts, yet at other times, I will embellish the story for story telling sake.

As the heavy condensation filtered over the tree top canopy, the forest floor, damp from the decay of countless deteriorating leaves, smelled foul, as the pungent odor of decaying vegetation permeated the thin morning air. A slight breeze, one unable to move through the thick dense forest below, wafted through the treetops. Thin rays of morning sunlight randomly penetrated the upper barrier of thick leaves to strike at the dark almost impenetrable world below.

Two worlds existed, one high up, and one down low, each a macrocosm created by the presence or absence of light. Creatures, adapted to one world or the other, scurried, jumped or flew about, some living entirely inside one sphere, never entering the other one.

As the early morning dew evaporated from the upper world, a man walked silently through the underworld. One cautious step after another, he moved through the forest, tracking an elusive, solitary creature. The lone man, around 40 years old, carried a large caliber rifle in his hands. The occasional ray of light, cast down from the high canopy above, glimmered off the cold, steel barrel.

The hunter, paying extra attention to detail, walked slowly through the sub-tropical jungle. He positioned himself against the wind, to hide his scent from his potential quarry. The morning coolness wore off as he traveled deeper and deeper into the unfamiliar forest. The dew on the leaves evaporated in the warming air.

He came to a small creek, one that ran down slope and vanished somewhere in the valley below. The water was a cool relief from the rising temperature of the late morning sun. The heavily bearded man washed his face and hands in the refreshing water then decided to travel along the creek up slope to reach a higher vantage point and gain elevation. If he could find an opening in the thick forest above, he would sit and watch a game trail in hopes of finding his elusive quarry.

The stalking hunter traversed the difficult terrain, slowly moving farther and farther up the steep, riverbank. The dense forest stopped just short of the rocky riverbed which allowed the hunter to evade the thickest areas of the foliage. He walked for hours, stopping often to listen and survey the surrounding area for the slightest noise or tiny flash of movement, either by animal or rustling leaf.

By mid-day, the man reached the top of the creek where it pulsated through a rocky opening in the sandstone cliffs which littered the upper part of the valley. The hunter, now able to look back down the meandering creek, could see just how dense the sub-tropical forest was. Some of the trees were over 100 feet high, as they strained to gain the life-giving rays of sunshine cast down by our enigmatic star.

The tired hunter stopped briefly to rest and re-energize in the cool creek water. He moved to the bank and carefully examined his rifle magazine. The rifle held up to six cartridges, each capable of dealing out death to any unsuspecting creature which crossed his path. The focused hunter, satisfied that the rifle had all six bullets in it, stood up and entered a small cavern in the sandstone cliff and vanished out of sight.

The dark, humid cavern, carved out by running water for millennium, allowed the hunter a passageway from one part of the forest to another. He walked for about 100 yards before the light reached him from the cavern opening on the other side. The man, out of caution, stopped before exiting the cavern. A slight breeze blew towards him, which was a good omen. He was up wind from his potential quarry, which gave him an edge.

After sensing no danger, the hunter moved out of the cavern and into the forest once again. On this side of the forest, the atmosphere was heavy and the climate gloomy. A constant drizzle layered the leaves and drenched the dense ground. The absence of sound perplexed the hunter as he slowly walked away from the sandstone cliffs and deeper into the forest.

The dampening drizzle kept the persistent insects at bay, which was a welcome relief to the tired hunter. He leaned up against a massive eucalyptus tree, its thick branches extending towards the heavens. The immensity of their leaves offered some protection from the chilly rain.

The weary hunter pondered his quandary. Should he start back, returning to his vehicle for the night, or take his chances and stay in this strange unfamiliar forest? If he left now, he might make it back before nightfall—perhaps. Either decision was a risk. He could easily become disoriented and find himself lost or slip and fall and injure himself on the journey back to his vehicle.

The man decided on the latter and searched for a place to shelter for the night. He needed both security from prowling beasts and protection from the harsh elements of the rain. He walked for a mile until he spotted a rocky outcrop, jutting out on the far side of the forest. It looked promising, so the man picked up his pace to cross the last stand of giant trees and reach the rocks.

He reached the outcrop as the drizzle turned to a heavy, thunderous rain. A small cave, carved out by thousands of years of rain and erosion, rested, partially exposed some ten feet off the ground. The hunter searched until he found a way up the rocky outcrop and onto the ledge which supported the cave. He pulled out a blanket from his pack and placed it on the ground to help alleviate the dampness of the stone.

Once done preparing his bedding, the hunter took some jerky from his pack and took a long refreshing drink from this canteen. He settled in for a long night. All the wood in the general vicinity was wet or rotten due to the heavy rainfall, so a fire was not possible. He would have to survive the night without the warmth and added protection a fire gives.

The man dozed off temporarily. His mind was heavy with thoughts of his family. A son he barely knew, a wife he rarely saw. He traveled all the time in his job and with his free time he hunted. His son, now just ten years old, spent most of his time with his mother and her family.

A loud cry shattered his self-brooding sleep. The hunter snapped out of his dreaming state and popped up from his blanket. The piercing scream penetrated the night air like a heavy burst of thunder. The tired, startled man crept back closer to the wall of the cave and peered out into the pitch-black night. He strained his eyes as he focused on one area of the pitch-black forest to another, trying to find the direction of the mysterious sound.

The strange sound rattled the hunter. He had killed many a beast in his time, but this sound in the dead of the night shook him. The sound did not break the silence again, and before long the tired hunter dozed off in the relative security of the hidden cave up on the out-crop shelf.

The hunter woke up as the light of a new dawn broke the misty morning dreariness. He stood up to stretch his tired bones before climbing down the ledge, back down to the small opening below. The night had been long and chilly, but he hoped the inconvenience would culminate with the prize he looked for.

The man, now fully alert, slowly entered the thick forest to search for his unsuspecting prey. He moved through the trees without making a sound. He could see a small opening some distance ahead and moved towards it, slowly testing the air for sound and scent. The giant trees parted just enough to expose a small meadow; a small beacon of green grass nestled in amongst the massive guards of various tree species.

The hunter suddenly stopped at the edge of the meadow, cautiously hiding behind a giant tree. He looked over the clearing for any sign of impending danger before moving out into the open. About halfway into the meadow, the cautious man bent down to look at a print in the mud. The print was faint, but his experienced eye recognized the tell-tale sign. It was the print of a Thylacine, also known as a Tasmanian tiger.

The Thylacine, an exceedingly rare Marsupial carnivore, once lived in this part of the world. When the last known specimen died in a zoo in 1933, the species made the extinct list. There were many sightings of the marsupial over the years since 1933, but no solid proof or documentation through photographs of its existence ever surfaced.

The hunter knew otherwise. Word had spread about a sighting in these parts, and he quickly set up travel plans to search for the secretive creature. It would make a fine addition to his collection of rare species to hang on his wall. To the hunter, the rareness of the beast did not penetrate his comprehension. It was but one more thing to dominate and conquer.

The man, now on full alert, searched the immediate vicinity for any visual sign of the creature. Not seeing the beast, he followed the tracks back into the trees. The prints of the solitary animal led in a wide circle around the outer edges of the meadow. They led him into the trees and back into the meadow several times before vanishing in the forest.

By mid-day, the trail had gone cold, but the hunter, now invigorated by the adrenaline of his rare find, pressed on after his elusive prey. He followed the last tracks deep into the thick foliage, hoping to pick up the trail once again. The under growth was damp from the constant barrage of moisture, moisture which assaulted the forest daily. Soaked from the waist down from trampling through the thick wet grass that grew abundant in the rainy, humid environment, the hunter pressed on.

Several hours later, the man spotted the tracks of the Thylacine once again. The lone beast headed back in the direction of the isolated small cave, the cave the hunter had spent the previous night in. Motivated by his discovery, the hunter followed the tracks back through the forest, towards the outcrop and the small cave.

The tracks led directly to the outcrop. The hunter cautiously stopped at the edge of the forest, just a few hundred yards from the cave. He checked the wind direction, quietly chambered a round, and patiently waited. He pulled out his binoculars and surveyed the area beneath the ledge which led to the entrance of the cave, and then around the opening to the cave.

Not seeing the creature, the hunter crept closer to the large outcropping. The sun started to set and the evening gloom slowly filtered in. Soon the natural light would fade, leaving the hunter no choice but to give up the hunt. This could be his only chance he thought as he quietly pushed forward towards the cave. His adrenaline surged as he neared the rock outcropping.

A faint sound broke the evening air waves. The hunter froze, all his senses on alert. He strained to see through the fading light, further hindered by the murkiness of the persistent rain. The sound reoccurred, this time from up on the ledge in front of the small cave.

The hunter, sure the sound came from above, lifted his rifle up to his arm and looked through the scope. The sound continued and grew louder as the hunter moved towards the rocks once again. He was ready to squeeze the trigger as he slowly walked forward.

A shape appeared on the ledge. A lone creature exited the cave and walked to the edge of the shelf to sniff for danger. It peered over the ledge in the general direction of the hunter. The wind shifted. A faint breeze blew towards the solitary animal, coming from the direction of the hunter. The beast wheeled to flee.

The hunter, fully aware of the changing wind direction, stopped and raised his rifle. He focused on the ledge, straining to see in the dimming light. He spotted his prey as it bolted from the edge of the ledge and then he fired his rifle.

The hunter heard a tremendous thud as the bullet hit flesh and bone. His heart raced as he chambered another round. He ran towards the rock outcrop, stopping just beneath the ledge. He realized he hit his mark, but in no way could he be sure the creature was dead.

The beast, as it tried to wheel and run, felt the sting of the bullet as it entered its flesh. It let out a thunderous cry as the bullet tore through its body. Blood poured from the fatal wound on to the rain cleansed rock shelf. The struggling creature moved towards the cave entrance, entering the darkness of the cave and collapsed.

The energized hunter heard the shrill scream of the dying animal and the hair on the back of his neck stood erect. He realized his bullet had hit its mark and he pressed on. He climbed up to the rock shelf in front of the cave and stopped. A mortally wounded animal is a dangerous animal. The hunter knew from the death cry of the beast that his quarry would die, it was only a question of when.

The hunter walked to the opening of the cave and stopped. It was dangerous and unwise to follow the wounded creature into the dark cave, but unsure of where the cave led, he did not want the injured creature to escape through an opening at the rear of the cavern, so he withdrew his hunting knife, the stainless steel blade glistening in the faint light, and entered the lightless cave.

The cave, now pitch black, due to the encroachment of night outside, opened to a large cavern. The hunter quickly clicked on his flashlight to allow some light to filter into the cave directly in front of him. The man struggled to hold the flashlight and keep his right finger on the trigger of his rifle. If the wounded animal attacked, he had but an instant to fire his weapon.

He continued deeper into the cave until he heard the faint sound of laborious breathing, which caused him to abruptly stop. He cautiously moved the flashlight from side to side, looking for the wounded Thylacine. The sound of the dying beast, taking its last gasps of oxygen, made the hunter overzealous and he picked up his pace to find the suffering creature. The man, now confident his bullet hit its mark, frantically searched for the dying marsupial. He pressed on only a few feet before the light from his flashlight reflected off the eyes of the injured animal.

The hunter quickly moved towards the Thylacine and stopped just a few feet in front of the lethargic beast. He moved his light over the body of the marsupial to see if the creature could move. The Thylacine gasped as it labored to take in oxygen into its massive chest. It tried to crawl off but collapsed only a few feet from where it had lain.

Not wanting the animal to suffer, the hunter put down his rifle and continued with just his large hunting knife. He moved towards the dying animal. The suffering Thylacine stared at the hunter with questioning eyes and uncanny bewilderment as the human closed in. This encounter would be the Thylacine's only one with the human species.

The Thylacine's breathing slowed even further as the hunter moved in to finish the kill. The hunter, realizing the animal did not have the energy to fight back, knelt next the dying Thylacine and placed his hand on the striped fur of the marsupial predator and gently stroked the dying beast.

The man did have compassion for the creature and quietly muttered some words before plunging the knife blade into the heart of the fading beast. The Thylacine let out one last deep gasp as the hunter held onto the knife with one hand the held the creature down with the other.

As life left the body of the Thylacine, both man and beast vanished without a trace. The last Thylacine, also known as the Tasmanian tiger, killed deep inside a cave, miles inside an ancient forest, was now extinct. **(Image 1: Thylacine: page 128)**

Chapter 2

The Site

The notes from the manuscripts abruptly ended about the hunter and the now extinct Thylacine. Before reading on, I searched through the material looking for any supplemental information revealing the strange disappearance of both man and beast, but I won't reveal their role in the tale at this point for story telling sake. Their involvement struck me as very odd, but to this juncture, the entire series of events seemed unnatural, so I continued to read through the manuscript. From here on out, I will try to stay out of the narrative and do my best to detail the story without further interruption.

The story picked up again several decades later with a man named Eric Asvaldsson, a young professor at Montana State University in Bozeman, Montana. Eric was a tall, muscular man, standing around 6 feet 5 inches tall. He taught Anthropology and Archaeology with exceptional enthusiasm, trying to pass his exuberance on to his students. Every year in late spring, the entry level class in archaeology would work a pre-historic chert mine above the Missouri River, several miles from the town of Three Forks. Three Forks derived its name from the convergence of three rivers, the Gallatin, the Jefferson, and the Madison. These three rivers merge to form the beginning of the mighty Missouri River in Montana.

For decades, the students, all tasked to work at least 40 hours at the site, traveled to the mine to dig and shift through the layers of dirt and rock. They searched for any sign of early human activity. This chert mine dated back some 10,000 years to the Pelican Lake people. The mine, often visited by these early humans, supplied this precious mineral, one highly prized for making tools and weapons. The class offered acuity into the physical aspects involved in archaeology. It takes 1000's of hours of sweat and labor, sometimes in harsh conditions, to un-earth the past mysteries of our world.

Eric Asvaldsson, eager to set up the site for the new group of fervent laborers, enlisted the help of five of his friends. Some were former students, and some were just friends. Eric became a professor at an early age, which closed the gap on himself and some of the older students, so naturally he found friendship and shared similar interests with many of his past students.

Spring came early that year, so the group decided to visit the dig site and set up the equipment needed to work the mine. They brought camping gear, so they could stay at the site for several days. The group included Eric Asvaldsson, Takoda Fire Eagle, Lexa Carerra, Maka Dove, CeCe Davis and Hope Alexander.

The six friends were eager to escape the dreary, winter confinement, confinement that kept them from journeying into the great outdoors. Each member, for individualized personal reasons, looked forward to the adventure, the companionship, and mostly the escape from the everyday monotony of life. It was a welcome relief to leave the books behind, replacing them with fishing gear and outdoor camping equipment, as they eagerly ventured into the wilderness.

The outdoors relaxed them, allowing each the opportunity to marvel at its immense beauty and peaceful solitude; the sway of the trees, the sound of the river, the rush of the wind, all contributed to this tranquility.

It was April, a little early for overnight camping, but the group needed the break, so they decided to risk the weather. The nights were cold this time of the year, so they planned appropriately, bringing wintry weather apparel and gear to keep them warm during the night once they left the warmth of the fire to enter the tents.

The group arrived in the early afternoon as the temperature for the day reached its highest point. The warm rays of the sun penetrated the forest floor along the river, beginning the thawing process, which in a few weeks would lead to the explosion of plant growth on the forest floor—below the upper canopy of the trees. Lush grasses, flowering plants, succulent raspberries, and a multitude of other plant species would spring to life to feed the myriad of creatures suppressed for months by the frigid winter.

They unloaded the equipment for the dig site on the upper plain close to the mining site. This consisted mostly of screens for shifting through the dirt removed from the mine. Many fascinating artifacts, unearthed at this location remain on archive back at the university, and remain on display to this day. These consisted of projectile points, bone tools and even a prehistoric pygmy dog.

The party settled on a secluded spot down by the river, out of the wind that constantly blew above the river, on the open plain which spread out on top of the bluff. A storm could form at any time and drench them if they placed their tents out in the open, but the riverbank offered the protection of trees, their tiny forming leaves giving some relief if it rained.

They agreed to pitch the tents under a tall stand of pine trees to help reduce the chance of getting wet if the weather suddenly changed as is so often the case in the Rocky Mountains. Eric and Tak went off to gather firewood, disappearing into the thick underbrush of fallen trees and snapped off branches, scattered around the area by violent displays of raw nature.

The other members of the group stayed behind to get the camp organized. They built a large fire pit so they could have a big fire. One of the primary reasons for going camping, besides enjoying the peaceful tranquility, was the flame. Humans have a primordial urge dwelling deep inside them towards the power of the flame—so, the more firewood the better to burn big, hot, and deep into the night.

The group always searched for a few good stumps while out collecting firewood. Once fully ignited, a stump would burn intensely hot with a large mesmerizing, flickering flame, silently weaving its way through the tangled maze of what was once a trees root system.

Eric and Tak came to a large opening in the trees and found an abundant source of dead fall that would make a good dent in the fuel needed to burn deep into the night. They spotted at least two good stumps they could return for later if they needed too.

Eric turned to Tak and said, "Hey, hold out your arms and I will load you up."

"Why don't you hold out your arms instead? Your wingspan is much larger than mine and you can carry more wood."

The native laughed as he held out his arms.

Eric loaded Tak up with as much wood as he could carry, then held out one of his own arms, stacking the wood up as high as he could. He then grabbed a large stump with his free hand and the two headed back towards camp.

"We'll have to make a few trips to get enough to burn all night."

Tak shook his head in acknowledgement. The two had a good relationship and often razzed each other.

They carried the load of wood back to camp as dusk was just starting to cast its shadow on the treetops.

"We have arrived with the means to create fire," Eric jokingly shouted.

Eric liked to make offbeat comments, comments with satirical meanings that others did not always grasp. He could not understand their inability to see the same humor he found in these comments.

"We come in peace," Tak added as he dropped the firewood on the ground by the fire pit.

CeCe responded back, "Well it's about time. We thought you two got lost."

CeCe was a talker not a worker. He would exercise all day to play football, but when tasked with manual labor, he usually found something else to do or vanished briefly.

The girls, familiar with the smack talk between the boys, just shook their heads. Occasionally they would take part in the banter, but usually they just ignored it.

"We have the tents and the sleeping bags set up already," Hope answered back as she laughed.

Lexa and Maka both smiled, joined in on ribbing the men, then went down to look at the river. The women were very task oriented, always finishing a task with speed and efficiency.

The fire started quickly as the flames engulfed the dry wood. Within thirty minutes, the embers were large enough to sustain even the largest pieces of wood. The group gathered around the fire as dusk fell upon the mountains and shadows started to appear high up in the trees. The smoke from the flames rose into the cool, brisk evening, flowing out over the river, traveling downstream just above the strong current.

It was common for the temperature to rapidly drop when the sun faded this time of the year in the mountains. As the fire grew larger, the group moved closer to its radiant heat and talked about the break from school, a much-needed escape from its hectic pace.

In a few short months, some of the group would graduate, which meant the end to carefree days, the end to long nights of deep conversation, and the end to these magnificent camping trips. They would move on to pursue their individual careers, each going their separate way. This was their reality, one chapter ending, while another one began.

Although graduating would be an accomplishment, it also meant the end to the close bonds they had developed. Distance has a way of alienating friendships as time erodes the intricate layers of commonality. They would miss the outdoor trips together, the endless discussions deep into the hours of the day or night, and the closeness they now shared. Deep down, they each realized this might be the last time they would all be together, and a quiet sadness was ever present. The relentless revolving sphere of life was continually pulling each of them in their own direction. The time was nearing for each of them to enter a new phase in their own personal evolution.

The group cooked up some steaks, grilled to perfection on the open flame. They enjoyed the civilized luxury afforded them by way of the cooler—ice cold beverages, steaks, mushrooms and baked potatoes with all the trimmings.

After dinner, the small group sat by the open fire and enjoyed the heating embers as the coolness of the night air settled in. As soon as the sun vanished on the horizon, the temperature dropped drastically. A deep chill blew in from over the wide river, as the air mixed with the cooling water, water sourced from deep inside Yellowstone National Park.

As the night went by the flames dwindled, and the embers quietly sizzled, as the light from the flame started to fade. They drifted off to the tents one by one until only Eric and Tak stayed by the glowing embers. They gazed up at the star filled sky, deep into space. The Milky Way lit up the night sky with its brilliant display of intense flickering light. It was times like this when Eric and Tak felt their insignificance; the small role the Earth, a small pebble in a sea of cosmic clutter, has in the scope of the universe.

The full moon finally peaked over the mountains, lighting up the night sky. They talked for a few more hours, until they too wandered off to bed. The sleeping bags felt soft and comfortable, quickly erasing the night chill, a chill that invaded the body once they left the warmth of the fire.

The temperature outside dipped once the fire died out, the once brilliant flame reduced to a smoldering pile of dying embers. The sound of the nearby river pulsated, as it had for centuries, throughout the campsite. It was extremely late in the night when Eric and Tak finally drifted off to sleep. Silence fell upon the camp, leaving only the natural sounds of nature to fill the nighttime airwaves.

Abruptly awakened by a strange smell, Eric tried to raise his head as a thick fog enveloped the camp. He heard the heavy trampling of feet and shouted out to Tak. Tak did not respond. Eric cried out to the girls but received no answer. As he tried to stand up, he fell back down. The shuffling sound of footsteps came closer to the tents.

Eric could barely make out the shape of a giant beast looming outside the tent as it approached the tent doorway. He shouted out once more, then everything went dark.

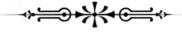

Chapter 3

Strangers in a Strange Land

Eric slowly regained consciousness. He found himself sprawled out on the dirt floor of what he thought was a primitive hut. He could smell the dank scent of the stale air permeating throughout the small, dark, enclosure—the musky smell of decomposing leaves stung his nostrils. The floor of the hut, a combination of dirt intertwined with the various stages of decomposing vegetation, stayed damp in areas where the decaying plants released their last puffs of moisture as he crawled about in the blackness. The lack of light in the pitch black, humid prison, distorted Eric's assessment of the situation, increasing his anxiety, anxiety funneled by the unfamiliar.

Unable to detect the presence of his camping mates in the absolute blackness, Eric called out to them several times, but he heard no response. If they were here, he thought it highly possible they were still unconscious, lying just feet away from him in the darkness. His hands, bound by a thin rope, were numb, but oddly enough his legs were free, so he stood up to stretch his legs.

The ceiling of the enclosure was extremely low, causing Eric to hunch over after he scraped his head on the ceiling as he moved cautiously around the room. He bent down and crawled to the far side of the structure, which in the absence of light, was impossible to see. Eric felt around in the darkness, until he bumped up against two bodies sprawled out on the floor. He nudged the two lifeless figures, who he guessed were Tak and CeCe, until they finally started to move. He could not see his friends, but he could feel and hear the thud of his kicks on their legs.

The two figures, startled by the nudging, abruptly tried to stand up. Eric moved back towards the far wall of the hut to gain some distance from the two bodies, just in case the two other occupants of the hut were not his friends. If the two bodies were not CeCe and Takoda, he could be in serious trouble, so he wanted time to react to any inauspicious situation. He reached the outer wall of the hut where he decided to speak.

"Is that you Tak? Is that you CeCe? What happened to us and where are we?"

The two simultaneously responded, "I don't have any idea."

CeCe and Tak were slowly coming to their senses, as the fog, which obviously held a type of sleeping agent, began to wear off. The two men fought to break the thin rope bonds that held their hands tightly together. The darkness of the enclosure made it impossible to distinguish by sight, who was who, but the moon, casting slight rays of light into the enclosure, was just coming up.

CeCe and Tak shook their pounding heads in total disbelief at their current circumstance. A nauseating feeling overcame them temporarily as the drug wore off.

"Does anyone recollect anything? I remember going into the tent, getting inside my sleeping bag late at night, then nothing. At least nothing until now!" Takoda said.

"That is about all I can remember too," CeCe said as he stood up, his head banging into the top of the rudimentary prison.

CeCe was a big man, standing six feet seven inches, with arms as big as many a man's leg. His voice boomed in the enclosure, as it echoed off the walls in the tight quarters of the hut. His size gave them an advantage over the captors if a serious scuffle were to break out or if they had to fight to escape. If given the opportunity, all three men would resort to violence to escape from their mysterious captors.

The three men moved closer together, sitting back to back, trying to free themselves from the restraints on their arms. Tak, with his long, stringy fingers, eventually made some progress on Eric's bonds, loosening the first knot, which made it possible to untie the rope and free Eric. The blonde Norseman quickly went to work on freeing the other two prisoners and untied Tak and CeCe as the light in the hut faded once again.

The men naturally assumed it was a cloudy night as the moonlight temporarily faded in and out, lighting up the interior of the hut. None of them had any idea where they were, or how they got there. It was too dark to make out the time in the blackness of the hut, so they had no idea how long it would be before dawn. The darkness deeply confused the men. According to their internal clocks, it should be approaching day not night. Eric and Tak entered the tent along the Missouri River late at night, only hours before dawn, so how could the moon be so bright? The only plausible answer was they had been unconscious for some time.

The three men huddled together as Eric whispered, "We have to come up with a plan to get out of here."

In no way did Eric want to leave his fate in the hands of who or what had kidnapped him.

CeCe responded, "Let's at least try to find a way out of this enclosure and see where we are."

CeCe wanted to see what was outside the hut; to see if they were still on the river in Montana.

The three men quietly discussed their options at length, eventually agreeing on a course of action. They started to crawl around the hut, stopping to feel around in the dark at the edges of the structure.

The hut, constructed of mud and sticks tightly interwoven, extended ten feet from one side to the other, and was surprisingly strong for its rudimentary nature. There had to be a way in, which meant there had to be a way out too. The bottom of the enclosure, strategically lined with large rocks, rocks that were at least three feet thick, created a base wall that ran around the entire structure. A mixture of mud, which had hardened like concrete, cemented the rocks together. The thickness of the stones made it impossible to go under the structure to escape. The sides, constructed of what felt like bamboo sticks, had a heavy layering of mud to keep out the weather and to strengthen the walls. The men continued to crawl around the room looking for some way to breech the enclosure.

"I found an opening. It feels like a door," Takoda called out.

The Sioux brave stood up to look for a handle, his fingernails scraping along the surface of the door until he found the latch.

Eric and CeCe quickly crawled towards the sound of Tak's voice, stopping once they reached his side, where they stood up to test the strength of the door. Tak gently cracked open the door which at once slammed shut. A large chunk of mud fell from above the door, hitting Eric squarely in the head, which he just shook off. All three men tried to push open the door simultaneously, but the door did not budge. Something was holding the door closed, and whatever it was, it had the bulk to stop the door from moving. They tried once again, but the door would not move.

"Don't try to escape! It would be to your peril," replied a thunderous voice in a low, grumbling tone; a tone heavy with guttural inflection.

Eric shouted out, "What do you want with us? Where are we? Who are you?"

Eric held back CeCe and Tak from pushing on the door to attempt escape once again. Both men wanted to make a break for it while they heard only one voice outside the door. There were three of them and only one voice outside, which might be their best chance of escape they thought. To them it was utterly insane to stay put in the hut until the abductor could decide their fate. They needed to control their own destinies.

"All in due time. I suggest you try to rest. We can't protect you once you venture away from the hut and our encampment," the mysterious voice responded back, cautioning the humans in an extremely commanding tone.

The humans could tell by the fading footsteps that whatever was keeping them prisoners had wandered off from the area around the hut. This alerted the men to the possibility of another attempt at escape.

CeCe quietly muttered, "What did he mean by we can't protect you? Is there more than just one captor? Where could we be? How could we go from camping in our tents to this unknown place just like that?"

CeCe, obviously distraught by their current predicament, was beginning to get worried. It made absolutely no sense to him why anyone would kidnap them and keep them hostage inside a primitive hut. He needed to visually inspect the area that surrounded the hut to figure out if they were still around camp.

The three men stared into the darkness, each one trying to grasp the unexplainable situation they now found themselves in. How was it possible to be camping along a river in the Rocky Mountains one moment and wake up in some unknown place the next? It just didn't add up Eric thought. He was confident it had to be some backwoods lunatic who somehow drugged them, abducted them, and brought them to this strange land. He further realized that just one person could not pull this off. Did the group somehow infringe on someone else's property or territory? Was it a frontier extremist thing or a poaching ring?

The latter made more sense to Eric. The group must have come into the area at the wrong time, stumbling upon an illegal poaching operation. If that were the case, then he realized they could be in grave danger.

This dark notion was on his mind when he said to CeCe and Tak, "Do you guys think poachers captured us? Did we camp in the wrong area?"

Tak quickly interjected, "Then why did the voice say protect us? What could be outside of the encampment that is so terrible? Did you see how easily it held the door shut with all three of us pushing against it? That would take tremendous strength."

CeCe interrupted, "It just doesn't make any sense. We are in a different place. Can't you hear the strange sounds coming from outside?"

He was obviously incredibly nervous, which resonated in the tone of his voice.

Eric and Tak paused to focus on the strange noises coming from out beyond the darkness. The sounds, made up of hideous screams followed by guttural growls, resonated from the land outside. It was the first time they concentrated on the bizarre sounds coming from beyond the tiny hut. It sounded like a primordial nightmare, one playing out just beyond the walls of the hut, just beyond the enclosure. What protection could this rudimentary hut give them?

Eric was growing increasingly concerned about the whereabouts of the girls. They too would surely be wondering what was going on, wherever they were. For now, he decided to keep this concern to himself. There was no need to worry about the women's whereabouts with CeCe and Tak. It would only lead to more conjecture and anxiety; anxiety they could do without.

Eric realized escape was pointless until the light of day, so it was with a tempered voice that he recommended they try to get some rest until the light of day returned, which would allow them to visually assess the situation. He hedged that a new hope would come with the light of dawn, a dawn that would offer some reasonable answers. Surely, there had to be a simple logical explanation about what happened, or so he hoped.

So, it was with nervous restlessness that the three men stretched out on the dirt floor of the hut to wait until the daylight. They slept in shifts, so at least one of them was on guard during the night. The strange noises, terrifying in nature, reverberated throughout the long night. It was obvious to the men, based on the brutality of the sounds, that life and death struggles were unfolding on a regular basis out in the shadows, merely yards from their primitive lodging.

The hideous screams made it almost impossible for any of the men to sleep. The noises sometimes sounded nearby, but most echoed from a distance. The three humans tossed and turned all night, as an unknown silence, one precipitated by fear, hung over them while they quietly waited for morning.

It seemed pointless to cogitate what creatures roamed the land outside. None of the men recognized any of the odd sounds. Takoda, the Sioux native, was remarkably familiar with the back country and had experienced many sounds in the night, but nothing like this. It did not frighten him; however, it did concern him.

Eric, on the other hand, realized these sounds were coming from beasts of giant proportions. The screams were quite loud, some high pitched, others low pitched, as they resonated from all directions. They could hear the heavy, thundering clashes of giant beast as they pounded into one another. The safest place was in the shelter for the time being, away from the terrifying sounds of the hostile night. They could assess the situation visually in the morning light. Light brings with it a feeling of greater safety, a safety supported by the rational connection between the eyes and the mind.

Finally, after what seemed an endless night, the light of dawn began to filter into the blackness of the hut, allowing some vision. The three hostages began to stir, each trying to stretch tired muscles as they stood up. The spine–tingling screams died down during the early dawn until they eventually ceased altogether. The men learned one valuable lesson that night. Night was hunting time in this place. If they did escape, they would need to find shelter before nightfall every night to hide from the menacing beasts that roamed the darkness.

CeCe blurted out, "What a night! Those noises and loud screams were almost unbearable. I don't know where the heck we are, but we could be in some serious trouble. I've never heard such eerie sounds."

"I'm with you. We need to get some answers from our captors. What do you think Eric?" asked Tak.

"I'm worried about the girls. We need to find them. They could be in deep trouble, left all alone with who knows what."

Eric realized it was time to address the women with CeCe and Tak.

Eric looked around at the inside of the hut, which was finally beginning to lighten up from the arrival of dawn. He could now see the primitive design of the structure. It was beyond his comprehension how this simple enclosure could keep out the aggressive beasts that frequented the area during the night. If something wanted in, there would be little to stop it from knocking down the walls of the hut, gaining access to the flesh inside.

Eric knew they had to escape to search for the missing girls. He hoped there was another hut nearby, but it did not explain why there was no answer when he called out for them. This put doubt in his mind. Was it possible the women went somewhere else? If that were the case, the situation just intensified, escalating the importance of escaping. Hope, Lexa, and Maka could be the victims of torture or some other unthinkable atrocity committed by a group of extremists or backwoods hillbillies. They had to escape the hut first, then elude the captors, before they could search for Maka, Hope, and Lexa.

"We need to try and escape again so we can find out where we are and where the girls are being held."

The urgency resonated in Eric's voice.

The other two men agreed so they surrounded the door of the hut. CeCe placed the bulk of his heavy frame up against the door. Eric and Tak braced themselves on each side of CeCe.

"On the count of three, we rush the door," CeCe cried out.

"One, two, three!"

They threw all their might at the door, which flung open, almost coming unhinged from the velocity of the push. The bright light, from the sudden emergence from the dimly lit hut, blinded them momentarily. They could taste their freedom now, or so they thought, as they flew out of the enclosure, each sprawling to the ground when the unmanned door slung open, surprising the men.

Eric, regaining his feet first, quickly rushed around the hut, closely followed by Tak and CeCe. They bolted for the open field which led to the forest—the forest they hoped to escape into. Eric led the way as he sprinted, at full capability, towards the forest. The tree line loomed a good fifty yards from the hut, separated by a field of tall grasses. The morning dew clung to the green fibers of the long, narrow threads of grass, soaking the men from the waist down as they ran to the safety of the forest.

"Run!" Eric yelled as he reached full speed.

Takoda gained Eric's side within moments. He looked over his shoulder to see the heavier CeCe falling behind. The big man had the power but lacked speed.

"Run CeCe," the native yelled.

Eric and Tak reached the edge of the forest, stopping just behind the first row of tall trees, to wait for CeCe, now a good twenty yards behind. They screamed for CeCe to increase his pace as he neared the forest.

CeCe stopped suddenly, mid stride, just before reaching the safety of the trees. His face went pale, his body went limp, as he pointed past Eric and Tak.

The two men hastily turned around to confront the object of CeCe's distress. From the trees directly above them, a massive, brutish looking beast, one that stood over 12 feet tall, dropped to the floor of the forest, blocking any avenue of escape. The creature emitted a hideous growl as it gently landed within feet of the terrified men.

The feeling of hope quickly evaporated when the three men saw two more imposing figures come from around the hut and trot towards the trees. The three creatures, all gargantuan in size, were ferocious and terrifying in appearance.

Fear at once entered the hearts and penetrated the minds of the escaping prisoners. These creatures were giants, brutes easily capable of restraining each of them with only one hand or killing them with little effort if they so desired.

The escape route now cut off, the humans had nowhere to turn, and they could not outrun or physically compete with these imposing behemoths. All three of the men, terrified by the three unimaginable creatures which now stood before them, surrendered without incident.

In an instant, Eric, Tak and CeCe knew they were strangers in an extremely dangerous world.

Chapter 4

What About Us?

Maka Dove, the first of the women to wake up, rolled over onto her knees and vomited. There was a faint buzzing in her ears. The roaring sound of a waterfall reverberated in her ears, intensifying the pounding in her head. She did not recall hearing this thundering sound by the camp along the river. By the river, there was the sound of the water rushing by, the sound the trees made from swaying in the wind, but not the loud roar of the rushing water hitting the rocks below.

Her face, damp from the spray of the mist drifting in from the waterfall, was pale white. She felt nauseated when she first woke up, but that feeling soon faded after several minutes. As the grogginess cleared from her head, Maka looked around at her surroundings. She slowly stood up, stretching her stiff muscles while surveying the area around her for the other members of the group. The natural light inside the cave was fading, so she rationalized it was getting close to evening which did not make sense; sense would mean it was getting light. By all logic it should be morning not evening.

Maka gazed into the dimly lit room until her eyes met a wide stream of water plummeting down, covering the opening in the front of the cave. She was unable to explain her vision. Behind her, the cave became longer, wider, and higher, until she could not see any farther, due to the lack of light. Then she heard a voice.

Lexa's voice broke the silence, "Are we behind a waterfall?"

The Latino shook her head. She too, now wide awake, looked in the direction of the cascading water.

Maka responded, "I think you are right. This is very strange. Do you think the guys somehow drugged us and put us in here? If so, they are going to pay for this. I woke up with a sick feeling that had to be from some type of drug."

Maka was a proud native woman who prided herself on her self-reliance; self-reliance that did not leave room for manipulation.

Hope chimed in, "How is this possible? There must be a logical answer, but I feel mildly sick too," her soft voice was barely audible over the roar of the falls.

It was the teacher coming out in Hope. She always looked for the reasoning behind things—the reason and the goodness. Hope, the optimist, had a sensitive soul, a kind heart, and an undying devotion to always do the right thing. She continuously tried to resolve things before they reached deeper, arcane consequences. To Hope, everything had a reasonable solution, one solved by proper preparation through logical formulations of thought.

Maka answered, "You're probably right, Hope. Even they could not have pulled this off. Besides, I don't recall a waterfall like this along the river. I have been fishing up and down this river and have yet to come across a waterfall of this size."

"There is not a waterfall on the Missouri where we are camping," chimed in Lexa; her voice becoming louder, her facial mannerisms more animated, all hinting towards her growing apprehension and fear.

Lexa was known to heat up quickly, speak her outspoken mind, and erupt into rare instances of rage, often to the chagrin of her friends. Her friends accepted this trait, considering it to be part of her spark plug personality. If a dispute did erupt, it was best to have Lexa on your side and not be the object of her fury. Her personality was in deep contrast to Hopes, but this made the two even closer friends. Their relationship was more of an attraction of opposites, one if put together to form a whole, would make a very well-rounded individual.

Maka suggested they explore the cave behind the waterfall to look for another way out of the cavern. The camp could not be that far away, she rationalized. If they were still somewhere on the river, they could find their way back to the camp, back to the safety of the vehicles, then they could drive out and find help.

The three women went off in different directions to survey the depths of the cavern. It was difficult to see in the cave once they moved beyond the penetrating light coming through the waterfall, as it plunged down in front of the cave opening. The cavern was sizable as it opened to a massive room. Its depth was greater than its length and it was not long before the three women met in the middle of the large room. Hope still had in her possession her flashlight, which she always attached to her belt in case she needed to get up in the middle of the night while camping. When in the outdoors, Hope thought it best to prepare for everything, and to her, it was better to be over prepared than under prepared.

They decided to explore the depth of the cave, to see if it led to an avenue of escape. As they went farther into the cavern, the air became warmer and stickier, which meant a natural hot spring or river flowed somewhere beneath them. The moist, warm air was a welcome relief from the much cooler temperature of both the original camp site and the outer region of the cave. The air, thermally heated, warmed them from the core and brought momentary physical relief. It was the psychological strain that worried Maka. Waking up in this unexplainable predicament would eventually take a toll on them, especially if they could not find a reasonable explanation to rationalize the oddity of the event. She particularly worried about Lexa and her quickness to become frustrated. It would be a challenge to keep her calm.

"At least we won't freeze tonight," Maka jokingly remarked, trying to play down the situation.

Maka often used humor to cover up uncertainty and awkwardness.

"That's true! You know I have thin blood," laughed Lexa.

"I'm glad we slept in our clothes. It would be beyond awkward to be standing here in our underwear," Hope mockingly chimed in.

"What should we do now?" remarked Lexa, ready to further explore the cavern to find any answer to this riddle.

Maka once again took the lead and said, "We have to keep searching for a way out. Somebody put us in here, so it's up to us to find a way out."

The tone of Maka's voice echoed with confidence.

The three women continued, slowly moving deeper into the dark abyss. The light of the day faded as nightfall set in on the other side of the waterfall. The cave, now pitch black without the light from outside, seemed terrifying as the continual rumbling of strange noises echoed from the river below. It was a great relief that Hope had her flashlight. It is amazing what a tiny light can do for the inept eyesight of humans. We feel safer in the light and we feel terrified in the dark. Humans are a daylight species, a species fearing the darkness; just one prehistoric instinct left over from our early days when predators came out at night—forcing us to climb into the trees to avoid dangers from the beasts that roamed the plains.

Hope, Lexa, and Maka searched and hunted for a way out of the cave but could not find one. All avenues led to dead ends, fortified by eons of eroded rock which entombed the cavern. They even tried to venture down into the earth to the source of the heat but to no avail. A large crevice led down to a super-heated river running beneath the cave which later deposited its heated water to the cool river below. They knew it would eventually run into the river outside, but the water was just too hot for them to risk entry. The scalding water was too dangerous, so they re-surfaced to the confinement of the cave. At this point they were growing frustrated, fatigued, and concerned the flashlight would go out at any minute, leaving them stranded in the darkness of the cavern, so they decided to rest and wait until morning. In the morning, they would try to find a way out of the cave again once day light filtered back into the cavern through the waterfall. It was futile to keep searching in the darkness.

They came part way back out to the front of the cave, closer to the waterfall, where they picked a flat spot on the edge of the large open room, one that was warm and comfortable, to settle down for the night. Sleep was out of the question. They still had no idea what happened or where they were, and they worried about the men. Where were they? Was this a hoax? Did something terrible happen to the men as well? All were legitimate questions without answers.

The women stretched out on the dirt floor of the cave and tried to rest. The silence was at once interrupted by a strange shrieking noise coming from beyond the falls. The terrifying sound became louder and shriller. A piercing scream, one loud enough to break through the constant roaring of the falls, penetrated the night. There were other sounds as well. Deep muttering growls followed by shrieking high-pitched cries often echoed on the air waves during the night. The girls were fortunate to be in the cave, hidden away from the searching eyes of predators, the perpetrators of the peculiar sounds coming from out beyond the falls in the darkness.

At this point the three captives were grateful for the protection of the cave behind the falls. Things could be much more perilous on the other side. It sounded like life confronting death outside. The ominous sounds would continue all night, sometimes subsiding, causing the cavern to fill with unusual noises created by the heated river far below. In the darkness, these noises played havoc with the women's imaginations. It was best to keep the eyes closed and not strain into the blackness.

"I don't know what's going on out there, but we're not in Montana anymore girls. These sounds are completely alien to me," Maka apprehensively said.

There was an element of fear in the native's voice. As a child and teenager, Maka went on long hunting trips with her father and brothers while growing up in South Dakota, where she held her own, but never once had she heard such horrific animal sounds. She was familiar with using weapons, some of which were self-made, and was very apt in the art of outdoor survival. The Sioux native realized she may need some of these traits in the coming days. If this place was half as dangerous as it sounded, then everyone would need weapons to survive.

"What are we to do?" shrieked Lexa, who was becoming nervous and anxious.

Lexa liked to approach things head on and not wait. The air of uncertainty, complicated by the fear of the unknown, could cause her to reach her boiling point quickly, as patience was not her strong point. She needed solvable situations.

Maka forcefully spoke up in a supportive tone, "We're safe in here for tonight. I suggest we try to stay calm and conserve our energy. Tomorrow we'll have more time to explore this cave and find a way out."

If they could not find a normal way out, she quietly thought to herself, they may have to go through the falls, which might be a considerable risk, but what other options would they have. She knew starvation would eventually set in and their options would dwindle as time passed if they continued to stay in the cave. It would be a gamble to risk going through the falls, plunging to possible death on the rocks below if the pool of water below were too shallow or surrounded by large boulders.

None of the women knew what was below the falls or how far down it was to the river. If they survived the fall, it was entirely possible the strong current could carry them away, downstream to some unknown territory—if they survived drowning. It would assuredly be a long shot if they all survived, but on the other hand, they might be able to climb down to the river below. As Maka dozed off, she knew they would have to find another way out.

It was difficult for the women to sleep. Every time they drifted off to sleep, the loud shrieking sound would pierce through the falls, resonating throughout the cave. The high pitch of the noise jolted the women to alertness—terrifying them. What could make such a sound?

The shrieks, followed by chilling growls, ghastly grunts, and morbid moans, permeated throughout the night, until they finally subsided as the light of day approached. The light began to leak through the waterfall, gently filling the area just inside the cave with rays of light, filtered by the water. It was the start to a new day.

Hope, startled from her fitful sleep in the early dawn by a sudden noise, quickly sat up and faced the opening to the cave. Her eyes slowly adjusted to the contrast between the dark and light. She was still foggy with sleep. The restlessness caused by the frightful sounds that echoed throughout the cavern all night made her tired. She focused, straining her vision, on one area by the opening in the cave where she saw a slight movement.

Hope cried out to the others in a tone of distress, "Wake up! Wake up! Did you hear that?" she whispered.

She was very animated, which was unusual for Hope who was the constant, levelheaded one.

"I just heard a loud noise coming from over there," she screeched as she pointed towards the corner of the cavern.

Maka and Lexa, startled to consciousness by Hope's cry, instantly popped up fully alert. Both looked in the direction where Hope was pointing. By now Hope was motioning them to keep quiet by raising her finger to her lips to signal silence.

Maka and Lexa gazed at Hope with confusion on their faces. Hope again pointed to the outer part of the cave on the left side of the waterfall. Maka and Lexa strained to see in the dim light. After a moment, their eyes adjusted to the new light, and a shape started to appear by the wall on the far side of the cavern. The shape, enormous in size, started to move towards the women.

Hope, Maka, and Lexa jumped to their feet, quickly moving to the back of the cavern. The creature slowly followed. They could see the giant outline of its shadow up against the transparent waterfall in the background. It covered the distance between them with just a few strides. All three of the women screamed as loud as they could to try and confuse the intruder, who just kept coming towards them.

The assailant, now within a few feet of striking distance, suddenly stopped when a gargantuan creature flew through the waterfall into the cavern opening, landing in the cave. The avian beast's enormous size momentarily blotted out the waterfall as the water collapsed behind it. The women simultaneously screamed.

"Run into the cave!"

Then one of the creatures spoke causing the women to freeze in their tracks.

Chapter 5

Captives

Eric, Takoda, and CeCe attempted to flee from the three gargantuan beasts—but to no avail. One of the three behemoths blocked each avenue of escape. A giant ape blocked them from entering the forest as the other two brutish creatures closed the gap from the rear. The massive ape emitted a terrifying guttural rumble that halted the men in their tracks.

Trapped with no place to escape to, the men stood in shock as the two creatures approaching from behind them quickly reached them at the forests edge. The monstrous beasts were too big, too strong, and too intimidating for the men to challenge. It was very conceivable they could end up on the dinner plate for these three monstrosities.

Normally, all three men would fight to the death if necessary, but with these creatures, they were physically at their mercy. They could not outrun them or overpower them; all they could do was yield, hope for the best outcome, and try to escape later.

CeCe and Tak turned to face the two approaching attackers, while Eric held his ground against the huge hominid blocking their retreat into the forest.

CeCe was a big strong man, one that could hold his own with any human, but these things were not human. Using only one arm, one of the creatures grabbed CeCe, lifting the big man off the ground with relative ease. The terrifying beast, which stood 15 feet tall, had powerful muscular legs, with dog–like claws, claws that could easily disembowel any unfortunate victim that crossed their sharp pointed path. The brute's arms, chiseled in muscles that looked like sculpted stone, easily restrained CeCe like a human would handle a small child. The hair on the grizzly giant, the consistency of stiff bristle, had a reddish–brown tinge to its color. The hair around the animal's neck and chest area was longer and thicker than the rest of its body hair and was so stiff, it could rub a man's skin off like rough grit sandpaper.

CeCe had no doubt he was a goner. If this beast wanted to kill him, there was nothing he could do to stop it. Just one look at the brute's massive head, powerful jaws, and razor–sharp claws terrified CeCe.

The creature had an elongated snout full of triangular crowns intended for crushing bone or tearing flesh. At the front of its snout were two large, dagger–like canines that protruded down below the bottom jaw line. These two fangs were readily visible to CeCe, whose face rested only inches away from the sharp, pointed ivory. The big man could see a faint crack, surely gained during fighting or killing, running down one of the brute's incisors. CeCe was just a mere snack to this beast.

The behemoth had dark, black eyes, eyes which were oblong, and quite large, as they gazed at the helpless human. Huge, pointed ears, stood erect, reaching past the top of the massive head of the leviathan. Both physical features led CeCe to believe the creature had excellent vision and hearing.

CeCe stopped struggling and to his astonishment, the beast spoke.

"I am **Creo**. I am from the family of mammals known as **Creo**donts and I mean you no harm," the strange beast said.

The imposing captor's voice was low pitched, a faint rumble, but deep.

"I'll put you down if you don't try to escape. I know you have questions, and they will all be answered in time," it growled.

The giant Creodont glared at CeCe while it spoke, then it dropped the African American to the ground.

"I won't try to flee."

CeCe was in shock from the sight of the terrifying creature which was now speaking to him. He could only imagine what an animal this size could do to him if it really wanted to. CeCe decided it would be best if he just went along with the thing for now, and hopefully an opportunity to escape would come later. But escape to where? What other unimaginable beasts lived in this strange place?

While CeCe ceased to struggle with Creo, both Eric and Tak were dealing with their own terrifying encounters.

A second creature placed one of its large hands on Tak's shoulder, quickly dispatching the proud native with the same ease. It resembled a bear, a bear with a much shorter face. It, like Creo, was enormous in size, standing around 15 feet in its bipedal form, and like Creo, it had large defined muscles that exuded strength and power.

Tak looked at its massive claws, which he figured were at least 10 inches long, and quickly gave up resisting. The massive bear beast had long, thick black fur with a strip of white running up its neckline, ending at the top of its head. The upper torso of the creature was exceptionally long in relationship to its lower body. If it stood on all four legs, the creature would be higher in the front than in the back. The legs of the brute, well developed with longer muscle tone, stopped at enormous claw tipped feet. Tak, convinced the creature had tremendous power and speed, quickly realized running was not a possibility. The arms of the beast hung down past its waistline, ending with long, claw-tipped hands. As with the beast Creo, this bear was not a creature to mess with. Then it too spoke.

"I am **Arcto**. I am from the species known as **Arcto**id. You need to remain calm."

Arcto possessed a powerful jawline filled with bone crushing teeth. His eyes were kinder in comparison to Creo's. His gaze was not as terrifying but was more inquisitive. Arcto dropped Tak to the ground.

Tak quietly sat down and shook his head. His mind reeled as he tried to somehow rationalize the situation, one he and his friends now found themselves in. How was this possible? Where were they? What were these things? All were questions without answers. He and his two friends were at the mercy of these giant monstrosities. If they did escape, where would they escape to?

Eric confronted the last of the three beasts, a giant ape-like creature, which stood over 12 feet tall, and blocked the escape route into the forest. He guessed, judging from the beast's tremendous bulk that it weighed over 1,200 pounds. It had arms that were very muscular and extra ordinarily long.

The brutish ape, covered in thick, long brown hair, glared at Eric. The chest area of the creature, chiseled and defined, was darker in color in relationship to the rest of its body hair. The brute could easily crush him with one blow from its mighty arms or sever his throat with one bite from its long, protruding canines.

The ape had enormous hands tipped with long fingernails, nails blackened by dirt, dried blood, and animal skin. Eric recognized the ape beast as Giganti**pith**ecus blacki, the largest ape hominid to ever walk the Earth. It roamed the Earth for a million years, before going extinct around 100,000 years ago.

The ape did not speak but instead unleashed terrifying guttural sounds that sent chills through the humans. Eric concluded the brute was serious, so he followed Tak's example and walked back to the hut, sat down, and leaned up against the side of the structure. They could not escape from the three captors; they were too fast, they were too strong, and they had the advantage of knowing the surrounding dense jungle.

Eric, Tak, and CeCe would wait for the opportunity to escape later if the chance presented itself. Eric was confident the chance to flee would present itself at some point; creatures of this size would eventually need to eat and sleep. Eric knew they would be safer with their captors for now, safer until they could learn more about this strange land. They needed to find out more details; details that would help them find the girls and explain their mysterious abduction.

He motioned for CeCe to come and sit with them by the hut. Together they would develop a plan for future escape. All three humans, now resigned to their fate, quietly sat down, stared at their ferocious looking captors, and waited.

The three creatures huddled together, each taking a turn to speak. Eric concluded that Creo was the leader from the way Arcto and the ape beast addressed him. Creo was a powerful looking specimen, one that demanded respect. Eric assumed he was the enforcer of the group.

The bear-like creature would often gaze over at the three humans and point as it responded to Creo. The ape-like creature just stood there looking intimidating. The men never heard the ape speak. It would sniff the air from time to time, emit a low terrifying growl, and then break into an uncontrollable laugh. Eric perceived the giant ape to be the slow minded one. A slow minded, extremely dangerous brute, capable of inflicting great bodily harm if provoked or driven into an uncontrollable fit of rage. He whispered this suspicion to Tak and CeCe as they sat by the hut quietly analyzing the three beasts. If the opportunity to escape became available to them, it would be when the ape-beast was guarding them. They could trick the dim-wit Eric thought.

Finally, the Creodont spoke. "Which of you humans is known as Eric Asvaldsson?"

Creo's tone and body language pivoted to one of a profoundly serious nature. The creature gazed, with a penetrating glare, at each of the men while long canines clanged against its lower teeth as it spoke. The three captives hesitated to answer it back. How could this Creo know one of their names? That was impossible.

"We know one of you is him. It's better you just tell us. We're here to help you and have no intention of harming any of you."

"I am Eric Asvaldsson. What do you want with us? Where are we?"

Eric looked the lumbering Creodont straight in the eyes. He wanted to look confident, so he stood up to confront the giant.

Creo shook his enormous head but did not answer the human's questions. The three men now assumed he was a male Creodont. They thought Arcto was also a male of his species, but they were not sure about the ape. They thought it was a male but with all that hair they could not be sure.

Eric decided to name the giant ape Squatch. He told this to Tak and CeCe and all three had a good laugh. The big ape looked at the three men and scowled. The men felt less intimidated by the lumbering beast after Creo assured them no harm would come to them by the hands of **Pith**, which was the ape's real name. If anything, the lead creature seemed honorable; a creature of his word. There were no other options, so the three men had to trust the captors, trust them for now.

The huge Creodont spoke once again, "You three will go with us tomorrow on a journey to see our leader. He will answer many of your questions. I suggest you return to the hut before nightfall."

Eric introduced Takoda and CeCe to the three ominous beasts. The creatures responded to this gesture by barely nodding in acknowledgment. Such a custom was unheard of in their world. In the world they came from, it was kill or be killed.

At this point both Arcto and Pith, who now had a name, sprinted off towards the thick undergrowth of the forest. They effortlessly traversed the open field and within moments they disappeared into the heavy vegetation. Arcto vanished into the forest from the ground, while Pith swung effortlessly into the canopy, disappearing in the entangled branches and leaves.

Watching the two beasts vanish into the overgrown forest was the first time the three humans focused their attention on the surrounding jungle. The abundant trees, each fighting to gain unfiltered access to the sunlight, were the tallest trees any of the men had ever seen. There were hundreds of tree species, some familiar, some never seen by the human eye. The forest, including great palm trees, multiple types of conifers, beeches, maples, and many other unidentified species, encroached on the environment, creating diverse levels of life, each rich in its own diversity of species. Hardwood trees seemed to thrive just as well in the warm humid conditions. The observations of the three men ended when Creo spoke.

"They have gone to get you food. They'll be back shortly. You must eat and return to the safety of the hut by nightfall. This is an extremely dangerous place when the sun goes down. We can't protect you once the darkness of night descends. Your best bet for survival will be in the hut."

Creo's voice was serious now as his blazing stare fell upon them. His words commanded attention.

Eric asked inquisitively, "Where are you going to be?"

It made little sense to him why the beasts would not stay and protect them. How could they leave them alone in this hostile world? If there were more creatures like them, what chance would they have cowering in a hut?

Creo just gazed at Eric but did not reply. The giant beast just ignored the human's questions.

CeCe then spoke up and asked, "What about the girls? What have you done with them?"

The big man, deeply concerned about the whereabouts of the girls, needed answers. If they were in this odd world as well, they could be alone and afraid.

The giant Creodont just said, "They are safe for now," and shrugged his massive shoulders as he walked off.

Creo, growing tired of the humans and their questions, walked towards the forest and vanished into the thick green foliage.

Arcto and Pith returned shortly carrying some type of fruit and tossed it to the humans. Pith just grunted and wandered off to a safe distance to gorge himself on the succulent fruit.

Arcto came towards the three men and showed them how to crack the fruit open, to expose the tender sweet flesh inside.

It was the first time that Eric got a good look at the size and might of the bear-like creature. He thought it looked more like a cross between a giant bear and a giant wolverine. He had no doubt it could inflict great damage with those razor-sharp claws and huge blunt canines. Eric saw a scar about 20 inches long on Arcto's chest that had healed some time ago. He wondered just how a creature this powerful received an injury like that. He wanted to ask Arcto, but he thought it best to wait until they became more comfortable with one another, or became friends over time, if either were even possible.

Eric looked up at Arcto and asked, "Why can't you protect us at night?"

The lack of answers was really beginning to bother him.

The bear beast just shrugged.

"We still don't know where we are, how we got here or what you are."

Arcto could sense the growing anxiety in the men and stood up.

"It will be explained in time. Now hurry up and eat. We're running out of daylight."

The giant beast pointed to the hut as he passed by it on his way to the forest. He crossed the open field, stopped, and turned to look at the humans one final time. Arcto then disappeared into the forest, the thick undergrowth snapping back into place after his large bulky frame pushed through the impenetrable natural barrier.

Tak finally spoke up, "I think we should do as they say for now. I do not have any idea where we are but until we know we should be cautious."

Tak was talking words of wisdom now. It was his Native American intuition, that extra sense he had which told him when to heed caution. Eric and CeCe knew when to give in to it.

They finished the refreshing fruit then went back into the hut for the night. CeCe latched the door from the inside of the hut to help keep it closed during the night. The three men spread out in the hut to try and cover as many angles as possible. If attacked, it was better to have at least one of them close to the attempted breech point to battle back. They would need to react swiftly to any attack on the hut.

Once again, when the light was gone, the strange grotesque screams, mingled with low muttering growls, began. All three men hoped the hut would protect them during the night from the denizens of the surrounding jungle and they all wished they could watch, from the safety of the trees, any battles unfolding just out beyond the hut. What types of animals could make such terrifying sounds?

"I wish we had some weapons to protect ourselves with," Eric said.

Eric realized they would need weapons to fend off the creatures that roamed this world during the night. He wished he had his pistol with him; the pistol he left in his vehicle back in his world. What good would a spear do against monsters of these proportions?

"I agree. I have made many weapons before, but I especially like making bows," Tak answered.

In his youth, Takoda learned the skills necessary to survive outdoors. He was proficient in making knives, spears and the bow and arrow. Once given the chance, Tak would make weapons for defense. If these creatures were really on their side, what objection would they have to the humans having weapons?

The men were once again prisoners to the walls of the hut. The intermittent noises, randomly penetrating the night, created the image of a savage world just outside the confines of the hut. It was readily clear that nighttime was a brutal time in this primordial place. Even if they did escape, they would have to hide in the trees at night to avoid predation.

So far, they had only heard the beasts hunting at night, while their prey victims uttered their last death wails, but surely there were creatures just as brutal that stalked and killed during the daylight hours. If they did escape, they would need to be on guard all the time. This place was full of dangers night or day. As the men learned more information about this place, their concern for the girls grew rapidly.

Eric sat in the corner of the hut lost in his thoughts. He could not explain the unusual beasts, Creo, Arcto, and Pith. What they were was a mystery to him. The world outside was a foreign one, one the likes no human had experienced. It was Earth at some point in time. But when? Eric, by way of his archaeological background, was familiar with Creodonts and Arctoids. He had seen their fossilized bones, but in no way, could he imagine them in this form. He knew the time periods when these creatures lived, but those were vast spans of time, time spans which equated to millions of years.

As the grotesque noises flared up once again, the men knew they were in for a long, frightful night in the hut. All they could do was wait for the light of day, when at least they had a slim chance of surviving.

Chapter 6

Beyond the Falls

The water from the falls sprayed into the cave, soaking Hope, Maka, and Lexa, as the second intruder flew through the flowing curtain of water. The women, all terrified by the gargantuan size of the first beast, were wide awake now.

The mass of the second intruder momentarily blocked out the light filtering through the water fall from outside. Once the creature gained solid ground, it folded its massive wings, which allowed light to once again filter into the cavern.

Completely caught off guard by the intrusion, the girls retreated farther back into the depths of the cavern. Without weapons to defend themselves, retreat was the only sensible choice. All three women feared for their lives at this point, until one of the intruders spoke.

"We are here to protect you," said one of the creatures in a high pitched, screeching voice, one that verged on splitting the three women's ear drums.

The avian beast moved towards the women, who upon hearing the drenched raptor talk, halted their retreat into the interior of the cave.

"I am Aves, and we're here to help you. Don't be afraid," it said as it lowered the tone of its voice once the humans stopped their retreat.

Maka, followed by Lexa and Hope, moved out of the shadows, back into the light to get a closer look at the two invaders. Aves, a massive brown eagle-like creature, stood around 9 feet tall with a wingspan of just under 18 feet. Around the neck of the avian brute, was a white band of soft long feathers. The eagle's beak, which had a predominant curve to it, was solid yellow and very thick. It looked powerful enough to cut a human in half or make an opponent defenseless if needed.

The eagle shook itself violently to scatter the remaining water from its enormous wings. The cool water drops, flew throughout the cavern, saturating the women for a second time. At the base of its hairless, muscular legs, were two massive talons, which could puncture the toughest hide or grasp with unequaled power. Aves stared, with black piercing eyes, at the three terrified women as she spoke.

"Where are we?" asked Maka, who questioned the giant eagle in a commanding tone, her brown eyes fixed on it as she spoke.

The beast's words calmed her initial flight or fight instinct, so she moved out farther from the depth of the cave. The gigantic eagle petrified her, but she also felt compelled to trust it. The eagle did not show aggression towards the humans as it spoke, which gave the women some solace.

"What do you want with us?" said Lexa, who was ready to flee to the back of the cave.

This Aves creature scared her. This entire event, which seemed completely impossible to her, was unbelievable. This thing could easily pick her up and carry her off if it wanted to. If the eagle were lying, to lure them into a false sense of security, there was little she could do to stop it.

Lexa moved a few steps into the interior of the cave, so she would have less ground to cover if the giant eagle attacked. She bent down and picked up a rock, concealing it in her hand, just in case she needed to thrust it at the flying fiend.

Hope, standing off to the left side of the cave while the other two women were pre-occupied with the giant eagle, glared at the other creature in the cave. The beast, a gigantic, bulky behemoth, looked like a cross between a rhinoceros and an elephant, with a hide that looked rough and plated, like that of a rhino. The brute had two prongs, which resembled a Y in shape, protruding from just above its nose.

In the form it was in, the beast towered 13 feet tall, standing on thick, massive, powerful legs which supported its immense size and weight. Oddly enough, it had hoofed toes, and each leg had four of these. The neck of the animal was enormous in size which was necessary to support the tremendous horns that jutted out from just above its nostrils. The gargantuan ogre personified strength and power.

"What is that thing?" Hope shouted, as she pointed in the direction of the second antagonist, a brute the likes she had never seen before.

The other two women shifted their focus towards Hope and the second creature. They could see confusion, and fear on Hope's face. The second intruder carried enough ramming bulk to knock a hole in the cave if it wanted to. It would make a great battering ram.

"I am **Bronto** of the **Bronto**theres," it calmly said in an extremely low voice, its massive neck muscles flexing as it spoke.

Bronto's ears and eyes were surprisingly small in proportion to its immense body, which led the humans to believe it had poor vision and poor hearing. The women realized the giant relied on smell to sense danger. Due to its slingshot horns, the women assumed the beast was a male. One side of the Y was missing the tip that had broken off at some point during the creature's violent life.

Maka spoke up once again and asked, "If you're here to help us, how do we get out of this cave?"

She fixed her intense gaze on Bronto.

The Brontotheres did not blink, it just stared at the fragile humans. He moved closer to Maka.

Maka had seen enough; she was in a cave in an unknown land staring at an enormous eagle-like raptor accompanied by some other massive beast. Both of which could talk. The native wanted to get out of the cave to search for a way back home.

The freedom of being outdoors would give Maka a sense of being more in control of her own destiny. Trapped inside the cave created uncertainty for her. For her own mental stability, she needed to escape the cave, move onto the land below, where she had faith in her abilities to adapt to situations within her control. Trapped behind the waterfall left her out of control.

Before Maka could finish her thought, the behemoth Bronto grabbed her with one arm and leaped through the falls. Maka could feel his powerful strength as he pressed her to his side. He had enormous bicep muscles, muscles that felt like steel against her soft bronze toned skin.

They plummeted towards the bottom of the falls, their momentum increasing as they free fell. The beast did not let go and with a tremendous splash, they landed in a deep pool of water that rested at the bottom of the falls. The water was cool, but not cold like the river by the campsite.

Maka and Bronto came up from the deep pool and separated, both swimming rapidly to the bank, where they climbed out of the water. Maka, delighted she survived the fall, shook herself to throw off the excess water. She estimated the fall must have been at least 75 feet. She walked over and slapped Bronto in the face.

"You could've killed me. What were you thinking?"

Maka was a proud woman, one that always stood her ground in conflict. She was not going to leave the event unchallenged.

The giant Bronto just stared at her in bewilderment then let out an enormous burst of air filled with water from his nostrils, soaking the Sioux native. They both broke into laughter simultaneously as they briefly connected. It was nice to see the creature had a sense of humor. Maka feared everyone in the party would need a sense of humor to survive in this hostile, primitive place. If the last couple of days were a prelude to events to come, then all the members of the group were in danger.

From the vantage point on the ground below the falls, Maka and Bronto could see a shape fly out from the opening behind the falls and quickly descend towards them. It was Aves with Lexa hanging on for her life.

Maka could barely see the shape of Lexa clinging to the back of the great avian raptor. The giant eagle plummeted down the waterfall, dramatically increasing in speed as it descended. Lexa struggled to stay on the back of the eagle, nearly losing her grip around its huge neck. The eagle broke off and flew parallel to the ground gently landing beside Maka and Bronto.

Lexa had made it down alive. She at once jumped off the eagles back and fell to the ground. It was good to be out of the cave and back on open ground once again.

Aves then leaped into the air, flapped her powerful wings, and flew off again, flying back up to the cave behind the waterfall. Within a matter of minutes, she disappeared once again into the cave behind the waterfall. The water parted as Aves appeared from the cave with Hope tightly holding on. It was now Hope's turn to enjoy the free fall. Aves plummeted, Hope held on, and they effortlessly landed on the bank by the river next to the other members of the group.

The sunshine felt wonderful to the women who were growing tired of the dark cave. Its rays were warm and comforting in the early morning hours. The temperature outside was warmer than the dusky cavern behind the falls, which was virtually black inside from the absence of light.

"That was incredible," shouted Hope as she jumped off the eagle's back.

Hope sounded like a little kid on a carnival ride for the first time; that first time when you lose all control to the laws of gravity and speed.

"Speak for yourself," replied Lexa.

Lexa was content to keep to the ground and travel on her own two feet. If it were up to her, she would not be flying again anytime soon.

Finally, Bronto broke in and said, "We need to keep moving. We have a lot of ground to cover before dusk. First, we have a long journey through this forest, and then across the open plain, to reach the great swamp, which is quite dangerous. We must reach the forest on the other side before nightfall. It will not be safe for you three once the sun goes down and the denizens of the night come out."

This sent a chill through the girls, who were still waiting for answers to the questions, what, where and why. They had no idea where they were, what these strange creatures were, why they were here, or what happened to Eric, Tak, and CeCe.

"What happens when the sun goes down?" asked Lexa.

Lexa was the one of the three that needed concrete facts not abstract logic. She believed in controlling situations to her advantage. The growing fear was clear on her smooth bronze face, a face that was beautiful even when scared.

Bronto snorted and said, "This world returns back to the time as it once was, before time could change it."

The brute motioned for the rest of the band to follow him. He understood the urgency to reach the forest on the other side of the swamp before nightfall. If caught out in the open after dusk, the girls would be subject to the ferocious species that roamed the night, beasts which could easily kill them. The only choice was to reach the forest on the other side of the swamp before night set in.

This comment, which the girls did not understand, made absolutely no sense to them now, but in time they would grow to understand Bronto's meaning. They felt compelled to trust him. They did recall the strange noises, the screams and the growls, coming from outside the cave last night, but they had no knowledge of what made the eerie sounds, which convinced them that nighttime in this place was very treacherous.

So, the three women, the eagle–like creature Aves, and the beast Bronto all headed away from the river, moving inland towards the mountains, where a series of tall mountain peaks jutted towards the sky off in the distance.

The mountains were volcanic in nature, an observation supported by black, cooled lava fields that stretched out for miles below their summits. It was these mountains that the band looked to reach after navigating the great swamp.

The unlikely band of misfits, both human and non–human, made their way across the plain to the forest, towards the open swamp. The forest, primarily coniferous and deciduous trees, many of which were over 100 feet tall in some areas, entirely blocked out the sunlight from reaching the forest floor. The largest trees stretched out trying to reach the sun–lit heavens to horde the rays of the life–giving sun. The girls were familiar with many of the tree species, but others, oddly shaped with strange leaf patterns, were unfamiliar.

While the group walked, sometimes the vegetation grew so thick, it was difficult to navigate through its entangled maze. The humid wet conditions allowed hundreds of species of plants to thrive wherever the sun penetrated to the floor beneath the canopy. Small fern–like trees along with other leafy plants littered the forest floor. Many shot out long vines to capture more sunlight. Even the vegetation in this land fought to survive.

Insects tirelessly assaulted every living organism. Giant dragonflies the size of small birds zoomed around, passing by the travelers like little dive bombers, each on their own banzai mission. They were blue, turquoise and green in color. When the sunlight hit them at just the right angle, they became iridescent.

Other insects, the size of small rodents, scurried in and out of the vegetation searching for food or trying to escape from being food. Giant centipedes the length of small snakes, crawled from beneath the decaying leaves that littered the forest floor, eagerly waiting to pounce on any species small enough for them to devour.

It was a foregone conclusion that many of these insects emitted poison of one type or another, which further complicated the matter if one of the humans fell victim to a sting or a bite. Persistent biting flies continually ravaged every living species during this time. It was impossible for any of the traveling band to escape the onslaught of the insects. The mosquitoes were three times the size of ordinary mosquitoes and left large welts after feeding on the blood of their victims. Hope, Maka, and Lexa all wished they had some insect repellant to help fend off the relentless attack waged on them by the insect kingdom.

The group traveled for most of the day until it came to the edge of what seemed an endless swamp, consisting of miles and miles of wet, muddy slime that bogged down the group with every step. The smell of dead and decaying organic matter mixed with the occasional rancid odor of foul stagnant water filled their nostrils. Hardly any green vegetation grew anywhere as the group slowly trudged through the shallow water. The water level, consistently a couple of feet deep, did not fluctuate often.

Occasionally, the group would come across a mound of exposed earth, reaching out above the swamp, which offered a momentary respite from the rancid water. The diverse band of travelers would huddle on these elevated islands to rest for short periods of time. The small islands of dirt allowed the women a brief break from the foul water, a water that was brownish in color, a color created by silt deposits from the surrounding water ways.

The women could not see below the surface of the water, which was a good thing, yet this inability to see into the water caused anxiety and uncertainty for the girls. They were sure some creature would rise out of the swamp at any moment and swallow them. The group had no other choice but to continue the slow journey through the swamp. It was crucial they reach the forest before nightfall to allow them time to seek shelter before darkness fell, un-leashing the carnivorous hunters.

Aves, the prehistoric navigation system for the party, would fly ahead of the group, surveying the land for any approaching dangers. The three humans struggled to keep pace with Bronto, who considered this an ordinary jaunt through a swamp. The huge beast would at times wander far out in front of women, leaving the girls vulnerable to attack by any hidden carnivore lurking below the surface of the murky water.

On one of these occasions, Hope noticed a movement, a slight ripple in the shallow water. She turned her attention on the spot where she had seen the movement. Aves had been gone for some time to search for the easiest path through the swamp ahead. The girls could not see

Bronto in the distance. The giant had inadvertently wandered out in front of the defenseless humans once again.

Even Aves, with her incredible eyesight, could not see everything that lurked beneath the surface of the swamp, but the women were sure she could see into the water better than them with her superior eyesight. The huge eagle had the advantage of altitude, which allowed her the ability to look over a vast amount of territory, while effortlessly soaring overhead. She surely would have seen the ripple in the water. The swamp, as with everything in this land, was unforgiving. The ripple in the water caught Hope's eye once again.

"Did you see that?"

It was larger this time and moving fast.

The other two women looked in the direction Hope was pointing. Maka and Lexa simultaneously noticed a movement in the water as it came directly towards them. They could see a black scaly ridge barely breaking the surface of the swamp as it swam directly towards them.

Maka screamed, "Something is attacking! We have to make a run for that strip of land."

Fear was clear in her terrified voice as she turned to flee.

All three girls dashed for the mound of dirt as the creature making the ripple in the water narrowed the distance between them at a tremendous speed.

Chapter 7

Nightfall

Trapped inside the hut for a second chilling night, Eric, Tak, and CeCe, huddled together. The three creatures, Creo, Arcto, and Pith had vanished right before dusk, disappearing into the thick, lush forest. Before leaving, Arcto gave the humans a waxy substance, a substance used in place of a candle. At least this night, while in the hut, they had some light to help ease their minds from the terrifying thoughts brought on by perpetual darkness. Though the light was slight, it gave some solace to the three men. At least now they could see one another in the tiny hut.

The growls and low–pitched mutterings randomly came and went, but it was the blood curdling screams that made the men uneasy. These would break the silence; sometimes near, sometimes from far away. The startling screams penetrated the tranquility of the nighttime air waves, overriding the constant pulsating sound created by the millions of insects scuttling about, camouflaged behind the cloak of darkness.

Finally, Eric broke the silence and said, "Guys, I think I know where we are, but it will sound crazy."

"Where?" replied Tak, eager to hear Eric's hypothesis.

"Yea, I would like someone to explain it to me too," mumbled CeCe.

CeCe was usually the talker of the group. No one could talk like CeCe, but he had been unusually quiet since waking up in the hut. He was eager to listen to any explanation if it made sense.

"Ok! I know this seems impossible...but I think we're somewhere in the history of the past Earth. I would say in the Eocene Epoch, which was between 54-38 million years ago."

"That is impossible," screamed CeCe, a look of confusion readily clear on his dark face.

His expression was one of both fear and unbelievable denial.

Tak looked at his good friend and asked, "What makes you think that?"

Tak knew his friend well and was aware of his background in archeology and paleontology. The native realized they were lucky to have Eric's knowledge on the pre–history of the Earth if that is where they really were. Tak knew they would need to draw on his knowledge more than once if they were going to escape this place and return to the campsite along the river in their world.

"One of the beasts called himself Creo of the Creodonts. Creodonts were the first successful carnivorous mammals that evolved were the first successful carnivorous mammals that evolved during the Paleocene Epoch around 65 million years ago, shortly after the mass extinction event known as the Cretaceous–Paleogene (K–Pg). During the Eocene Epoch, 56 million years ago to 36 million years ago, Creodonts were the top predators on the planet. They existed long before the modern carnivores evolved on Earth and towards the end of their reign on Earth, they subsisted alongside them. Creodonts died out for a few reasons. One major reason was due to their size. Many were large, some were giant, and this made them slow runners. They walked flat footed on short legs, tipped with claws. The modern carnivores, from the order Carnivora, replaced them in part because they were faster, smarter and could catch the evolving prey species. As the Earth began to cool down, which changed the environment, prey species evolved to run faster. The world, once covered entirely in forests and swamps, changed. It slowly transformed into a world with a drier, cooler climate and many forests died out and gave way to plains and grasslands. This opened the world to the hoofed animals which evolved to run faster. Creodonts, predators that evolved over millions of years to be ambush hunters, could no longer keep pace with these new faster food sources."

Both Tak and CeCe looked at him in astonishment. How could they go to sleep one minute and end up 50 million years earlier just hours later? They both shook their heads in bewilderment.

"Are you sure about this Eric? I know you're the expert, but how is this even possible? I can understand it because I can see it, but it's still unbelievable," commented the proud Native American.

There was no questioning Tak's bravery, a trait passed down from an extensive line of proud Sioux ancestors. He was not afraid of anything. As a young man, he went on his vision quest, braving the harshest elements possible for days without food or water. This made him a stronger person, one who learned to endure stress and adverse conditions while keeping calm and in control. The unbelievable notion of all three of them now trapped back in time terrified him but it also fascinated him.

"I know it sounds incredible, but it has to be true. How else can it be explained?"

Eric, well versed in the science of fossil searching, had spent the last three summers in the field at many different archeological dig sites throughout Montana and Wyoming. From an early age, the history of the Earth always intrigued Eric, which led him down the path to study paleontology and archaeology. Life on planet Earth intrigued him.

"I believe it!" cried out CeCe, who was prone to be more superstitious in nature.

CeCe grew up in the Deep South and was aware of the strange practices of voodoo and black magic. He grew up around his aunts who lived in New Orleans and dabbled in the dark sciences. CeCe had seen their supernatural powers firsthand. He was a believer in black magic, but not necessarily time travel.

"It's the only rational explanation I can come up with," Eric simply added, having difficulty hiding his excitement.

"So, what about the other two beasts?" Tak asked.

"Well, I would say the ape-like creature **Pith** is the extinct hominid called Giganti**pith**ecus blacki. It was one of the largest apes, standing over 9 feet tall and weighing over 1200 pounds, that ever-roamed Earth. This ape lived in existence with our ancestors, disappearing around 100,000 years ago. It could break CeCe in half with one blow from its mighty stump-like arms," he jokingly said as he let out a laugh.

Eric liked to get the big guy going when he could. It was always in playful fun, and besides, he learned at an early age that humor helped to diffuse tense situations.

"But we better be careful with him."

Eric assumed the monstrous ape was a dim wit capable of sudden outbursts of rage. A giant that big could dispatch a human in seconds, so it would be wise for them to stay on good terms with the ape and try to befriend him. In that moment, he decided to call him Squatch after the mythological creature Sasquatch. They all got a good laugh from this and if the ape-thing were as dim witted as Eric thought, it would not know the difference.

"Then what about Arcto?" asked CeCe, who thought to himself, what could that thing be?

"He would be an Arctoid. These evolved over 42 million years ago. They are also known by the term canoids. There were four families of Arctoids: canids, mustelids, ursids and procyonids. One group, named Canids, included extinct bear-dogs, wolves and other similar beasts. A second group called Mustelids evolved into otters, weasels, and badgers. Ursids include bears and the giant panda, while Procyonids went on to become raccoons, the lesser pandas, and coatis. It would be safe to say this Arcto is an ursid because he resembles a bear."

CeCe scoffed, "I don't care what they are, and why are they running around on two legs like us?"

CeCe had made a valid point. Both Creo and Arcto were four legged animals from a time long ago. In fact, Megistotherium was one of the largest known Creodonts to roam the Earth and weighed up to 2000 pounds. It preyed on earlier forms of mastodons as well as other giant ungulates. Megistotherium was one of the many Creodonts that ruled the Earth for millions of years and were phenomenally successful during their reign as top apex predators.

It was hard for the humans to grasp the concept of a creature capable of bringing down something larger than any elephant living today; by itself. Today, it takes a pride of lions to kill a modern-day elephant. What chance would ordinary humans have in the world of Creodonts and Arctoids?

"Why they're on two feet, I don't know yet. What's fascinating is that around 26 million years ago, another branch of species split from the Arctoids to become known as the pinnipeds, a group that went on to evolve into seals and walruses. Let's hope we don't run into any of them walking on two feet. They went from land animals to sea dwelling predators."

Eric laughed! "We have to keep positive," he said.

He knew it would take intelligence to survive in this ancient primal world, a world where humans were absent for a reason.

"We'll need to make weapons to help us survive here. I wish I had my backpack and my hunting knife. It would be nice to make some spears and even a bow and arrow," Tak said.

The native did have the knowledge and the skills to do this. Not only to make them but use them as well.

"You're right. If we're in the Eocene, we're but small morsels to the fierce predators of this time," replied Eric.

Eric understood they would need some type of protection, yet what good was a knife against the size of the beasts that dominated this period? He realized they would have to stay close to the three strange creatures now guarding them, guarding them at least during the light of day. Where did they go at night? This was the question that perplexed the blonde Norseman.

The fascinating narrative ended when a loud growling sound started close to the hut.

"What was that?" whispered CeCe, his nerves on edge.

He lowered himself to the floor of the hut and squatted down.

"I don't know," replied Eric and Tak simultaneously, as they sat down on the floor of the hut.

"One of us should move up against the door," whispered Eric.

He realized the only way into the enclosure was through the door, so it needed fortification.

"CeCe, you are the biggest and heaviest of us. You should be the one to hold the door," Tak said.

CeCe moved over and leaned up against the door of the hut. He put the bulk of his 300 pounds against the door and braced himself by digging his heels into the dirt of the hut floor.

The low-pitched snorting sound came closer and closer to the enclosure. The men could hear the heavy thud of footsteps as the animal sniffed around the outer walls of the vulnerable structure. Whatever it was, had great bulk and tremendous size. At one point the beast brushed up against the hut, testing the soundness of the enclosure. The walls shook violently but held fast.

Tak and Eric moved closer to CeCe to help support the door in case the unknown monstrosity attacked them. The intensity of the situation escalated when they felt the movement of air filter through the cracks in the door as the beast exhaled through its nostrils.

The scent of the creature's breath was foul with the distinct smell of decaying vegetation. It was close to the men now, just beyond the few inches of protection the door offered. They could feel it press on the door as the door began to push inward from the massive bulk of the giant animal just inches away from the defenseless humans. It let out a low grunt as it strained to gain entrance.

The three men dug their heels deep into the dirt floor of the primitive hut and strained to keep the attacking beast out. The creature pushed harder, and the three men slid farther into the interior of the hut. They were no match for the strength of the monstrous animal outside the door.

Suddenly the men heard a loud terrifying scream, which caused the brute outside the door to abruptly stop pushing up against the door and flee. Something had frightened the intruder, causing it to flee for its life.

The three men could hear the petrified animal running for what they thought was the open field that led to the forest. The creature's thudding hooves stopped suddenly when some other primitive monster violently attacked it.

The three humans could hear a fierce battle for survival begin, coming from the field around the hut. They heard bellowing and screaming mixed in with horrific growls. The clash sounded fierce, of epic proportion. Some type of carnivorous predator had attacked the animal that had been sniffing at the door of the hut. The outcome of the fight could save the humans from the beast outside the door, but it could put them into more danger from the second creature if it won the fight. Only time would tell.

The two creatures battled for what seemed hours to the trapped humans. They could hear the heavy blows as one beast violently clashed into the other, followed by chilling screams and cries of agony. The battle waged on as one of the combatants would momentarily gain the advantage, then counter moves by the other one would equalize the fight momentarily.

Finally, loud screams took over, and the three men, convinced that the creature outside the door was losing, waited in silence inside the tiny hut. The low grunting, which had dominated the early struggle, started to subside.

CeCe, the anxiety of the unknown finally winning out, cracked open the door to see what was happening outside. The three humans, astonished by the outside spectacle, peeked through the narrow crack in the door.

There was a huge rhino sized animal battling an enormous dog–like monster just outside the hut. The big herbivore was in a struggle for its life as the enormous dog–like carnivore lunged, trying to slash deep gashes into the thick hide of the giant plant eater.

"I think that rhino-sized thing is called Uintatherium and the other thing is a Sarkastodon," Eric enthusiastically whispered.

"Incredible!" he softly said.

The Uintatherium was larger than any rhino they were familiar with. It had three sets of horns that protruded from its gigantic head in different directions and a hide that was rough and thick like an elephant or rhinoceros with a thin layering of hair. The massive sets of horns, used for battle with others of its own species and to fight off attacks from predators, dripped the blood of the giant Sarkastodon. It was an imposing beast, one that could tip the scale at over 4,400 pounds with a length of up to 12.5 feet. This Uintatherium was in a battle for its life and it was losing. **(Image 2: Uintatherium: page 129)**

The Sarkastodon was a huge hyper carnivore that could weigh up to 900 pounds with a length of 9 feet. It looked like a cross between an enormous type of dog-like creature and a weasel. It had bone crushing, powerful jaws like a hyena. It could crush bones with its strong molars, feasting on bone as well as flesh. It was an intimidating, powerful predator that roamed the Earth as a top predator for millions of years. **(Image 3: Eocene animals of Asia: page 130)**

The two massive combatants lunged at each other. The carnivore would attack, and the huge herbivore would counter with mighty blows from its solid, sharp horns. This went on for close to 45 minutes, as each beast countered the other's moves. At one point the Uintatherium drove a horned blow to the Sarkastodon's shoulder, and the massive predator fell to the ground.

The three humans, watching the life and death struggle, thought the battle was edging towards the vegetation eater and were relieved that the mighty carnivore was losing. They felt their odds increased with the rhino-like beast winning. They knew if the meat eater won, it was possible they could be the next meal for the carnivore.

The fight raged on. Blood was streaming down the side of the Sarkastodon as it struggled to regain its footing. It bolstered the energy for one last lunge and thrust itself at the snorting Uintatherium. The momentum of the lunge knocked the giant herbivore to the ground, rolling it onto its back, which exposed its vulnerable underbelly. Within a matter of seconds, the hyper carnivore, seizing the opportunity, applied the death grip to the exhausted Uintatherium's throat, which struggled for a few minutes, the last minutes of its life, then let out a horrific gasp. The battle was over—the predator the victor.

The Sarkastodon let out a monstrous scream as the Uintatherium's body went limp. The scream was so terrorizing that it caused Eric, CeCe, and Tak to quickly close the door to the hut. They feared they were next. What chance would they have against the vicious power of the winner of the epic battle they had just seen? They could only hope the beast was too exhausted to attack them. Besides, it had all the food it could need with the gargantuan herbivore lying just yards away from the hut.

"That was extraordinary," replied Eric, who was both frightened and fascinated by the savage display of carnal ferocity.

"No, that was frightening," uttered CeCe.

The fear was clear in the expression on his face.

"How do we survive in this hostile, cruel place?"

CeCe was a powerful man, but he realized this meant nothing in this primordial place, a place where they dwelled close to the bottom of the food chain.

"I don't know. But we must. We need to find the girls. Hopefully tomorrow in the light of day we can get some answers from our captors," Eric forcefully stated.

"I'm with you, Eric. We need to keep our wits. The girls could be anywhere, but with any luck, maybe they didn't even wake up here," Tak answered.

This was a thought none of them had realized until now. Perhaps Maka, Hope, and Lexa were back in the real world looking for them right now. They would not give up on them.

The three men leaned up against the door for hours. They could hear the carnage outside, as the victor savagely tore off large chunks of flesh and cracked bones with its powerful jaws. It was inconceivable to them how one creature could gorge itself to that extent. The massive Sarkastodon was devouring hundreds of pounds of meat just outside the tiny hut. They were nothing more than a snack to this thing. They realized their insignificance in this place; a savage world, one that existed millions of years ago.

The light of early morning was beginning to break as the three huddled together in the hut. It was almost impossible to rest, but they took turns throughout the unnerving night. The carnage continued for hours, finally stopping around dawn.

Takoda was the first to hear the rustling of the nearby trees. He quickly nudged CeCe and Eric. He motioned them to keep quiet. The heavy sounds of footsteps moved closer towards the hut. The men could hear deep breathing as the creature slowly rounded the side of the hut and approached the door. Deep, horrifying growls, growls that terrified the hut inhabitants, reverberated off the structure. The creature crept to the door, slowly running its hardened claws down the wooden frame. The terrified men moved to the far edge of the hut. Then the door swung open.

Chapter 8

The Swamp

The ripple in the water, now moving at a tremendous speed, came bearing down on the women. They tirelessly fought the suction like grip of the thick mud of the swamp with each step as they tried to flee the inevitable attack from the cloaked menace, hiding just below the surface of the murky water. The assailant quickly closed the gap between itself, Maka, Lexa, and Hope, as they continued to struggle free from the mud below the surface of the swamp. Each step took considerable effort to pull loose from the quicksand like sludge that lined the bottom of the fowl water and hindered the women from reaching the tiny island jutting from the swamp in the distance ahead.

The women labored with every motion as the slithering monster creating the ripple bore down upon them. They had to reach the small island that rose from the swamp before the unidentified foe reached them. The island would offer solid ground for the girls to stand on, but it would give them little protection from the pursuing creature if it could breathe oxygen and leave the water.

"Run!" screamed Maka.

Maka could now see the outline of a giant serpent swimming directly at them. The slinking reptile, coming straight towards the women, was obviously hunting and the women were on the menu. The women could not see Bronto anywhere; the brute had inadvertently strayed too far ahead of them to offer speedy protection.

Aves, flying ahead to scout the area, had been gone for hours. She often flew ahead of the party to use her superior eyesight to search for the easiest way through the swamp and to guide them around any impending danger.

The three women, all running for the closest island, were on their own now. The muck slowed their progress with every step. Escape was futile; they could not outrun the serpent. Their only choice was to stand and fight, fight with the only weapons they had, fist, foot and teeth. If they could jab the snake in the eye, causing injury, it might buy them some time to escape.

They huddled together, back to back, to form a circle. Without the two super creatures to protect them, they stood little chance against the massive serpent. The one advantage they had was their wits. They would have to outsmart it until Bronto, or Aves returned. If they could somehow avoid the snake's strikes, they could drag out the fight.

The monstrous snake was within 10 yards of the girls when they recognized just how enormous the serpent was. It was over 80 feet long, python-like, with huge armor-like scales. Its head was exceptionally large, large enough to swallow a horse, a human or all three humans. The scales on it were grey and black, colors which helped it blend into the environment very effectively. A massive red, head, with yellow menacing eyes, crowned the top of the snake's slithering body. The serpent's body was at least four feet in girth, girth easily wide enough to swallow and digest something much larger than a human. It was hungry with one thing driving it, dinner; and the girls were the main dish.

The reptile, now within striking distance, raised itself slightly out of the water to gain a better sense of where the women were by flicking its large tongue in and out. The women could see several rows of razor-sharp teeth, slightly curving backwards, in the serpent's powerful jaws when it fully opened its mouth. These backward curving teeth allowed it to move any unfortunate victim down into its great body for digestion.

The snake struck, slightly lifting itself from the swamp with huge jaws extended, as Maka, Lexa, and Hope jumped to the side and out of its path. The giant serpent missed its mark as the women stepped out of harm's way temporarily.

The giant snake recoiled and turned to attack once more. Then something miraculous happened. A giant crocodilian reptile, the size of a small dinosaur, thrust itself out of the water and seized the mighty snake around its mid-section. A tremendous battle ensued.

The crocodile's powerful jaws latched onto the snake, clamping down like a steel vise. The struggling, surprised serpent wrapped itself around the amphibious beast to squeeze the life out of it with its crushing death grip. The crocodile spun itself violently with great force to untangle the serpent. The serpent applied constant pressure, as the two intertwined giants slipped beneath the surface of the water to continue the battle in the depths of the murky swamp.

The humans, seizing the opportunity to escape, ran towards the tiny island in the distance. None of them looked back to see which creature won or if either of the two reptilian monstrosities even resurfaced. They needed time to put distance between them and the victor of the brutal battle. The epic encounter opened an avenue of escape, so the girls took advantage of it. To them, it did not matter which beast won. There was little doubt in their minds, the crocodile was hunting them just as the giant snake was. Either of the creatures could have easily killed one or all of them that day. They were lucky this time. This close encounter was the first time all three women utterly understood the savage brutality of this hostile world, a world where it was fight and kill to survive.

They ran through the swamp, battling the mud and water with every step, until they came to the small island, a strip of land covered by primitive palm-like trees. The island, one of the larger ones they had come across, was the size of a football field. It was safer on dry land so the three climbed out of the knee-deep water and stood on the dry ground. It was good to be out of the water for the first time in hours.

The three women were exhausted, so they took the opportunity to rest. The incident with the giant serpent pushed them beyond their endurance level. The ordeal seemed surreal; to be that close to death terrified the women.

"What do you suppose happened to that snake? I've never seen a python that big before. We're lucky to be alive," Hope exclaimed.

Hope was familiar with the green anaconda that lived in the Amazon, but it was nothing compared to the size of the lurking reptilian predator that lived in the swamp.

"I don't know and don't care. I'm just thankful that croc came along when it did," replied Lexa.

Lexa was deathly afraid of snakes. While on a hiking trip in the American southwest when she was a teenager, a rattlesnake bit Lexa. It took her months to recover from the serpent's bite. Since that time, she tried to avoid snakes at all cost.

"I'm glad we didn't stick around to see which one won. They were both giants if you ask me!" Maka added.

Maka realized they had just barely escaped death. The encounter came awfully close to ending in disaster, so she needed to make sure Bronto and Aves stayed closer to them for protection. The two beasts were vital to their surviving long term in this primitive place.

"Just wait until I see that Bronto and Aves again!"

Maka was truly angry at the two super beasts, beasts in charge of protecting them. Their carelessness could have gotten one or more of them killed and swallowed by a prehistoric python.

"I'll give them a piece of my mind! We're lucky to be alive."

The three humans rested, trying to regain their composure from the intense release of adrenaline. They were about to trudge on when Aves flew in. The giant bird of prey lightly landed on the island sanctuary of vegetation.

Aves was a magnificent creature with eyes the color of bronze. Her glare was transfixing and she no doubt could see for miles and miles from high above the swamp. She defined grace and fluidity.

Maka, unable to let things rest, went up to Aves and forcefully asked, "Why did you fly off and leave us alone? A horrific snake almost killed us, and we had to flee for our lives. No thanks to you!"

Maka was flailing her arms around and pointing her finger at the avian behemoth. The eagle just looked at her and shook its massive head. Then it let out a loud screech and Maka stopped talking.

"I had to fly ahead and see how much farther we needed to go before we lose the light of day," the raptor calmly replied.

Aves was quite calm and took Maka's criticism very well. She either took it well or was just ignoring the animated human's comments. This seemed to just further anger Maka, but she realized arguing with the eagle was pointless, so she kept quiet.

Shortly after Aves returned, Bronto reemerged, covered in a thick layer of mud, which had dried to his great body. The three girls told him the story of the snake, the crocodile and the frightful battle that had ensued. He solemnly apologized for getting too far ahead and vowed that it would not happen again.

Bronto, while out searching for a faster route through the swamp, became mired in a deep pool of quicksand and struggled for some time to escape. At one point, he feared for his life, as he fought to free himself. Once freed he continued until he found a way around the quagmire. He then returned as quickly as he could.

"I found a way out of the swamp and back into the forest," he told Aves and the three humans.

The massive brute was near exhaustion from his exploits.

"We'll need to hurry to make it into the forest before nightfall."

The three girls, noticing the apprehension in Bronto's tone, quickly got up to resume the journey. They had seen what the swamp had to offer and felt solid ground would offer more protection, protection at least from the strange monsters that inhabited the swamp. What hideous creatures inhabited the forest was another matter.

The group traveled for a few more hours, until they finally reached the edge of the forest. The sun blazed down upon them as they left the foul, dank, swamp water behind and climbed out onto solid ground. It was a comfort to be out of the shallow water and on dry ground again.

The forest, primarily made up of redwood trees now, gave a wonderful reprise from the swamp cypresses that sporadically grew throughout the swamp. The temperature remained extremely hot, the air extremely humid, as the mid-afternoon sun beat down upon the land.

The small band stopped to eat some fruit they found growing at the edge of the forest, which refreshed them, offering sweet energy producing nectar. Hope, Lexa, and Maka were extremely exhausted by the long journey through the swamp. The rest was much needed, but they realized they needed to get as far away from the swamp as possible; they saw firsthand what perils the swamp had to offer and gaining distance from the swamp drove them on.

Bronto and Aves stood up to resume the trek, quickly followed by the three humans. Bronto took the lead, the girls followed, and Aves brought up the rear. They stayed close together this time. The task of protecting the three girls was now the priority of the two super beasts. There would be no more swamp mishaps while they were in charge. The band walked for a couple more hours before stopping in a small clearing.

The clearing, nestled between giant Sequoia trees on one side and old Beech trees on the other, stretched out for a couple hundred yards. The bases of the giant Sequoias were at least 25% larger than the current day Sequoias, due to the year–round warm climate and tropical rainy conditions on Earth during this time, which allowed all species to grow at an accelerated rate.

It was time to prepare for the night, as the light of day began to wane. Aves flew up into the treetops and quickly constructed a primitive nest for the girls to sleep in. Bronto stood guard on the forest floor at the base of the trees. The behemoth brute took his role as protector profoundly serious now, another mishap on his watch would not happen.

"Are we going to sleep up there?" Hope asked as she looked up at the great height of the tree.

The sleeping nest was around 30 feet up in the air. The tree itself was more than 100 feet tall with massive, sturdy branches that started around 25 feet up from the mighty base of the tree. Bronto assured them they would be safe from marauding predators at that height.

"What if I fall out while sleeping?" asked Lexa, obviously not thrilled about sleeping that high off the ground.

She did realize it would be safer up there than down on the ground, so she let the subject drop.

"If you fall, I guess we will continue the journey one short," mused Aves.

Aves was very independent in her own right. She had the ability to fly and go anywhere she wished, which allowed her absolute freedom. The mighty bird realized Lexa had some of these traits as well and admired the Latino for speaking her mind.

"That's not funny! You're supposed to be protecting us...Right?" Lexa snapped back at the avian beast.

"You are right. I was just having fun with you," Aves responded.

Aves then grabbed the Latino sass and shot up the base of the giant tree. Lexa barely had time to grab on. Aves landed on a branch next to the soft cushion of pine needles she had prepared for the humans to sleep on. She dropped Lexa and shot back down the massive base of the redwood and returned moments later with Maka. She deposited the native and then retrieved

Hope and within minutes, all three of the women were sitting 30 feet above the ground in the canopy of the immense redwood forest.

Dusk was quickly approaching as the two super beasts said goodbye. Aves returned to the forest floor where Bronto was patiently waiting. The Brontotheres quickly disappeared into the forest running along one of the many game trails until the thick vegetation swallowed his massive frame. Aves took to flight and was gone in a matter of seconds. As darkness started to set in, the girls settled down for the night. This would be the second night in this strange land.

Hope sighed and said, "We should get some sleep. Tomorrow will be a better day and I just pray there won't be another swamp in our way."

Hope had a positive outlook on life and always looked for the good in everything. She tried to project a calm relaxing energy.

Maka laughed and replied, "I'm with you! I never want to see another swamp, so I guess Florida is out."

Maka, tired from the long day of struggle and conflict while navigating the swamp, was ready for a good sleep. The day had been physically draining on the native.

"I hope your right Hope," responded Lexa, as she stretched out in the nest and soon fell asleep.

All three women were sleeping within minutes. They spent a great deal of physical energy traveling through the dangerous swamp but sometimes it is the psychological strain that can cause exhaustion. This day was a combination of the two which made sleep a much welcome agent.

The nest was surprisingly wonderfully comfortable, and the hot and humid climate added to the overall coziness of it. They were far enough off the ground to keep marauding forest floor predators from reaching them, but they had no idea what types of creatures lived in the canopy of the trees. The hours passed as the three women slept high up in the giant Sequoia.

An awful scream abruptly awakened the three girls. It was close to the tree, somewhere in the clearing below. The moon, which seemed closer to them in this odd world, was up and offered great lighting. The night was lighter than the moonlight on a night with a full moon in a snowstorm, the kind of snowstorm when everything becomes illuminated.

"Did you hear that?" whispered Hope.

She was nervous as she looked around the nest. The sound had abruptly ended her peaceful sleep.

"Yes!" replied Lexa.

It did not take much to scare her. She was already sitting up and peeking over the side of the nest.

"Stay calm," cautioned Maka.

She had a calming effect on the other two. She knew everyone needed to keep their wits to avoid unnecessary over reaction.

"Be quiet and don't move! We need to avoid being detected."

Maka knew silence was the best defense.

The night echoed with other terrible noises. There were harsh screams and deep moans coming from the thick forest. They could hear the rustling of branches and padded footsteps around the tree, coming from below, as stealthy denizens of the night roamed the forest, looking for food. Occasionally, they could smell the rancid odor of some marauding beast wafting up from the meadow below.

At one point, below in the clearing, they heard a horrid conflict erupt. They quietly peered over the edge of the nest to see the battle as it escalated. One creature, which looked like a cross between a small horse and a tapir, struggled to escape a predator. The other beast, the predator, reminded the observers of a monster weasel. It was weasel-like but larger than anything they had seen in the modern world; the world they called home.

The stocky predator pounced on the back of the horse–tapir animal, biting it repeatedly on the neck. The small horse kicked and bit at the attacker but could not shake off the furry vermin. Within minutes after gaining the back of the horse–tapir beast, the weasel brute sunk its fangs into the throat of the unfortunate victim and the struggle was over.

The three girls, shocked by the brutality of the attack, watched as the little creature took its last breath. The struggle of life and death in their world, rarely seen by the ordinary human, disturbed the women, but in this place, it was an everyday, ordinary event.

The weasel gorged itself on the flesh of its fallen quarry. Maka, Lexa, and Hope could hear the snapping and crushing of bones from high up in the canopy. It made them shutter. That could easily be one of them.

In this place, the struggle of life and death was a normal every-day occurrence. Their goal was to stay on the life side. The creatures in this world had no fear of humans. The girls could attest to this firsthand. Life was in jeopardy with every step, every turn, every path taken. How long could they survive in this hostile world?

Chapter 9

The Forest

Eric, Tak, and CeCe, hearing the lumbering footsteps outside the shelter, hopped up to battle the approaching intruder. The aggressors hardened fingernails scraping against the outside of the structure terrified the three humans.

The door to the hut flew open, sending the men sprawling to the dirt, as the huge hominid Pith burst inside. The men, quickly realizing it was the giant ape they had jokingly named Squatch, relaxed and regained their feet.

The ape grunted in a deep, low tone. A grunt was Pith's way of acknowledging the humans, who to this point had not impressed him. He considered them a weak and fragile species. Pith raised one of his massive hands and pointed to the doorway, a gesture to move the men outside.

"I guess he wants us to go outside," said Eric, who found it odd that Squatch did not talk as much as the other two creatures: Creo and Arcto.

Eric, convinced the ape-beast had a small inferior brain, assumed this was the primary reason for his lack of profundity in his speech.

Pith was a menacing specimen of savage brutality. His fangs were exceptionally long with yellowish stains from years of eating fruit and carrion. They protruded out from enormously powerful jaws; jaws capable of inflicting serious wounds on anything unfortunate enough the meet them. All three men realized it would be wise to stay on the giant ape's good side. The time might come when they needed his help.

"I agree. We better go outside," responded CeCe.

The three humans walked through the door, into the cool, refreshing morning air. The fresh air was a welcome relief from the musty, dank scent of the hut. To the men, freedom from the hut was the first step in finding out answers, answers to what and why they were here.

The three exited the hut followed by Squatch. That was his new name for now. The giant did not seem to mind his new name as he exited the hut, ran towards the forest and briefly glanced back at the humans. After flashing a menacing scowl, he climbed into the overhead canopy and vanished. Where he went was a mystery to Tak, CeCe, and Eric.

The three men moved to the clearing behind the hut, where they saw first–hand the carnage from the previous night. The ravaged carcass of the Uintatherium lay where the giant beast had fallen during the night. The Sarkastodon, after gorging itself for hours on the flesh of the plant eater, wandered off into the forest to sleep off the immense quantity of flesh it had consumed.

Tak went over to the carcass knelt and took a few morsels of meat.

"We need to get a fire going, so we can cook up some of this meat. No need to let it go to waste," he replied.

The native realized they needed protein to keep strong. Besides that, it was not every day they had the opportunity to eat the meat of an animal that lived 50 million years ago.

Tak, displaying a large grin, asked, "I wonder if it will taste like chicken?"

"I will get some wood," answered Eric, shaking his head as he disappeared behind the hut to find some branches and sticks for a fire.

Eric shortly returned with a large armload of wood and dropped the branches on the ground. He then lit the fire with a lighter he still had in his pocket from the camping trip. At least that had gone their way. He wished he had his knife and pistol, especially the pistol. The beasts in this land were flesh and bone, both susceptible to the bullet. He realized they would need to make weapons to survive in this hostile place. As soon as the opportunity presented itself, he would fashion a good knife made from either obsidian or chert, whichever mineral he found first. Confident both types of minerals existed here, he decided to search for them if they journeyed away from this area. He would keep an eye out for either type as they traveled.

CeCe cooked the Uintatherium meat, meat he had cut off from around the backbone of the fallen behemoth. He was the barbeque man. The pit-master. He placed the flesh of the Uintatherium on sticks to roast it. The delightful aroma filled the area around the hut, which alarmed the men. They were sure the aroma would attract unwanted predators, but all three were ravenous and needed to eat. The Uintatherium tenderloin would deliver the rich nourishment their depleted bodies desperately lacked. The fruit from the day before was great for hydration, but it offered truly little protein.

Tak, seeing his opportunity to razz CeCe, said, "You might be the first person to ever barbeque CeCe. Just think, this might be the first-time meat was ever purposely cooked."

CeCe just smiled and laughed. "This will be one story I will tell my entire life. Too bad no one will believe it," he joked.

He continued to cook the meat, all the while grinning, as he kept talking smack.

The three enjoyed the meal, which was the first real food the men had ingested since the abduction during the night a few days earlier. It was much needed sustenance. The warm protein revived them both physically and mentally. It was one less thing to worry about as they prepared for another day.

CeCe cooked extra meat to take with them if they did get a chance to leave the hut. It was time to start preparing for every trial or tribulation that befell them as they traveled in this strange, alien time.

The smell of the roasting flesh did attract others. Squatch re-emerged from the forest and loped across the open field. He looked puzzled by the fire, but even more so by the smell of the cooked flesh.

"What that?" the giant muttered in a low pitched, hoarse voice, resembling a growl.

The giant ape pointed at the fire and then at the meat on the stick placed in the fire. The meat sizzled as the aroma filled the mighty ape's nostrils. His expression was one of puzzled bewilderment. To the men it was obvious the giant ape had never been this close to fire before or even smelled roasted flesh, much less eaten cooked meat.

"It is known as fire," Tak explained to the giant hominid.

"We humans use fire for heat and for cooking food. It can also be used for protection against roaming predators at night," he further explained.

Tak was not sure the dim-witted ape could understand him as he tried to explain it, but he offered an explanation anyway. The ape just glared at the meat as it popped from the overheated oils in the flesh.

"I see," uttered the ape, who was obviously more interested in the sizzling meat now.

Squatch bent in close to the fire and sniffed the cooking flesh. Saliva began to run down his tremendous fangs, drip into the ash, which in turn caused small puffs of smoke to waft up into the morning air. The salivating beast seemed transfixed by the roasting meat on the stick.

"Do you want a piece?" asked Eric.

He reached down, picked up one of the sticks with a large chunk of meat on it, and handed it to Squatch. The perplexed ape grabbed the stick forcefully in one hand, turned and ran a short distance from the humans, then stopped. He bit down on the flesh with his mighty jaws and let out a loud, horrific scream when he burnt his mouth on the scalding meat.

"That's what we call hot!" laughed Eric.

"You have to let it cool down," added CeCe as he let out a thunderous laugh.

The ape glared at the humans with a heavy scowl on his face. It was clear the new sensation was disagreeable to his senses.

"You think funny?"

The men could see saliva running down his chin, as he scowled at them in deep disgruntlement.

Tak quickly shouted, "Hold on Squatch!"

Tak wanted to avoid any physical outburst by the giant. One such rampant outburst could lead to all three of them dead in a matter of minutes.

"Oh, come on Squatch! We meant you no harm," replied CeCe.

"You have to blow on it," instructed Tak, as he parsed his lips and blew out air to show the ape how to cool down the flesh.

The big ape imitated the human and blew on the food until it was cool enough to eat. He bit off a large chunk and quickly scoffed it down. The scowl on his face turned to joy once the rich flavor of the meat conquered his taste buds. Pith liked roasted meat and motioned for CeCe to give him another piece.

"Why you call me Squatch?" he asked with a puzzled look on his face.

The juice of the roasted flesh dripped down his long face, soaking his chest hairs.

Tak was quick to answer, "Where we are from, there is a myth or legend of a creature called Sasquatch, Yeti, or Bigfoot. There are many different names for this creature. It is a giant ape-like creature that people throughout history have reported seeing. Although the creature has eluded capture, reports of sightings, generation after generation continue. You remind us of this beast, so we call you Squatch. It is a nickname of sorts."

"Ok," replied the ape-man.

Whether the ape understood what Tak said was unknown, but he seemed satisfied with this answer. He went over to the nearby stream, bent down and drank his fill of water.

Up until this point, the three men had failed to notice the stream that ran right by the hut. They heard the water, while they huddled in the shelter for safety, but none of them had bothered to look for it. When they saw Squatch amble towards the stream, they became aware of their own thirst. They too went over to the stream and drank their fill. It must have been a colossal sight; a gigantic hominid, one that lived a million years earlier, with three modern humans, all bent down in the most primitive form to drink water from an ancient river. A camera would have been priceless.

They stood up from the stream after drinking their fill to see Creo and Arcto approaching. Both were formidable, powerful beasts. It was on this occasion that Eric, CeCe, and Tak first questioned their form.

"Why are the two of you bipedal in form...and not on all fours?" Eric asked.

Eric realized the two super beasts should be traveling on all four feet and be much bigger. In their time, they would have been massive beasts, beasts at the top of the food chain.

"And why can you talk to us in our language?" CeCe added.

If they could communicate in English, then walking on two legs was not that strange, he thought. CeCe was up for any explanation.

Creo stared at the humans and simply said, "Your questions will be answered when we get to the time of Megalo."

"How do we get there?" asked Tak.

The Sioux native did not like the sound of Megalo. It could only mean giant, and what could be bigger than their three massive captors?

Creo and Arcto just ignored the question. It was time to move on. Arcto instructed the humans to start walking towards the forest. Arcto led the way followed by Eric, CeCe, and Tak—Squatch and Creo took up the rear. They made it to the edge of the forest and entered the thick vegetation, where the dense foliage quickly swallowed them up, concealing any trace of them from the open field and the small hut.

The forest was full of lush green plants and endless tree species. Ferns grew at the lower heights, while maple, walnut, poplar, birch and many other types of trees fought for the sunlight at the top heights of the canopy. It was amazing to the three humans that a forest could embody so much diversity.

The number of animal species seemed endless. The forest reminded the men of a rainforest, a rainforest on steroids. It was inconceivable to see creatures never seen by the human eye. Species ranged from small, rabbit–like animals with long legs and slim bodies to massive rhino–like giants that varied in size. Some had peculiar horns, some had enormously long horns, and some had no horns at all. Life here astounded the humans. They saw giant warthog like beasts with multiple sets of tusks that could easily disembowel a man. One small creature, which they saw in large numbers, looked like the early ancestor of the modern horse. It stood only a couple of feet tall, had four toes on its front feet, and three toes on its hind feet.

Eric, Tak, and CeCe knew they were seeing life as it existed millions of years ago. This world, totally foreign to them, perpetuated evolutionary experimentation. Species exploded in every form to fill every niche, some environmentally unique, some uniquely common.

The reason they were here, in this place, continued to be a mystery to the men. What impact could three or six humans (if the girls were here) have on this complex eco–system? Takoda and CeCe now understood the words spoken by Eric the prior night: Paleocene Epoch, millions of years ago. How to survive here was another issue.

"Wow!" was all Tak could say.

Tak was an avid outdoorsman but this was beyond the scope of his reason. The native wanted to take back some of the strange horn patterns he was seeing. What a story they would make in front of his tribal council.

"This is incredible," replied Eric, fascinated by the reality of seeing these ancient species in their natural environment.

This was exactly why he pursued a degree in Paleontology and Archaeology. He was familiar with many of these species, but only through books, fossils, and research. Now he could see them first-hand and witness how they naturally existed and coexisted together. To him it was the chance of a lifetime, a chance to see the early evolution of the earth.

Eric also realized it was a dangerous place, a place where a multitude of animals could kill any of them at any time. Attack was possible at any moment, around any bend in the trail, from land or air. Humans were no match for the beasts that lived in this time; nature left out the human species for this reason. It would be millions of years before the first hominids safely left the security of the trees to journey on the ground.

The quicker the men could make weapons to help balance out this unbalance of power, the better. He had some ideas for weapons, spears, bows and sharp projectile points, but he needed time to find the right resources. Eric kept a close eye on the surroundings as the group journeyed deeper into the forest.

The band of odd companions continued walking for hours, making their way through the thick underbrush, underbrush including ferns, grasses, and primitive flowering plants. It was easy for the three super beasts to move through the brush. The great bulk of their immense bodies crushed the vegetation which in turn created an easier path for the three men to navigate.

They faced a multitude of strange insects on the trek, which ranged in size from tiny to exceptionally large—larger than any known insect in their world. Many of the insects were familiar; spiders, scorpions, and dragonfly like creatures. They were just bigger, like everything else in this world. Due to the hot, humid climate, insects thrived in the millions and many lived off the blood of other unfortunate species.

The humans, relentlessly attacked by these flying and crawling pests, fell into this category. In time, they would cake on mud to try and repel the swarms from constantly attacking them. They needed the knowledge of Maka, with her natural medicinal training, to concoct insect repellant, but they had to find her first.

The group came to a large clearing in the forest where Creo suddenly stopped and silently motioned to the others to be quiet. He pointed to a pack of wolf-sized beasts stealthily stalking something on the edge of the forest on the other side of the clearing. To this point, the pack did not detect the arrival of the odd group of travelers.

Creo motioned the men to stay in the safety of the trees. The two super beasts calmly walked out to the edge of the clearing to see the size of the pack. The wind changed direction, blowing from behind the group, spreading their undeniable smell to the predators.

One of the pack creatures, the leader, stopped and sniffed in the direction of the band of travelers. It turned towards the group, exposing its side, which allowed Eric his first opportunity to visually inspect it. The animal was the size of a large wolf but much thicker and heavier.

The beast had powerful elongated jaws with short, pointed canines. It was the Creodont known as Hyaenodon, a powerful predator that roamed Earth for millions of years. There were five of the brutes out hunting, which made them five times more dangerous. Just one could easily kill a lone human.

"It's a pack of Hyaenodons," whispered Eric, the astonishment prevalent in his expression and tone.

All three humans gazed across the opening at the carnivorous band of vicious predators. The creatures had long snouts, powerful teeth, and sharp claws. They were chestnut brown in color with a thin layer of hair covering the skin; there was little need of thick fur during this extremely hot time in the Earth's history. They could see the sharp rows of teeth, teeth made for shearing flesh rather than crushing bone like the modern Hyena. Their legs were long, supported by feet with claw-tipped toes. This true-life monster lived during the late Eocene and into Miocene times. The Hyaenodon existed for millions of years, roaming the world as a top predator. **(Image 4: Hyaenodon horridus: page 131)**

"Hyaena what," said CeCe, in a frightened tone.

Eric could hear the panic in his voice. The big man was frightened, a normal reaction, one they all felt.

"What should we do?" asked Tak, who was ready to run or climb a tree.

If he had a spear or knife, he would stay on the ground and fight, but without any form of protection, he knew the height of a tree was the only choice.

Arcto and Creo motioned for the humans to stay behind them in the safety of the trees. None of the group had seen Pith in some time, since he ambled off deep into the forest. It was normal for the giant ape-thing to wander off. Pith lived in his own world in his own time.

"Where is Squatch?" whispered CeCe. "He should be here to help us!"

By now, all the members of the pack, were looking and sniffing in the direction of the travelers. They sensed something was just across the clearing. The Hyaenodons split up into two groups of two, while the leader of the pack came straight towards the men.

The lead Hyaenodon cautiously approached the terrified humans, never taking his eyes off Arcto. The two groups of Hyaenodons tried to circle Creo, Arcto, and the men to prevent them from running.

Arcto and Creo charged out towards the two smaller packs, trying to head them off before they reached the men. It was obvious. The Hyaenodons were attacking!

"Run," screamed Eric, as he headed for the closest tree, followed by CeCe and Tak who sprinted behind him.

They reached a large maple tree that stood at the edge of the opening. It was close to where they waited in concealment. Eric jumped for the lowest branch catching it with both hands. He quickly pulled himself up and scampered to a safe height. Tak followed suit and within seconds, he joined Eric in the safety of the tree. CeCe, being much heavier than the other two, missed the low hanging branch and fell to the ground.

One of the Hyaenodons, the alpha, closed in on him. The attacking carnivore slowed down, approaching with caution, and momentarily stopped which allowed CeCe to gain his feet once again. By the Hyaenodons hesitant response, it was clear the beast had never met a human before. It was wary of the unusual quarry standing just feet in front of it. CeCe was strange looking and had an unfamiliar scent.

"Jump for the branch," shouted Tak. "You can do it."

Eric and Tak were ready to climb down and help their friend. They were not about to let their friend die in this place without a fight.

CeCe tried to jump once more but failed. The big man missed by at least a foot, but this time, he landed on his two feet, without falling. He turned to face the hesitant Hyaenodon.

"I can't reach it," he cried out as he clenched his fists.

The Hyaenodon continued to circle the strange human. It was waiting for re-enforcements from the pack before moving in for the kill. It walked slowly as it circled CeCe from a safe distance. The beast growled in deep guttural tones as it tried to get CeCe to turn and run which would expose the big man's back to a swift lunge from the hideous killer.

"We'll come down and help you!" shouted Eric.

He knew his friend was in big trouble. CeCe's life was on the line. He moved down the tree to a lower branch, so he could drop from the security of the tree and help his friend.

"No, you stay in the tree. There's no need for us all to die here today."

The pack did not come. The lone Hyaenodon let out a loud scream that terrified the humans. It was trying to call the pack for re-enforcements. But the pack did not come. Tak and Eric lost sight of Creo and Arcto in the confusion. They assumed the two super beasts were battling with the rest of the pack. They could hear loud growls and bellowing screams coming from the other side of the clearing. If these sounds were any sign, both Creo and Arcto were fighting for their lives just a few hundred yards away.

Tak and Eric knew CeCe was on his own. There was nothing they could do but watch the event unfold in front of them while they looked on from the safety of the towering tree.

CeCe stood tall and waited for the large beast to attack. He was no match for the super predator, but he had to fight. It was fight or die. The Hyaenodon cried out one last time for reinforcements. CeCe flailed his arms in the air to try and intimidate the brute. He needed to look as large as possible to try and daunt the predator.

The attacking Hyaenodon, finally realizing the pack was not coming, closed in on CeCe. It bared its sharp long fangs at the big man, growled and then charged.

It moved surprisingly fast for a large carnivore as it lunged for CeCe. The Hyaenodon catapulted itself through the air with one giant lunge, an attempt to knock the human to the ground upon impact.

The brave football player braced himself for a quick death. He clinched his big hands to strike at the primitive killer and screamed at the attacking carnivore as he jumped to meet the lunging beast head on.

At that same instant, a large figure swooped in from the tree canopy and landed on the back of the attacking Hyaenodon.

Chapter 10

The River

The battle for survival between the small horse-like creature and the giant weasel ended with the loss of life; one beast perished so another one could live. The women, saddened by the loss of the little horse, could hear the crunching of bone and the shearing of flesh coming from the feast of gluttony in the meadow below the tree.

The nest, high up in the safety of the trees, gave the women protection from the ground dwelling predators that thrived in the forest, but it did not silence the sounds of agony that penetrated the night. They were out of the reach of the brutal beasts that roamed the land below, but they still had no idea what might inhabit the trees.

The girls needed rest. The long arduous trip through the swamp drained them physically, while the encounter with the giant serpent tested them mentally. The huge moon reached its zenith around midnight, transforming the surrounding landscape into a world somewhere between the darkness and the light. It would have been a good night for traveling if they were in their world; the world without these insidious creatures.

Maka, the native Sioux, was the first in the group to wake up in the early morning. Something awfully close to the nest chattered vociferously, which disturbed her sleep. She looked around until she spotted a peculiar looking monkey, one with small grasping hands and elongated nails instead of claws. The small creature, extremely good at climbing trees, jumped from limb to limb while chattering incessantly. It reminded Maka of a cross between a squirrel and a monkey—more squirrel than monkey. It excitedly chattered at the three strange looking humans who now encroached on its territory. Within minutes there were more of them, coming to see the strange curiosity that had invaded their tree top kingdom. The tiny creatures were curious about the three intruders, three intruders from another time.

Soon, Lexa and Hope were awake looking at the unusual primates. The monkeys scampered about the tree, stopping around the edges of the nest to peer at the humans, then scurried off to the safety of a nearby tree, where from a safe distance, they threw pinecones at the human trespassers. They were overly excited by the presence of the weird looking humans.

"What are they?" asked Hope, as she reached out to touch one.

The frightened little animal scurried higher up the tree, stopping just above the sleeping nest to peer down at the unfamiliar intruders.

"I think it's a primitive monkey," replied Maka, who thought the furry pest didn't really look like a real monkey, although it acted like one. "Or it's an ancient squirrel of some kind."

Maka had no idea what it really was, but it had to be one or the other she thought. The native was becoming familiar with the unfamiliarity of this place.

The wandering tree top herd soon lost interest in the three humans and moved on to forage other food sources in the area. They vanished as quickly as they had appeared. All three of the girls were wide awake now. They heard many sounds, some coming from up in the trees while others came from down on the forest floor.

The forest, transformed by the new light of the morning, sprung to life, as hundreds of daytime species once again ventured out from their nighttime hiding places to search for food. There were many types of birds flying from tree to tree or bush to bush. Some resembled modern-day woodpeckers, brandishing shorter, thicker beaks. They ranged in color from black, white, red, silver and even blue. They were busy at work searching for insects, insects that lived inside the bark of the many species of trees which existed in the thick forest. Primitive species of doves, finches and other songbirds flew about from tree to tree while strange chicken-like birds roamed the forest floor, chasing insects and small rodents. The diversity of species astonished the women.

The vivid variety of life amazed the three humans as they watched from the nest high above the forest floor. It was like being in a look-out tower overseeing an ancient eco-system lost in time. They could see in every direction from their perch high up in the sequoia tree.

The humans spotted the shape of the now familiar Bronto coming towards the tree. He was a massive beast with incredible bulk. He walked on two powerful legs with his mid-section covered in some type of leather. Leather, no doubt, from the hide of some unfortunate adversary, an adversary fallen during a fierce battle to the death. His arms were enormous and bulged with giant muscles. He had a large head with two horns that projected out from just above his nostrils. The horns were several feet in length and formed a Y pattern above his mouth and nostrils.

Bronto called up to the women, "Is everyone safe?"

His booming voice filled the morning air.

"We are all alive and well," answered Hope, relieved the light of day had returned.

She felt much safer in the light of the day, even though the moon had lit up the forest the former night.

"That is good to hear," replied the giant ungulate.

Bronto was a Brontotherium and belonged to the family known as Brontotheres. They thrived in all northern continents around 51-28 million years ago. They were also known as odd-toed ungulates or Perissodactyls. In the case of Bronto, who was a Brontotherium, his front feet had four toes and his rear feet had only three toes, deriving the term odd-toed ungulate. The only problem was that this Brontotherium was walking on two legs.

Horses formed another sub-order of these odd-toed ungulates and both (Brontotheres and horses) came from the same common ancestors called Condylarths, which were more primitive animals, ones that had claws instead of toes in their earlier evolutionary molding. Most Condylarths ate plants but some still ate flesh. They ranged in size from a marmot to the size of a bear. Condylarths evolved shortly after the disappearance of the non-avian dinosaurs around 65 million years ago and existed until around 40 million years ago. Horses are another matter for another time.

Soon after Bronto arrived, Aves flew in and landed on the nest. She was a magnificent creature, a marvel of both grace and power.

"Are we ready to begin the day's journey?" she asked as she picked up Lexa and shot down the tree, gently placing the Latino next to Bronto.

Aves shot back up the tree twice more to retrieve Maka and Hope and soon all were standing on the forest floor. They ate a peculiar fruit, one tart and bitter, which offered vital nutrients while quenching their thirst. The crisp morning air, although still warm, was a welcome relief to the sweltering day sun which within hours would increase the daytime temperature dramatically.

Bronto once again led the way through the heavily brushed forest, followed by Maka, Lexa, and Hope. Aves, of course, took to the sky and every so often, when they entered an open meadow in the forest, the girls could see her fly overhead, soaring magnificently above the tall trees. It was hard to miss a bird with a eighteen-foot wingspan.

The group walked for a few hours until they came to a river where they paused to get a cold drink of water. Bronto knelt and took a long drink. The girls followed his example. They were thirsty from the excursion through the forest. The shaded ground beneath the giant trees gave some respite from the hot humid climate but it was still very warm.

"Where are we going?" Lexa asked as she looked up at the strange brute Bronto.

"You must have some type of plan for us," chimed in Hope.

Bronto thought for a moment and then answered, "We are going to the time of Megalo. He will answer all your questions. We are here to only guide and protect you."

That is all the ungulate would tell them. Bronto was a Brontotherium of few words. He stood up, looked around and then pointed up stream.

"We will go that way," he said, as he started to move up the stream.

The three humans fell in line and followed the big ungulate as he weaved his way around the large boulders strewn about the riverbed. They had no idea what the time of Megalo meant or where it was, but without reaching it, they knew they would never get solid answers to their questions from Bronto or Aves. Maka, Hope, and Lexa realized they needed to keep close to the super beasts to find answers, answers to what happened to the men, so they could all unite and find a way to get back home.

The terrain gradually became steeper as they navigated through the rocks and boulders that littered the banks of the river. The river, aqua green in color, slowly meandered its way through steep canyons, heavily treed forests, and through open flat lands. The group walked into an insect hatch of some type, as thousands of tiny flying bugs swarmed everywhere along the riverbank briefly pausing before flying out over the meandering stream to deposit their tiny eggs which drifted downstream.

The fish noticed the hatch too. A type of large salmon, feeding on the tiny protein rich insects, jumped out of the current, grabbing as many of the small insects as possible. There were hundreds of these large salmon feeding in the river. They looked like normal salmon, silver and red in color, but they had rows of dagger-like teeth which left massive gash wounds on the smaller unfortunate salmon who swam into the frenzy. These salmon were true river monsters, powerful swimmers, which effortlessly navigated the strong, swift current. Many were up to 8 feet long as they swam against the current, cannibalizing on the smaller fish during the chaotic feeding tumult.

As the group watched the feeding glut, they decided it was best to stay out of the river. Fish that large could inflict serious bite wounds on them; intentionally or incidentally. They continued to travel upstream which meant going up in elevation. At times, this became a grueling task, as navigating the boulders meant walking on varied sizes of rocks on uneven terrain, which was hard on the feet and increased the chance of injury to a foot or an ankle.

Aves flew above and scouted out the best route through the maze of boulders and downed trees. She landed occasionally to talk with Bronto, conveying what was up ahead before taking to the air once again, disappearing high in the sky. They traveled up the river for about 10 miles until Bronto halted the group for a much-needed rest.

"You're probably tired, so we'll stop here for a rest," the behemoth said as he motioned for the women to stop under a large tree in a shaded area along the river.

Bronto was not tired, but he could see the hard journey tested the tiny, weak humans. They lacked the physical attributes needed to survive in his world. Besides, he could use a snack, so he went over to some bushes and began to graze on the lush green leaves.

"We just need a few minutes," replied Maka, who wanted to project strength not weakness.

Maka was a proud member of the Sioux nation and would never admit to fragility. Giving up without a fight was not in her nature.

"I sure wish we could catch some of those fish and eat them," Hope said. "If they are a type of salmon, we might be able to eat them raw."

Hope, hungry from the harsh morning trek, recognized the fish would be a significant source of protein which would rejuvenate them for the continuing journey. They needed to eat to sustain the rigorous pace set by Bronto.

"Great idea!" answered Lexa. "We need Aves. I'm sure she could fly in and snatch us a couple at a time. We could even take some with us for later."

They waited for a short while until Aves finally returned to check on the resting group. The journey was easy for her. She did not have to spend the same amount of energy as the rest of the group. Once Aves reached the correct elevation, she used thermal drafts to effortlessly soar as she surveyed the land below. The great eagle could travel great distances in one day.

"Can you catch us some fish?" asked Hope.

Aves came over and asked, "How many do you want?"

The great eagle was up for the task. She gracefully took off, swiftly gaining altitude, and was quickly flying above the river. She maneuvered into a steep dive then lightly swooped down, grabbing a large salmon from the river with her sharp talons. She then flew back towards the girls and dropped the fish on the bank. The great eagle performed this several more times, each time depositing a larger fish on the riverbank before she gently landed where the group was resting. It was that simple.

The humans and the giant eagle ate their fill of the fish. It was a delicious meal; the best one the women had eaten since arriving to this new world. They were ready to resume the trek once more, so Bronto took up the lead again while Aves took to the air. The girls, now refreshed from the meal, followed the big bodyguard. They still had no idea where Bronto was taking them, but they hoped they would arrive there soon.

The group traveled for a few more hours in the heat of the mid-day sunshine. The climate, hot and humid in this place, never really seemed to fluctuate. The only respite came in the early morning or late evening when the blazing sun relinquished its hold on the world.

They climbed higher and higher in elevation as they followed the stream up towards its source. A light mist began, a welcome relief from the heat as the water cooled the travelers. The light mist helped disperse the insects too. The smaller insects retreated, hiding in the plants to wait out the tiny droplets of moisture that made flying too difficult.

The larger insects were relentless. Several types of biting flies incessantly swarmed the group looking for the chance to land and draw blood. The exposed arms of the three women were targets for the biting insects which left large welts and dried blood; welts caused by the biting pests, and blood by squashing the unrelenting pests, making the insects short lives even shorter. In their world, the humans called them deer flies or horse flies, but here they seemed more like elephant flies, flies much larger with bites more painful.

The women needed insect repellent to fend off the merciless pests. Maka was sure she could find a natural repellant from the surrounding forest once she had time to search for one. In the meantime, they were at the mercy of the tiny, ruthless, legionnaires.

The group continued to press on until they reached the source of the river. The last few hundred yards were arduous. A large formation of sandstone cliffs, carved out by eons of erosion, created a long narrow rim. The river dropped down through a thin passage between the rims, which created a beautiful waterfall that plummeted for 50 feet until it landed in a deep, wide pool at the bottom of the sandstone cliffs.

To navigate the rim here was much too dangerous, so the group with the help of Aves found a much easier place to ascend to the top of the cliff. Once they gained the top of the rim, the landscape flattened out, which made travel easier.

They continued until they found the source of the river. A shallow lake, surrounded by trees, sourced the nutrient rich water forming the headwater of the river. The lake was large, the size of fifteen acres. Beyond the lake, the trees gave way to land which opened into a great plain. The water in the lake was clear, filtered by a thin layer of white sand and rock. It was magnificent.

From on top of the rim, the group could see the path they had taken to gain the rim. The winding river raged, picking up speed as it dropped in elevation, until the flattening of the terrain slowed it down. They could see for hundreds of miles down into the valley below. An expanse forest of trees covered the entire area below them.

The climb, at times, was difficult for Maka, Hope, and Lexa who struggled over the large boulders. The physical trek did not seem to bother Bronto at all. He never showed any signs of fatigue. This surprised the women because of the enormous size of the beast.

"Bronto, how can you not be tired from that climb?" asked Lexa, who was in great physical shape herself and the long climb had at times tested her natural endurance.

The big giant just looked at her and said, "I do not think of such things."

Bronto then jumped into the lake and soaked his tuff hide. The massive ambling beast relished the cool water.

"That was a tuff journey," added Maka, the long-distance runner.

Hope chimed in, "It was a long climb, but we made it. Just look at the beauty of this place."

She was always the optimist.

They decided to go for a swim. The water, besides refreshing them, would clean off the sweat, the blood from the insect bites, and just the grime in general. All three humans leaped into the cool, refreshing water. They splashed around trying to get Bronto to lighten up, but the big brute would have none of it. He was, as usual, all business. It was good that he took his role as protector to heart, especially after the swamp incident, but the girls hoped he would eventually ease up, so they kept trying to engage him with humor. The massive ungulate was just too serious a brute.

The three washed up as best they could and returned to the lake bank to dress. The clothes they put on would have to last for as long as they stayed in this odd world, or until they found a suitable material to make new clothes from.

Once finished dressing, Bronto led the women around one side of the lake while Aves soared above keeping a watchful eye out for trouble. The majestic bird effortlessly floated on the air currents moving in a circular pattern. It was good to have an air borne sentry. She could see predator's way before Bronto could smell them. They walked for a couple of hours then stopped again.

"This is the place," spoke Bronto, now with a cautious manner about him—a look of nervousness on his face.

Aves dropped down and landed by the group. She had a seriousness demeanor about her as well. The two super beasts quietly conversed, just soft enough so the humans could not hear their words.

Bronto and Aves moved a few steps out in front of the women, where Bronto picked up a broken piece of tusk–like ivory horn hidden between two rocks. The polished ivory glistened in the bright sunlight.

The last thing Maka, Hope, and Lexa remembered were the words the mighty Brontotherium Bronto spoke, Pleistocene Epoch 3-5-0-K.

Then they all vanished!

Chapter 11

Attacked

CeCe, Eric, and Tak watched in amazement as the hairy Giganti**pith**ecus they nicknamed Squatch landed on the lunging Hyaenodons back. The enraged ape-beast emitted a blood curdling scream as his immense weight knocked the carnivorous Hyaenodon to the ground.

The Hyaenodon, in a futile attempt to shake off the giant ape, violently convulsed while snapping its powerful jaws in the air. The startled, infuriated beast growled and howled as the ape gained the advantage by securing one of its powerful arms around the pack hunters' muscular neck. The Hyaenodon tried to roll its body in a last-minute effort to dislodge the giant ape, but the immense weight of the hominid pinned the flailing brute to the forest floor.

Squatch then positioned his other arm around the carnivore's burly neck to apply the final death grip. His long fingernails penetrated the Creodont's thick skin, and blood started to flow from the slicing wounds. The massive ape then sank his powerful fangs into the neck of the writhing predator as he pulled back with all his strength on the throat of the beast.

Within moments, the three humans heard the unmistakable sound of the Hyaenodons neck snap and the carnivore's body went limp as the last vestiges of life slipped from it. The Hyaenodon was dead—it died as it had lived—violently.

The giant primate beat his chest with both fists, then let out a hideous scream...a scream meant to warn other creatures to stay away. The beastly Gigantipithecus, Pith, had just saved CeCe's life.

"Unbelievable!" shouted Eric from the safety of the maple tree.

Eric realized he had just seen an unbridled display of savage brutality, that thin line between life and death. The fierce fight was simply incredible to observe. To see such a raw display of carnal savagery simply astonished the human.

"Wow!" exclaimed Tak as he dropped down to the ground from the branches of the mighty maple tree.

What a story, one passed down from generation to generation, this would make—if anyone would ever believe it!

CeCe, still shaking from the adrenaline released during the encounter, dropped to his knees. He had just narrowly escaped the clutches of death, and he knew it. CeCe, a physically powerful man, was no match for the savage Hyaenodon, a beast that lived to kill and killed to survive in this dissonant world, a world that belonged to the savage species that inhabited it, a world without humans.

The colossal ape walked over to CeCe and placed a strong hand on his shoulder and simply asked, "You ok human?"

That was all the blood-soaked hominid said.

CeCe, still shaken by the close call with death, smiled and nodded to the ape beast and said, "I'm in debt to you."

The adrenaline now fading, CeCe felt weak and fatigued, a normal response to the chemicals released into his body during the ordeal. It would take a little time to return to his normal self.

"That was a close one CeCe. I thought you were done for," Tak said.

"Me too," added Eric. "Just another few second...and bam...that beast would have been on you."

"Try to explain that one to my family. I disappeared somewhere in time and got killed by a carnivorous predator that lived millions of years ago," CeCe joked.

"You have to admit, even if no one believed you, it would be a fascinating story to tell," answered Eric.

Pith vanished while Eric was ribbing CeCe. He returned shortly with Creo and Arcto, both covered in the blood of the other Hyaenodons. Arcto had a deep, long gash on his left arm. The men could tell the two super beasts had just been in a violent battle.

"What happened to you two?" asked Tak, concerned by Arcto's bleeding wound.

Creo answered, "We went after the two groups that split off to surround us. One of the Hyaenodons either saw us or smelled our scent and let out a terrific howl, which alarmed the other members of the pack. Within seconds, all four beasts rallied to attack us. They were on us by the time we trans-shifted. One of the Hyaenodons came straight at me and went for my throat. I could see yellow eyes and razor-sharp canines as it launched itself off its hind legs to gain momentum. I turned just in time to catch it by the nape as it flew by me. Once I gained a firm grip, I merely crushed the life out of it, and it slumped to the forest floor. The second Hyaenodon attacked me from behind as I finished dispatching the first one. It bit at my hind legs, so I quickly turned to meet the foe head on. At this point I became the aggressor, the Hyaenodon the victim, as it ran for its life. I hastily caught the fleeing beast as it tried to reach the safety of the forest. With one mighty bite, from my vice grip jaws, I severed the carnivore's spine. I left the dead adversary sprawled lifeless in the grass just before it reached the safety of the trees and went to see how Arcto was fairing with the last two vermin. The other two had simultaneously attacked the giant bear. Their attacked on him, obviously better coordinated than the one on me, put him at a disadvantage. This is when one of the loathsome creature's bit Arcto on the arm. It attacked Arcto while he focused on the other Hyaenodon. Arcto, in a primal fit of rage, seized one of the vile beasts, crushing its skull in his strong jaws. The remaining Hyaenodon turned to run, but I was able to intercept it and kill it by piercing its jugular vein. Then Pith came along and told us what happened to you and we came at once."

The event, the men's first encounter with death in their new world, had been a narrow escape for CeCe, one he would never forget. It was the first time the three men, once carefree and living life unassumingly, realized the stakes were high in this world. Situations could turn life threatening at any time and all three men now recognized it was crucial to stay alert if they wanted to survive.

Eric, Tak, and CeCe were growing increasingly worried about the girls. They had yet to receive any real answers from their three guides, who continued to reveal little information to them. The near miss with the Hyaenodons brought home a new reality, one that left them gravely worried about Hope, Lexa, and Maka. If the girls were here, the men hoped they had good guides like Creo, Arcto, and Pith. They felt the other members of their camping group were here somewhere in this strange place and if they were, they more than likely were worried about them as well. They knew the women would worry about their whereabouts.

The three super beasts, now ready to resume the trek, motioned to Eric, Tak, and CeCe to move out. The attack by the Hyaenodons was already a past thought to them. Eric wondered how many times similar incidents had crossed the super protector's paths. It seemed an ordinary event to the primitive beasts.

Once more the group took a game trail, one worn down by the countless footprints of creatures of the past. The forest, alive with the sounds of the forest dwellers—both large and small—echoed the sounds of daily life. Learning the different sounds of the animals that inhabited the forest would be vital to the human's survival, so Tak, the native, intently focused on this task, becoming especially diligent in learning the bird calls, one of which could signal danger. The group came to a small stream and stopped to quench their thirst.

"Creo, can you tell us what happened to the rest of our party?" Eric asked, growing more concerned for the well-being of the girls.

A few days had passed since himself, Tak, and CeCe had mysteriously woke up in the hut and this worried him. The girls, if they were here, could be in imminent danger from even more brutal species from a different period.

"I can only say that you will see them soon, when we get to the time of Megalo," the Creodont responded.

Creo was a formidable, impressive beast and Eric could see how this creature could have easily severed the Hyaenodons spine with his mighty jaws.

"Thank you," the blonde Viking said in an appreciative tone.

Eric now knew the three girls were here somewhere. It was a relief to know where they were, but their safety was still unknown. Eric could only assume they had protection as well.

"Then we must hurry," Tak added, his voice strong with conviction.

CeCe and Pith, now called Pith out of respect by CeCe, were still down by the stream when they noticed Eric and Tak waving to them to return to the group. The big man and the primate, their thirst satisfied, took off at full speed towards the others. It was a close race, but the giant ape won on this occasion. The two were becoming friends, or at least as friendly as one can be with a giant ape. Within minutes they were by the sides of the other members of the group and Eric explained the news about the women to CeCe. He was excited by this turn of events and like Tak was at once ready to set out in search of the women. To the three men, there was little time to waste. The girls could be in trouble and need help.

The group, its resolve now heightened by the news of the girls, set out from the stream and entered the forest. This time the band moved silently, with renewed vigor, through the forest. They had a new focus, a new focus to find the girls.

The pace was much quicker now. The super beasts, sensing the men's haste, were more than happy to pick up the tempo. Creo and Arcto moved effortlessly along the ancient game trail while Pith raced through the canopy, swinging from tree to tree on some type of large, thick vine. The men still had no idea where they were going so, they aimlessly followed the two guides.

The band traveled for some time journeying deeper into the forest. The foliage began to change from primarily trees to a denser brush. The trees became sparser with less variety. A type of evergreen now dominated the landscape as they randomly shot up to the sky. They were very tall without any needles or branches until way up towards the top, which allowed more sunlight to reach the lower levels, which in turn supported a wider variety of plant life, as it flourished on the floor of the forest.

The explosion of diverse plant life on the forest floor now slowed the groups pace. This made foot travel extremely difficult as the group continuously struggled to force its way through the thick vegetation. Pith had to travel on foot now. The change in the species of trees, as well as the distance between them, allowed no mobility through the treetops.

They came to a small clearing and decided to stop for a quick rest. The continuous struggle of fighting their way through the underbrush used a lot of energy. They had made considerable progress since finding out about the plight of the girls, but they needed to rest. Creo, Arcto, and Pith huddled together and talked about something, as Eric, Tak, and CeCe stretched out on the ground surrounded by small ferns. The momentary pause felt good.

"I needed to rest," sighed CeCe.

CeCe's big frame made it particularly difficult for him to move through the thick brush. It was easier for the smaller, slender Eric and Tak to squeeze through the foliage. The three super beasts, with the advantage of their great mass, could walk through it by shear force.

"We all could use a break," added Tak as he curiously observed the three super beasts.

Tak was eager to see the girls, but he knew they needed to be patient and not make any drastic errors in judgment. Any injury could jeopardize the progress of the entire group.

"I just wish we had better answers and I hope this Megalo has some explanation to why we're here," remarked Eric.

The burden of the unknown was beginning to weigh on them all.

Tak and CeCe nodded in agreement—they too were ready for answers.

Creo, Arcto, and Pith, once done with their huddle of the minds, came over to the humans.

"We should get moving again," said the Creodont, his demeanor now profoundly serious. "I'd like to get there before dusk."

The men were all too familiar with what happened at dusk. The super creatures would then vanish into the night leaving the humans to fend for themselves. Night was a brutal time in this world and what little security the hut gave was long gone now. They too were eager to resume the trek into the unknown and find a safer place to stay for the night far away from the terrors that came out once the sun faded.

The group pushed on through the thick brush until it gave way to an open woodland. The woodland, now scattered with shrubs, trees, and dead fallen tree trunks, was more open than the earlier forests they had traveled through. The men could see for greater distances now as opposed to the narrow vision the forest had provided.

They saw a large group of Uintatherium, like the one they saw fight for its life and lose to the giant Sarkastodon outside the hut. In the light, they could see the enormous size of these sub-ungulates. There were small groups of perissodactyl, or odd-toed ungulates, made up of horses, rhinoceroses, tapirs and other strange horned beasts. These were mesmerizing to Eric, who marveled at the scene of evolutionary progression. He was getting the opportunity to see the very things he had spent so much time studying.

Unable to hide his exuberance, Eric said, "Do you see those horse-like animals? Those are early horses with three toes."

The primitive vision before his eyes, amazed him.

They pushed on toward a distant mountain that rose high above the woodland beyond the dense forest. The mountain looked to be volcanic and still active like Mt. St Helen's in Washington State back in the human world. If this were the case, it could erupt at any time if they were really in the Eocene Epoch.

The band continued to push on but with more caution now. Where there were grazing ungulates, there were predators. They had to be on the lookout for Hyaenodons again and other more menacing meat eaters like the mighty Sarkastodon. It was time to keep quiet and move silently through the open woodland. They headed for the forest on the far side of the valley towards the active volcanic mountain.

Creo and Arcto led the way, followed by the three men, while Pith, the giant ape, guarded the flank. They tried to stay concealed, keeping to the more wooded areas and blending in with the landscape. The wind was blowing directly at them, which kept them undetectable to the nostrils of both predators and prey; danger by scent would have to come from behind them and go through the massive fierce ape.

Pith was an intimidating brute, and they were lucky to have him on their side. He had already saved CeCe once and this revealed his loyalty. The men were starting to grow fond of the massive Gigantipithecus blacki.

They walked silently towards the forest keeping all senses alert for danger. Just yards away from the edge of the trees, they stumbled upon a conflict between a smaller, juvenile Sarkastodon and a bear–size creature that Eric called a Patriofelis.

The two brutes were circling one another, each trying to gain advantage over the other. The Patriofelis resembled a fusion between a cat–like creature and a tree martin. The mid-size predator, long and lean, with a broad head equipped with powerful jaws designed for crushing bone, was much smaller than the young Sarkastodon. In size, the Patriofelis was no match for the larger Sarkastodon, which could tip the scale at over 1,800 pounds when fully grown. It would have to rely on its quickness and agility.

The two carnivores snarled and growled at each other, both trying to intimidate the other into backing down.

The super beasts and the humans tried to sneak past the ongoing stalemate and gain the security of the trees. Creo, Arcto, Eric, and CeCe made it to the concealment of the tree line while Tak and Pith lagged just long enough for the Sarkastodon to notice them, which distracted the great carnivore just enough for the smaller Patriofelis to seize the opportunity to escape. It turned and ran off, disappearing into the woods just down from the rest of the group. Somehow it instinctively knew to flee if it wanted to survive.

By this time, Tak and Pith caught up with the rest of the group in the trees. The Sarkastodon naturally ran after the Patriofelis but then stopped and turned towards the direction of the group. It let out a frightful scream and charged.

Pith was the first to see it coming and grunted to the rest of the group. He was a beast of great strength but was no match for a predator the size of a Sarkastodon. Creo and Arcto stopped to let the humans get in front of them as they quickly turned to face the oncoming threat. There was no place to hide and they could not reach the lowest branches of the trees. They had two choices, run or stop and fight the mighty creature.

Then something spectacular happened.

The humans heard Creo shout Megistotherium and Arcto yelled Arctodus simus and to their amazement the two guides trans-shifted, a term the humans later would fully grow to understand.

Both turned into the real specimens; Creo into a Megistotherium and Arcto into a real life Arctodus simus. They instantly transformed into the terrifying super-carnivores that roamed the planet eons ago.

The Megistotherium, one of the largest land carnivores to ever walk the planet Earth, was a giant Creodont that weighed up to 2,000 pounds and preyed on early forms of mastodons. It had powerful canine teeth for killing and strong limbs, tipped with sharp claws. It was the top apex predator of its time no question.

The Arctodus simus was the largest bear that ever lived on Earth. It could weigh over 1,800 pounds, making it also a contender for the largest land omnivore. The gigantic bear was a successful Arctoid, one capable of running as fast as a horse. **(Image 5: Arctodus simus: page 132)**

One of these species alone was enough to tackle the smaller Sarkastodon, but both posed an insurmountable obstacle and the smaller predator turned and fled for its life. It shot off at full stride and entered the safety of the forest. The event was short-lived and the two super creature's trans-shifted back into the familiar guides the humans had spent the last few days with.

Eric, Tak, and CeCe were both enthralled and baffled by what they had just seen. The transformation was both incredible and terrifying.

"What just happened?" asked Eric, fascinated by the inimitable transformation.

"Can all of you do that?" questioned Tak, his curiosity peaked by this strange new ability the protectors had.

"We all have certain abilities," was all Creo offered in response.

The great beast was back to his elusive self again.

Arcto offered no response and started off into the forest. The humans, still in shock over seeing the event, fell into line and followed Arcto. Their only hope was that this Megalo would answer their questions, questions they were sure Creo, Arcto, and Pith would never fully reply too.

They walked for a few more hours until they came closer to the volcanic mountain. The vicinity around the mountain was strewn with petrified trees from eons of lava flows. It was getting close to dusk now and the humans feared what the coming night might offer.

Eric, CeCe, and Tak had survived two horrific nights in the primitive world and experienced incredible battles between warring species in this primordial place. A third night out in the open would test them even further.

Creo suddenly stopped the group, huddling with the other two super beasts for a moment. All three super creatures looked around at the surrounding area while briefly talking.

The men, standing together, over-heard the giant Creodont say this is the place. Arcto and Pith both agreed and then Creo picked up a horned ivory object nestled in the cavity of a large, petrified tree and said, "Pleistocene Epoch 3-5-0-K", and they all disappeared.

Chapter 12

Time Shift

The last thing Hope, Maka, and Lexa remembered hearing were the words of the giant Brontotheres as he spoke the words Pleistocene Epoch 3-5-0-K. This opened a vortex and the two super beasts along with the three humans passed from one time in Earth's history to another in a matter of seconds. Somehow, they traveled from the Eocene Epoch, 35 million years ago, to the Pleistocene Epoch, 350 thousand years ago. **(Image 6: Pleistocene animals of Eurasia: page 133)**

The Earth, now covered in vast ice shields, was remarkably different from the Earth during the Eocene Epoch. The climate was harsher, the temperature was colder, and many of the creatures of the Eocene had vanished from Earth, replaced by smarter, faster and better adapted species, species which drove many of the Eocene species into extinction. The planet now resembled a colder version of the world the three women lived in: current day Montana. Glaciers and ice covered all of Antarctica and large parts of Europe, North America and South America. The average temperature was 40-50 degrees colder than today.

Heavily treed forests, thinned by harsher, drier conditions, relinquished their dominant hold on the planet, as many tree species, particularly the warm climate varieties died out. These tree types were unable to adapt to the colder drier climate. The once immeasurable forests, which covered most of the Earth during the Eocene, vanished, slowly replaced by smaller forests that dotted the colder Earth, intertwined between the broadening plains and the vast oceans. Trees like conifers, conifers such as pines and cypress, along with broadleaf trees, like beeches and oaks, still flourished in certain areas.

Prairie grasses, which propelled the evolution of the grazing species, now dominated the open spaces, replacing enormous regions of once forested land. New grazing herbivores formed expansive herds, herds that traveled from one area to the next, searching for the life sustaining nutrients the grasses bestowed. Varying species of predators followed them, continually on the lookout for the weak, the old, or the injured to give the life supporting nutrients offered by blood, flesh, and bone.

"Where have you taken us?" asked Maka, as the group landed millions of years later.

Hope and Lexa, both dazed by the incredible time travel, shook their heads in disbelief. The dramatic change in the environment astounded them. The temperature drastically dropped in the blink of an eye, as they traveled through time. The warm, humid, favorable climate of the Eocene, only seconds removed, vanished, replaced by a frozen, frigid, unforgiving world. They would need warmer clothing to survive in this harsh environment, and once again, they wished they had the camping gear from the camp along the Missouri River in Montana.

Bronto looked at the bewildered group and explained, "We have the ability to travel to and from different time periods in the world of the extinct. When you meet Megalo, he will answer your questions in more depth. We are merely protectors."

The giant Brontotherium gazed at the three women. The girls could sense his sympathy. The beast felt sorry for them. He understood their anxiety and fear...fear and anxiety brought on by the absence of reason and logic. Bronto may have been a giant ungulate but he was beginning to like the girls and the kindling of an odd friendship was developing. He would gladly give his life to protect the humans if necessary. Protecting and guiding the women was now his purpose.

Maka, Hope, and Lexa were eager to move on to find this Megalo. They needed answers, answers that involved them and answers that explained the fate of the men. The girls hoped the men somehow dodged this nightmarish trek into the strange world of the extinct but deep down they realized the men had to be here somewhere. They could be anywhere in time, a time that spanned millions of years. The chances of finding them on their own were next to zero. There had to be an explanation, one that would reveal the true reason for them being here.

"How will we ever find Eric, CeCe, and Tak?" asked Hope, realizing the three men could be anywhere in this world.

For all Hope knew they could be millions of years apart, stuck in a time where the primitive beasts were even more savage and brutal than in the Eocene Epoch where she had just come from. She shuddered at the thought.

"Surely, they would have these protectors also," answered Lexa.

Lexa could only imagine what type of super beasts were leading the men. It was hard enough for her to believe Bronto and Aves were real.

"You are probably right," responded Hope, who deep down, wanted to believe the guys had great guides like Bronto and Aves, which would give them a chance to survive in whatever time they were in.

Aves had been quiet up until now. She was eager to get moving again. They only had a few hours until dusk and she wanted to get to Megalo before darkness descended on this colder world.

"We need to get moving," the giant eagle screeched.

She was ready to take to the air to allow her keen vision to scout for any impending dangers out in front of the group.

Bronto nodded as he took up the lead once again. Aves took one great leap with her powerful legs and within moments was soaring high above the small band. The girls were lucky to have Aves, who flew air reconnaissance and could see danger way before the group stumbled upon it. The terrain during the Pleistocene Epoch consisted of open plains and the powerful soaring avian giant gave the humans the visual advantage. Unlike the perpetual forests before, the openness of the grasslands allowed Aves the ability to see for great distances from the air. She could spot danger for miles ahead now.

The group traveled out onto the plains. They could see trees, mostly conifers, on the distant horizon. The openness of the plain left them vulnerable to prowling carnivores. This period was full of predators like the saber-toothed cats, hyenas, cave bears and cave lions, as well as many other daunting predatory beasts. They stalked these very plains the girls now found themselves navigating.

Except for the two super protectors, the women were powerless against these super predators without any weapons to defend themselves with. They would need to manufacture weapons if trapped here for any length of time. Maka was confident she could make razor sharp projectile points from obsidian or chert. To do this they would have to find a prehistoric obsidian or chert mine. She could make knives and spear tips from the same materials. If they could find the men, she knew Tak could make bows. The arrows would be simple for him to make.

Once out on the plains, the group came across several grazing species. Camels, early horses, deer, antelope with very odd sets of horns, and long horned bison roamed in large numbers. It reminded the humans of the Serengeti except the Serengeti in a cold climate. The herds continually migrated, constantly looking for grasses to sustain them, while the carnivores followed the herds or waited in ambush. This was also the time of the mastodon and the woolly mammoth. The diversity of creatures was extraordinary.

Bronto led the group around the bigger herds trying to stay close to whatever brush he could find for extra camouflage. The best outcome for everyone would be to pass through the area undetected by both the carnivores and the herbivores.

They were within a few hundred yards of the trees when Aves dropped in. She gracefully swooped down on the group, landing effortlessly on the ground, before the humans even realized it. She seemed overly excited. The big eagle went to Bronto and whispered something into his ear. The massive Brontotheres listened as the screeching eagle spoke at a quick pace. He acted alarmed by the news and halted the group. He came over to the women, calmly signaling for them to be quiet.

"Aves spotted some strange humans coming in our direction," he whispered.

"I didn't get a close look at them. I veered off so I wouldn't fly directly over them and cause them to be suspicious," the giant eagle screeched.

Aves and Bronto were nervous. It would be easy to dispatch the group of travelers if called for, but it was their intent to avoid conflict unless unavoidable. If this band of humans were really from Pleistocene times, they could be the early ancestors of the three women. They would be primitive hunter and gatherers with precarious rituals and superstitions. Early humans would not understand that the women were from a world in the future. They would more than likely think the girls were spirits or demons or even both. They would fear the women, fear which could have unexpected consequences. The best solution would be to avoid the new traveling party.

Certainly, the sight of the walking, talking Aves and Bronto would create panic and fear among the primitive humans. The women were terrified when they first saw the two super beasts as they rushed through the waterfall, into the hidden cave. Hope, Maka, and Lexa had traveled a long way since that day; one could say they had traveled across millions of years. At this point in time, they were only a few miles from possibly the first contact with early humans. It was compelling, but they knew it was best to heed the advice of the giant ungulate and avoid any encounter with the primitive group.

So, the girls followed Bronto and Aves in the opposite direction of the approaching humans. It was best to keep some distance between them and the traveling band to avoid any hostility. Bronto quickly picked up the pace while Aves and the women stayed close together, looking for any signs of danger.

They kept to the shrubs when possible, trying to avoid the open spaces. The group came to a waterhole that ran past a small patch of trees. The terrain, a mixture of clay and sandstone, littered with boulders and small rocks, was quite arid. A steep bank, riddled with many game trails, ran down one side of the waterhole to the edge of the life-giving liquid. There were several creatures drinking the cool murky water.

Aves took to the air to survey the surrounding area for approaching danger and to check on the location of the humans she had seen earlier in the day. Bronto led the rest of the group into the trees to avoid detection. The heavily branched trees concealed the women from view and supplied protection from the beasts visiting the waterhole, or those that cautiously crept by on their way to drink from the communal well.

A waterhole can give life and it can take life. It is a favorite location for predators to hunt and a dangerous place for those who come to drink. It is a place where the savage brutality of nature plays out daily. All creatures need water, in one form or another, whether it be by water or blood.

The safest method was to stake out the waterhole before moving in for a drink. Bronto and the women watched as massive elephants, of different varieties, visited the water hole and drank vast amounts of the life-sustaining fluid. There were giant ones, with tusks approaching 14 feet long, and massive hairy ones, like the Mastodon.

A small band of the long-tusked elephants journeyed down to the water hole to quench their thirst. They were incredibly large, some standing as tall as fifteen feet. They numbered six in all. Three were full grown adults, two were obviously juveniles and one was a small calf. The older elephants heavily protected the tiny calf by surrounding it.

Bronto, Maka, Lexa, and Hope watched as the group drank from the waterhole and splashed about. It was amazing to see the same similar behaviors of modern-day elephants on display some 350 thousand years ago; an elephant is an elephant regardless of the time in which it lived.

The little calf frolicked around in the water and sprayed its juvenile siblings. Maka, Hope, and Lexa all smiled at the little instigator, who was having an enjoyable time bonding with the older members of the herd. The humans could see how important each member of the family was to the good of the herd. It was a peaceful display of emotional interaction of a very closely aligned group of proboscideans.

The young calf, now covered in wet mud, frolicked towards the bank to exit the pool of refreshing water, when Maka noticed a slight movement in the water. It was a different type of ripple than the one from the giant snake in the swamp. This ripple, wider and more powerful, displaced more water as it stealthily approached the unsuspecting calf.

The calf reached the bank and was about to get out of the water when an enormous splash erupted from the waterhole. A huge, hair covered reptilian monster lunged at the poor helpless calf, barely missing it by mere inches.

The terrified calf let out a loud bellow which alerted the three large behemoth adults who jolted to its defense. Thousands of pounds of raging, infuriated flesh backed by immense power, descended on the water hole.

The reptile made one final attempt to grab the vulnerable calf and drag it back into the depths of the waterhole. The iron plated beast lunged for the hind legs of the little proboscidean. The calf continued to trumpet at the top of its capacity as the deadly jaws of the reptile snapped shut on one of its hind legs. The reptilian monster tried to turn with the calf in its jaws and retreat into the waterhole when the largest of the adult elephants rammed into it.

Bronto and the three women watched in awe as the primitive spectacle played out right before their eyes. This was life and death. The humans felt sympathy for the little calf while Bronto seemed indifferent. He was a product of this world, and to the giant Brontotheres, this was an ordinary experience. None of them could turn away from the event unfolding in front of them.

One adult Mammuthus imperator, obviously the matriarch, rammed the prehistoric reptile a second time with such momentum and force that it lifted the slithering beast out of the water. The two fourteen-foot, ivory tusks of the queen matriarch penetrated the side scales of the ambush assassin, passing completely through the silent killer's body. The slithering behemoth dropped the little calf and tried to free itself, by violently convulsing and trying to twist its body.

By this time, the other two adults, seeing the commotion, came to the aide of the calf, lifted it to its feet, and moved it to solid ground. The two guardians nudged the tired little tusker to solid ground a slight distance from the waterhole.

The skewered reptilian creature shook itself violently, trying to free itself from the death grip of the massive tusks. After a few moments, the reptile went flaccid, succumbing to the internal injuries it suffered during the attack.

The matriarch swung her head violently back and forth, which dislodged the dead reptile from her tusks, then tossed it up on the bank. The three adult elephants trampled, mutilated, and disjointed the body of the large reptile until they were certain all vestiges of life were gone from the deadly ambush assassin.

The secret audience, hiding in the small grove of trees, gasped at the horrific display of violence. They were all relieved the little calf survived the attack and watched as the small herd of prehistoric proboscideans trekked off from the waterhole as if nothing had happened. The small calf, left with only a slight limp, followed its mother, staying close to the giant matriarch.

The humans were hungry as well as thirsty, and the fresh kill meant meat. They quietly approached the waterhole, trying their best to be extra cautious. Where there was one slithering reptile, there could well be another.

Bronto led the way down to the edge of the waterhole and took a long drink. The girls followed suit, quenched their thirst, and then retreated to the bank where the mutilated carcass of the reptile now laid. They tore off chunks of flesh and returned to the trees.

Bronto followed the women, where he stood guard while the humans made a fire to cook the meat of the dead reptile. The smell of the cooking flesh was overwhelming. It brought to the forefront just how hungry the three women were. The raw salmon from earlier in the day seemed a distant memory. The energy exerted on the long trip had left them famished. A good, cooked meal was essential to restoring the vital nutrients their bodies needed from the long day of physical exertion.

Bronto did not understand why anyone would purposely burn the food they were about to eat, and being an ungulate, he moseyed off from the stand of trees. This practice was foreign, primitive, and barbaric to him. It made him ponder which of them were more savage, the humans or him.

Aves had been gone for some time by this point. The great Brontotheres was beginning to worry about his comrade. She was good at checking in periodically to let him know of any dangers. He knew she was either in trouble or was watching the small band of early humans they had met earlier in the day. He hoped it was the latter.

Maka, Lexa, and Hope finished cooking the reptilian meat and ate their fill. The meat was tough but had a good flavor. It gave them much needed protein, so they were glad to have it.

"It doesn't taste like chicken," laughed Hope, just satisfied to have a meal.   .

Fruits and plants were all right, but meat gave her energy, it revitalized her.

Lexa and Maka just laughed as they finished the last few morsels. The three went back down to waterhole for a final drink. They kept silent, always on their guard, constantly looking for any signs of danger. They took turns drinking from the waterhole while the other two stood guard. Once finished, they hastily returned to the minimal security of the trees where Bronto had returned from his intentional escape from the horrific display of cooking of flesh performed by the girls. He just shook his head in bewilderment.

"We saved you some," replied Lexa as she grinned at the great beast.

She was trying to lighten up his plain disgust at their cooking methods.

The behemoth just frowned and mumbled something under his breath. He did not want anything to do with that practice. He was about to say something when Aves landed nearby and ran over to them.

"They are coming," Aves shrieked in an overly excited tone, her high-pitched tone shattering the sensitive eardrums of the humans.

"Who is coming?" snorted Bronto.

"The strange humans and three others!"

"What did the humans look like?" Maka asked the overly excited bird.

Maka was curious as to what type of human they were about to meet. Were they brutal savages or simply humans more like them? That was the question she wanted to know. Would they be less intelligent?

The great bird looked at the three women and said, "They look more like you. There are three of them and they have similar wearing's as you three. One is white like Hope; one is red like Maka, and one is a darker color."

Maka cried out, "It's Eric, CeCe, and Takoda! They've found us!"

"Finally!" yelled Lexa, relived by the finding of the men.

"It is so," said Bronto.

Bronto knew the men were in the extinct world somewhere. He had been with the other super beasts when they kidnapped the six humans in the middle of the night along the Missouri River, in the real world. Aves was not with them then, she joined Bronto sometime later, and this explained why she was incapable of connecting the dots. As for Bronto, he was a simple beast and the thought never even crossed his mind that the group of humans avoided earlier in the day were the second half of the group from current Earth.

Now, it would only be a brief time before the whole group reunited.

Chapter 13

Reunion

Eric, CeCe, Tak, and the three super beasts Creo, Arcto, and Pith, surged through time, exiting a strange vortex, which transported them from the Eocene Epoch to the Pleistocene Epoch, 350,000 years ago. The group traveled millions of years within an instant—in the blink of an eye.

Eric rapidly regained his senses, senses momentarily distorted by a feeling of nausea, which wore off quickly. Tak and CeCe seemed unaffected by the jaunt through time and space. All three humans, confused and baffled by the odd series of events, looked to Creo for answers.

The men scrutinized the new landscape. They were astonished by the environmental changes, the climactic changes, and the drastic contrasts to the world they had left only moments before. The immense forests of the Eocene were gone, replaced by smaller forests, many of which consisted of entirely new tree species.

The Earth was much colder now and vast ice sheets plugged up the mountain valleys. It would be centuries before the glaciers entirely receded, releasing their frozen stranglehold on the ice entrenched world. Snow covered entire continents, continents once populated by a wide variety of plant and animal life. Millions of acres were slowly transformed from thick, lush forests into vast open prairies and grasslands. These new land masses remained locked in a world of snow and ice.

The carnivores, the ungulates, the reptiles, the insects, and virtually every other living organism had undergone drastic changes since the Eocene Epoch. Evolutionary experimentation, now narrowing the field of species diversification, focused on one species, one that would alter the lives of all other living creatures: the human.

This new world, a world vastly different from the Eocene world of warm humid temperatures that covered the entire Earth, still became an ecological dish full of genetic experimentation. Thousands of species, some growing to enormous size, thrived in this colder environment. The Pleistocene, also known as the time of the megafauna, would produce many of the same species that inhabit the Earth today.

Besides obvious environmental changes, Eric understood the presence of early, primitive humans and the possibility of interaction with them would be inevitable. This was a new threat, one that hinged on which continent they were on. If they were still in North America, it would be thousands of years before the human species crossed over into this continent. If they were in Europe or Asia, the risk of contact was highly conceivable.

Eric further realized the carnivores of this time would be smarter and significantly faster than their earlier ancestors of the Eocene. This period on Earth was potentially more dangerous to the humans than the world they had just left behind. They would need weapons to defend themselves and warmer clothes to survive here.

"Creo, what just happened?" questioned CeCe.

The big man, still in denial, could not understand how any of this was possible. He knelt to the ground and shook his head; the non-stop turmoil of this place was beginning to take its toll on him.

"Somehow, we just passed through time and ended up 350,000 years from our time," answered Eric.

The tall Norseman did not feel the need to tell the others about the highly evolved predators in this time or the other lurking dangers that could befall them; surviving the climate would be challenging enough, without the added pressures of the carnivores. It was best to deal with what they could see for now.

"We need to get moving," ordered Creo.

The massive Creodont was out of his element now. He was the result of one evolutionary experiment during the Eocene Epoch which his species ruled for millions of years. The Creodonts, specie by specie, slowly went extinct, replaced by the smarter, faster modern carnivores—the carnivores living in this time.

At one point, Creodonts ruled the Eocene as top predators until the gradual change in the environment, one that brought a cooler climate and massive deforestation, altered the course of many species and led to the demise of the mighty Creodonts.

Much of the Earth, now covered in vast savannahs of open range, allowed horses, antelope and other ungulates to become faster, giving them the edge in speed as they roamed these immense areas. The Creodonts were too big, too sluggish, and too dim to keep up with the evolving ungulates. Eventually this led to their extinction. Such is the story of our planet.

Arcto and Pith motioned for the three humans to move out. The group headed towards the sun, trying to keep in the trees when possible and quickly moving through the exposed plains when unavoidable.

Tak was unusually quiet. The Sioux brave had not spoken since they traveled through time. The patient Native American had a serious demeanor about him now. He was all business. His mood, now solemn, was a drastic departure from his normal gregarious nature. Tak's spirit, burdened by apprehension and dejection, weighed on his conscious. The native Sioux's deportment was now one of reflection and sadness. Something was weighing heavily on the proud native.

"Why haven't you spoken since we entered this new world?" asked CeCe, worried about his friend and his departure from his normal persona.

Tak, usually soft spoken and respectful to all things around him, seemed detached from the group. When he spoke, there was often some type of learning or enlightenment that came with his words. If trapped in his thoughts, he did not speak, leaving him only vaguely aware of his surroundings.

"Tell us what's on your mind?" pleaded Eric.

Eric knew his friend very well and realized something relevant was causing his silence. This distraction needed resolution right away before it allowed one of them to make a mistake which could jeopardize the whole group.

"I have a powerful sense we were brought here for an inevitable conflict. I can feel my ancestor's voices calling to me in the wind."

The tall native, his long braids blowing in the wind, looked at Eric and CeCe with coal black eyes. They knew the proud native would risk his life to save them, but they also knew when to heed his words.

"Time will tell us this. Why else would we be here?" replied CeCe, who did not understand any of this either, but he knew there had to be a reason for them being here.

"We must get to this time of Megalo and find out as much information about this place as we can. He can tell us why we are here," Eric interjected, his voice was strong and determined.

He wanted to encourage Tak.

This ploy seemed to snap Tak out of his brooding trance. That long-lost look finally left his eyes as he now focused on getting to the time of this Megalo, whatever that was. It had to hold the key to some explanation. He passed Eric and CeCe and took up the lead behind Creo and Arcto. Pith followed behind as usual, often disappearing, only to re-emerge at erratic intervals.

The group walked for miles without seeing anything, not a bird or even an insect. This landscape was desolate compared to the Eocene Epoch they had left behind just hours before. One world was moist and warm, filled with an unbelievable array of life forms and the other was a cold, less inhabited world.

The group stopped momentarily in a small strand of evergreen trees when they noticed a great flying creature circling nearby. It approached them and then suddenly veered off in the opposite direction. The men quickly hid behind the trees to escape detection. They assumed the ploy worked when the great bird flew out of sight.

"What was that?" cried out CeCe, with a look of apprehension on his confused face.

"It was just an eagle," uttered Pith as he emitted a deep growl and continued into the trees.

"That was a massive eagle. I've seen lots of them and that one was at least ten times bigger than any I've come across," Tak said.

Eric and CeCe were glad to see their friend's demeanor return to normal after his momentary lapse into the spirit world.

"It's gone now, and we need to keep moving," commanded Arcto.

The massive bear-like creature wanted to get going. It would be dusk soon and the humans would have to defend themselves. The great **Arcto**id knew, although they had not seen much animal activity up until this point, that this place had many beasts that could easily slay the humans. This world had fierce predators like the Smilodon, Dire Wolf, Short Faced Bear, Cave lions, and many other dangerous species. Primitive humans could pose a dangerous threat to the modern humans as well. To Arcto these were potential risks to the fragility of the modern humans. This was the world Arcto inhabited.

They traveled on, staying in the trees for protection, trying to avoid detection from scavenging eyes. The group came to the edge of the forest where the tree line abruptly ended, opening into an extensive plain. They spotted a water hole in the distance. Rays of sunlight reflected off the smooth surface of the water like light off a mirror held at just the correct angle.

It was wise to avoid this potential death trap, but they needed water. Their last drink had been early in the morning, so they had little choice but to risk it. Water supports life and water creates life. It is just that simple.

Creo finally broke in and said, "We need water and there is a water hole off in that direction. It will be dangerous out on the wide-open plain, so everyone must stay focused and look for any sign of approaching danger."

The Creodont pointed off in the direction of the water hole and the others calculated the distance to be a mile or two away. Each of them knew they needed to get to the water hole, get the life sustaining fluid, then get back into the safety of the trees as swiftly as possible.

The group headed straight for the water hole. Creo and Pith led the way, followed the humans, while Arcto now took up the rear. The menacing look of the Gigantipithecus would help deter any ambush from lurking predators or scare off approaching danger. Why the giant ape took the lead now was a mystery. One never knew what was going on in Pith's brain. He was a savage brute but ferociously loyal to the death. Eric stopped momentarily and pointed at a wisp of smoke, rising above the trees, in the distance.

"Look...smoke up ahead."

Eric, excited by the possibility of meeting some prehistoric humans, urged the group to pick up the pace. Would he be able to understand them? Would they be friendly? All were questions he was eager to find the answers to.

"I see it too," replied Takoda. "We should avoid whoever made the fire."

Tak was warier than Eric. He understood the dangers. Primitive people meant primitive ways to Tak. There were still many in his tribe who believed in antiquated rituals.

"Who could it be?" CeCe asked, a slight wavering in his voice.

CeCe wanted no part of anything prehistoric. If left up to him, they would go around the water hole and find a different source of water.

"We will approach with caution," warned Creo.

The Creodont knew they needed to get to the water hole for water, then get the humans to a safe place to wait out the darkness of night. Darkness was closing in fast.

Creo and Arcto led the way. They calculated the fire makers would see them coming and flee. Any early humans would be superstitious, and the presence of the bipedal beasts would be unexplainable to them. They would flee in fear.

When they got within a mile of the waterhole, they once again saw the giant eagle flying overhead. This time it flew closer and undoubtedly spotted them. It quickly veered off and returned to a small grove of trees, the trees in which the smoke from the fire was coming. The eagle landed somewhere around the trees and the waterhole. Was it guarding a kill or the waterhole itself? The approaching troop could not be sure until they got closer to the trees.

Pith decided to take the lead and raced off in front of the men and the two other super beasts. Leave it to Pith to take on danger straight away. The brutish giant, all business in his demeanor, reached full speed and began uttering a terrible, frightening growl followed by a wailing scream. The ape-man was out of sight when the loud screams and low growls ended. The last thing the men saw was Pith disappear into the trees. Upon the cease of his vocal utterances, the others picked up the pace towards the waterhole by the trees.

The three humans and the two remaining guardians slowed their pace when they got within 100 yards of the trees. It was best to be cautious. They had not heard a sound from Pith since he entered the trees. They walked past the waterhole and directly by the freshly killed carcass of some reptilian beast. The men thought it would be a great idea to come back and get some fresh meat for dinner after attending to Pith.

Creo and Arcto spread out as they closed in on the small band of trees. Eric, Tak, and CeCe followed just a few yards behind. They were tired and hungry and urgently needed to find out where Pith vanished to, and who was behind the fire coming from the area around the trees. Nervous tension filled the air.

Creo motioned for Arcto to rush the trees when a loud cry came from beyond the trees.

"It's the men! We've finally found them," yelled Hope, the tone of her sweet voice, filled with relief and excitement, was music to the men's ears.

Maka, and Lexa along with both Bronto and Aves turned in the direction of the men. Pith was sitting on his haunches reveling in some of the cooked meat the women had prepared. The giant ape, once again oblivious to his surroundings, had no sooner entered the trees when the roasted meat sidetracked his brutish brain.

"It's no wonder we didn't hear Pith," laughed Eric, pleased by the sight of the three girls.

He moved in and gave Hope a big hug. Eric had always had a big crush on the tall beauty but was afraid to make his feelings known.

"Finally, we're together again," said Maka, relieved to see the men. "We've been worrying about you since we woke up in this strange place."

The humans all embraced each other one by one. Although it had only been a few days, it seemed like an eternity to the group. They exchanged the tales of the earlier days and the events that had befallen each group. The women, the attack of the giant snake in the swamp and the men's encounter with the pack of Hyaenodons in which the courageous ape-beast saved CeCe.

Of course, CeCe played down the event and assured the girls the situation was completely under total control. To this both Tak and Eric laughed hysterically. They would expect nothing else from CeCe—they just shook their heads.

"Yea, that's how it happened," joked Tak. "If you could have seen the look in CeCe's eyes as the snarling beast launched itself at him...you would have seen how he had the situation under control."

"Totally in control," jeered Eric.

CeCe just laughed and pointed to Bronto and Aves.

"Who are these two?" he asked.

"I am Bronto of the Brontotheres and this is Aves," the massive ungulate spoke. "We were sent to protect the girls from harm."

Bronto and Aves gazed at the three men. They were sizing them up. The two super beasts seemed obviously unimpressed by the three men, who were such small insignificant creatures in their world. The two super beasts had become fond of the three women, growing to genuinely worry about them, and now they had to deal with the interactions of three more humans. Change was no different for the super beasts. They too met it with resistance.

The rest of the group introduced themselves to each of the protectors. The now five strong super beasts all converged to discuss the plan for the approaching dusk. They needed to somehow protect the humans from the territorial predators brought out by the darkness of night.

The men went down to the waterhole to get a much-needed drink while the women stayed in the trees. They shortly returned with more meat from the reptilian carcass and tossed it on the fire to cook. The smell was intoxicating. It had been a day since they had a healthy meal. The meat was tough, but the men did not seem to care. They each wolfed down a sizeable amount and then returned to the waterhole for one final drink before nightfall.

The five super creatures, having finished their conversation, returned to the waterhole. Each one took turns drinking while the other four stood guard. This was an observation the humans took note of. They had been careless when they approached the drinking hole. One or more of them could have fallen prey to hidden ambush by anything lurking in the depths of the water; ambush by another reptilian creature or even some other primitive life form.

The group, now finished at the waterhole, headed back to the safety of the trees. The humans were talking about the events of the past few days again. It was good they were all together again, one less obstacle to hinder their return to the current world. Now they could focus on returning home. Each member of the camping party would have searched and scoured this place until they were all together. This was just one less mystery to solve, and now they could focus on returning home.

Dusk was beginning to fall. Creo, obviously the leader of group, motioned to the others to construct a primitive structure to protect the humans for the night. The super beasts quickly went about forming a primitive shelter around a strand of trees. They constructed an almost impenetrable fence to keep out wandering carnivores and other dangerous threats.

Pith and Bronto brought in a good cache of wood to keep the fire burning all night. With the enclosed structure and the fire, the humans had a better chance to stay safe until morning. It was the best Creo and the others could do with the limited time left before darkness fell.

The massive Creodont closed the opening behind him as he left the inner circle.

"Try to survive until morning," he said as he sealed the entrance to the enclosure.

In a flash, all five of the super protectors vanished. Eric and the others had no idea why the strange beasts left or where they went at night. It was another of the many unexplained mysteries in this strange world. Something compelled the protectors to leave as darkness descended, only to return after the light of dawn. It was one more question with no answer. The humans had more questions than answers at this point.

"Why do Creo, Arcto, and Pith leave every night?" asked Tak. "They stay with us all day and never let us out of their sight but vanish just before dusk."

"It's the same with Bronto and Aves," answered Lexa.

Lexa was curious as to the explanation as well. It made no sense to her why the creatures would leave them vulnerable during the most dangerous time of the day, the treacherous night.

The group of humans, happy to be together again, talked into the night about the strange animals they met during the last few days. Eric explained his hypothesis on the period of the Earth they were now in and where at least the men entered this place at. The women told the men about waking up behind the waterfall and traveling across a great swamp. They described the odd creatures they met while journeying to this time. Eric surmised they were in the Eocene Epoch as well, but just a different time span. Each Epoch lasted for millions of years and during that time, there were many evolutionary changes. Plants, animals and landscapes went through many adaptations, some minor some drastic.

Eric decided to take the first watch, while the others tried to rest and sleep as much as possible.

The night brought out the stalking creatures of the darkness. Strange guttural noises came from outside the protective fencing. The fire attracted as many beasts to it as it drove off. Some came in close to sniff at the primitive shelter while others avoided it all together.

Down by the waterhole even more bizarre noises filled the nighttime airwaves. It was the one source that brought all the species together, some to drink and some to ambush prey. Nighttime brings out a multitude of species, ones that hope to avoid detection and others to hunt.

Darkness was an extremely dangerous time for the ungulates. Especially during the Pleistocene Epoch, a time when carnivores were many and dominated the Earth. There were Cave Lions, Dire Wolves, Saber Toothed Cats, Short Faced Bears and many more, all eagerly awaiting the opportunity to pounce on unsuspecting prey. Humans were prey as well if the opportunity presented itself.

The terrifying screams continued throughout the night as the weaker creatures fell prey to the marauding predators. Tak relieved Eric for the second watch. The blonde Scandinavian fell quickly into a deep sleep, while Tak kept the fire burning bright to thwart off any inquisitive beasts that passed by during the night on their way to the waterhole.

Several times during his watch, Tak could hear the footsteps of a massive beast passing by the enclosure, just out of visual sight of the fire light. He knew it was large, but it crept by silently as if trying to avoid detection.

Other smaller creatures managed to crawl under the protective walls of the temporary structure and scurry in and out of the light. Some reminded Tak of field mice with larger ears. They darted in and out of the light trying to hide in the darkness. He threw out a few small scraps of meat and the tiny intruders raced for them, temporarily forgetting to stay out of sight. He laughed at how easily they abandoned the need to be safe for the chance at a free meal. Some even attacked others and fought over the tiny morsels of the life sustaining flesh. Survival in the end is the true denominator.

Tak continued to keep guard deep into the night. It was a clear night, and the stars were shining bright. The moon was almost full, which helped his vision once he let it adjust from the light of the fire. He could make out shapes but nothing definitive. The passing shapes came and went throughout the night. The shapes seemed to know to avoid the firelight and most passed by without stopping to sniff at the enclosure. Occasionally, one would stop and circle the enclosure, then eventually move off.

The night passed without any life–threatening events for the humans. Down by the waterhole was a different story. Tak could hear the death cries as one creature fell to another. He was sure the carcass of the dead reptilian beast brought in the carnivores who disrupted the normal flow of animals that frequented the waterhole.

As dawn approached, the traffic around the waterhole dwindled. It had been a chilly night and without the warmth of the fire, it would have been a long miserable night for the humans. Eric and CeCe were the first to awake.

"Anything usual happen last night Tak?" asked CeCe.

"Just the occasional passerby."

"Have you seen any sign of Creo and the others?" Eric asked, all well knowing they would be coming with the dawn.

"No, not yet," answered Tak, who was tired from keeping the late watch.

All the humans were awake now. Hope was stretching, trying to relieve the stiffness from sleeping on the ground. Maka and Lexa followed suit and soon all three were talking about the fortunate series of events that led to the finding of the men. It was good to have everyone back together again. The chances of them finding each other would have been zero without the help of the super beasts, regardless of how strange they were.

"What was that?" whispered Maka as she pointed to the far side of the enclosure around the door.

"I heard it too," answered Lexa as she pointed to the doorway. "It's coming from the door to the enclosure."

Everyone now focused on the noise coming from outside the enclosure. The sound became louder as the temporary wall of the structure shook violently. Something was trying to get in.

"Who is it?" yelled Eric.

"It is I, Megalo," a deep voice articulated.

All six of the humans looked in awe at each other as the giant, powerful, beast Megalo entered the enclosure.

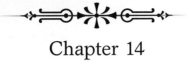

Chapter 14

Megalo

The door to the enclosure abruptly swung open and in walked Megalo. The humans, awestruck by his enormous size and equally mesmerized by his powerful presence, moved closer together for protection as the colossal creature entered the enclosure.

Megalo stood fourteen feet tall in his current form, with gigantic horns that spanned over ten feet from tip to tip. His eyes were noticeably big, completely black in color, yet they suggested intelligence and kindness. His magnificent ivory antlers, supported by bulging, remarkably defined neck muscles, glistened in the early morning sunlight. Each side of his imposing horns were astonishingly symmetrical with ten tines on each. The giant was heavily furred, fur that was brownish cream in color, varying in length from short on his underbelly to extremely long around his sizable neck.

"He is a **Megalo**ceros giganteus," Eric said.

"A Megalo what?" asked CeCe, as he gazed at the enormous, horned cervoid.

"A Megaloceros giganteus. It lived up until roughly 2,400 years ago and was one of the largest of the deer family to ever live."

The huge deer entered the enclosure, his massive antlers barely clearing the doorway. He surveyed the humans until his eyes locked on Eric.

"I am **Megalo**. You must be Eric Asvaldsson," he said in a commanding tone, his coal black eyes seeming to look through the surprised human.

Eric quickly answered, "Yes, that's me. What do you want with us?"

The Megaloceros giganteus moved closer to the group, quickly followed by Creo, who stayed within a few feet of the giant deer. Arcto, Pith, and Bronto stayed outside of the enclosure. Aves, the giant eagle, had not yet returned from the night before.

Eric and the others could now see the true mass of Megalo and his remarkable horns. They were not only impressive, but they were magnificent, a combination of pure white ivory with distinct patterns of black granular lines running through them. Megalo began to unveil the mystery.

"You and your friends are in the world of Extinctus."

"Extinctus is the world where all extinct species that lived on Earth still exist; they exist in the same form, the form they lived in when they roamed the Earth. 99% of all species on Earth are extinct, which amounts to over 5 billion species. Many of these species faded from your world long ago, but many are fading as we stand here speaking. All extinct species are here in Extinctus, living as they did during their time on Earth."

The giant cervoid, whose tone sounded very solemn, gazed at the humans with his dark coal eyes and transfixing stare. The unbelievable number of extinct species shocked the humans. This meant only 1% of the Earth's known species still survived, a statement which stunned the humans.

"That is shocking," responded Maka, deeply affected by the grim words of Megalo.

Her name meant "Earth" in Sioux, which made her feel a deep connection to the planet.

"It is what it is," replied Megalo.

The Megaloceros giganteus motioned for the humans to exit the enclosure and move out into the trees. The humans followed one by one until they reached a small clearing, where they all huddled together.

Megalo continued, "We take on this bipedal form to better communicate with you and not overwhelm you with our actual size. We can take on many forms. Take **Creo** for example; he is a **Creo**dont and can turn into any of the creatures that make up the family of Creodonts. Creodonts have two sub-families: deltatheridians and the hyaenodonts. Creo can turn into any of these animals or even a combination of one or more. All of us have the same ability... some like Creo and others like me can turn into any specie or a combination of the species which share the same prefix or letters in their name. You see me now as a Megaloceros, but for example, I can also be a Megalosaurus, a monstrous dinosaur, or Megalodon, the largest shark to ever live in the ocean, or even a combination of all these creatures."

"That's utterly astonishing," replied Eric, his keen interest peaked by this startling new information.

The ability of these creatures to 'shape shift' fascinated him, but the ability to change into a combination of animals intrigued him. To this point he had not seen this capability. The men had witnessed Creo and Arcto turn into just one form of their respective species to thwart off the attack by the Sarkastodon but had yet to see any combination of species.

"Why do they leave at night?" asked Hope.

The disappearance of the super beasts every night, which left the humans vulnerable, was an area of contention for Hope. She believed it was careless. They were there to protect them but instead, they left them in the darkness to fend for themselves when the carnivores of the night were the most active.

"That's the one weakness we have. We don't have the ability to sustain ourselves in the darkness. We turn back into our normal forms and spend the night eating which in turn rejuvenates our ability to change in the light. It takes quite a bit of food to keep our massive bodies sustained. There's a certain type of ivory that can give us the power to sustain this form, but it's rare, and we only use it sparingly. I know much of this is unbelievable to you, and more will be revealed in time."

Megalo pointed to Eric before speaking again, "You're the one we came for because you descend from the Asvaldsson line and are the key to saving your species."

Megalo hesitated as he spoke. The humans all looked at him with confused bewilderment on their faces.

"How could I have anything to do with saving humanity?" asked Eric. "There are billions of people on Earth now."

"It started with your grandfather; Asvald Asvaldsson."

The huge deer locked eyes with Eric and continued his story, "Your grandfather entered Extinctus some 47 years ago. A bizarre series of events unfolded which allowed him to cross over into our world—the world of the extinct. Asvald killed the last known Thylacine, also known as the Tasmanian wolf or tiger. He shot the beast one wet morning on a high ledge outside a dark cave, but the mortal wound did not finish the creature quickly. When Asvald found the wounded Thylacine, the dying animal clung to life with labored breath. Asvald then plunged his hunting knife into the heart of the beast. When he committed this act, since it was the last one of the species, it opened up the portal to Extinctus and both were pulled in."

Megalo paused and then pointed to Eric again.

"I know this is hard for you to comprehend, but I assure you this is very real," he said.

His coal black eyes did not stray from Eric or the others as he spoke.

"We were able to get to Asvald in time and gave him an ivory device, one that allowed him to travel to different time periods in Extinctus. Since I gave him the device, we haven't been able to find him, although we've searched for decades. It has been many decades and we have no idea if he still lives. We've searched and searched, but you must understand that Extinctus spans millions of years and your grandfather could have gone anywhere in time. From time to time we would hear stories about a white human and travel to investigate these stories but always to no avail. We arrived too late or Asvald kept well hidden."

The story so far sounded absurd to Eric and the others. Eric had never known his grandfather or his father. His father left before he was born. He knew him only from a few photographs his mother still had. There had been no contact from his father since he left.

"I never knew my grandfather. Since my father was gone before I was born, I never learned about him as a person. Now he would be over 80 years old."

Megalo, eager to get back to his narrative answered, "I'm aware of this. It's possible he's still alive though. I've seen stranger things happen."

The strange tale mesmerized the humans, but they had difficulty understanding the connection between it and saving the human species.

"After Asvald killed the last Thylacine and entered the world of Extinctus, this phenomenon caused a ripple of events. Asvald entered Extinctus during the time of the Miocene Epoch around 18 million years ago. It was there that I found him and tried to help him. I explained to him, as I now explain to you, the mysterious series of events and the role he now played in these events. At first, he didn't believe me, but over time we came to trust one another, and he finally understood his peril. I taught him the ways of Extinctus and gave him the ivory device that would move him through time. This turned out to be my mistake. He vanished somewhere in time," the giant shook his massive antlers and sighed.

Eric could hear by the tone of Megalo's words that the giant was truly fond of Asvald.

"So, what does this have to do with me, and why did you kidnap all of us?" questioned Eric, unable to understand what role the others had to play in this mysterious journey.

"We weren't sure which one of you was the grandson of Asvald. Besides, if we had left any of you, it would've caused suspicion and investigation. I decided it was best to take our chances and bring all of you here."

"It was very unfortunate that all of you were together, but we could not wait any longer to abduct you," spoke Creo, who up to this point remained silent.

It was the first time the Creodont had spoken since Megalo arrived. Eric could now tell that Creo was the protector of Megalo. It was his duty to make sure Megalo was safe. He was his bodyguard.

The big cervoid continued, "After your grandfather disappeared, I looked for him for months but always seemed to just miss him. When I would get close to him, he would travel to another time and the hunt would begin again. In some ways, this helped Asvald to survive. Consumed with rage and revenge, the last **Thylac**ine, now going by the name **Thylac**, vowed vengeance on the bloodline of Asvald. He concocted a plan to annihilate the blood line of Asvald and reverse the extinction of his species. Thylac falsely believed that if he killed Asvald while the human was in Extinctus, it would be as if he never existed, which would put his species back on Earth. So, he searched for Asvald with every resource he had."

The humans, now engulfed in the story, were beginning to see the link to Eric. This Thylac, along with his henchmen, could have easily abducted them, and who knows what evil demise would have befallen them if that had happened.

"Then what about Eric's father?" asked Tak.

"We don't know what happened to Tolf. We know he came looking for Asvald but that is all."

The giant horned beast looked at the enthralled group of humans and then continued in a tone of dire conviction, "We can't take the chance that Tolf still lives. That is why we had to come and abduct you. Humanity, as you know it, is now in jeopardy. Thylac has given up his quest to wipe out the Asvaldsson bloodline and has set his sights on the very link to you humans. Since he has given up his original quest, we surmise he has never found Asvald or Tolf. If he succeeds, none of you will ever have existed."

"We must stop him!" yelled Creo.

The other super beasts all joined in and yelled in unison. They rallied to Megalo's support as he further explained the predicament.

"If a species becomes extinct in Extinctus, which we call re-extinctionification, it will fade from both worlds. It would be as if it never existed at all. I know this is a lot to take in, but your very existence depends on the outcome. It's vital we keep you alive until we can defeat Thylac and his helpers. If Thylac learns you're here, he will stop at no end to kill you. He has devised a plan to annihilate an early hominid, one which he feels is the link to your species, but he would relish the opportunity to exact revenge on you or any of your bloodline. We brought you here to slow down his plan and keep your species safe inside of Extinctus."

"So, you want to use me as a decoy?" asked Eric, the heaviness of the burden beginning to unfold on him.

"Yes, in a way, but we will protect you," interjected Creo.

The giant Creodont smiled at Eric and the other humans.

"This is the only way to distract Thylac until we can determine what hominid species he has set his aim on and so we can contrive a plan to defeat him. We are the protectors of Extinctus, prohibited from causing re–extinction, and we have an obligation to stop others from successfully trying it," Megalo explained.

"So, you are Super–Extinctos?" interjected Tak, laughing at his new term for the beasts.

"We are whatever you want to call us," Megalo simply responded.

"What about my friends? I don't want to put them in any danger," asked Eric.

It was one thing to use him as a hostage, but quite another to jeopardize the safety of his friends. If anything, the Extinctos should return them to the camp along the Missouri River in Montana.

"We're all in this together," replied Hope, who was very fond of Eric and would stay by his side no matter the circumstance.

The other humans all one by one offered to stay and help Eric and the Super Extinctos save humanity. They had journeyed far from the camp on the Missouri River in Montana, to the land of the extinct, and would stay until the end; for they all had a significant stake in the outcome.

The giant deer further explained, "We'll have to split up to confuse Thylac. If we travel to several different time periods, it will cause him to spread out his henchmen to search for us. By now Thylac will know Eric is in Extinctus and this will distract him while we search for the hominid he intends to annihilate. He won't know where we've taken Eric, and waste valuable time searching for him. Once we learn which early hominid...he intends to wage war on... we'll be able to go in and protect the species. Each group of Extinctos, sent to separate times, will find and add more species to aide in our fight for Extinctus. But first, we'll need to decide who goes where and we'll need more Super Extinctos."

Within a matter of hours more Super Extinctos started arriving on the scene. Four of them walked into camp within minutes of each other. Like the Extinctos already with the humans, they were massive creatures of gigantic proportions.

One was even a tree, named **Arc**, named after the order of trees, known as the **Arc**haeopteridales. This one was an **Arc**haeopteris, long thought to be the earliest known tree. Archaeopteris, Greek for ancient fern, flourished during the Upper Devonian to Lower Carboniferous periods 383 million to 323 million years ago and reached heights of over 33 feet.

The next Extincto, named **Perris**, from the order of **Periss**odactyla, a group of creatures which included horses, rhinoceroses and tapirs, arrived soon after Arc. Perissodactyls, like Bronto, were odd toed ungulates. They evolved over 56 million years ago and are one of two surviving orders of the hoofed animals still around today. Perris took on the form of Pliohippus, the first one toed horse that lived during the Pliocene Epoch. Compared to the other Extinctos, Perris was short, only standing six feet tall. In her true form, she would have been a horse around 4 feet tall. She was very slim, very athletic, and incredibly fast.

The third Extincto was a terrifying creature named **Gorgo**. He was from the suborder **Gorgo**nopsia, from the order of Therapsids. Gorgonopsians were mammal-like reptiles that evolved during Permian times 266–250 million years ago. They were the primitive ancestors to mammals and ranged from dog size to bear size. Gorgonopsians were one of three groups that made up one group of Therapsids known as Theriodonts. Theriodonts were the largest carnivores during the late Permian. Gorgo took on the form of one of these Gorgonopsians named Inostrancevia. Inostrancevia was the largest Theriodont known and was the size of a bear. It was a strange looking reptile-like carnivore with 5-inch-long saber-like teeth. It was somewhere between a reptile and mammal with both tough scales and hair. The humans were glad Gorgo was on their side.

The last Extincto, **Arti**, was from the even-toed ungulates known as **Arti**odactyls. Artiodactyls, which number over 200 species, evolved around 50 million years ago and are still evolving today. Some of the more well-known species are pigs, deer, camels, hippopotamuses, alpacas, giraffes, antelopes, sheep and cattle. Other Artiodactyls split off to form their own sub-order called Cetacea, which included whales, dolphins and porpoises. Arti took on the form of **Andrewsarchus**, a powerful Artiodactyl that lived during the Eocene Epoch. It was one of the largest land carnivores to ever live and had a snout over 3 feet long filled with dagger-like teeth. It is hard to imagine that it belonged to the even-toed ungulate family, a family of animals we associate with deer, sheep and the like. **(Image 7: Andrewsarchus: page 134)**

After introducing the new Super Extinctos, Megalo decided Hope would go with Eric, along with Creo, Aves, and Arti. Takoda and Maka would travel with Arcto, Perris, and Arc while CeCe and Lexa would travel with Bronto, Pith, and Gorgo.

For added measure, Megalo decided the humans would not know the location of each other, in case Thylac or any of his allies captured any of them. This was for their own protection.

The Super Extinctos talked amongst themselves for several minutes. They needed to work out the coordination of where to meet and when. They would be the only members of each group that had this information.

The humans would be alone if all the Super Extinctos perished while amassing Megalo's army. Each Extincto in the group carried an ivory device, one made from the tusk of some prehistoric animal, to travel around Extinctus.

The group numbering 16 strong now traveled from the waterhole to a large clearing in the trees. Here the giant Megalo pointed to several back packs positioned under a tree.

"Here are your belongings. I had them brought to Extinctus for you."

Megalo bid them farewell and pulled a polished, pointed ivory horn from beneath his belt and uttered the words, Pliocene Epoch 2.5-M-Y-A and vanished.

One by one the other groups produced similar pieces of ivory and one by one they also disappeared in time.

Chapter 15

Eric and Hope

The three groups, consisting of both humans and Super Extinctos, vanished in time, traveling to different periods in the extinct history of the Earth. To tighten security, Megalo kept secret the location of each group to ensure the safety of each human, in case of capture by the ruthless Thylac or his sinister henchmen.

Eric, Hope, Creo, Aves and Arti traveled to the Cenozoic Era, a timespan from 65 million years ago to the present. Within moments, the group traveled through time, arriving to a time rich in species diversification.

The Cenozoic, also referred to as the Age of Mammals and the Age of Birds, was an era that saw a rich variety of species evolution. The extinction of many large non-avian dinosaurs led to an explosion in diversity among mammals and birds. Mammals expanded from a few small species to a disparate assortment of land mammals, birds, and marine creatures. The climate began to gradually cool down, which slowly altered the size of the forests, but opened vast grasslands, which in turn offered new food sources for the growing populations of grazing species. This produced a rich diversity of carnivorous predators, which preyed on the endless supply of flesh.

Many of the species today started as early forms during the Cenozoic Era. The first horse, around the size of a fox, evolved with three toes. Early elephants, which were plentiful in both numbers and experimental forms, thrived. Gigantic rhinos, swift antelope, stealthy carnivores, behemoth birds, deadly snakes, multi-horned deer, and many other species evolved during this period, many only to disappear from existence, as they journeyed down evolutionary dead ends.

Millions of species survived by adapting to the ecological conditions of their time. Some species, ones that evolved as the Earth evolved, are still around today in their more recognizable, modern forms. Evergreen trees, along with countless other plant species, evolved during this time, a time of vast experimentation of species—some strangely familiar and many too incongruous to understand.

During this time, one species appeared that would transcend all others, leaving everlasting impacts on all every other species and the planet itself—this species was the human species.

The Cenozoic Era, rich in predators and grazers, was now where Eric and Hope found themselves. To be more precise they ended up during the Miocene Epoch, one epoch during the Cenozoic, which spanned from 23–5 million years ago. This epoch followed the Oligocene Epoch (35–23 million years ago) which in turn followed the Eocene Epoch (56–35 million years ago), the epoch where Eric, CeCe and Tak first entered Extinctus.

The humans were now some 17 million years later in time than during the Eocene. The climate, now cooler with seasonal rains, still favored species adapted to a warm climate, but Earth was beginning to cool down due to the mountains rising in the Americas.

Large savannahs, rich in grass species, colonized the open spaces left vacant by the countless forests that vanished as the planet turned colder and drier. The oceans cooled down which created a new ecosystem, one rich in nutrients, brown algae, and kelp forests. This explosion of plant life in the sea, allowed mammals, fishes, and invertebrates to flourish in the oxygen enriched sea water.

This group, led by Creo once again, entered the new time, quickly moving into the cover of the thick forest. The forest now consisted of evergreens and hard woods like maple and birch. The larger hard woods towered over the shorter evergreens.

Aves took the air to scout the region. With one great swoop of her powerful wings, the giant eagle lifted herself off the ground, quickly vanishing above the tall hard woods. The humans watched in awe as the massive raptor effortlessly floated in the daytime sunshine.

"We're in a time of great diversity," said Eric, overhearing the words spoken by Creo moments before the group traveled through time.

"What are we to do now?" asked Hope in a tone that revealed frustration and apprehension.

Hope, the planner, needed a plan to feel secure. Her world needed to make sense all the time and she struggled with abstract, disorganization.

"We need to find support for our fight against Thylac," Creo declared.

The massive Creodont understood the gravity of Thylac's twisted plan. The loss of a species in Extinctus, could throw the entire world into chaos. Creo and the other Extinctos main purpose was keeping the balance of power neutral in Extinctus.

"I will travel to get the support of many of the **Arti**odactyls," Arti said.

There were thousands of odd toed ungulate species to recruit from in the Miocene. Arti would focus on the big and powerful ones first then recruit the smaller species for reconnaissance. He would search not only the Miocene Epoch for Artiodactyls, but the other Epochs as well until he was confident in his numbers.

"That's a great idea. I'll get the support of as many Creodonts as possible," answered Creo.

Creo knew Thylac, along with his henchman, would try to recruit the same species. Time was critical. They needed to leave at once.

"Aves can travel to get the aerial support."

Creo knew the avian menace would span the world of Extinctus and bring back the flying species to help with the battle in the air. War would certainly wage in the air as well as the land and sea once the inevitable conflict started.

"What should Hope, and I do?" asked Eric, who wanted to help in any way.

"You'll need a safe place to hide while we're gone. We don't have time to help you build a shelter or fashion any kind of weapons."

Creo feared the humans would be defenseless while he, Arti, and Aves went to gather help. It was risky to leave Eric and Hope alone but he felt he had little choice; the fate of all humans hung in the balance. He knew he could travel faster alone, without the humans to slow him down. It was a judgment call, a call that would leave the humans vulnerable. Originally, it was important to protect Eric from Thylac, but with Thylac's focus now shifted, the goal was to stop his more sinister plan, the plan to wipe out the human species.

Creo and Arti left at once, heading back out onto the prairie, where they met several herds of odd-looking antelope roaming the grassland. The smaller grazers were intermingled with the occasional enormous beasts, beasts which resembled bison, rhinos, and elephants.

Eric and Hope went deeper into the forest to find a suitable shelter, one that would offer them security as well as refuge from the elements. They journeyed deep into the forest until they found a large outcropping that spread out on a hillside in the forest. It looked promising, so the two humans searched the area around the out cropping for a hidden cave that would give them shelter and protection.

They found a small cave with two large boulders on both sides of it surrounded by a thick row of trees that ran down from the top of a hill. On top of the rock outcrop was a wide strip of grass. Trees grew from the top of the hill down to the bottom of the outcrop.

The only unsecured area of the cave was the entry way. Eric and Hope were confident they could build a suitable door from fallen tree limbs, so they set out to gather as much debris as possible.

It was miraculous that Megalo possessed the wherewithal to bring their belongings to Extinctus. Eric had in his backpack a knife, a small hand axe, rope, fishing gear and several other objects. These items would prove to be priceless in Extinctus.

Eric grabbed his axe and began stripping off the branches of several small trees until he had a series of long branchless poles, which he tied together to construct a large door. The branches gave strength to the door while the rope held everything together.

Hope started digging a trench along the opening of the cave. The idea was to put the bottom ends of the poles into the ground and bury them, which would make the door structure stronger and harder to penetrate. Eric and Hope worked exceptionally well together as they constructed the primitive door. They were highly compatible, which made them an effective team.

Once the door was in place, they packed dirt around the bottom of the poles to help support it. Eric constructed several longer poles, sharpening one end of each, with his axe. These he placed in the ground in front of the door with the pointed ends sticking out from the door to impale anything that tried to come into the cave. He hoped this would prevent any attack on them by roaming predators.

Once finished with the door, the two humans built a fire pit inside the cave to cook meat on and to heat the interior of the cave if the weather turned cold. They spent the next few hours gathering wood, enough to burn throughout the night and enough to last for a few days. Proper preparation was key to surviving in this place, so Eric and Hope spent the time necessary to survive. A little effort now could make a significant difference later.

Food was now the priority. What could they find to eat? Building the door and gathering firewood took energy, energy needing replaced by water and food.

"We need to find a good water source and scout the area for possible game," spoke Eric.

Eric realized the quicker they solved finding the necessities, the more time they could spend on hunting for food.

"I am ready to explore," responded Hope in her positive tone.

They decided to search the area around the cave for a water source, while they hunted for small game. Eric fashioned a couple of fine pointed spears for hunting and to use for protection when necessary. These he sharpened with his hunting knife until the points were razor sharp, capable of penetrating the thickest hides. He gave one to Hope, keeping a longer one for himself. They were slim and easy to throw. If they could get close to some small rodent or rabbit, they had a chance of impaling it.

Eric led the way. He slowly moved through the trees cautiously signaling Hope to do the same. They stayed together for protection. Hope spotted a strange looking gopher–like creature in a small clearing around 200 yards from the shelter. It had two horns projecting upwards from above its eyes.

The gopher, obviously a burrowing creature, was eating supple blades of grass in a small opening in the trees. The rodent, oblivious to what was happening around him, continued to dine on the grass, as Eric and Hope crept closer. They could see a series of burrows as they silently approached the unsuspecting quarry.

Eric motioned Hope to stay still as he moved closer to the target. He was within 10 feet of the rodent when it spotted him. The vermin ran for one of its many burrow openings as Eric launched his spear. His aim was on the mark, as the spear penetrated the side of the primitive creature, killing it instantly.

Dinner secured, the humans moved back into the trees to hunt for water, which was now the focus. The search drove them deeper into the forest. It was late evening and the lower reaches of the forest, now cast in long shadows, shadows caused by the waning sunlight, made the forest an eerie place.

They walked about a mile deeper into the forest before deciding to head back to the shelter. The two humans took a different route on the way back, one which brought them through on the forest side above the shelter. The light of day was beginning to fade so they picked up their pace.

Hope spotted a trickle of water flowing up out of the Earth from an underground natural spring. Both drank their fill of the cool, refreshing water; the purest of water without man made pollution or chemicals. In their haste to explore the region, the humans forgot to bring a pan to carry water back to the cave in. They would need to construct some type of container for hauling water.

Dusk, that time when dark shadows fill the forest floor, was slowly creeping in, so they hurried back to the security of the cave. This landscape, filled with life threatening dangers, unfamiliar terrain, and carnivorous creatures, was alien to them. They had to make it back to the cave before it got completely dark.

Eric and Hope reached the tree line above the cave just in time. Hideous screams and howls were beginning to fill the night air waves. Beasts, some sounding their ownership to their territory, others bellowing their last death tones, came out of the shadows as darkness descended on the primitive world.

Ominous sounds echoed all around Eric and Hope as they hurried down the hill and entered the cave. Eric secured the door while Hope built a fire next to the doorway so most of the smoke would filter out of the cave and the flames would aid in keeping the denizens of the night at bay.

Once Eric secured the doorway to his liking, he focused on cleaning the horned gopher and preparing it for roasting on the fire. It was small, not enough for them both, but it was better than nothing. Eric knew there was food all around them and he would look for bigger game in the light of the new day.

Eric and Hope relished the tiny offering of meat, which was more than likely the first time a human had ever eaten the small mammal. Eric guessed it was a rodent named Epigaulus, a small mammal that was very abundant during this time span and afforded a much-needed food source for many of the carnivores and birds of prey that lived alongside it.

Hope and Eric, thrilled to have something to eat after the long day, did not complain about the small portions. Both had spent a great amount of energy building the shelter. Soon they were sound asleep. They huddled close to each other directly in front of the fire for heat. The shelter allowed them some respite from the brutal carnage that played out, just yards from them, outside the shelter.

The strange screams and growls continued throughout the night. The humans were too exhausted to notice and were quite content in the safety of the cave. They slept uninterrupted until sometime towards the latter part of the night, when a series of loud growls and howling awakened Eric.

Eric stood up, nudged Hope and said, "Wake up Hope, I think we have company."

Hope, now fully awake, stood up and moved close to Eric.

"What is it?"

The loud noises were coming from just outside of the cave. At least two or three beasts were clawing and biting at the pointed poles that blocked them from entering the doorway to the cave. They continued to growl at each other, in deep tones, trying to communicate with each other. This went on for a considerable amount of time until it suddenly ceased when the creatures ran off.

It was then that it dawned on Eric and Hope. This cave must have been a den. Eric grabbed a large stick, burning on one end, and moved towards the back of the den. The burning stick was dim, but it helped break through the darkness at the back of the cave. He walked back into the cave about 200 feet when he saw four tiny eyes reflecting the light from his primitive torch. Eric found two small pups huddled together staring up at him. He approached them as they growled and hissed at him. It was the first time they had ever seen a human and the first time a human had ever seen one of them.

He quickly grabbed them by the nape to paralyze them, so he could bring them to the front of the cave. He called to Hope, and she met him as he returned to the fire.

"What are those?" she asked as she moved closer to look and the tiny, hiding hostages.

"I'm pretty sure they're bear dogs, but they're young, and I can't tell for sure in the darkness."

Eric knew if they were bear dogs, they were in for trouble from the adults. Bear Dogs were neither bears nor dogs. The correct name was Amphicyon galushai, a species related to both bears and dogs. He also knew they were vicious killers and hunted in packs like modern wolves. They grew up to 8 feet long, were heavily muscled, and reached weights of up to 1200 pounds. **(Image 8: Amphicyon giganteus: page 135)**

"What do we do with them?" Hope asked.

"We need to get them back to their parents," replied Eric, convinced the pack would stop at nothing to get to the pups.

The adult bear dogs returned to the front of the cave again and at once started digging at the stakes which held the door secure. They tried to dislodge the pointed stakes, buried deep in the ground, to gain access to the cave. If successful, it would only be a matter of time before they reached the primitive door and attack the humans. Eric and Hope, defenseless with their primitive spears, were no match for the three giant beasts; they were just no match for their immense size and ferocity.

The bear dogs continued to dig; one by one the stakes fell. By this time, the early light of dawn broke, lightening the darkness of the night.

Eric and Hope could now see the immense size of the bear dogs. Eric had been correct in his assumption—they were indeed bear dogs. The brutish beasts were long and heavily muscled, which reminded Eric of a fusion between a lion and a pit bull. They were tan in color with white on the chest and they had an exceedingly long, thick tail. The bear dog, a formidable omnivore, ate both plants and meat.

The menacing pack, now to the door, continued to dig vehemently. Three of the giants were visible to the humans, but only one could get to the door. The other two stood guard.

The one at the door dug at the poles with hardened claws and bit the rope with powerful jaws. Eric grabbed hold of the door and leaned back with all his weight. Hope threw heaps of wood on the fire to increase the size of the blaze to frighten the beast. This was the only line of defense they had; they did not have any guns to drive off the creatures from a distance, just primitive weapons, the spear, the knife, and the axe, all weapons incapable of fighting off such a massive animal if it gained entrance. They needed the superior strength and power of the Super Extinctos who could be gone for days or weeks or forever.

Hope tried to squeeze the pups through the opening in the door without success. They were too big to fit through the narrow opening. To open the door to place the pups outside was risky, but it was the only way.

Instead, she picked up one of the spears and jammed it between two of the poles at the bear dog. It hit the beast in the shoulder and penetrated the thick skin of the mighty predator. The injured beast quickly backed away from the door.

This tactic could save them from attack, but they still needed to get out of the cave to get food and water. Daylight was upon them now and the pack momentarily left the cave entrance. They too had to eat and drink.

"Where do you think they went?" asked Hope as she peered out of the doorway looking for any sign of the carnivorous pack.

"To get water, but they will be back," answered Eric.

Eric knew the pack would not give up so easily and leave their pups behind. If anything, they were loyal to each member of the pack large or small.

"We should open the door and let them out," replied Hope.

"Good thinking. Maybe if they get the pups, they will leave us alone," answered Eric.

Hope slowly opened the door, cracking it open just enough to squeeze one pup at a time through the tiny opening. Eric grabbed each pup and placed them on the other side of the doorway. The pups were young and did not move from the spot Eric had placed them in. They just whimpered. Their soft cries attracted others and soon the three pack members returned to the front of the cave.

One pack member, which Eric and Hope assumed was the mother, slowly approached the pups. She moved in slowly, using caution. The smell of the humans was something entirely new to the bear dog. She sniffed the pup and started to pick one up by the neck when the other two members of the pack emitted ferocious growls.

Eric and Hope heard another sound coming from outside the door. It was a loud lion–like roar. The mother at once left the pups and turned to join the pack.

Hope and Eric peered through the door trying to catch a glimpse of what event was unfolding just feet in front of the shelter. They could see the three bear dogs standing side by side facing the same direction in a defensive posture, their teeth bared, exposing powerful jaws.

The bear dog's snarling kept getting louder. Two of the ferocious beasts split off and the group spread out. The onlooking humans continued to gaze through the door in suspenseful anticipation.

A few moments later, they could see what was commanding the packs attention. There was a much larger, heavier built carnivorous beast, facing the bear dogs. It was massive in size, with a head at least two and half times the size of a modern–day Kodiak brown bear.

"It's a Megistotherium! One of the largest Creodonts that ever lived from the same family as Creo. This could be a battle to the death," whispered Eric in a tone of utter astonishment.

The two humans looked on as the pack of bear dogs tried to protect their den and pups. The Megistotherium came closer emitting a fierce growl. It outweighed the bear dogs by 800 pounds. It was the true giant of the time but was in the last stages of its evolution and would vanish from Earth a few million years later.

The bear dogs would not yield to the gigantic predator or give up their pups. They simultaneously attacked the giant Creodont from all sides. A vicious fight to the death played out right in front of Eric and Hope. The bear dogs were quicker than the Megistotherium as they darted in and out, biting at its legs. They were trying to move the attacker away from the den and the defenseless pups. They could have easily out distanced the brute but the necessity to protect their young was too compelling.

One of the bear dogs rushed in and distracted the foe while the others bit at its defenseless backside. This strategy seemed to work until one of the bear dogs stumbled, a misstep which allowed the Megistotherium the opportunity to seize the smaller beast and crush it in its clamp like jaws. It crushed the helpless bear dog's spine in one mighty bite and flung the lifeless form to the side, at once focusing its attention back to the two remaining bear dogs.

In the end, the Megistotherium's superior size gained the upper advantage and once the second bear dog stumbled and fell to the ground, the immense weight of the Creodont crushed the life from the heroic beast trying to save the pups. They were no match for the brutal beast's size and savagery.

The last bear dog, the mother of the pups, tried to run at the last minute but the massive Megistotherium knocked her down in front of the cave, in full view of Eric and Hope. She tried to get up, but her effort was futile. The giant Megistotherium pounced on the weaker bear dog and with one tremendous bite around the neck, the last bear dog faded.

The victor violently shook the lifeless body of the mother bear dog then wandered out to check on the two other lifeless forms. The wounded Creodont moved towards the lifeless bodies of the first two bear dogs, sniffed the motionless corpses then fell to gorging itself on the flesh of the fallen beasts. The entire episode took less than a half hour but changed the life of the two pups forever.

Eric and Hope were both fascinated, stunned, and deeply saddened by the horrific display of brutality; life playing out 17 million years ago. Eric quickly opened the door just enough to grab the poor, now pack-less pups, and bring them inside the cave. He returned the door to its original position and handed one of the pups to Hope.

They silently moved the pups farther into the cave and away from the front door. Eric returned and began throwing wood onto the fire to increase the blaze. The new wood quickly caught on fire and the cave filled up with light as the flames flickered higher. He quickly returned the spears, so they pointed out from the doorway once again. They heard a low rumbling noise coming from outside the cave. The two humans peered through the primitive door.

Eric pushed Hope behind him as he moved closer to the doorway to investigate the low guttural noises. He looked out into the sunlight of the early morning and saw the tremendous head of the Megistotherium, its massive jaws covered in the blood of the bear dogs, approaching the entrance to the cave.

Chapter 16

Maka and Takoda

Maka, Takoda, Arcto, and the two new Super Extinctos Perris and Arc stayed in the Pleistocene Epoch. The group merely transported to a different time span. They landed 30,000 years ago to a cold, hostile, formidable world. The climate and environment, now extremely colder with glaciers covering much of the land mass on Earth, seemed completely foreign compared to the period when the humans first entered Extinctus—the Eocene Epoch.

Vast forests still existed on Earth, especially in the southern regions of the globe. Open grassland took hold in the drier, colder climates of the northern latitudes. Many species of animals, drastically changed by millions of years of climate change and further evolutionary molding, moved south in mass migrations to escape the encroaching ice fields, while various other species stayed to live in the new harsher climate. The warmer seasons, both spring and summer, were shorter, varying as much as 50 degrees colder in comparison to the climate of modern Earth today.

Warm clothes, a warm shelter, and access to a bountiful food source would decide the success of Maka and Takoda in this time. The struggle to survive in this inimical, dangerous world would test the native's resolve. If they endured the climate, the predators, and possible interaction with primitive humans, they might return home one day.

This era, during the Pleistocene Epoch, would later become known as the time of the megafauna. The continents, separating eons earlier, were in the same positions as they are today. There were mega species during this time such as the mammoths, several species of bison, short-faced bears, sabre-tooted cats both Machairodontinae and Metailurini types, horses, mastodons, rhinos, and many other species. Some species grew to enormous size, adapting to the new world, and flourishing in the cooler climate. They developed thick, heavy coats of hair or fur to fight off the persistent freezing temperatures.

Arcto, the short-faced bear, Perris, the 6-foot horse-like Extincto and Arc, the giant tree all huddled together, discussing their plan of attack. Their mission was to secure support for Megalo in the battle against Thylac, the acrimonious Dark Extincto. It was mid-day by the time the three finally reached unanimity and approached Takoda and Maka.

Arcto approached Maka and Takoda and simply said, "We're going to split up and travel to find help. You humans will need to find shelter, but don't stray too far from here so we can find you when we return."

"How long will you be gone?" asked Tak, who knew it would be dangerous for them without the protection of the Super Extinctos.

"However long it takes," replied the massive, short-faced bear.

"You will need to find a safe shelter, food, and a good dependable water source," added Perris in a soft voice, a voice which revealed a deep concern for the welfare of the humans.

The two super beasts and the giant tree Arc bid the humans farewell, then headed west towards the sun, quickly vanishing from sight, leaving Maka and Tak alone in the new, cold world. The natives wondered if this would be the last time, they saw the giant creatures.

The two Sioux began searching for a suitable shelter, one that would offer both protection from carnivores and the weather. They were on the edge of a vast plain that ran in one direction towards a mountainous region to the west and a deep forest, one that zigzagged along the edges of the sprawling grassland, to the east.

They decided to move into the trees, where the crown of heavily leafed branches would offer some protection from the rain or the snow, while they pushed deeper and deeper into the gloomy forest. They found a large section of dead fall, trees pushed over by the winds during extremely violent weather patterns and decided it would be worth investigating.

"How about this dead fall?" asked Maka. "We could build a safe structure here."

Maka spent long hours building shelters while growing up, many of which she made from animal skins, stretching them over poles to make a tepee or over downed trees to construct a quick shelter used for only one night. She wished she had a mammoth skin now.

Tak looked over the deadfall and remarked, "This looks good. I'll get smaller, straight branches to make poles which we can lay over the deadfall to make the shelter stronger. We can use pine needles to help keep the weather out and the warmth in."

Takoda emptied the contents of his backpack to see what was still in it from the original camp along the Missouri River. The pack held his hunting knife, some rope, a compass, a lighter, fishing gear, a water bottle, clothes, and a small hand saw. He was glad the protectors had thought to bring the backpacks. His pack even had an iPod with a solar charger. He could listen to music in this primitive world. He could hardly wait to try it on Pith.

"Maka, what do you have in your pack?"

Maka took off her pack and dumped out the contents. In it were clothes, matches, a knife, a water bottle, some dehydrated food, a small tin pot, a deck of cards, a bottle of ibuprofen, a tablet with writing instruments, and a couple of miscellaneous items. She too was glad to have her bag. It had warmer clothes in it, clothes much needed in this colder world. Maka at once put on another layering of clothing to help keep out the cold.

Tak took his folding saw and headed to a nearby stand of smaller trees, where he cut multiple branches off, stripping them down to poles. He carried the poles back to camp then returned to retrieve the cut branches which still had the green pine needles clinging to them. The pine needles would insulate the inside of the shelter from the cold temperatures while giving some element of waterproofness. He made several trips back and forth from the stand of trees until he thought he had an adequate supply that would completely cover the shelter.

Maka cleared the loose debris from under the dead fall so the floor of the shelter would be smooth, free of rocks, broken limbs, and other annoying obstacles that would make sleeping uncomfortable.

The dead fall offered protection from four sides: the top, the back and the sides. The humans left the front of the shelter open for access while they worked on the shelter.

To gain access into the shelter, Tak and Maka had to get on their knees and crawl through the small opening. They filled in any open spaces with the poles, leaving some to build a door at the front of the shelter. Next, they placed branches in the gaps between the poles and the dead fall until no light could penetrate the walls of the shelter. When finished, the shelter looked more like a mound.

The small shelter was secure on all four sides. It would take a significant amount of effort for a carnivore to gain entry. The natives were hedging a carnivore would spend too much energy trying to gain access and give up. Tak used his hunting knife to sharpen both ends of the poles left over and thatched these together using some of his rope. He attached this to the front of the shelter and secured it from within.

With the shelter now finished, Maka and Tak set out to stock up on firewood. They made several trips into the surrounding area to find dry wood and built up a large stockpile which they stacked beside the doorway to the shelter. Maka built a small fire pit just outside the doorway to the shelter. She hoped the burning fire would further dissuade any attacks by predators.

"I will stay here and get a good fire burning with hot coals to keep predators from visiting our shelter," Maka said.

"Sounds like a plan. I'm grabbing my pack and heading out to scout the surrounding area."

Tak went off to find water. He walked at least a mile from the shelter before he found a large natural spring, a spring which formed a large pool. He filled up both water bottles and headed back to the shelter.

The native suddenly froze in his tracks when he spotted a large cat sniffing the air about a hundred yards away. The prowling cat, not detecting him, kept sniffing the wind for any type of scent. **(Image 9: Smilodon gracilis: page 136)**

Luckily, the wind was blowing in Tak's face, so he knew the predator could not smell him.

The cat started to move in his direction. It was a Smilodon gracilis, one of the apex predators of the time, and it was hunting. It was the size of a lion with dagger like upper canines used for impaling its victims. The animal had extremely thick fur, fur light brown with black spots in color, which ran in random patterns to help conceal and hide the feline during hunting.

Tak's heart rate increased as his adrenaline kicked in. He slowly moved further back into the trees, out of the sight of the carnivore, and ran. He sprinted about a half a mile at top speed before he stopped to see if the killer cat was stalking him. The Smilodon gracilis was nowhere in sight, so Tak anxiously walked back to the shelter where he told Maka of the encounter.

It was a narrow escape, one where the direction of the wind could have drastically altered the outcome. Tak realized the danger was far from over while the predator roamed in the vicinity. They would have to keep on guard throughout the night. A carnivore of that size could easily slay the humans if given the opportunity to do so; the two humans were just another food source for the imposing cat.

Maka and Tak crawled inside the shelter, placed more wood on the fire, and heated up some water in the tin pot. Once the water was boiling, Maka added a packet of dehydrated food she removed from her backpack. This was the extent of their first meal together in the tiny makeshift shelter, somewhere in the Pleistocene.

Tak closed the door to the shelter, crawled into the darkness, and stretched out as best he could to wait out the night. Maka, already resting on the far side of the shelter, lit a match so Tak could see her.

"It will have to do until we can find something more permanent," Tak said.

"It'll be fine for now," answered Maka. She was content to be with the tall, handsome Tak, but she remained fearful of the unknown creatures that roamed the forest during the night.

The light soon faded, leaving the two humans alone in the darkness of the shelter. The small fire supplied minimal light to the interior of the shelter, but it did help ease their fears, fears that can be exaggerated when humans are left in total darkness. For further protection, Tak cut four long branches, stripped off the pine needles, and crafted spears from them. He sharpened the ends of the poles with his hunting knife and placed them with the pointed tips protruding out of the small doorway to further discourage entry to the shelter. Between this and the small fire, the two humans felt a minor sense of security. The roaming Smilodon gracilis left them anxious and created a real sense of fear in their hearts. Could the shelter stop such a beast? The two exhausted humans eventually drifted off into a light sleep as small embers from the fire cracked and flew out into the cold night where they were quickly extinguished by the coolness of the nighttime air.

Tak, awakened by the sound of rustling branches, quickly sat up inside the small shelter. The moon had reached full zenith which meant it was at least past midnight. The light outside the shelter was bright, but within the shelter it was still pitch black. He quietly nudged Maka to wake her up. She quickly rose and came closer to Tak, who was peering through the doorway.

"What is it?" she whispered in the darkness.

"I heard a rustling noise coming from the branches."

Tak handed Maka his longer hunting knife while he reached down and grabbed one of the spears.

They heard the distinct sound of a branch cracking under the weight of some creature; some beast out hunting in the stillness of the night. More rustling of branches followed this sound. The sounds were getting closer to their hidden sanctuary deep under the fallen trees.

The night stalking beast was obviously on top of the fallen trees that created the deadfall, walking over the branches the humans had added to the top of the shelter for added protection from the elements and predators. The creature continued to creep closer. Tak and Maka could hear the top of their shelter straining under the weight of the beast as the creature moved directly above them.

The only deterrent between Takoda, Maka and the creature were the intertwined branches stretched out over the fallen trees, the branches now beginning to sag under the tremendous weight of the attacker. The beast started growling loudly as it intensified its effort to gain entrance to the shelter.

The unidentified assailant started to pounce up and down, trying to throw its entire body weight on the branches. The branches were failing. Tak quickly grabbed two more spears from the doorway and braced them between the floor of the shelter and the branches that made up the roof. It was a tight fit, but he managed to get three of them in place before he grabbed the last one from the doorway.

Maka moved as close to the doorway as possible and positioned herself to quickly remove the door to allow for a quick escape if needed. The fire died out, leaving only a few smoldering coals.

Tak motioned Maka to hand him the knife, so she moved towards him and passed it to him, then quickly returned to the entrance. Tak positioned himself just to the side of the upright spears on the doorway side of the enclosure. The beast continued to pounce up and down on the roof while growling incessantly. The branches started to snap one by one and then the roof failed.

The remaining branches, branches that formed the roof, all snapped under the great weight of the attacker, causing moon light to flood into the shelter as the beast fell, impaling itself on the three spears.

The impaled animal writhed in agony, trying to dislodge itself from the wooden spears. It was the Smilodon gracilis from earlier in the day, the one Tak encountered while searching for a water source.

The beast had long canines supported by massive neck muscles which gave it an extremely powerful bite. The rest of its body had tremendous muscle tone, chiseled for a life of brutal battle and carnage.

One of the spears penetrated the giant cat in the chest, penetrating the beast's heart, which was the mortal blow that ended the magnificent feline's life. It let out a hideous death cry as Tak, for further measure, drove home his hunting knife. The carnivore died as it had lived; brutally.

Takoda and Maka both looked at the incredible specimen that now lay dead in front of them. They felt both relieved and sad. Relieved they were alive but saddened that they had to take the big cat's life.

The moon light lit up the shelter in the absence of the roof, and they gazed at the now dead Smilodon gracilis. The two Native Americans gave thanks to the beast for giving its life in the traditional Sioux way. If possible, they would use as much of the beast as possible to honor its spirit.

In the morning, they would skin the beast, dry out the pelt, and use it for a blanket. The dagger canines would make good spear tips and Tak decided he would sharpen them with his saw and knife. If they were to live in this world for any length of time, they would need to use its resources to survive.

Morning finally arrived. The two humans were eager to greet the light of day. It was a new day in this fierce world. The two humans exited the now roofless shelter and quickly set out to harvest the Smilodon. It took both to drag the hefty beast from the now destroyed shelter.

Tak went to work skinning the dead cat as Maka started the fire again. He returned with the pelt and hung it to dry on some nearby branches. Maka would scrape any remaining flesh off the hide in a couple of days and then let it dry until it was suitable for use.

This was the first time the two Sioux would use the given resources of Extinctus to survive. In less than one day, while left alone, they survived attack by one of the fiercest predators this time had of offer and had survived.

After the fire built up a good bed of coals, Maka went to the carcass of the Smilodon and cut off several strips of meat. She returned to the fire with the strips of flesh in her pot and placed it down in the coals to cook. The meat was not the ideal meal for the humans, but they had to eat whatever was available to help them survive. She cooked the meat until completely done, then gave a large piece to Tak, who gulped down the meat.

"It's not so bad...but it tastes like an old goat."

Maka replied in a sarcastic tone, "We could be eating it for a while, so you better get used to it."

"We should finish here and take as much meat as we can and move on, the carcass will attract scavengers," Tak said.

"I agree," answered Maka, ready to find a more suitable shelter, one they could defend easier from predators and one that would offer more protection from the elements.

They prepared as much meat as they could carry in their packs and rolled up the skin of the Smilodon. It was time to move on. Their first shelter in this new world was primitive but they had survived an attack by the apex predator of the time. It would be a story that would last for generations.

The natives put out the fire and headed back into the forest to find a new shelter. Although Arcto warned them to not go too far from where they had left them, they had no choice after killing the Smilodon gracilis. This area, tainted by the flesh, bone, and blood of the saber-toothed cat was not safe anymore. Scavengers would soon descend on the area for the dead carcass. Tak and Maka needed to put some distance between themselves and this area of the forest.

The forest became thicker as they moved farther into it. Maka and Tak had gone about ten miles when they heard a low pitched, light growling coming from a nearby rock outcropping. The outcropping, surrounded by trees and encompassing an area around 35 yards in length, rose from the floor of the forest about 40 feet.

The noise continued as they approached. It was a soft growl, faintly audible. Tak motioned Maka to stay put, and he slowly advanced towards the outcropping. He had his knife in one hand and a spear in the other. He was ready for anything at this point as he quietly advanced towards the muffled sound. There were several trees close to the rocks, so he momentarily stopped to survey the vicinity from the protection of the tall trees. He could see a small opening in the outcrop. It was the size of a small doorway; just large enough for a human to crawl through.

The sound was coming from within the cave. Tak silently advanced to the opening with his knife and spear ready. He knelt by the entrance and peered inside. There was a crack in the rocks from above which allowed light to filter into the cave, so he could see inside the cave incredibly well.

Tak cautiously peered into the opening, searching for the culprit making the barely audible growling sound, but he did not see anything in plain sight. The low growling noise stopped all together. He clutched his knife and crawled into the opening, which opened to a large cavern.

Once inside, the native could stand fully erect and the lighting was terrific for a cave. He surveyed the inside of the cave, looking for the source of the sound. Somewhere from the very back of the cavern, the low growl started again and continued. He walked towards the back of the cave with spear and knife ready to dispatch the creature. The growling continued to increase as he approached. Then he saw it.

It was a Smilodon gracilis cub and Tak instantly realized it was the cub of the massive saber-toothed cat he had killed during the night.

He dropped his knife and spear and yelled for Maka.

Chapter 17

CeCe and Lexa

CeCe, Lexa, Bronto, Pith, and Gorgo passed back through time in Extinctus, exiting the portal during the Paleocene Epoch, a period between 66-55 million years ago. The group landed at the end of the Paleocene, 55 million years ago, just one million years before the beginning of the Eocene Epoch, the period all the humans found themselves in when they first arrived in Extinctus.

The Paleocene Epoch was the first epoch in the modern Cenozoic Era. The climate during this time was extremely humid and exceptionally warm. Subtropical plants grew as far north as Greenland and as far south as Patagonia. Tropical palm forests covered most of the Earth during this time, a time vastly different from the Montana CeCe and Lexa were familiar with.

The Paleocene followed the Cretaceous—Paleogene K-Pg extinction event that ended the reign of the non-avian dinosaurs. This extinction event, caused by a massive asteroid striking off the coast of Yucatan, Mexico some 65 million years ago, devastated the planet. Millions of species wiped out by this catastrophic event—vanished from existence forever.

The world of this time was quite different from the world today. Shallow equatorial seas separated North and South America, while the Rocky Mountains continued to lift from the Earth's mantle, a process that would not end until much later during the Eocene Epoch. South America, Africa, Australia and Antarctica were just beginning to pull apart from one another and end the super-continent known as Gondwanaland.

The ocean currents, which circumvolved the entire planet, were warm during this period, but most oceans were devoid of marine life. The K-Pg extinction event wiped out most of the marine life from the earlier Cretaceous Period, yet by the end of Paleocene Epoch marine life had once again rebounded to become diversely abundant. Corals evolved during this period and with the extinction of most of the marine reptiles, sharks evolved to be the apex predators of the seas.

Mammals evolved to replace the niche left by the non-avian dinosaurs. These new life forms spread throughout the planet, adapting to and conquering all climates and terrains. Fern trees rapidly multiplied to cover much of the Earth, as modern plants began to evolve after the K-Pg extinction event. Cacti and palm species colonized the now humid and warmer world, while modern vegetation, many of which are still living today, colonized the planet. The world was a pleasant place weather wise, but by the end of the Paleocene Epoch, the planet was extremely dangerous, a world full of capable predators and massive prey animals of epic proportions.

CeCe and Lexa landed in a primitive pre-historic era of drastic change and diversity, a world that would test their limits. Bronto, Pith, and Gorgo discussed their plan to mobilize support for Megalo. Bronto called the humans over to the group.

"We must split up and find support for Megalo against Thylac," the giant Brontotheres spoke.

His expression was one of urgency and deep concern for the well-being of Lexa and CeCe.

"What are we to do?" asked CeCe, not keen on this idea, which left Lexa and himself unprotected in this hostile place.

"You and Lexa must find a safe shelter from predators and stay in this area until we return," he answered.

"How long will you be gone?" asked Lexa with a terrified expression on her face. "You can't just leave us here without protection."

"I don't know how long it will take. We will scour this time for support for our army and will return when finished," is all the massive ungulate said as he walked off, obviously torn between his feeling of responsibility for Lexa's safety and his obligation to Megalo and the fight for the human species.

Pith and Gorgo followed the bulky beast to a small clearing in the trees. Within moments all three disappeared, leaving CeCe and Lexa alone in the Paleocene.

The two humans looked at each other in utter despair—Lexa's usual spunkiness reduced to apprehension and uncertainty and CeCe's usual boisterous self, now rendered completely silent.

"What should we do? Where will we go?" asked Lexa, her voice filled with a nervous anxiety.

"We need to find shelter before nightfall because we need to hide during the night," replied CeCe.

CeCe had no idea what types of monsters lurked in this violent world, but he wanted to be as safe as possible. Within just the brief time in Extinctus, he had seen plenty of disturbing events—most involving a violent death at night.

The two humans followed the trail left by Bronto and the other two Extinctos deeper into the fern forest. The forest was thick in vegetation, a combination of fern trees, palms and other plant species. The air was warm and humid so the need for warmer clothes was not an issue like before when they were in the Pleistocene Epoch.

For food, they could forage on the wide variety of plant species available, until they found suitable protein. CeCe was a large man, a man that needed a lot of calories a day to stay energized. He attended Montana State University on a football scholarship where he excelled as a defensive lineman. He grew up in New Orleans, raised by his two aunts, aunts who occasionally dabbled in the depths of black magic. This made CeCe susceptible to a belief in spells, potions and mysticism. He had seen their power on several occasions.

Shelter was the priority and after that, the hunt for food would be second.

They walked for a few hours until they stumbled upon a section of bamboo forest. The bamboo forest sat directly in the middle of a meadow nestled between giant ferns on one side and tall palms on the other. CeCe stopped and motioned to Lexa.

"We could use this bamboo for both shelter and to make weapons," he said.

"We should check our packs to see what we have in them," Lexa answered, obviously agreeing to the spot CeCe had chosen.

They sat on the ground and emptied the contents of their packs. CeCe had a knife, a spool of fishing line, a flashlight, matches, a hand axe, some rope, a water bottle, and a few other items. Lexa dumped her pack out on the ground. She had a water bottle, a multi-tool, a lighter, sunscreen, insect repellant, a tin pan, and several other items. Both CeCe and Lexa had notebooks and pencils which would be valuable in capturing their time spent in Extinctus. Someone needed to record this bizarre adventure.

Once they finished inventorying the packs, both went about the task of cutting bamboo for the shelter. They decided to build the shelter in an area surrounded by thick ferns; ferns that would hide the shelter from the eyesight of roaming predators.

CeCe drove the bamboo poles deep into the ground with the flat side of his axe. The total area of the shelter was 10 feet in width and 15 feet in length. Since CeCe was a tall man, he made the inside roof 8 feet high, which would give him the ability to stand up in the shelter.

After driving the bamboo poles into the ground, Lexa and CeCe used fern branches to cover the roof and sides of the hut. For further protection, they cut bamboo poles and sharpened one end to a fine point. They positioned these bamboo poles between the wall poles with the sharp point protruding just outside the outer walls, which would keep out unwanted predators who risked the possibility of impaling themselves if they tried to gain entrance into the shelter. CeCe and Lexa thatched the bamboo together in sections with the rope from CeCe's pack. This added strength to the overall structure of the shelter. They examined their work and were both quite pleased with their design, marveling at the stability of the hut.

Once satisfied with the shelter, CeCe went off to gather firewood as Lexa collected stones for a fire pit. He made several trips, each time returning with arm loads of good dry wood. To help burn long into the night, he found several large logs and couple of dead stumps.

Lexa built an impressive fire pit out of large stones she had found by a nearby stream. She was the engineer so designing and building were her hallmark trait. She built the fire pit inside of the hut and funneled the smoke out through a series of chambers she constructed that ran the entire height of the shelter. These chambers routed the smoke up and out of the shelter.

"Very nice! It will give us light and warmth," praised CeCe.

"We don't know how long we'll be left here alone, so we might as well be comfortable," the bronze Latino replied.

The light of day was fading, so they decided to retreat to the shelter without any food for dinner. It would be too risky to wander outside in the darkness, so they went to bed hungry on their first night in the Paleocene Epoch.

Lexa and CeCe sprawled out by the fire. Tomorrow they would search for food, both meat and plants. They had an endless supply of wood and a good water source from the stream nearby. In the light of a new day, they could explore the area and look for food sources. They would be able to make deadly weapons from the bamboo stalks which were very sharp and extraordinarily strong. The small groves of bamboo trees, intermingled between the fern and palm trees, would provide them with all the bamboo stalks they needed.

"When do you think Bronto and the other Extinctos will be back?" asked CeCe.

"In a few days, after they recruit the species needed to fight Thylac."

"What kind of help and what for?"

CeCe was not sure how all the pieces fit together. They were trying to save Eric but from what?

"I just don't know. Nothing in this place makes sense."

"I heard that!"

The talk gradually faded as the hours clicked by. They both drifted off into a deep sleep. The fire flickered for hours, its embers only dancing to unseen eyes, until it too was out.

Except for the smoke from the fire, the shelter stayed almost undetectable, nestled deep in the ferns. Only small rodents and insects stumbled upon it by accident. Some crawled into the sanctuary while others scurried away, away from the strange smell of the humans. The smell was alien in this world, and if anything, this would help the humans.

The night was quite uneventful as Lexa and CeCe slept. There was an occasional loud scream coming from somewhere off in the distance, but nothing in their immediate vicinity, so, their first night in the new shelter was a safe and restful one.

The light of dawn brought a new confidence to the two humans. The relative safety of the shelter gave them one less thing to worry about, one less weakness. Now the search for food became the primary goal.

CeCe and Lexa exited the bamboo shelter hidden in the thick fern underbrush. The structure nestled deep inside the ferns, almost undetectable from sight, lay hidden deep in the forest millions of years before the presence of any humans. It would be by mere chance that a roaming predator stumbled into it.

"We should stay together and search for food."

Lexa knew it would be safer to travel together. Two sets of eyes and ears doubled the chance to spot or hear danger and allow ample time to escape.

"I agree. We'll take a few of these bamboo spears for protection."

CeCe placed his knife sheath on his belt to place his knife in, then he stuck his axe handle through his belt while he grabbed one of the longer spears.

"If we head towards the sun, we'll have a direction to follow and we can reverse our course to find our way back easier," Lexa said as she pointed in the direction of the sun.

CeCe and Lexa exited the thick forest and walked into the sunlight. The warm rays of the sun felt good on the skin. The fern trees were still plentiful, but many other trees species competed for the sunlight as well. They decided to travel along the edge of the forest for security from preying eyes.

The forest was amazingly dense, with thousands of plant species, each trying to squeeze out the competition, while striving to horde all the sunlight. It was entirely possible that this forest was one of the first early forms of a tropical rain forest. During the Paleocene Epoch, tropical, sub-tropical and deciduous forests, covered most of the Earth. They were thick due to the lack of large plant eating ungulates, which were just beginning to evolve after the extinction of the large grazing dinosaurs. A new world was evolving.

During this time span, placental mammals evolved at an unprecedented level, one never again duplicated, and by the end of the Paleocene they were the most successful species. They exploded in both number and size. The weather was warm and humid which allowed reptiles to flourish all around the globe even in areas that are too cold today. Creatures ranged in size from tiny to gigantic. Some were peaceful grazer's while others were carnivorous monsters.

In some ways, this early new explosion of species, was helpful to Lexa and CeCe. The population of the various species was still low due to the evolutionary clean slate caused by the mass extinction some 10 million years earlier. This gave the humans a lower encounter rate with other species of the time.

The two humans were closer to the end of the Paleocene around 55 million years ago. The Paleocene Epoch would usher in the Eocene Epoch in around 3 million years and with it the explosion and development of many new more modern species.

Lexa and CeCe traveled for about a mile when they found a small stream, about the width of a two-lane road. From the bank, the stream looked swift and deep. Large deciduous trees like poplars, walnuts and maples, grew along its banks. It was strange to see these types of trees mixed in with ferns and palms. They seemed out of place in comparison to the smaller ferns and palm trees.

Below the walnut trees, nuts littered the ground. Lexa collected them and added them to her backpack. They would be a useful source of protein and vitamins once she dried them out by the fire.

CeCe wondered down to the stream to collect water. There was a small opening between the overgrowth of trees and smaller vegetation which led down the bank to the river. The river, lined with rocks and dead timber, moved along at a swift pace on its way to empty into one of the larger waterways downstream before emptying into the ocean somewhere further down the line.

CeCe navigated the thin trail, one trampled down by the heavy footprints of the other thirsty inhabitants of this world and stopped just short of the streams edge. Just beyond the edge of the stream, he could see a deep pool, deepened by a large boulder that slowed the pace of the stream. He could see fish in the deep pool so CeCe memory marked the spot for a future food source. At this point, he was glad for the water, so he moved to the edge and bent down. He filled his bottle and took a long drink. The water was cool but not as cold as the water from the Missouri River in Montana.

"Come down and fill your water bottle," he shouted to Lexa.

Lexa came down the trail and stopped next to CeCe and filled up her bottle. She took a long drink, re-filled her water bottle and then backed up from the edge of the stream.

"I needed that. We now have a second water source and some nuts, but we need to forage for plants. Should we do that now?"

CeCe pointed to his pack and said, "We have fish in this stream, and I've got fishing line and hooks. We just need bait if we want to try our luck."

CeCe took out his axe and moved back up the trail to the top of the bank where he walked over to the trees to look for insects. Lexa followed him up the bank, taking out her axe as she walked up the steep embankment. She found a large tree standing alone just off to one side of the bank, and this is where she decided to dig in the rich soil for worms.

CeCe found several strange looking insects and collected them. They were large insects, some up to 5 inches long, all covered in a primitive beetle type armor. There were black ones, black and red ones and even a light green one. He found a small growth of bamboo and cut two long poles which he stripped down to become fishing poles. Lexa continued to dig up the soil until she found earthworms for bait. They were like the worms from her world just longer. She collected them while CeCe put fishing line on the poles.

"Now we can go fishing," CeCe laughed. "I don't know what type of monster we'll catch but I'm hungry, and I'm going to eat it."

"I'm hungry too! Give me one of those bamboo poles," Lexa said, pointing to the makeshift fishing poles in CeCe's hands.

She would eat anything they caught. Just think, a fish without any man-made chemicals affecting it from a pure non-polluted stream.

The two walked back down the trail and stopped along the streams edge. They moved about 15 feet apart and dropped their hooks into the pool. CeCe tried the green insect while Lexa used the first earthworm in history to fish with.

It was only seconds before they had action. CeCe set the hook and began pulling the line in by hand. The fish, strong and defiant, put up a good battle. It jumped out of the stream, just long enough, for the humans to see how big it was; it was a hog. It looked like a salmon variation, one CeCe estimated to be six feet long—remember we are talking about CeCe who loved to exaggerate.

The primitive fish fought hard for around 5 minutes, until becoming tired, which allowed CeCe to haul it into the bank, where it flopped violently on the rocks until he hit it in the head with the backside of his axe. It did resemble a salmon but had longer, sharper teeth. It would make a delicious meal and more importantly CeCe and Lexa now had a steady source of protein.

"It's a monster!" CeCe yelled out. "It's the largest fish I've ever landed."

They would return later to put some set lines out to catch the giant salmon at night. The stream would give them a valuable resource—all the fish they needed to supplement their diet. They were the first human fishers in the history of the planet.

"Wow!" exclaimed Lexa, as she dropped her pole on the rocks and hurried to help CeCe.

In a flash, her pole was gone, disappearing into the deep pool. Some monstrous river creature had taken her bait and pole!

"My pole is gone," she yelled, barely catching a glimpse of the tan bamboo stalk as it disappeared under a large boulder at the bottom of the deep hole.

As Lexa gazed into the deep pool, she caught the glimpse of a large menacing creature coming down the bank. She could see its terrifying shape in the reflection of the pool. She at once turned around to see a massive creature, at least 15 feet tall, approaching. Behind the first giant monstrosity was a second more hideous beast. She turned around looking for CeCe.

"Run!" the terrified Latino screamed.

Thylacine
Pleistocene - Holocene of Australia (2 million - 70 years ago)

Uintatherium
Early to Middle Eocene of North America (56-38 MYA)

Eocene animals of Asia

1. *Andrewsarchus mongoliensis*
2. *Sarkastodon*
3. *Aktautitan hippopotamopus*
4. *Embolotherium ergilense*
5. Tapir-type herbivore

Hyaenodon horridus
Eocene - Middle Oligocene of North America (40-20 MYA)

Arctodus simus
Pleistocene of North America (1.8 million to 11,000 years ago)

Pleistocene animals of Eurasia

1. *Panthera spelaea* (Cave lion)
2. *Bison bonasus* (wisent or European bison)
3. *Bos primigenius* (Auroch)
4. *Mammuthus primigenius* (Woolly Mammoth)
5. *Megaloceros giganteus* (Irish elk)
6. *Coelodonta antiquitatis* (Woolly rhinoceros)
7. *Ursus spelaeus* (Cave bear)
8. *Palaeoloxodon antiquus* (straight-tusked elephant)
9. *Bison priscus* (steppe bison or steppe wisent)
10. *Camelus knoblochi* (Eurasian camel)
11. Extinct wild horse
12. *Homotherium* (also known as the scimitar-toothed cat)
13. *Pachystruthio dmanisensis* (Pleistocene ostrich-like bird)
14. *Crocuta crocuta spelaea* (Cave hyena)
15. Deer
16. *Ovibos moschatus* (muskox)
17. Canis lupus (wolf also known as the "gray wolf" or "grey wolf")

Andrewsarchus
Middle Eocene of modern Inner Mongolia, China (48-41 MYA)

Amphicyon *giganteus*
Oligocene - Miocene of Europe (16.8-7.2 MYA)

Smilodon gracilis
Pleistocene of North America (2.5 million to 500,000 years ago)

Megistotherium osteothlastes
Early Miocene of Africa (23-11.6 MYA)

Pleistocene animals of North America

1. *Homotherium* (also known as the scimitar-toothed cat)
2. *Arctodus simus* or short-faced bear
3. *Canis dirus* (dire wolf)
4. *Miracinonyx* or American cheetah
5. *Mammuthus columbi* (Columbian Mammoth)
6. *Equus scotti* (Scott's horse)
7. *Aiolornis incredibilis* or Teratornis

Diatryma (*Gastornis gigantea*)
late Paleocene and Eocene of Eurasia and North America (56-45 million to 11,000 years ago)

Dinocrocuta gigantea
Middle Miocene - Late Miocene of Eurasia and Africa (11.2 - 4.5 MYA)

Platybelodon
Middle Miocene of Africa, Asia and Caucasus (15-10 MYA)

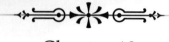

Chapter 18

Miocene Epoch

The rancid breath of the Megistotherium mixed with the blood of the now dead bear dogs, filled the cave as the victorious carnivore cautiously peered into the cave. Hope and Eric had just enough time to pound the stakes back into the ground and re-secure the door before the colossal carnivore reached the entrance to the cave. They each grabbed two pointed spears and quickly placed them through the openings between the branches used to construct the doorway. **(Image 10: Megistotherium osteothlastes: page 137)**

The humans could see the massive size of the Creodont's powerful jaw muscles as the giant carnivore moved in to inspect the strange smell coming from inside the cave. The jaws of the beast, designed for tearing flesh and crushing bone, had two long fangs that dropped down below the creature's bottom jaw line. The beast had a thick, muscular build with massive shoulder muscles designed for extreme bursts of power during the ambush. A dense, light brown hair covered the animal's gargantuan frame.

Creodonts lived during the late Eocene times until well into Miocene times. The modern carnivores, a group of new agile and efficient hunters, slowly replaced the Creodonts, who eventually over millions of years vanished entirely from the planet.

Eric, his head still reeling from the brutal battle between the Amphicyon galushai and the lone Megistotherium, doubted his ability to stop the huge carnivore from breeching the doorway.

The battle between the stoic bear dogs and the grisly Creodont, a keenly contested fight, could have gone either way. Eric and Hope would have preferred to face neither of the monstrous creatures, but at least with the bear dogs, they had a better chance of surviving by placing the pups outside the cave.

Unfortunately for the humans, the bear dogs lost the battle, leaving behind two defenseless pups; such were the ways of the early primitive world, a world where survival of the fittest and sometimes just the fortunate ruled.

Eric could now see only one Megistotherium and in his rationale, that was better than three bear dogs.

Hope and Eric held firm to the spears, bracing for the attack. The Megistotherium, confused by the new smell of the humans, a smell it was unfamiliar with, hesitated at the front of the cave. There was little doubt it could still smell the pups as it constantly sniffed the ground where the pups, just moment before, had laid just outside the doorway. The Creodont, to reduce competition, would have killed the pups instantly after dispatching the adult bear dogs if the humans had not intervened. Less competition meant more prey for the gluttonous brute and less danger of injury during territorial disputes.

The carnivorous behemoth, overcoming the fear of the new human smell, slowly gained the nerve to attack. It rushed the door and slammed into it with the full might of its elongated snout.

The door strained under the hard hit and cracked but held. The lunging beast just missed the protruding spears and cautiously stepped back. It rallied for a second assault by moving farther out from the door, to gain more distance, which would allow it to increase its speed. This time it sprinted in a primal burst of unbridled power as it flung its full body weight into the poles.

This proved to be the beast undoing as it collided into three of the sharp, pointed spears with such great force that they penetrated its thick hide, causing the injured brute to let out a tremendous scream as it tried to pull free from the spear tips. One of the spear tips entered just behind its right shoulder and the other two just missed its spine.

The wounded Megistotherium finally shook itself loose and moved back from the doorway as blood poured from its open wounds. It let out a horrific scream as it charged the door, in one last fit of rage, for a third time.

This time, one of Eric's spears landed squarely below its elongated snout and pierced its jugular. Eric pulled back on the spear which caused it to snap off becoming lodged in the creature's throat. The fatally wounded animal reeled from the doorway and crawled off into the forest to die.

Eric and Hope had survived two attacks in their first night in the Miocene Epoch. They slowly relaxed their guard, now confident the Megistotherium was either dead or at least had left the immediate area to tend to its wounds. They were both shaking from the adrenaline released during the episode and sat down to calm themselves.

"That was unbelievable," cried Eric, astonished they had been able to kill or at least gravely wound such a giant apex predator of such enormous size.

"I think we got lucky," replied Hope, who, unlike Eric, abhorred the deadly encounter.

Life in this place would be one long, dangerous journey if the events of one day were any indicator.

"We'll need to be on our guard always, but if we stick together and protect each other, we might survive this place," Eric calmly said.

"I hope you're right."

She went back into the cave and picked up one of the pups. They were small, which led her to believe they were incredibly young.

"What are we going to do with these little ones?"

"We'll keep them and make them part of our pack. When full grown, they'll make fierce allies. We'll be the first humans to have pets," Eric laughed. "Let's call the male Amp after his scientific name Amphicyon galushai."

"Let's call the little female Shai then," Hoped chimed in.

She smiled and they both broke out in laughter. Eric and Hope now had pet bear dogs, ones that would grow to become loyal protectors and companions.

They decided to leave the two young pups and journey from the cave to assess the damage from the earlier night. The pups were sleeping so they left them in the back of the cave and opened the door. They exited the cave and re-fortified the door as they closed it behind them. They were confident the pups would be safe while they ventured out to get food, water and survey the area around the cave.

It was just moments before they saw the carnage from the night before. The three bear dog carcasses spread out over a 30-yard area were brutally dismembered. Two of the losers, partially consumed by the Megistotherium, were mere reflections of their once powerful selves, while the mother, the last to die defending her pups, was intact just a few yards from the cave.

The mother bear dog had given her life to protect her pups. Each member of the pack died protecting the newest generation. It was a grisly scene of vicious carnage.

Eric shook his head at the gruesome scene and said, "We have to remove these carcasses before they attract more predators."

"We'll have to cut them up and carry them out of the forest to the edge of the plain," Hope replied.

"That makes sense."

Each bear dog weighed over 1000 pounds when fully intact. The two partially consumed bear dogs were still quite heavy, which made it a physically challenging task. It would take a considerable amount of time to take them to the edge of the forest.

They spent most of the day cleaning up the area around the cave to remove the scent of the dead bear dogs. They did not find the dead body of the Megistotherium anywhere in the vicinity, so they assumed the beast had survived. The two humans were less than eager to go searching for it, so they decided to keep an intensified guard for a few days just in case the beast returned.

The meat from the Creodont would have supported them and the pups for days but it was safer to wait a day or two before looking for the carcass. It was strenuous enough to dispose of the three bear dogs. They finished the laborious task of removing the bear dog carcasses, then placed branches and scattered debris from the forest floor over the areas of blood to mask the smell. It was not perfect, but it did give them some peace of mind.

It was time to get water and continue the search for food. Hope and Eric dismissed the thought of eating the dead bear dog flesh now that the two pups were in their care. This was a human trait. They would wait a few days and then search for the wounded Megistotherium, hoping it had succumbed to its fatal wounds.

Eric and Hope went to the natural spring and drank their fill of the cool refreshing water. Hope then filled up a water bottle from her backpack for the pups. The pups previously hydrated by their mother's milk, would now have to switch to water and learn to eat meat. Only time would tell if they could survive the change.

"We should head back to the cave," Eric calmly said.

Late afternoon gloom was settling in and Eric did not want to be outside when darkness fell. If the events from the prior night were any indicator, it was safer to stay hidden during the night. This was a violent and cruel world with humans being quite low on the evolutionary food chain.

"You're probably right, but maybe we'll see something to eat on the way back," replied Hope in an optimistic tone.

"Keep your eyes open for game and edible plants," Eric whispered.

They walked back towards the cave, keeping to a game trail that led to the natural spring. Hope found a variety of plant species that were safe to eat along the way. She spent a considerable amount of time in the mountains growing up and her mother had shown her what plants were safe and what plants to stay away from. The only problem was this was not modern times and although some of the plant species looked familiar, it was not a sure thing. It would take time to learn the plant species that flourished in the forest and on the plains, learning from trial and error which ones were safe to eat.

Eric walked in front of Hope, his lean tall frame easily adapted to hiking and trekking into the wilderness. Hope was gaining a great appreciation and fondness for the blonde Norseman and she was happy the two were together in this hostile world. What stories they would have to tell when they returned to their time. She hoped the journey would make them stronger together so when they returned, they could stay together. Hope was falling in love with Eric.

Eric suddenly signaled Hope to freeze. He pointed to a small opening in the trees just in front of them. Standing, oblivious to the humans, was a pig-like creature. It was over three feet long, resembling a wild boar or peccary. It was grey in color with long legs and canine teeth. It would be an abundance of meat for them and the pups if he could bring it down.

He whispered to Hope to stay hidden behind a tree as he moved slowly and cautiously towards the primitive beast. Wild boar in the modern world were dangerous and could gouge a man easily so he assumed this one would be no different.

The wind was blowing in his face, so he knew the boar would not smell his approach. He grasped his spear in one hand and held his hunting knife in the other as he continued to silently approach the boar. Eric knew how important the opportunity was.

He was within 10 yards from the unsuspecting beast when it turned and ran towards him. It let out a deep, chilling grunt as it charged.

The boar was running for its life, not attacking. Within moments Eric spotted the reason for the pig's distress. A mountain lion like carnivore pursued the fleeing boar. Eric recognized the large cat as Dinictis, an ancestor to the biting and stabbing cats that followed it later in time. The early cat like species died out sometime during the Miocene.

The primitive cat moved swiftly after the boar but lagged some 50 yards behind it. The boar continued to run towards Eric and Hope, so the blonde hunter readied his spear for launch. He hedged that his surprise attack on the boar would thwart the attack of the Dinictis and cause the medium sized cat to veer off after seeing the human, an unknown sight to the beasts of this time.

The boar reached the tree where Eric was hiding and instantly the human hunter launched the wood spear. It impaled the large peccary through the upper part of its body just under the spine, sending it stumbling to the ground. The injured beast let out a tremendous grunt as it slid across the dirt and dead leaves that littered the forest floor.

The boar re-gained its feet and continued heading in the direction of Hope while Eric reeled to face the Dinictis. The great cat, confused and bewildered by the human intervention, stopped in its tracks. The medium sized cat growled at the human thief, seeming to gauge the odds of injury if it attacked, then ran into the forest and disappeared into the trees.

The wounded boar continued to emit loud screams of agony, while running towards the tree Hope was hiding behind. Part of the spear had broken off during the frantic rush, but the tip remained lodged in the wild boar.

"It's coming your way!" shouted Eric, his adrenaline pumping as he burst into a full run trying to catch the incurably injured peccary before it attacked Hope.

Hope stepped out from behind the security of the tree, into full view of the screaming boar, which at once ran at her, lashing out in blind rage at the first thing it saw.

Eric, a short distance behind the feverish beast, quickly closed the gap between himself and the injured boar. It was clear the spear had fatally injured the creature as its pace slackened from rapid blood loss.

It ran straight towards Hope, who raised her spear to defend herself from the attacking pig-like monstrosity. The boar now in a frantic state, ran for its life as blood gushed from its grunting, screaming mouth. Hope in a desperate spot, had to make a quick decision. The blunt protruding canines of the boar could inflict great damage on her or easily kill her.

Hope had to hold her ground, running was not a possibility at this point. She boldly drew her right arm back and launched the spear as hard as she could at the oncoming menace. Her aim true, the spear hit the boar directly in the mouth, penetrating the back of the creature's head. The entire event took only minutes, but the outcome was decisive. The boar dropped and fell dead within inches of Hope.

"Wow!" yelled Eric, impressed by Hope's decisive determination.

She had boldly faced the pig-beast and dropped it.

"I think you must have fatally wounded it," she laughed.

"It was a united effort," answered Eric.

It was the first time Eric truly realized he had deep feelings for the beautiful blonde teacher from Montana.

Hope and Eric looked at the dead boar then dislodged their spears from its lifeless corpse. It would give them and the pups a good supply of protein. As a team, they had made their first kill in their new world.

Eric quickly dressed the carcass, cutting large strips of meat to carry back to the cave. He then took the rest of the boar and tied his rope around its hind legs. After this, he tied a rock to one end of the rope and tossed it over the highest branch he could reach by throwing the rock over an outstretched limb. He then pulled the carcass up over the branch until it was out of the reach of the forest dwelling carnivores. Eric secured the rope by tying it around the base of the tree and then he and Hope journeyed back to the cave.

Tonight, they would feast on primitive peccary.

"I think it's a Platygonus. It was one of the pig-like animals that lived during this time. Just be glad it wasn't from the family known as Entelodonts. They weren't called hell pigs for nothing," the young professor said.

"I have heard of those," replied Hope as she followed Eric back to the shelter.

The pups met them at the entrance to the cave. Both were hungry and thirsty. Eric opened the door to the cave and both he and Hope entered. The male pup, Amp, met him eagerly and emitted an apprehensive growl. Eric gently spoke to the confused and frightened pup now entirely dependent on the humans. This seemed to work as the little bear dog began wagging its tale and approached the human. Eric knelt and stuck out his hand. Amp slowly came close enough for the human to pet him. This was the first time the two had really connected.

Hope moved closer and called for Shai to come. The little female bear dog, recognizing it was safe, came over to Hope and rolled overexposing her belly. This was a sign of submission and Hope reached in and scratched her chest. The four were now friends for life.

Hope started a fire to cook part of the peccary meat for dinner. It smelled wonderful, as the scent filled the cavern. The delightful smell made Hope and Eric realize just how hungry they were. They gave both cooked and raw meat to the pups which did not seem to make any difference to the tiny carnivores who devoured both in the same manner. All four members of the newly established pack took a long drink of water and settled in for the night. The pups came over by Eric and Hope curled up and went to sleep. They had accepted them as their pack leaders.

"We now have a family," Hope said. "They're our responsibility now."

"They'll be invaluable when they're fully grown. They will grow fast, needing enormous amounts of meat, so the hard part will be keeping them fed," Eric laughed as he scratched the little male's belly.

Eric knew they would be the size of a full-grown wolf in just a few weeks, eventually reaching a length of 8 feet and weighing as much as 1200 pounds once they reached adulthood. They would need to hunt for themselves at some point.

The days passed as Eric and Hope waited for the return of Creo, Aves, and Arti. They originally thought the giant Extinctos would only be gone a week at tops, but the weeks had now turned into months, and they began doubting if they would return at all. If not, they needed to prepare for the worst-case scenario, one that involved spending the rest of their lives stuck in the Miocene Epoch.

The two humans often wondered about Tak, Maka, CeCe, and Lexa and how they were surviving in their time zones. Hope kept track of the days by recording the events in her notebook. In her pack, she had a computer notebook that she kept in power with a solar charger she luckily had placed in her backpack. She kept a count of the days on the cave wall for simplification. For this she simply used a sharp rock to scratch out the number.

The weeks turned into months and the bear dogs grew larger and larger. Amp was the protector and Shai the mischievous one. They grew to be very loyal and offered not only added protection for the humans against predators, but they also were a type of early warning detection system as well. They could see, hear, and smell danger or prey way before the humans could. They were indispensable to Eric and Hope as they followed the two humans devotedly, everywhere they went.

Eric and Hope realized it was time to move on and build a more permanent structure to live in. The cave had served its purpose, but it was now too small for the four of them. They needed a new shelter, one that would give them better light and 360 degrees of visibility. It was time to explore the area at great length.

They had purposely stayed in the general vicinity so the Extinctos could find them, but with the passing of time, this became less important to them. For all they knew, Creo and the others were not coming back at all. The possibility of the Super Extinctos perishing while recruiting other species to help Megalo's cause was now a deep concern for the humans.

Hope and Eric decided it was time to live their life the way they wanted to and if the Extinctos returned hopefully they could find them. Aves could fly and cover vast amounts of range to search for them, they just needed to make a shelter visible from the air.

So, it was with heavy hearts that Eric and Hope packed up the contents of the cave dwelling and headed out to the open plain to search for a new permanent home, followed by the loyal, courageous bear dogs, Amp and Shai.

Chapter 19

Pleistocene Epoch

Maka Dove swiftly crawled through the opening of the cavern when she heard Takoda's excited voice. Once inside the cave, she stood up looking for Tak, who by now had ventured deeper into the surprisingly well–lit cavern. She could hear the low growl of some small creature, coming from back in the cave.

"What is it?" she called out.

"It's a Smilodon cub! It must have belonged to the one we killed last night."

"That's sad. What are we going to do with it?"

"I don't know," replied Tak, well knowing that without their help the poor orphan cub would not survive long.

"We can take care of it until it's large enough to fend for itself," responded Maka, who at heart was kind and gentle, especially when it came to animals.

"We'll do what we can."

The cavern would make a great shelter thought the Sioux native and the Smilodon cub already lived in it, so all they had to do was move in. Anyway, it would only grow into a big cat, he reckoned.

Maka and Tak left the orphaned cub in the back of the cavern and crawled back out into the sunlight, where they collected their belongings, brought them to the opening to the cavern, and placed them by the doorway.

Once finished, they journeyed back to the natural spring to fill up the water bottles and use the opportunity to scout the surrounding area. On the way back to the cavern, they collected as much firewood as they could carry to begin building up the necessary reserves to combat the colder elements.

The Pleistocene, a cold and unforgiving world, would test not only their hunting, gathering, and defensive skills, but it would equally test their endurance against the frigid temperatures and momentous snowfall, snowfall that measured in feet during the harsh winter months. **(Image 11: Pleistocene animals of North America: page 138)**

Maka entered the cavern and started a fire while Tak continued to collect wood. It was getting close to evening, so he piled a large stockpile of wood by the entrance to the cavern before wandering back towards the spring to search for some meat for the cub. It seemed unnatural to feed the cub the Smilodon gracilis meat from the earlier night. To make matters worse, it was the cub's own mother. Tak even felt reservations about eating it himself, now that the orphaned Smilodon gracilis was part of his native pack.

The native stopped at the edge of the trees and patiently waited, surveying the area in and around the large spring. The spot offered him ample protection from visual detection by predators and gave him an unhindered vantage point to the area around the natural spring.

Tak made sure he was down wind, so his scent would not betray his presence as he surveyed the proximity near the spring. Dusk was quickly approaching, which increased the activity around the spring as a myriad of creatures, both large and small, traveled to drink from the life giving well one last time before darkness fell. Once darkness descended on the forest, the carnivores silently appeared from their daytime hiding places in search of unsuspecting prey.

A giant beaver, known as Castoroides, ambled down to the spring for a long drink and to eat the tender, supple saplings that grew around the life sustaining water. The beaver, a brute the size of a large black bear, moved in and out of the trees, testing the flavor of the various saplings that bordered the spring.

At over seven feet long, the huge Castoroides was capable of inflicting physical harm to any assailant, so attacking the giant buck–toothed beaver was too risky. Tak could not take the chance on getting injured; he needed something smaller to feed the Smilodon cub. In time, he might tackle the larger prey once he was proficient with his weapons, but for now it was safer to tackle smaller game.

He heard loud crashing coming from the trees on the far side of the spring. His first impulse was to run, but he decided to stay still until he could see what was coming towards him. He watched as a small band of prehistoric elephants rambled into the spring. They were enormous in height and were much larger than the modern elephants from his world. They were Mammuthus Imperators, the second largest elephants to roam the Earth.

The matriarch stood guard as the young ones drank first. The Castoroides fled the commotion as soon as it picked up the scent of the obtrusive invaders. It vanished into the forest as quickly as it had appeared.

The band of elephants drank their fill, frolicked in the water then turned back into the trees. Tak heard snapping branches as the massive herd of Proboscideans left the area, returning to the forest for the night, to continue the endless task of grazing.

The disruptive invasion caused by the lumbering elephants, created a chaotic upheaval around the natural spring. Several types of small rodents darted to the edges of the natural spring, drank the water, then scurried back to the safety of the trees. A couple of these smaller vermin would make a satisfying meal for the Smilodon cub, so the heavily furred rodents now became the focus of Tak's hunt.

Tak silently moved out from the protection of the trees, walking slowly towards the spring, where he speared three mice–like varmints the size of rabbits. He gathered the medium sized rodents, then quickly hurried back to the shelter to share the bounty with his new pet.

The native made it to the opening to the cavern as the last fading rays of light disappeared from the forest floor. He tossed the rodents to the Smilodon cub, who pounced on the fresh meat. Tak then returned to barricade the opening to the cavern for the night. He would build a stronger, more secure door to the cave in the light of the next day. For now, spears tied together with rope would have to hold off intruders.

The cub, the size of a large Bobcat, devoured the rodents. It was difficult for Maka and Tak to imagine the orphaned feline growing up to be larger than a modern lion with large dagger–like canines supported by massive neck muscles. If they could keep it from being too wild and independent, it would make a formidable pet. The issue would be trust. Would they ever be able to trust it? Only time would reveal this.

"What should we name it?" asked Tak.

The human, unsure if it was a male or female, walked over to the now gorged cub and rolled it over, rubbing it underneath its belly. It began to purr and Tak could see it was a female.

Maka replied, "I don't know. I will think of a good strong Sioux name."

She tossed some strips of meat into the small tin pot and placed it on the fire. Soon the meat was popping and crackling, the rich aroma filling the cave.

"It smells good! I am hungry," replied Tak.

Maka placed some of the cooked meat on a piece of bark and handed it to Takoda.

"How about Canowicakte for a name?"

Canowicakte, Sioux for Forest Hunter, seemed to fit. Maka knew the Smilodon cub would eventually grow into a great hunter, one that would rule the plains and the forests of the Pleistocene Epoch.

"That's a good strong name."

He liked it.

Maka and Tak finished the sizzling meat, following it with a long drink of the refreshing water from the natural spring. Tak went and tossed some more wood on the fire. The fire light flickered against the side of the cavern like dancing spirits. The crack at the top of the cavern allowed fresh air and sunlight to filter into the cavern during the day and moonlight on nights when the moon was out. Tomorrow Tak would begin to build a rock fireplace to funnel the smoke directly up and out of the cave.

The natives had no idea how long Arcto, Perris, and Arc would be gone, so they decided it was best to plan on a prolonged stay and try to be as comfortable as possible while they lived in this hostile period on Earth. The weather could change at any time, becoming even more frigid in the winter. The Pleistocene was known for cold and snowy conditions all around the Earth. They would need a good stockpile of wood and some animal skins for warmer clothing. The better they prepared the better their chances for survival would be.

The two Sioux laid down by the fire. The cavern, quite cozy and warm, offered a high-level of security for the humans. It would make an adequate home if the Extinctos for some reason did not return. Takoda was confident they would return soon but he wondered how the rest of the humans were faring in their time periods. It would be great when they all met up again to share their tales with one another. He was sure CeCe would have an exaggerated experience to share with them all.

"It will be good when we all get back together again," he said to Maka as he stretched out by the fire, enjoying the warmth of the blaze.

"I can only imagine the stories," she said with a hearty laugh. "We've only been here for a couple of days and we already have a pet Smilodon."

Canowicakte the Smilodon gracilis cub, although still wary, came closer to the two Sioux natives. She rolled over on her back and went to sleep. Time would tell if she ever would totally accept the two humans.

Soon all three creatures were fast asleep, oblivious to the outside world in the cavern some 30,000 thousand years ago. It was hard to imagine a different time, a different place, in a different space.

The night was uneventful, the first night without incident since the native's abduction into Extinctus.

Canowicakte was the first to stir in the morning. The little orphan cat sat at the opening to the cavern, emitting a low cry, obviously a call to her dead mother.

This woke up Maka who stood up and walked over to the distressed cat. She bent down and gently stroked Canowicakte's head. The cub continued to cry for its dead mother. Maka felt saddened by the cub's inability to understand the loss of its mother, so she tried to console the little orphan as much as possible. Her persistence eventually won out and Canowicakte stopped her crying and rubbed up against her, emitting a constant purr. This bond, formed that morning, would last a lifetime.

Tak awoke and re-started the fire. There were some coals left over from the preceding night, so he threw more wood on the coals as he blew on the ashes to start a fire once more. What he would give for some coffee.

"Do you think coffee beans were growing in this time?"

"Who knows? We might stumble upon some when we survey the area, but I think it's too cold for them to grow here," Maka softly replied.

"It would taste so good in this cold place," Tak replied.

He went over and opened the door to the cavern. Canowicakte rushed out, vanishing into the thick undergrowth of the forest. Maka followed the cat, catching only a glimpse of it as it disappeared behind the trees. Maka wondered if Canowicakte would return at all.

While outside, Maka set about gathering wood to carry back to the shelter. Takoda collected rocks to build his fireplace. One by one he carried the larger rocks into the cave to make his base. It was slow work but in the end the fireplace wall would keep the cavern warmer and the air quality purer; both of which were essential.

Tak stopped around mid-day. It was time to go hunting while he surveyed the surrounding area. Maka decided to go along and look for Canowicakte. They put on their backpacks, grabbed their spears and headed east. It seemed like a good direction to go towards the mid-day sun.

The two Sioux natives walked a few miles until they came to the edge of the forest. The forest opened to a vast plain, filled with sporadic plants, bushes, and trees. They could see a large body of water, which they assumed was a lake, off in the distance. A small river flowed from the lake down to the valley floor.

Tak pointed towards the stream and lake and said, "We should head for that body of water. We can try fishing the river along the way and put out set lines in the lake once we get there."

"Sounds good. I'll make a net when we get back to the cavern to help bring the fish in."

The two humans walked towards the river, constantly surveying the area for danger. The openness of the plain left them exposed for the first real time. Up until now, they relied on the forest to keep them hidden from the keen eyesight of predators. Predators were not the only beasts they had to fear. Early primitive humans populated this time as well. If they ran into a primitive hunting party, the consequences could be fatal. They would have to rely on their superior intelligence to stay undetected and if contact occurred, outsmart them. Primitive humans would think they were spirits which could be either good or bad. Takoda and Maka would use this spiritual mysticism to their advantage to manipulate the primitive humans if necessary.

Anatomically modern human development was in the beginning stages during the Pleistocene Epoch. If Tak and Maka did run into a band of hunters, would they have language, abstract thoughts and symbolism to express creativity in art?

This all depended on which continent they were stuck on. If they were in North America, it would be thousands of years before early humans entered the continent from Europe and Asia. Tak and Maka had no idea which continent they were on, but assumed it was North America. This offered them some psychological security from the possibility of meeting early humans.

Tak searched the plain for danger then hand signaled Maka to follow. The two modern humans headed directly for the stream. It was narrow in width but deep as it flowed from the large lake in the distance. They could see a large herd of grazing herbivores in the distance on the opposite side of the river.

Both Tak and Maka carried two sharp pointed spears for protection. Tak carried his knife on his belt for quick access if needed. They were too slow to outrun the predators of the time, so they had to rely on weapons and stealth for protection.

In the days to come, Tak would make a couple of bows with arrows for hunting and protection. If time allowed and if he could find the right materials, he would make a forge to heat and shape his own weaponry; but for this he would need to find metals. To make his arrows he would use either obsidian or chert, both of which were excellent materials for flaking and sharpening. These materials were highly prized and used for tool making by later Pleistocene humans.

For now, the spears and the knife would have to protect them. They cautiously approached the river which was slightly lower in elevation than the plain. Tak led the way down a small bank, one that headed to a rocky, dried up river bottom, left exposed by the lower water level. He could see the river swelled during the brief warmer periods to the top of the bank. Luckily, now the river was low and he and Maka could easily fish the isolated deeper pools.

Tak tied fishing line to two of the spears and added hooks. Maka turned over rocks until she found several worms along with multiple types of slower moving insects. They tried the worms first to see what the fish would bite on.

In a matter of seconds, they were getting action. Tak landed a large salmon that had sharp teeth like a modern-day tiger fish. Maka brought in a similar looking fish except it resembled a trout species. The fish added a new staple to the native's diet. In time, they could catch more fish, drying the fillets for use later. Dried fish or smoked fish would last for months if properly preserved. It gave them a sustainable food source; one they could carry with them while they explored the region.

Tak cleaned the fish then placed them in his backpack. It was time to move on towards the lake. The river would supply them with fish, but they were interested in surveying the lake to see what treasures it might provide.

The humans needed to find obsidian or chert to make weapons. Chert would be easier to find and was more abundant than obsidian. Obsidian was extremely rare in North America, only found in a few places. If they were still in North America, the chances of finding the rare mineral were slim.

The Sioux natives walked for a couple of miles towards the lake when they came to a rocky outcrop that dropped down to the lake shore. It was 30 feet above the lake and gradually transitioned to the shore. From on top of the ridge, they could see the vast delta as it stretched out for miles. In the distance Tak saw a small herd of primitive horses.

The horses he spotted, named Equus, were very much like the modern–day horses in build, resembling modern day Zebras, and stood around five feet tall. Horses make up the Perissodactyl, or odd–toed ungulates, a family made up of horses, rhinoceroses and tapirs. It is one of two surviving orders left living today.

Perissodactyls evolved over 54 million years ago. The first known horse, Hyracotherium, was a horse the size of a mid-sized dog. It had four toes on its front legs and three toes on its rear legs. Over millions of years, these toes would evolve into hoofs.

Horses originally evolved in North America, slowly spreading to the rest of the planet, until they died out in North America. Early humans from Europe re–introduced them to North America thousands of years later when they came to explore the unknown Americas.

"I think we should try and capture some horses for transportation," Tak said in a curious tone as he pointed at the herd of primitive horses.

The native was an avid horseman, one who had broken many a wild horse in his time. Horses, once captured and trained, would give the humans superiority over game and predators in the land. On the swift horses, the natives would be able to outrun predators when threatened and chase down game for meat and skins.

"That's a great idea. Do you think we can catch them?"

"It won't be easy, but we have to try. We'll drive them into a corral of some kind."

"We'll start building one tomorrow, but now we need to get down to the lake and catch some more fish for dinner," the native beauty replied.

The two climbed down the rocky outcrop and walked up to the edge of the lake. They had no idea what types of creatures lurked in the depths of the lake, but they felt it was too cold for crocodiles or alligators, so they jumped in.

The lake depth dropped drastically just out a couple of feet from the shoreline. They could see the lake was deep and could only guess how big the fish might be. The water was cold, but it felt good to get in and get clean.

The temperature of the water escalated the washing process, and soon both exited the cold lake. Tak decided to make a couple of set lines so he set off to gather the materials needed to construct them. He attached his heaviest weights from his fishing tackle to long sections of fishing line.

Once again, the forethought of Megalo to bring the humans their backpacks paid off.

Tak tied on his strongest hooks and threw the lines out as far as possible. Once satisfied with his casts, he tied the fishing lines around heavy boulders, to keep whatever denizens from the depths took the bait, from pulling the line into the water. He was confident the boulders would work, but only time would tell if the test of the fishing line would be heavy enough to keep a giant fish from breaking it during the struggle to free itself.

Maka searched the lake shore for signs of chert. She was certain chert would be easier to find than obsidian, so she left the shore and decided to focus on the rocky outcrop. The outcrop ridge, made primarily of sandstone, jutted out of the dry grassland just above the lake. It was a good place to start looking for chert.

Chert is common around sandstone outcrops: sometimes buried beneath the soil and sometimes scattered on the surface of the ground. Early humans journeyed to the same regions year after year to mine for chert.

Obsidian was highly prized but was rarer to find. She continued to search the rims as Tak finished the set lines.

"I found some chert," Maka yelled.

It was a good find. One good chunk of chert could make many arrow tips or a fine knife blade.

"I'll be right up," replied Takoda as he quickly climbed up the bank and hurried over to where Maka was digging.

"That's a great piece. You've found an excellent spot."

She filled her backpack with several large pieces of highly the prized chert.

"We now have a working mine," Maka laughed.

"That was a fantastic find which could save us in this place. We need weapons to protect ourselves from the predators here. We better head back to the cavern before it turns dark," Tak said as he pointed back down the valley.

The day was getting late—that time when the light becomes grey before turning to darkness. Tak and Maka both knew they had to get back to the safety of the cavern before nightfall. They guessed they had walked at least three miles to reach the lake. They would have to hurry to reach the cavern before darkness fell and the stealthy carnivores of the night came out.

On the way back to the shelter, they came across several herd animals. The bison of the time were significantly larger and extremely more dangerous than their modern–day relatives, so the humans went out of their way to avoid them. Perhaps once they domesticated some horses, they would try to bring one of the behemoths down.

At least four types of Bison roamed the Pleistocene Epoch, any of which would offer not only meat but many other usable materials. The open plain teemed with odd looking ungulates, some obviously related to the antelope species but with very unusual horn patterns. There were camels, horses, various deer types, elephants, and rhinos just to name a few.

It was the predators, which were both widespread and diverse, that worried Tak and Maka. Giant bears, several Smilodon species, cave lions, dire wolves, were among some of the apex predators of the day. These were the beasts that the two natives had to protect themselves from; for around every corner or out in the open, these powerful beasts could hunt them at any time. Therefore, it was imperative for them to make the most advanced weapons for protection as possible. Every day would be a struggle in this hostile time and place. If the predators did not get them, the freezing weather might.

They were within 200 yards of the trees when Tak noticed a pack of roaming Dire Wolves. The beastly pack was hunting on the edge of the plain, following just outside the tree line and slowly moving in the direction of the humans. They were menacing looking beasts, much larger than modern day wolves.

Luckily the two natives were up wind of the pack which removed smell from the equation. The pack would pursue the humans if they saw or smelled them; the natives were just another meat source to the wolves. Maka and Tak were at least a half a mile from the marauding pack, which gave them a slight flight advantage.

"Be quiet and stop moving. There's a pack of wolves," Tak coolly said to Maka as he pointed in the direction of the dire wolves.

Maka froze in her steps. She looked towards the pack and looked back at Tak.

"What are we to do?"

The situation was serious. If the beasts detected them, the natives would have to flee for their lives, trying to out distance the lethal predators.

"Move slowly towards the trees," whispered Tak as he pointed to the tree line.

Tak and Maka moved silently towards the trees, trying to avoid detection. Once inside the forest, they were certain they could give the beasts the slip. They just had to make it to the trees.

The pack, now within a quarter mile from the humans, unknowingly continued to travel in the direction of the natives. At least three members of the pack were visible to Tak and Maka. The wolves stayed on the edge of the tree line to patrol both the forest and plain for unsuspecting quarry.

To the chagrin of the unlucky humans, the wind direction changed. The lead wolf froze, sniffing the evening breeze by lifting its muzzle straight into the air. It turned its large head in the direction of the natives. The alpha wolf had picked up their unfamiliar scent.

The creature let out a loud howl and the pack sprang into action. They loped towards Tak and Maka.

Tak shouted to Maka, "Head for the forest!"

Chapter 20

Paleocene Epoch

Trying to distance themselves from the imposing threat, CeCe and Lexa dropped their fishing equipment to the ground and ran upstream. Both were good athletes, athletes that could reach top speed rapidly. CeCe glanced over his shoulder as he ran along the riverbed. The odd shaped boulders littering the riverbank made solid footing impossible. He could now see the cause of Lexa's panic; two enormous beasts, similar in appearance to the Extinctos, were chasing them.

The first one, a hideous looking reptilian creature, part mammal and part reptile, pursued them with extreme conviction as it covered great distances with each stride. The beast had thick reptilian like skin covered in a fine brown hair, which grew in splotches around its chest and legs. Long, sharp claws, claws easily capable of eviscerating any foe it combatted, protruded from its long hands and enormous, broad, flat feet.

CeCe and Lexa would later learn it was a Theriodont, early flesh eaters that flourished about 249-168 million years ago. The only difference between these early mammal-like reptiles and later mammals was how the jaw and hearing mechanism evolved. This early design was primitive; it would take millions of years of experimentation before the modern carnivores of today evolved with a more specialized design.

The huge Theriodont, closely followed by another sinister looking Extincto, gradually gained on the two humans, who tried to outmaneuver the pursuing monsters by dodging in and out of the large boulders along the riverbed.

The second creature, a type of early carnivore, looked like a giant warthog with exceptionally large bumps protruding from the sides of its head. It belonged to the family of species known as Entelodonts, an early even-toed ungulate that lived some 55 million years ago. Some of these creatures were larger than the modern-day Bison, and they reigned as a top predator for 10 million years in North America until the emergence of the adversarial Bear Dogs. It was huge, grotesque, and terrifying as it trotted behind the Theriodont.

"They're gaining on us.! What should we do?" CeCe shouted to Lexa.

"Keep running. We can outlast them with our endurance."

Lexa, confident she could run at top speed for an extended time, was unsure if the big football player could sustain the pace. CeCe, built for power and short burst of speed, lacked endurance.

The two humans kept up the frantic pace until they reached a deep pool, one that formed at the bottom of the large waterfall that plunged down from the rocky cliffs high above the river. There was no time to stop to survey an escape route, so without hesitation, they jumped into the deep pool, swimming for the far side of the stream. Their only hope rested on the slim chance the pursuing Extinctos could not swim.

The two pursuing beasts stopped when they reached the bank by the deep pool. They hesitated just long enough for the CeCe and Lexa to reach the opposite bank of the stream.

"They're stopping," shouted CeCe, as he climbed out of the river.

"I think we should keep running," answered Lexa, as she looked over at the two creatures on the opposing bank.

The two ominous beasts seemed to be arguing over something. The brutish Entelodont squealed in an uncontrollable fit of rage as it watched the two escaping humans climb onto the opposing bank across the deep pool.

Lexa sucked in as much oxygen as she could, yelling at CeCe to do the same.

The terrified humans heard a loud splash as one of the Extinctos jumped into the river.

Both humans turned to flee, but instantaneously stopped as a ghastly, winged creature hovered directly in front of them blocking their escape route. The presence of the gruesome flying demon froze the humans in their terrified tracks.

A massive, reptilian winged, flying monstrosity with a carnivorous mammalian head landed gently on the rock littered riverbed directly in front of the two shocked humans. It resembled a type of pterosaur spliced together with a hyaena–like carnivore. The creature had thin reptilian skin, a head covered in hair, and dagger sharp teeth that were visible even when the monster had its mouth closed, obviously the consequence of having a tremendous overbite.

The atrocious beast let out a spine–tingling scream which halted the humans in their tracks. There was no escape!

The lead Extincto exited the stream, shook itself violently, then cautiously approached CeCe and Lexa. It glared at the two humans with a loathing scowl and a blazing stare. Lexa and CeCe, for the first time, could see the terrible monster up close—it was hideous and monstrous.

The Theriodont looked exceptionally cruel as it glared at the two insignificant humans. The hog–like Entelodont was missing; it had simply vanished.

The new flying beast scowled at the humans as it jumped in the air and pumped its enormous skin covered wings, emitting a cloud of dust, dust filled with small rocks, which sprayed CeCe and Lexa.

The humans could tell these Extinctos were quite different from the ones who had helped them when they first arrived in Extinctus—these fiends exuded cruelty.

I am Therio...don't try to escape or we'll kill you!" sneered the creature as it clambered out of the river. It bared its sharp protruding canines to terrify the humans.

The dreadful **Therio**dont seemed to relish its role of antagonist. It was obvious a brute that had no qualms about killing anything.

"What do you want with us?" demanded CeCe as he tried to be firm, to hide his growing fear.

"You're now our prisoners," Therio answered as he pointed to the other creature and said, "This is Odon, don't mess with him. He'll be happy to kill you as well."

"What happened to the third one of you?" asked Lexa.

Therio laughed and answered, "You mean **Odon**?"

At this the terrifying flying menace transformed back into the wart–hog giant Ente**lodon**t.

"You see Odon can change into a variety of creatures, creatures which sometimes resemble many combinations of species. The giant Ente**lodon**t, known as Dae**odon,** is his current form. The flying creature from just moments before was part Dimorph**odon** and Hyaen**odon,**" jeered Therio as he let out a sinister spine–tingling laugh.

CeCe and Lexa, astonished by the ease in which Odon changed forms, now realized the complex capabilities of the Extinctos. It only took seconds to complete a total transformation. They were no match for these savage captors. They would have to bide their time wisely, hoping a chance to escape would present itself later.

"We will go with you and not try to escape," replied CeCe.

If the chance to escape without detection became available, CeCe realized they would try to escape, but for now, it was better to play along with their captors. The humans needed to learn their intentions first.

"Which one of you go by the name of Eric Asvaldsson?" the reptilian beast asked, obviously unaware of male or female names; in fact, he had no idea or concept of gender.

"It is neither of us," answered CeCe.

"We don't know what happened to Eric, and even if we did, we wouldn't tell you anyway," Lexa bluntly replied, her tone adversarial...almost defiant.

"You will tell us in time," declared Odon for the first time.

The enormous razorback grinned as he spoke in a high–pitched, squealing voice.

Lexa and CeCe knew from Odon's demeanor that this foul beast would be extremely dangerous to deal with. They could see it had a very short temper, one that could be very volatile, causing it to fly into a fit of rage at any moment and inflict mortal injury before coming back to what little sense it had. Both Lexa and CeCe felt it would be wise to not agitate or provoke the primitive beast until they could figure out how to manipulate its weaknesses to their advantage.

"Follow me," commanded Therio.

The titan reptile-mammal took the lead, followed by the humans, while Odon followed behind. They headed up stream navigating through the boulders and dead fall that littered the area around the stream.

The temperature, very warm and extremely humid, caused both Lexa and CeCe to sweat profusely. The forest, which covered most of the world during this time, was extremely dense caused by the unchecked growth of trees, shrubs, flowering plants, and grasses. Nature flourished in the miserable humidity and heat of this time, but to the humans, it was wearisome.

Once the rocky stream banks subsided, a thick deciduous forest lined both sides of the river. The group, once they reached the top of a large waterfall, headed into the thick forest. The forest thinned out as they reached the higher elevation.

The band followed a game trail, traveled for millennium, as it weaved in and out of the trees and through open meadows as the group journeyed farther away from the top of the cliffs. When the sunlight reached the forest floor, the meadows filled up with flowering plants and lush plant life. This gave a pleasant reprise to the darkness of the forest.

Mammals during the Paleocene were just beginning to evolve. Smaller mammals survived the mass extinction known as the K-Pg extinction event which wiped out the non-avian dinosaurs. These early mammals thrived on the rich insect diversity of the time.

By the middle to later Paleocene, mammals had adapted, ranging in size from exceedingly small to extraordinarily large. The oceans and seas were warm but low in diversity after the K-Pg extinction event, but these became truly diverse later in the Paleocene Epoch due to warm tropical conditions that helped give rise to coral reefs.

Danger, the type which usually ended in death, existed around every corner and in every water way. Rivers and seas, now filled with varying types of crocodilia, champsosaurs, and other frightening beast, always looking for the next meal, still covered much of the Earth.

Most of the bird families are traceable back to this time in origin. They exploded onto the scene to fill every niche. Giant flightless birds later called terror birds roamed the open plains and forests during the Paleocene as top predators, while smaller predatory mammals were just beginning to evolve.

This was a time meant to be without humans, who could not easily survive in these violent times. Early prosimian, relatives to modern lemurs and tarsiers, lived in the trees for protection. They were no match for the carnivores who waged war on the ground. The world was not ready for man during this time.

CeCe and Lexa along with the two Extinctos continued to move through the forest at a steady pace. The forest, filled with the cackles and screams of exotic birds, sounded alive as the group silently passed through one forest and into another. This was a foreign unrecorded world.

Insects buzzed around, constantly pestering the group. It reminded the humans of Africa or the North reaches of Alaska in the summer when large swarms of insects continually attacked all other living mammals. The only difference between then and now was the size of the insects themselves as they swarmed all living animals searching for blood.

CeCe and Lexa, as they traveled through the region, fought off some of the largest insects to ever exist. Giant dragonfly like insects with double even triple sets of wings hovered around them in a strange fixation. They hovered over the humans more out of curiosity than designed purpose. It was a journey through an alien world of both climate and species interaction.

The humans had no idea where they were going, but they had no choice but to follow. They could not escape or overpower the beasts and more importantly, they needed their protection to survive in this brutal world until they became more familiar with its dangers. They were a long way from their bamboo structure that gave them protection from the creatures that roamed the area. Now they were out in the open, away from their shelter, which meant they needed the protection of these hostile Extinctos.

The group stopped at the tree line which yielded to a small clearing, littered by downed trees. The area looked like a microburst had flung the trees around and dropped them like toothpicks. Some resembled trees knocked down by a bulldozer, their roots up ended to expose large holes in the earth. Other trees, picked up and tossed violently against standing trees, splintered, their exploding particles of wood scattering in every direction. It was a violent display of the power of nature.

CeCe and Lexa weaved their way through the fallen trees, all the while fighting off the hordes of relentless insects.

Suddenly, Therio stopped and motioned to the others to be quiet. He sniffed the air with his long snout. Odon, the wart-hog demon followed his lead. The hideous wart hog shook his head from side to side, trying to move more air through his giant, wart riddled nostrils. A small amount of saliva dripped down his elongated jaw line and landed on his thick leathery foot.

The two beasts looked at one another then quickly took off in the direction of the tree line on the far side of the meadow. CeCe and Lexa tried to keep up, following around 20 paces behind. It would have been an opportune time to try and escape, but the humans were deeply afraid of what caused the two Extinctos to flee, so they cautiously followed their two captors towards the trees.

CeCe and Lexa reached the far side of the forest. They could no longer see Therio or Odon, so they slowed to a walk. Lexa forcefully grabbed CeCe, pulling him behind a large tree for cover. Both humans turned to look back in the direction from which they had fled.

Entering the open meadow littered with fallen trees, was a small group of giant flightless birds. They were over 6 feet tall with huge beaks and long claws. They were "terror cranes", beasts capable of killing large omnivores by disemboweling them with their claws and crushing their skulls with their powerful beaks. These were killing birds best avoided at all costs. **(Image 12: Diatryma (Gastornis gigantea: page 139)**

The two humans watched as the cranes slowly moved into the lush meadow. There were four of them, all obviously adults, between 6 and 7 feet tall, covered in thick feathers of varying colors, primarily black and grey. Their beaks, large, pointed, and curved, were yellow with black tips.

CeCe and Lexa silently backed away, trying to sneak deeper into the forest to avoid detection. They needed to put some distance between themselves and the terror cranes. Therio and Odon had vanished, so the two humans devised a plan to circle back in the direction they had come from. The plan was to give the meadow a wide birth, avoid the pack of hunting cranes, then return to the trail once they circled around the occupied meadow.

Lexa motioned for CeCe to move quietly across the game trail, back into the trees, to the right side of the trail. The two crept into the safety of the trees and started the slow trek around the meadow. They had to fight their way through the dense vegetation that grew everywhere, left unchecked by the absence of large herbivores. The game trail was just too dangerous to navigate which forced them into the thick jungle.

The forest, thick in vegetation without a defined trail, made navigation difficult. The insects persisted. They were now more interested in the sweat on the humans caused by the increased physical exertion.

Lexa then remembered the insect repellant in her pack. She whispered to CeCe to stop and they both hid behind a large growth of ferns. Lexa pulled out the repellant and sprayed CeCe then herself.

"We're the first humans to use insect spray," Lexa whispered to CeCe as she laughed.

"I'm glad you remembered it."

"We better get moving so we can put some distance between us and those terrible birds," Lexa softly whispered.

Lexa and CeCe started moving once again through the thick vegetation. They made it to the far edge of the meadow, the edge they had entered from, and decided to head back towards the trail. They finally spotted the game trail, so they picked up the pace to reach it. In their minds, they had circumvented the terror cranes and it was safe to resume travel on the trail once more.

Once on the trail, they ran. They needed to put as much distance between themselves, the killer cranes, and Therio and Odon as possible, so they ran as fast as they could. It was about a mile later when Lexa could see another opening in the trees. She slowed her pace and stopped on the edge of the clearing.

"Wait," she said to CeCe.

CeCe stopped right behind Lexa as she surveyed the open meadow for danger. It looked safe, so they apprehensively entered the meadow. This second meadow, covered in tall flowering plants that grew around the large depressions left in the earth by the fallen trees, appeared empty.

Lexa led the way. She darted from one downed tree to the next one for cover. They were halfway into the meadow when they heard a loud shrieking sound.

Lexa and CeCe dropped down into a depression in the earth created by an up rooted tree. The depression offered cover from sight, especially when they both laid flat. It was like a fox hole used during war.

Lexa peered over the top of the depression, looking for the culprit of the loud sound. CeCe continued to lay flat to hide his tall frame. He crawled up next to Lexa but stayed low to avoid detection.

The shrill sound broke the silence once again, quickly followed moments later by several added shrieking sounds, which were coming from somewhere in front of Lexa and CeCe. The other sounds could only mean the creature was not alone. CeCe and Lexa felt trapped.

"What should we do?" asked Lexa.

The shrill screams terrified her.

"Can you see anything?" answered CeCe who wanted to know if they could outrun whatever was making the sounds.

"Not yet," Lexa replied as she peered over the top of the depression once again, this time raising her head a little higher to get a better view.

The sounds continued to get closer. It sounded like the creatures were trying to communicate with one another.

"It's the giant cranes. We need to get out of here CeCe."

Lexa jumped out of the hole she was hiding in and ran back in the direction of the trees. CeCe was right behind her. She looked over her shoulder, instantly spotting the killer cranes in pursuit. They were picking up speed, trying to run down the two humans.

The leader of the pack let out a hideous, piercing scream, answered at once by the other cranes in response. The pack of cranes ran after the fleeing humans.

CeCe and Lexa, now in a death race to the finish, had two choices; one hinged on climbing into the trees, while the other one relied on dodging in and out of the trees to escape. They opted for the first one.

Lexa jumped as high as she physically could, barely grabbing a low hanging branch. She had the natural athletic ability to swing herself onto the strong branch, then climb up the tree until she reached a safe elevation. She yelled at the cranes to distract them while CeCe attempted to gain the security of a tree.

The terror cranes, momentarily confused by the Lexa's action, briefly halted their pursuit.

After gaining their dim wits, two of the cranes ran to the base of the tree where Lexa safely stood and began to squawk excessively. They were swearing in bird language. For now, Lexa, safely unobtainable in the tree, could only helplessly watch the events unfold below.

CeCe leaped for the lowest branch he could find on a tree next to the tree Lexa waited in. As the big man tried to pull his large bulk up to the branch, one of his legs dangled below the tree branch. The leader of the terror cranes, filled with uncontrollable rage, followed right behind him. It lunged at CeCe as he struggled to raise his remaining leg up to the branch.

With one great thrust from its powerful legs, followed by a strong flap from its flightless wings, the crane shot off the ground and clamped its beak onto CeCe's left shoe. The African American let out a loud scream as the tremendous power of the crane's beak compressed his left foot.

CeCe tried to shake off the beast by kicking it with his right foot, but the grip of the beak was too strong. The weight of the crane put a tremendous strain on CeCe's body as he slipped down from the branch. He was a strong man, but the crane weighed around 200 pounds. CeCe slid his other leg down from the limb, kicking violently at the beak and head of the crane. Once he even kicked it in the eye, but the beast would not relinquish its hold—CeCe was dinner for the pack.

Lexa could only watch the battle unfold from the security of the tree she found refuge in.

"Keep fighting CeCe," she yelled over the loud screeching of the terror cranes.

The other members of the pack, realizing Lexa was out of reach, turned their attention to the struggling CeCe dangling from the branch of the nearby tree. They rushed to the aid of the leader crane. Each one took turns leaping off the ground, trying to reach CeCe's other foot, but each time they failed. The terror cranes would not relent.

"I can't hold on much longer," screamed CeCe.

The big man was tiring fast, his grip on the branch was weakening. He kept trying to kick at the terror crane to free himself, but without any luck. The giant flightless bird would not yield as it continued to constrict its neck muscles to pull the human to the ground.

The other terror cranes stopped leaping at CeCe. They were content to wait for their meal to fall to the ground. When this happened, they would pounce on the defenseless human and tear it apart.

As Lexa watched the scene, a deep feeling of helplessness fell over her. Was she about to see the death of her good friend? The situation was desperate, she knew CeCe could not continue to hold on much longer. Lexa could only watch the scene below take its course. Then she heard the faint crack of the branch.

"The branch is going to break CeCe!"

Within seconds, the branch snapped, plunging CeCe and the killer terror crane to the forest floor where they landed in a massive heap on the hard ground.

Chapter 21

Livelihood

Eric and Hope abandoned the small cave, the cave where they found the two loyal bear dog pups Amp and Shai, to search for a permanent home in the Miocene Epoch. The two humans, saddened by the thought of leaving their first real home, took one long last look at the tiny cave before heading out towards the plain. They realized that if the Extinctos did not return, it was up to them to survive in this hostile time, a time filled with capricious environmental challenges, hostile landscapes, landscapes populated by giant ungulates, hunted by vicious predators.

They traveled onto the sweeping flatland in search of a good water source and a place to build a permanent home. It would be beneficial to build a solid structure on a high cliff with a 360-degree view which would provide them with good visibility to spot approaching danger well in advance and give them time to prepare to face the threat or flee it.

Several months had elapsed since Creo, Aves, and Arti forsook the humans in search of recruits to help battle the treacherous Thylac's army of abhorrent beasts. The humans, at this point, did not expect the Extinctos to return so they decided to move on with their lives, lives dependent on their own versatility and adaptability.

The only rational explanation Eric and Hope could believe in, revolved around the untimely demise of their powerful protectors. Thylac's barbaric horde of monstrosities must have gained the upper hand and eradicated the three Super Extinctos: Creo, Aves and Arti.

This probable notion deeply saddened the humans who had grown fond of the giant beasts. If all three of the magnificent creatures had perished, it was only conceivable that Eric and Hope would now have to fend for themselves and any chance of returning home died with the deaths of the Super Extinctos. It was time for them to become self-reliant.

Amp and Shai, the loyal bear dogs, led the group out onto the plain, in obvious sight of the myriad of creatures that lived and died there. The two animals were growing into powerful adults. Amp, now approaching 800 pounds, had long defined muscles, while the smaller Shai, now pushing 700 pounds, developed better overall agility. Both were fine specimens of

Amphicyon galushai with strong powerful jaws, long legs for running down prey, and beautiful brown multi-colored coats.

Eric and Hope, on several occasions, watched as the two bear dogs ran down much larger game with precision, coordination, and raw primal power. They worked well together in complete unison, easily capable of running down faster creatures by using their superior stamina.

The bear dogs supplied meat for all of them often. They were formidable pets, pets that would protect their masters at all costs. The humans were thankful they found them that day so long ago in the small cave. The two bear dogs made life in the Miocene easier to cope with for the humans. They gave Eric and Hope unmatched protection, security, devotion, and loyalty.

The group moved out into the open, revealing themselves to the wandering eyes of every beast that roamed the plains. Just months earlier, Eric and Hope would have been hesitant to journey onto the openness of the delta by themselves, but now, with the bear dogs as prowess protectors, they were confident in their ability to respond to all dangerous situations. Amp and Shai would meet the danger head on while Eric and Hope could escape if necessary.

Strange looking creatures ranged the vast grasslands in small herds, medium herds and large herds. The perissodactyl Moropus, a giant clawed relative of the horse, bizarre looking camels, various experimentally horned antelope-like ungulates, dwarf rhinoceroses, and of course a deadly variety of carnivorous hunters, both solitary ambush slayers and deadly pack killers, lived, ate, and died in this area. Many of these creatures met the humans at one time or another, as they travelled onward exposed and vulnerable, heading for a far-off bluff which rose from the valley floor, trying to touch the endless blue sky.

Then there were the giants like Diceratherium an early type of rhinoceros, Entelodonts like Daeodon also appropriately named the "hell pig", and many other forms of mammals. Herds of early horses roamed the immense grasslands, falling prey to dog-like creatures like Daphoeodon, a thin, long, tall capable hunter.

The world was quite dangerous during this time; but it was also just as beautiful, teeming with experimental natural evolution, as species evolved to fill every nook and cranny. This time brandished a wide variety of species, some exploding in numbers while others dwindled, navigating down an evolutionary dead end until vanishing from the face of Earth.

Eric pointed towards the horizon where the large bluff towered high above the plain.

"That looks like a fine place to explore."

Hope agreed by nodding her head, so the band turned and headed towards the blue horizon, in the direction of the towering bluff.

The two humans walked most of the day before reaching the bottom of the outcrop just below the tall bluff. Along the way, they passed several small herds of horses intermingled with other roaming ungulates, followed by the predators. The prehistoric scene reminded Eric and Hope of the massive migrating herds of Africa, only with larger species.

Both Eric and Hope felt this area would offer a steady reliable source of food for them and the two bear dogs, so they decided it was well worth investigating. If they could find a way up to the top of the bluff, a home perched high above the expansive plain would give them the visual advantage over prey and predator. A source of clean, reliable water would be the next obstacle to solve.

Eric and Hope decided to camp at the base of the bluff until morning; when they would go in search of a water source, a source that could make or break their new home site.

Eric found a small cave at the base of the bluff large enough to offer good shelter for the night. Hope started a fire and soon all the members of the Asvald clan were relaxing by the warmth of the fire. It had been a physically demanding day of extreme trekking through completely unknown territories filled with potentially life threatening, dangerous animals. Eric and Hope, relieved they had survived another day in the Miocene, settled in for the long night.

Amp and Shai slept for a while just outside the heat of the fire. They still feared fire, that instinctual urge to avoid the flame genetically engrained in them, even though they had been around the open flame since they were pups. They could only tolerate the heat for short periods of time.

Eventually, the two bear dogs got up to journey out into the blackness of the night. Although they were pets, they were still wild beasts, ones that lived to hunt and kill and it was time to go and investigate the unfamiliar territory they found themselves in. By learning the area, and the dangers, the two bear dogs would make this new home safer for Eric and Hope.

Hope watched as the two fierce protectors disappeared into the darkness and said, "It's time for them to roam and explore."

Hope often wondered where the two bear dogs went and what they did while they roamed the wilderness. It was difficult for her to accept that her loving pets were successful, experienced killers, capable of brutal carnage.

"They will stay close in case we need them," replied Eric.

Eric trusted the two Amphicyon galushai totally. To him, they were the ultimate pets.

"I hope we can get to the top of the bluff without too much difficulty. We have to make sure Amp and Shai can get up there also," replied Hope, who was deeply concerned with keeping the pack together.

"We will find a way," answered Eric, realizing the bear dogs were vital to their existence while trapped alone in the Miocene.

The night was clear without any wind. The stars were highly visible once the human eye adjusted to the natural light, overcoming the intense light from the flame of the fire. The moon, still hidden for a few more hours, allowed the rich illumination of star light to fill the nighttime sky.

The stars seemed closer to Earth 15 million years ago and the moon looked even closer than the stars. Eric wondered if the enormous size of the dinosaurs was in direct correlation to the moon being closer to Earth which in turn led to less gravitational pull. If this theory were the case, it would have allowed dinosaurs to move around easier like the first men walking on the moon.

Eric and Hope stared up at the night sky and wondered what was happening in their own time. They could only imagine the grief their families were dealing with caused by their sudden, obscure disappearance. They worried about CeCe, Lexa, Maka, and Takoda. What dreadful events were they dealing with, and were they all still alive?

So, it was with these somber thoughts on the mind that the two humans fell to sleep, in a small cave, somewhere on Earth millions of years ago. The long journey left them fatigued.

Eric, wrenched from his sleep by the sounds of Amp and Shai growling, jumped up, and peered out into the darkness beyond the fire pit. The bear dogs vociferously growled, signaling danger as they placed themselves between the humans and the unseen danger coming from the plain.

The fire smoldered; the once bright flame, reduced to a pile of wafting smoke, causing Eric to throw more branches and twigs onto it to revive the flames. A large flame quickly flickered up, spreading light onto the base of the cliff's wall.

Hope, now wide awake, stared out into the darkness.

"What is it?" she asked, as she turned and looked at Eric.

"I don't know yet."

Eric could sense something looming just out beyond the edge of the light. The hair on the backside of both Amp and Shai was standing up in alarm. This posture meant extreme danger.

"What is it Amp?" he called to his fierce pet.

The big bear dog turned, looked at him, them at once turned his attention back in the direction of the imposing threat.

Hope threw more wood on the fire to increase the light. The moon, just clearing the top of the bluff, would soon usher in the light of the full moon which would aid the human's inferior eyesight.

For some reason, the bear dogs stayed with the humans instead of leaving them to investigate the danger. In most cases Amp and Shai would rush out and instantly confront the antagonist, but the scent of this new threat must have been unfamiliar to them. They were still young pups, although extremely large ones, only about two thirds of their potential adult size. If the impending threat alarmed the two bear dogs, Eric and Hope had reason to be afraid.

The standoff continued for about an hour, until the moon finally came up, offering better vision to the humans.

Eric and Hope walked out in front of the fire pit to allow their eyes to adjust to the nighttime light. The light from the fire was now behind them and no longer impeded their vision. They carried their spears for protection.

Once their eyes adjusted to the moon light, the two humans understood the reason for the angst of the bear dogs. Amp and Shai stood by their sides, continuing to growl and posture. Around 50 yards out from camp stood a small band of Dinocrocuta gigantea, hyena–like carnivores. **(Image 13: Dinocrocuta gigantea: page 140)**

The menacing beasts, all heavily built with thick chests and bone crushing jaws, paced back and forth just yards from the humans. If adults, they could weigh up to 850 pounds each. Both Amp and Shai were close to the Dinocrocuta in weight but neither of them had experience in settling territorial disputes either by posturing or violence, and besides, the Dinocrocuta outnumbered them.

Eric grabbed more spears and handed two to Hope. They were primitive spears, just stripped down, straight, small trees with sharpened ends. Eric still had his knife and axe, so he handed the knife to Hope. He kept the axe in his belt just in case the potential conflict ended at close range, in a hand to claw battle.

The light of the moon penetrated the darkness. There were three of the savage carnivores pacing just outside the depth of the light. They walked back in forth, uncertain and bewildered by the strange scent of the humans. Amp and Shai, emboldened by the added presence of their masters, increased their guttural growls and deep barks. Amp and Shai considered Eric and Hope as added members of the pack. To the bear dogs, their pack, now outnumbered the Dinocrocuta four to three.

The savage beasts roamed the plains, out hunting for weaker prey and unfortunately the humans, although completely unknown to the Dinocrocuta, fit the description. Amp and Shai delivered the equalizer, making the impending fight closer to equal.

The two bear dogs, emboldened by the failure of the Dinocrocuta to attack, increased their posturing, becoming increasingly aggressive. They looked at Eric and Hope for the signal to attack.

The Dinocrocuta cautiously crept in, closing the distance from 50 yards to about 25 yards. The inevitability of attack, by the merciless beasts, was obvious to Hope and Eric who now realized the Dinocrocuta were not yielding; they posed a serious threat to both them and the bear dogs. It would be up to the humans and the bear dogs to fight them, kill them, or chase them off, preferably the later.

Eric began shouting as loud as he could to try and deter the creatures. This seemed to help as the three hunters stopped. It was the first time the creatures had heard the strange screams of a human.

"Hope start yelling," screamed Eric, who figured two strange voices were better than one.

Hope screamed as loud as she could. Amp and Shai, taking the lead of the humans, increased the pitch and velocity of their growls and barks. All four members of Asvald clan screamed, growled, and shouted at the bewildered Dinocrocuta.

The Dinocrocuta increased their posturing as well. They let out horrific screaming cries comparable to the modern hyena. This war of sounds continued for what seemed hours. The stand-off was a stalemate; neither side would yield or give any ground. Resolution would take more direct action.

Eric walked back to the fire and picked up a large branch that was partially burning on one end. He walked back and handed it to Hope and then returned to grab another one for himself. It was time to end the stalemate and attack.

"Attack!" shouted Eric as he rushed the three Dinocrocuta.

Hope, Amp, and Shai followed Eric's lead and soon all four were running towards the three surprised beasts. They shouted as they descended on the pack. Amp and Shai seemed confident now that the humans were engaging the antagonists.

It took only minutes to reach the Dinocrocuta, which were reeling from the sudden attack. Two of them instantly ran back towards the plain while Amp caught the third one off guard and attacked it. A viscous battle broke out between Amp and the clear leader of the Dinocrocuta pack. Shai chased one of the fleeing creatures out onto the plain. Eric and Hope stopped just short of the ensuing battle between Amp and the pack leader.

Amp was at full speed when he thrust his whole body into the confused Dinocrocuta. The momentum of the attack crushed the beast, sending it instantaneously to the ground. It flailed wildly as it struggled to get up from the massive hit.

Amp, after colliding with the surprised creature, rolled over the Dinocrocuta and somersaulted two more times. This was his first fight. The male bear dog regained his footing and turned to re-engage the hideous hyena-like beast, which had scrambled to its feet after the first attack. The surprised beast, now worked into a chaotic frenzy, dripped foaming saliva from its snarling jaws. The battle was on.

The beast lunged at Amp in an obvious attempt to seize his neck and rip out his throat. Amp, easily dodging this maneuver, had the advantage of greater agility and quickness over the Dinocrocuta. The foe, a scavenging pack killer, was slower than the bear dog, but it did have a higher level of stamina. If running long distance, the beast had the advantage, but this was a battle to the death not a race.

Amp turned in retaliation to the lunge, biting the creature on the hind quarter, leaving an open gash that sprayed blood on both combatants. The injured beast turned to attack Amp once again, rushed in, and clamped down on Amp's shoulder on his left side. A large chunk of flesh ripped off Amp's shoulder as he twisted himself free from the powerful, steel jaws of the fierce Dinocrocuta. Both Amp and the creature were now bleeding profusely. Blood soon covered them both, even splattering Eric and Hope, as they stood watching the violent altercation.

Amp attacked the beast once more, thrusting his 800 pounds into the equally heavy Dinocrocuta. They locked jaws with one another, both uttering deep growls and screams. The powerful jaws and upper body bulk of the Dinocrocuta gave it the slight edge.

Once Amp reached his full adulthood, he would weigh up to 1200 pounds and this altercation would have been over in minutes, but he was still young, and this was his first fight. This gave the gruesome hyena-like beast a slight edge.

The Dinocrocuta rolled on top of Amp. Amp struggled to free himself, but the bulk of the attacker pinned him down to the ground. The young bear dog struggled to regain his feet.

It would be only moments before the foaming, frenzied beast dealt Amp the death blow. Amp was just too young to battle the experienced Dinocrocuta one on one.

Eric and Hope watched in horror as their beloved pet was on the verge of losing his life to the fierce Dinocrocuta.

Eric, disregarding his own safety, ran to the aide of Amp. He drew back his right arm, thrusting a spear deep into the side of the preoccupied adversary. He kept a firm grip on the spear to drive it in until it pierced the heart of the Dinocrocuta.

The dying Dinocrocuta let out a terrifying death howl as it lashed out in agony at both the man and the beast, the duo responsible for its painful demise, until its body went limp and slumped to the ground.

Amp regained his feet and came over to Eric, rubbing his blood-spattered body up against his leg. The loyal bear dog had nearly lost his first battle but had gained invaluable knowledge and experience in the art of combat, which he would remember far into his life.

Soon Shai returned with blood on her jaws. She had pursued the two fleeing Dinocrocuta as they fled from the preliminary attack. They were younger and smaller than the leader who now laid dead just a few feet from the fire. It was unclear to Hope and Eric what events occurred with Shai and the two other Dinocrocuta. They were glad she had returned without significant injury.

"Wow!" exclaimed Eric. "That was close!"

This was their first real battle out on the plain with the two bear dogs as allies.

"It was frightful. I'm glad everyone survived," replied Hope.

"We need to get back to the fire and tend to Amp's and Shai's injuries," Eric said in an anxious tone, the adrenaline still surging through his body.

All four of the Asvaldsson clan returned to the fire. Hope threw more wood on the fire and soon the light from the fire was bright enough to focus on the wounds of the bear dogs. Amp had a gaping wound on his shoulder that Hope gingerly tried to clean out with water.

The giant Bear Dog sat gently by Hope as she cleaned the wound. She would look in the morning for the ingredients to make a poultice to help it heal. Shai had only minor cuts on her jaws and these she easily cleaned.

"Amp will heal up nicely, but he may have a good scar," Hope said as she cleaned the wound as well as she could with the limited resources available.

In the worst-case scenario, Hope would put in stitches, so it could heal properly. She would try an herbal poultice first if she could find the right plants. Animals have a way of healing themselves usually by licking their wounds.

"We're lucky Amp and Shai were here," responded Eric. "We left ourselves vulnerable by camping out in the open. Tomorrow we'll climb up the bluff and see if we can find a better shelter for protection until we can build a permanent home."

Hope threw more firewood on the flames before laying down to sleep. Soon all four of the clan were sleeping in the dawn hours. The excitement was over for now, at least until the next time.

The intense battle drained the energy from all four of them, so they needed the rest. Hope and Eric were both confident the bear dogs would warn them if danger returned so it was with this feeling of security that they both drifted off to sleep.

Hope, the first to wake up the next morning, at once went to tend Amp's wound. The wound, now covered in dried blood, needed cleaning once again. She cleaned it as best as she could and woke up Eric.

"I will take Shai and go look for plants to make a poultice for Amp," she told Eric.

Eric nodded in acknowledgement. He was still tired, but he knew they had to find a safer shelter before nightfall. Even with Amp and Shai, sleeping out in the open was too dangerous, for both them and the bear dogs.

He surveyed the sandstone rims for a route to climb to the top of the bluff. Ideally, the trail would allow Amp and Shai to follow, but this would make the bluff accessible to other predators as well.

What creatures lived on top of the bluff remained unseen, and it would be weeks before Eric and Hope could survey the area and learn the species that thrived there. For all Eric knew, the bluff above could open into a large plain that stretched for miles. The same predators they now confronted below more than likely lived on the bluff above as well.

Hope finally returned with a variety of plants, which she ground up in a small cook pot she had in her backpack. She added water to the ground up plants to make a mixture and then put the pot on the fire. She stirred the healing poultice until it was thick enough to stick to the wound.

She called Amp over and placed the now gooey substance all over and around the deep wound. She tore off a piece of a tee shirt she had in her pack and wrapped it around the shoulder wound. She would apply the poultice every day until the wound healed. The poultice was to help fend off infection. The challenge would be to keep the giant dog from licking the poultice off.

Eric returned from his search for a way up the cliffs and onto the bluff above.

"I think I see a way up."

"Good, then let's pack up camp and head out," she replied as she finished cleaning and dressing Amp's wound.

Once they finished packing up camp and the fire was put out, Hope, Eric, Amp, and Shai headed down the cliff towards the spot where Eric had found access up the steep cliff walls. They traveled a short distance before Eric stopped and pointed up the cliff wall. There were a series of small ledges, like stairs, spaced farther apart running up the wall of the bluff. The problem was that the first step was twenty feet off the ground.

"How are we supposed to reach the first step," asked Hope, who could not see a way to climb up twenty feet.

"I found a small tunnel that we can crawl through and reach the first ledge."

"Will the dogs be able to follow?" Hope inquired.

She would not leave them behind. To Hope, they were part of the family or pack.

"They will follow us once we get them into the tunnel. We'll put them between us, so they have to follow."

Eric entered the small tunnel, pulling himself upward with his arms and legs. He called for Amp and Shai to follow behind him. The two bear dogs, skeptical about the request, cautiously entered the secret tunnel. Hope then followed Shai.

Eric easily crawled up the tunnel out onto the first ledge. Soon Amp, Shai and Hope exited the tunnel, joining Eric on the first ledge. Erosion from eons of water running through sandstone created the tunnel.

The secret tunnel, a perfect security system, isolated the top of the bluff. Large creatures would not try to crawl up the tunnel which left only smaller rodents the ability to come and go from the valley below to the top of the bluff. For added protection and security, Eric would return later and cover up the tunnel opening.

The rest of the climb up the cliff was easier. The next ten ledges were closer together allowing for easier access. The bear dogs leaped up the natural steps with graceful agility and were soon on top of the bluff as Hope and Eric slowly progressed each level.

Hope climbed up on Eric's broad shoulders to gain access to the difficult higher levels. On other levels, she could pull herself up without any help. Eric, being taller, could make the jump up to each level without much effort. He would later return to construct a series of ropes and ladders for easier access from the bluff to the plain below. The plain would be their hunting grounds.

Eric and Hope reached the top of the cliff by mid-day.

A heavily treed plateau, made up of both soft and hardwood tree species, spread out just a few yards from the top of the bluff. The bluff spread out for what Eric estimated to be equivalent to 50 acres. It would take him days to explore the area to predict its true size. The trees were both ferns and hardwoods. From the hardwoods such as maple, beech and oak, Hope and Eric would build a permanent shelter.

Eric and Hope had found a small paradise on top of the bluff and it was time to get to work.

Chapter 22

Life in the Cold

Tak and Maka raced towards the heavily treed forest, hoping the dense vegetation would offer some cover to help outmaneuver the pursuing group of dire wolves. They dodged in and out of the trees, trying to stay out of the sight of the hunting beasts. The dire wolves continued their relentless pursuit. They like modern day wolves could run for hours to bring down their quarry. The two natives could deceive the vision of the pack by zigzagging between the trees, but they could not fool the tracking predators' keen sense of smell.

The wind picked up, continuing to blow in an unfavorable direction for the humans, which guided the huge carnivores directly towards the two fleeing humans. If the wind did not change direction soon, Tak and Maka faced a tough decision; stop and face the menacing pack or climb the nearest tree. The wolves had great stamina, stamina the humans did not have. If it came down to a race, the wolves were certain to win. The natives, using their superior intelligence, would have to somehow outsmart the wily beasts.

The leader of the wolf pack, a grizzled old long in the tooth patriarch, had a large, long scar which ran from just below one of his ears to the tip of his nose. The creature had obviously been in a battle or two in his life, somehow rising to the top position in the pack.

The other two wolves were younger, smaller, and less experienced than the leader. One, grey and white with large canines, looked heavily muscled, while the other one, black and brown with much longer legs, was slimmer in build. Both lesser experienced killers followed the leader of the pack through the tangled maze of trees and overgrown vegetation, all chasing their quarry—the two native Sioux.

The three wolves were out roaming their territory looking for trespassers; displaced intruders trying to move in on the pack's resources, while always searching for any easy opportunity for prey. The wolves were abject opportunists, ones quick to pursue any easy meal.

Tak and Maka unfortunately fit both these categories. They were trespassing not only in the wolves' territory, but in the time as well. They were easy prey if caught out in the open, so they weaved in and out of the trees trying to lose the pursuing pack. The trees were older in this forest, so it was impossible to find a low hanging branch to climb onto to gain access to the higher elevations and reach the safety of the upper canopy. So, they had no choice but to keep running.

Tak motioned for Maka to take the lead. She was an excellent runner, one capable of running for miles, but neither had the speed to lose the dire wolves. Tak kept right on her heels, as he looked over his shoulder. The leader of the pack, with its blazing, greenish yellow eyes transfixed on its mark, was now within 20 yards of the fleeing humans. It would patiently wait and run its quarry to exhaustion before closing in for the kill.

"They're gaining on us. Keep running," Tak shouted to Maka.

"What else can we do?" she yelled back.

Maka ran towards an opening in the trees as Tak gained her side. They were running side by side now, weaving in and out of what cover they could find.

The trees stopped abruptly, opening to a small meadow, covered in short, thick evergreen shrubs and lush willows, which made hiding in them too risky. They were quickly running out of options.

On the far side of the meadow a pointed cliff jutted out from the meadow floor. Maka and Tak were on top of a tall mountain. The drop-off from the cliff plunged for at least 100 feet to the valley floor below. By the time they made it to the cliff and realized this, it was too late.

Tak and Maka spun around to meet the attackers. They brandished their pointed weapons, ready to fight to the death if necessary. Tak had his knife in one hand and a spear in the other. Maka had two spears, both razor sharp from the chert blades attached to the shafts, in her bronze hands. The two Sioux natives let out ancestral screams and shouted in their native tongues—they were not afraid to die.

The leader of the Dire Wolves slowed his pace as he approached his victims. He snarled viciously as he curled his top lip, revealing dark, deteriorated canines. The menacing beast was old, close to reaching the end of his reign, but still wielded a commanding threat.

The two younger wolves from the pack caught up to the old lead wolf but stayed at a further distance from the humans. Their demeanor, one of unfamiliar apprehensiveness, kept them from fully engaging the natives. They seemed inexperienced, unsure of themselves, wary of the strange creatures trapped in front of them. Tak and Maka were alien to them. It was the Pleistocene, when humans did live, but not in this modern form. Pleistocene humans, low in numbers, thinly dispersed, and primitive, had yet to cover many parts of the Earth. It was highly likely that these wolves had never seen a human before in their lifetimes.

Tak and Maka, trapped by the wolves in front of them and the deep gorge that plummeted behind them, had no place left to run. They would have to stand their ground, fighting to the death if needed.

The leader of the wolves stopped in front of them with the two younger members of the pack just behind him. Tak and Maka continued to yell at the looming beast. He snorted out a low, rumbling growl as he glared at Tak.

Tak braced for the attack by raising his spear to meet the oncoming wolf. The other two younger wolves did not attack, they were afraid of the humans. The pack alpha male, his size staggering up close, was just a yard away from Tak and Maka.

Dire wolves had extremely long legs built for the chase which made them giants compared to modern wolves. Even though the leader was old, he was huge compared to modern wolves, wolves' familiar to the natives. It would be difficult to stop the beast without injury or death to one if not both humans.

The cautious beast continued to approach, continuing to growl and stare at Tak and Maka as it paced from side to side. The hair on its back puffed straight up which made the beast much larger in appearance.

The old wolf, now within a couple of feet of the humans, lunged for the final strike. It dove at Tak, who was now standing in front of Maka to accept the charging brute.

Takoda Fire Eagle braced himself to receive the full thrust of the charge, fully realizing his life was but seconds away from ending. The native did not fear death. If it was his time to die, then so be it.

Suddenly out of nowhere, Canowicakte, the forest hunter, dashed in front of him to meet the attacking dire wolf. The young Smilodon cub hit the larger wolf from the side, sending them both to the ground.

The young cat interrupted the attack just long enough to allow Tak to quickly strike the confused dire wolf, forcefully plunging his spear into the neck of the old beast. The dire wolf leader let out a horrid scream that sent the other two inexperienced wolves fleeing for the tree line, where they ran into the forest, never once looking back as they fled.

The old wolf died instantly as Canowicakte plunged her mighty fangs into the throat of the beast for added measure. It was surely the spear that dealt the death blow, but the young cat had saved the humans from potential injury, even death. The ordeal left the two natives shaken, but they soon calmed down and were thankful for the intervention by the big cat.

With the attack over, Tak, Maka, and Canowicakte, headed back home to the safety of the cavern. The Smilodon pet, now part of the native clan, had shown it was loyal and trustworthy.

"I'm sure happy Canowicakte came to our rescue," replied Maka. "I didn't think she would come back when she ran off this morning."

"She needs us as much as we need her," answered Tak.

Until the Smilodon gracilis was full grown, Tak was confident she would stay with them. It was after she reached her full potential as an efficient killer that worried the native. In time, would Canowicakte stay loyal to the natives or strike out on her own?

The three members of the native clan made it back to the cavern just before sundown. Tak opened the shelter door and they all eagerly entered. The door to the shelter was primitive but the size of the opening was small, which caused the humans to crawl on their bellies to gain access. Tak used broken spears and rope to fabricate a primitive door. Next, he would find a boulder to cover the opening to make entry even more difficult for wandering creatures.

Once the doorway was secure, the only exposed entry into the cavern would be from the top opening which let in sun light and moon light. They would construct a net weaved from fibers to attach to this opening to allow in the light and fresh air but deter entry. Maka would set out to find the needed materials the next day.

Tak threw wood on the fire and soon the cave filled with fire light and started to heat up. The nights were getting colder now with the possibility of snow increasing as the barometric pressure decreased. Large storm patterns, dropping feet of icy snow, could move in at any time and last for days at a time, making life for the two Sioux even more difficult.

Soon, all three members of the Native clan were sound asleep. The day had been full of adventure filled with danger, but in the end, they had survived another day in prehistory.

Tak, eager to journey to the lake, got up early the next morning. Maka quickly joined him and they had a small breakfast of dried fish.

"I will go and check our fishing lines this morning," Tak said.

"While you do that, I'll go out and find plant fibers to construct a net to cover the opening in the ceiling of the cavern."

They exited the cavern and Maka and Canowicakte ventured into the forest while Tak headed out onto the plain in the direction of the lake to check the set lines. He paused at the tree line and looked out over the vast plain. There were several small herds of perissodactyls, or early horses, peacefully grazing on the cool, dew dampened grass.

Tak looked at the primitive horses; he needed to figure out a way to catch a couple of them. He was confident he could break them. He had extensive experience with horses, taming many of them, in the modern world. Tak considered himself to be a modern-day native horse whisperer. He attended university on a rodeo scholarship.

Maka and Canowicakte headed into the forest to find a suitable plant to strip into long fibers to construct a net to cover the open crack at the top of the cavern. They journeyed in a new direction, one unexplored to this point.

The trees were thick in this part of the forest, and the terrain was steep. Giant evergreen trees stretched towards the sun while ferns grew wildly covering the forest floor. The vegetation was surprisingly diverse for such a cool climate.

The two walked until they stumbled into a bamboo forest. This was what Maka was looking for. Bamboo fibers, strong and workable, would be perfect for making the net. The stalks, once stripped into fibers and put in direct sunlight until they dried, would make suitable roof netting. Bamboo is a strong, workable material. A net constructed of this material would be strong and offer added security for them while they stayed in the cavern.

Maka cut the bamboo into five-foot sections with Tak's small hand saw then tied the sections together in a large bundle with rope from her backpack. This she threw around her neck with an added piece of rope, which allowed her to keep her hands and arms free to carry her spear.

Maka and Cano, now the pet Smilodons nick name, retraced their steps back to the cavern. The forest was alive with the scurrying of rodents and the songs from several species of birds. Maka spotted three types of woodpeckers as they flew from tree to tree in search of hidden insects, insects just underneath the thin veil of bark covering the taller hardwood tree species. Of course, there were crows, large ones the size of small eagles that scavenged whatever they could find.

Tak crossed the open valley quickly, reaching the lake without incident. He pulled in the first set line which had a large odd-looking fish comparable to a ling on it. It was more eel-like than fish and was about two feet in length. Tak estimated it weighed in at about 20 pounds. It would make good eating. Ling, if cooked right, tasted like lobster.

He then grabbed the second set line and pulled it hard. The line obviously snagged on something, would not budge so he grabbed a piece of dead wood and wrapped the line around the middle of the wood. This gave him extra leverage as he pulled on the line, which suddenly moved, almost causing him to drop the line. He felt a strong tug on the line.

Something loomed large on the other end of the line. Tak continued to pull harder, that fine line between pulling and breaking the line. The lake dweller on the other end would not give up and continued to put up a strong fight.

The struggle went on for close to half an hour until the creature in the lake wore down. Tak could sense he was beginning to win the battle, so he pulled, with ever increasing pressure, while he walked back from the shoreline of the lake.

The unknown creature on the end of the line refused to yield as it tried to make a final surge out into the lake. This unexpected surge caused Tak to stumble and he fell onto the rocks. Luckily, he kept his grip on the chunk of deadwood as he plummeted to the boulder strewn bank.

Tak lumbered to his feet and with one mighty thrust, he pulled on the line as hard as he could. The thing on the other end of the line, worn out by the lengthy struggle, relinquished. Tak wound the line around the deadwood, pulling the fish towards the shoreline.

The played-out fish rolled up onto the lake shore, allowing Tak to see it was a giant salmon of some sorts, one close to nine feet long, with two small fangs hanging down from the front of its upper jaw. The large fish had two beautiful black stripes that ran along both sides of its body.

The lake monster was similar in color to that of a King Salmon: crimson red. It would make great eating and Tak guessed it weighed around 75 pounds. It was the largest fish he had ever caught.

Tak cleaned the giant salmon and buried the entrails in a deep hole by the lake shore. He would use these for bait later. He decided to return to the cavern with his bountiful conquest.

On his journey back to camp, Tak once again met a small herd of primitive horses, ones that resembled the modern-day horse but were a little shorter in height. His goal was to domesticate them, for work, hunting, and travel. Once he conquered the horses, he would be able to bring down larger game like the long-horned Bison that roamed the plains around the camp. The meat would last for months and the skins would make warm clothes and blankets.

Tak continued to walk on the plain as he returned to the cavern. He spotted several ground birds, like pheasants, grouse and prairie chickens, all of which would make great meals. He needed to make a bow and arrow, so he could kill the birds from a distance. This he would work on tomorrow he told himself as he reached the opening to the cavern.

The area around the cavern was quiet and peaceful with only the slight drifting of the smoke from within the cavern detectable from outside. The returning native bent down and crawled into the cavern where he found Maka cooking a meal. Canowicakte, watching with great interest, always hoping for a morsel or two, stood right next to the bronze beauty.

"You have returned," laughed Maka, in a playful tone.

"I caught a giant salmon," Tak answered, then added, "it will make a fine meal for us and Canowicakte can have the leftovers."

Maka looked over at the huge fish and smiled. She was beginning to enjoy life in the wild with Takoda. It was comparable to the life her ancestors lived with limited technology while hunting and gathering for existence. It was cold at times, but overall life was good. If destined to live the rest of their natural lives in this place, Maka, prepared to spend it with Takoda, was content.

Once they finished dinner, all three settled in for another quiet night inside the cavern. The fire warmed up the enclosure nicely.

"Today was a good day. I saw a small herd of horses on my trip to the lake and tomorrow I will start building a corral," Tak said in a confident tone.

"How will we drive them into the corral?"

"It'll take all three of us. You and I will funnel them into the pen once Cano spooks them towards us. Our best opportunity will be when the herd comes into the woods to drink water from the hidden spring."

The plan was far from perfect, but at least it was a plan. The humans needed only one horse to start with. Once trained, Tak could herd more into the corral by horseback.

"I will finish my net tomorrow while you do that."

Maka spent most of the afternoon stripping the bamboo into long thin fibers to construct her net. Once she finished the net, she would place it over the opening at the top of the cavern. The net would give them extra protection and keep entrance from above by wayward creatures to a minimum.

The next morning all three were up with the light of the day. The mornings were cold in this time in the world, but by mid-day, the temperature rose into the fifties. It snowed quite often and quite deep, but the temperature fluctuated daily, allowing the snow to melt quickly.

Tak and Maka did not know what to expect in this world or if it was winter or summer. They had no idea, which made them prepare as if it would get colder. They spent many days collecting and cutting firewood to fuel the cave fire pit. They wanted to be ready for every scenario. They had a good shelter which afforded them great protection and offered warmth from the outdoor elements.

"I wonder where the Extinctos are?" Maka asked while she put on a heavy layer of clothing before going outside into the cold morning.

It had been months since they left in search of soldiers and abandoned them in the Pleistocene Epoch.

"I don't know... but we must prepare ourselves for the possibility they don't come back at all," replied Tak in a gloomy tone.

He missed his good friend Eric.

Tak removed the door and all three slipped out of the cavern. Tak went into the forest to find the materials needed to build a primitive corral. He could re-enforce it later. He focused on the smaller trees, ones only a few years old and six inches in diameter. These would make good rails for the corral. For the posts, he gathered larger trees. The arduous task took all day.

Maka finished her net and climbed to the top of the outcrop to place it over the opening at the top of the shelter. She pounded small stakes into several fissures on top of the outcrop.

This secured the net from blowing off in the wind. She lined the outer edges of the net with large rocks to help keep it from blowing off during a severe storm.

Takoda spent several weeks constructing the corral. In the end, it was primitive, but he was sure it would hold horses. He would fine tune it later by placing rock walls around it to help keep predators at bay. Once Tak felt confident the structure would hold, it was time to capture some horses.

Tak monitored the herds' migratory habits for weeks to learn their patterns of movement. Every two to three days they entered the forest to access the natural spring to drink the life sustaining liquid. The primitive horses, like clockwork, journeyed to the spring early in the morning after the mighty predators of the night returned to sleep during the day. Tak felt this gave them the best opportunity for capture.

Tak, Maka, and Cano positioned themselves early one morning to try the first capture. They heard the herd pass by on their way to the spring early that morning and quickly ran to get into position. Capture would take a coordinated effort by all three of the native clan.

Tak positioned himself on one side of the corral while he motioned for Maka to take Cano close to the tree line on the other. When the herd came back through, Maka and Cano would rush from the trees and drive the herd towards Tak. Tak would then reveal himself and try to break up the wild band of horses, driving them in all directions. If all worked as planned, they would have a horse that day.

Everyone waited in position until the familiar sound of hoofs pounding the ground began to echo through the trees. The herd was on the move, heading back towards the plain to graze.

The leader, a strong, magnificent beast with a slender build, was comparable to a modern-day Zebra in size but had thicker hair for warmth to survive the brutal winters. It was tan with a black mane and was obviously the herd stallion. Behind him was a group of six other adult horses and two yearlings. These were the ones Tak wanted to catch. The stallion would be much too difficult to tame.

The herd approached from the forest trail. Tak motioned to Maka to unleash Canowicakte. The mighty Smilodon gracilis surprised the herd as it exited the tree line with a quick burst of speed.

The stallion bellowed out a loud warning cry which drove the remaining members of the herd into instantaneous panic. Some turned running back into the trees, while others sped up and galloped for the flat plain. The scene resembled unorganized chaos with moments of unbridled panic echoed by frantic cries and pounding hoof beats.

The stallion, trying to intimidate the young cat, ran straight at Canowicakte. The frenzied primitive horse kicked madly, thrusting skull shattering kicks into the open air. The distraction by the Smilodon was just enough to occupy the stallion, which gave Tak the opportunity to jump into action.

The horses, running for the plain, met the unnerving sight of the Native American waving his arms in the air and screaming at the top of his lungs. Two members of the frenzied herd veered to the left and directly towards the corral. The remaining members of the herd ran straight at Tak, causing the surprised native to dive out of the way of the enraged horde.

Tak quickly re-gained his footing and sprinted after the two horses heading for the corral. To boost the confusion, he screamed as he ran after them. His strange war cries filled the morning air.

This ploy worked perfectly. The two panicked horses headed directly towards the opening in the corral, their loud bellows echoing in the still, morning air as the heated steam from their laboring, deep breaths floated up to the sky.

Before realizing the trap, the horses entered the pen and Tak, now right behind them, slammed the gate shut.

The time traveling natives were now the proud owners of two horses.

Chapter 23

On the Run

CeCe and the dominant terror crane plunged to the ground resulting in a ginormous thud. CeCe landed squarely on the giant bird's neck, causing the fragile bones to emit a loud crack. The weight of the big man instantly killed the leader of the crane pack—its lifeless body now lay motionless on the forest floor.

CeCe rolled over the dead crane, jumped to his feet, and turned to meet the other members of the bird horde. The three remaining cranes, stunned by the outcome of the attack, appeared bewildered by the unbridled confusion brought on by the stillness of their once fierce leader. Fortunately, for CeCe, the remaining cranes were young, lacking experience in the art of killing. CeCe yelled at the befuddled cranes in his loud booming voice as he rushed towards them swinging his spear back and forth to baffle and threaten the young cranes even more.

To further create the illusion of a united front, Lexa, safe in the tree, screamed as loud as she could. This tactic helped perplex the younger birds as they squawked back and forth at one another, waiting to see which one would take the lead.

CeCe knelt and picked up a large rock to throw at the largest remaining crane. He hurled the rock striking the panicked flightless bird in the breast, which knocked the creature to the ground. The two remaining cranes, terrified by the attack, turned and fled back into the forest, where the two humans could hear their continued squawking until they finally left the area.

CeCe grabbed his knife from his belt, rushed over to the fallen crane, still stunned by the blow from the rock, and thrust himself upon the flailing beast before it could regain its feet. His momentum flattened the non-avian menace to the ground. With one quick motion, he ran his sharp blade through the fallen cranes main artery in the neck killing the giant bird instantly. CeCe and Lexa had survived the attack by the terror cranes.

Lexa climbed down from the safety of the tree and asked, "Are you all right CeCe?"

"I'm ok. Just a little shaken," answered the big African American, ephemerally overwhelmed with adrenalin.

CeCe momentarily turned to vomit; the encounter had been his second close brush with death since entering Extinctus.

Lexa turned to CeCe and put her arm around him, trying to console him. The big man dropped to his knees as the adrenaline left his body, leaving him shaking.

"Have a drink of water," Lexa said as she handed him her water bottle.

"Thanks," is all CeCe said.

He took a long drink from the water bottle then washed out his mouth.

"We should head back to our camp. We need to keep moving to avoid being re-captured by Therio and Odon," CeCe said as he started to overcome the trauma of the attack.

The two Dark Extinctos, the newly adopted name given to them by Lexa, were nowhere in sight. The humans contemplated why the two horrid beasts Therio and Odon ran off leaving them to the mercy of the terror cranes. Did Therio and Odon, once they realized Eric was not with them, decide it would be easier to just leave the weak humans to the mercy of this violent world? They did not need the fragile humans anymore, so what better way to get rid of them than letting the cruel world of the Paleocene Epoch deal with them.

CeCe and Lexa headed back to their camp. If Odon and Therio truly left them for dead, their bamboo house would be safe for a while longer. Surely, Bronto, Pith, and Gorgo would return to lead them out of this wilderness, which was the original plan, but months had passed since they last saw the Extinctos, who had left them to the mercy of the primitive beasts of this world.

The humans wondered what was taking the Extinctos so long to return. Were the three Extinctos killed while traveling throughout Extinctus looking for soldiers to aide Megalo in the battle to save the human species?

The two humans needed to move on and prepare for life in this hostile world, a life where they could be all alone. They could not rely on the Extinctos returning. They were merely an inconvenience to them. It was Eric who played the key role; he was the important one to the Extinctos. Keeping Eric alive and protected was the main goal of Megalo and the Extinctos.

CeCe and Lexa fully realized this, and at times became bitter towards their friend, until eventually, they would return to their senses and realize it was not Eric's fault; he was but a pawn in the overall game playing out in Extinctus. They were merely expendable after thoughts, brought to Extinctus as side notes.

Lexa and CeCe reached the bamboo shelter just as night set in. They built a small fire and cooked the fish they caught earlier that morning before the Dark Extinctos interrupted their fishing. The large salmon-like fish was still laying were it fell earlier that day. It was good eating and soon CeCe and Lexa were full. The day, full of turmoil and struggle against the terror cranes, left them famished and exhausted.

They quickly fell asleep, drifting into a deep sleep. They dreamt of life back home in their world—the carefree days of school, endless fun, and no responsibilities. That life, which now seemed long ago, was completely opposite of this life, a life of tremendous danger filled with daily life-threatening turmoil. Life here was for mere existence with the chance of daily catastrophic injury or death.

The next morning, they awoke with a new refreshed attitude. The sleep had done wonders at rejuvenating their mind set. Just in case Therio and Odon were still hunting them, it was time to move on. It was safer to keep distance between themselves and the Dark Extinctos. CeCe and Lexa had no idea if the two horrid beasts would return to recapture or finish them off, but they could not take any chances. It was time to move on and explore their new world.

They packed up their belongings, anything they could carry, and each took two bamboo spears with them for protection. They decided to travel for days, to leave the bamboo structure well behind them and journey in search of a new land far away from the forest where they first entered the Paleocene Epoch.

They journeyed east, toward the rising sun. The humans were fortunate to have a warm, humid climate, one that was tropical, rainy, and pleasant during this period on Earth. Cold would never be an issue if they stayed in the Paleocene.

A spot near the ocean would be ideal, but they had no idea what direction the ocean was or if the ocean existed here. All they could do was search for it and hopefully accidentally stumble upon it. CeCe and Lexa assumed the oceans still existed, but they could only guess in what direction. They knew the sun came up from the East, so they headed in that direction. What continent they were on was another mystery. Where they in North America, the continent they had vanished from, or somewhere else? They had no idea.

They traveled for a good part of the day moving through the thick rain forest. The only trails that ran through the forest were ones trampled by countless beasts as they moved in and out of one forest and into the next forest. Danger lurked around every bend in the trail.

On several occasions, CeCe and Lexa left the trail to hide in the thick vegetation, away from marauding beasts. It seemed the main predators in this world were the terror birds and various sized Creodonts. It would be another 20 million years before the modern carnivores would rise to rule Earth.

In this world, the Creodonts, were at the top of the food chain. This played into the human's favor as Creodonts were slower in speed and lacked the intelligence of the modern carnivores. They were still extremely dangerous beasts, capable of ambushing unsuspecting prey, and could easily kill an insignificant human. Numerous Creodonts grew to tremendous size; some of which were the largest land carnivores in the history of the Earth. Creodonts could still outrun a human and many had greater stamina, so it was best to avoid contact with them.

CeCe and Lexa traveled quietly through the forest, constantly on the alert for any sounds. They heard the common noises of singing birds and the relentless buzzing from the millions of insects that thrived in the endless tropical warmth. The insect repellant was priceless. Without it, the insects would have made life unbearable.

They stopped, always before dusk, to look for the safest places to hide during the dangerous night, nights filled with dreadful hunting beasts. Sometimes they nested in the trees, which offered sanctuary from the hunting creatures of the night, and at other times they found a cave to hide in for the night.

They kept traveling east, always beginning the day early and traveling in the direction of the sun. CeCe and Lexa faced many dangers along the way, but luckily each time danger befell them, they hid, escaping detection.

Days turned into weeks as they sought the ocean. The two Dark Extinctos, Therio and Odon, did not show themselves so as the weeks passed, both CeCe and Lexa felt less fearful of their return. The humans surmised the two terrifying creatures left them to die in the hostile world of the Paleocene.

After traveling a great distance from the now forgotten bamboo structure, CeCe and Lexa decided it was time to ease up on the grueling pace, one designed to out distance the two monstrous beasts, so they decided the next suitable, isolated location would be a permanent one; permanent at least long enough for them to make more weapons and stock up on meat.

In the distance, they could see a large bluff that rose above the forest floor. The trees were thinning which allowed sunlight to reach the floor of the Earth. It was the first time in weeks Lexa and CeCe could see more than 50 yards in front of them. It was a pleasant change from the thick under vegetation which lined the lower reaches of the forest.

In some places, grass was slowly beginning to appear. It would be millions of years before grasses populated the planet, creating vast plains. For now, it was a relief to walk without fighting the thick brush back to gain passage.

The humans continued, trying to reach the bluff before nightfall. Once darkness fell it would be too dangerous for them to stay out in the open. Nighttime was one danger all the humans faced in the world of Extinctus.

Lexa and CeCe, in an increased effort to reach the rocks around the bluff before the light faded, picked up the pace. At least in the boulders, they could hide for the night out of sight.

"We need to reach those boulders before dusk," Lexa spoke with distinct urgency in her voice.

The Latino beauty was completely aware of the dangerous consequences, consequences which included death, from the stealthy hunters of the night; the lurking, killing beasts, camouflaged by the blackness of the night before the moon light appeared, ending the total darkness.

"I agree," answered CeCe as he increased his speed to a jog. "I figure we have about two hours to reach the rocks."

Lexa passed CeCe and started to increase the pace. She knew CeCe would not move fast enough unless she took the lead and pushed him. He was a large man and needed added motivation.

CeCe unwittingly followed Lexa as she continued to speed up the pace. It was vital they reach the safety of the bluff before nightfall.

A warm breeze started to blow towards them. It would keep their scent from reaching the nostrils of predators ahead of them but give them away to hunters coming from behind. They kept up the increased pace, making it to the first rocks just before dusk.

The large rocks, scattered as if dropped from the sky by the art gods, littered the base of the cliff. Thousands of years of erosion had caused larger boulders to splinter off and tumble from the long ridge above. This created a vast number of hiding places for the many creatures over the countless millennium. Lexa and CeCe were ecstatic to reach the boulders before nightfall.

The two travelers searched the area around the cliff until finding a ledge that was 15 feet off the ground. From the ledge, they could see the top of the bluff towering above them. Trees lined the top of the bluff, which suggested another forest started on top of the cliff.

The ledge was barely large enough for CeCe and Lexa to fully stretch out on, but both humans, exhausted from the series of events of the day, fell fast asleep within minutes. They escaped the clutches of the Dark Extinctos and eluded certain death from the terror cranes, but now they were homeless and on the run.

The night was excessively dark, without the presence of the moon. Lexa woke up to the sound of a strange noise coming from below the ledge. It was a low growling sound. She nudged CeCe from his deep sleep.

"Do you hear that low groaning sound?" she asked.

The annoying sound lasted for a moment then stopped, only to start again a couple of minutes later.

"I do hear it. What could it be?" moaned CeCe. "Is there ever any piece of mind in this place? Can we ever get a break?"

CeCe and Lexa strained to see in the darkness, but neither could see without the light of the moon. They decided to concentrate on the direction of the sound, hoping to figure out where the sound originated from. The sound continued from directly below them in the boulders.

Some unseen creature, sneaking around the rocks below searching for a meal, created the nerve-racking sound that alarmed the humans.

CeCe picked up a small rock and tossed it down from the ledge. The small creature quickly scampered towards the sound of the rock as it crashed off a boulder. CeCe picked up another rock and threw it as far as he could in the other direction to lure the nighttime nuisance away. The nocturnal beast scurried off in that direction and the sound stopped altogether.

After an hour or so, Lexa and CeCe were fast asleep once more.

It started to rain early the next morning, which interrupted the fitful sleep of the humans. CeCe and Lexa woke up to a wet and humid morning.

The clouds, hanging incredibly low in the morning sky, just slightly above the bluff, created an atmospheric vision of gloom, one heightened by the dampness of a drizzling rain. The bluff cliffs, soaked by the early rain, presented a safety hazard for Lexa and CeCe, who had little choice but to wait out the storm.

Luckily, both had a rain jacket, the type that rolls up into a ball and fits in a tiny bag, in their packs. One again the wherewithal of Megalo paid off. Fortunately, they found themselves in a time when the weather was hot, and rain was a relief from the heat for most species.

About mid-day the weather broke, the clouds giving way to the sun, allowing the blue sky to appear. Within less than an hour, the rocks were dry once more, so CeCe and Lexa decided to navigate the bluff.

The climb was arduous and took hours as they cautiously and meticulously climbed from one crevice to the next. Both had some experience in rock climbing from attending extracurricular activities in college—now this knowledge was paying off.

Lexa being much smaller in frame, had little trouble moving up the bluff, but for CeCe, who was a giant man, the climb was much more strenuous. CeCe persisted, never giving up, and soon both he and Lexa reached the top of the bluff.

From on top of the cloud concealed bluff, CeCe and Lexa looked down onto the treed valley, the one they had navigated just days before. The towering bluff allowed the humans a great vantage point to spot the Dark Extinctos if they were still pursuing them. Deep down both Lexa and CeCe knew they would see the menacing Therio and Odon again someday.

For now, all they could do was stay hidden for as long as possible until Bronto, Pith, and Gorgo returned to find them. It had been months since the three Extinctos left them isolated and alone in this primitive land before the time of humans. If they returned, Lexa was intent on giving them a piece of her mind.

CeCe and Lexa turned to survey the area stretching out from the top of the bluff. A dense forest, not very deep, stretched along the top of the bluff. As they walked into the trees, the heavy clouds rolled out over the valley, opening the bluff up to the deep, blue sky.

After 200 yards the tree line stopped, giving way to a large flat plain which abruptly ended a mile later. The humans could not see beyond the open plain, so they decided to venture in that direction. The sun appeared, quickly heating the areas not cooled by the protective shade.

Lexa and CeCe surveyed the area for danger, looking in both directions. After not spotting any living creature within eyesight, they moved out onto the open plain.

The forest behind them teemed with singing birds, often muffled by primitive screams, so both humans were eager to leave it behind and head for the far side of the bluff. The dangers of the forest, more hidden and unexpected, directly contrasted with the dangers of the plain. On the plain, danger, usually visible, gave the humans time to react by running away from the threat or climbing a tree to avoid it all together. Both the forest and the plain caused unique challenges for the two humans.

Lexa took the lead, at once breaking into a run. CeCe had no choice but to follow.

"We should make it to the far side of the plain as fast as possible," she yelled back at CeCe.

Lexa wanted to see what was below the bluff.

"You just keep running and I'll keep up."

Lexa continued to set the pace while CeCe followed. The plain stretched out for just over a mile and within ten minutes they were nearing the end. The land gently slanted downhill and then abruptly ended. Lexa eased the pace stopping just shy of the edge of the bluff. CeCe shortly reached her and stopped as well.

"There it is! We made it to the ocean," Lexa cried out, as she pointed to the endless sea.

CeCe stopped to catch his breath while looking out at the immense body of water.

"It does exist," he shouted and then jokingly said, "I wonder what monstrous beasts live in it?"

"I'm sure many that would like to eat us," Lexa answered back, with a small grin on her face.

"What do we do now?" questioned CeCe, temporarily winded by the mile run.

They stood on top of a tall ridge, one that jutted out from the Earth on both sides. On one side was the valley of trees, where they had come from, and on the other side was the ocean. They found themselves in the safest place in the area, on top of an isolated bluff. If this mass of land elevated on both ends as well as the sides, then the bluff would be isolated, allowing only creatures that could fly or were agile enough to climb up the walls of the bluff to reach the top. It could be the safest place for them they thought.

"I think we should stay up here on the ridge. It could be safer with fewer predators," Lexa said.

"I agree, but we should go back to the forest to build a good shelter. The trees will give us better protection from the weather and predators. We can find a way down to the ocean another time."

Lexa and CeCe, now feeling more relaxed by the isolation of the bluff, returned to the forest on the other side of the bluff. The day was getting late, so they decided to climb into the trees and make a temporary nest for the night.

Both humans fell to cutting branches covered in lush leaves. These they interwove to create a safe and sturdy sleeping nub. The temporary structure would suffice for at least one night, or until they could construct a permanent home.

They had a small fillet of the salmon left so they divided it equally and washed it down with a long drink of warm water. It was time to settle in for the night.

CeCe dejectedly said, "I just can't understand what's happened to us. One minute we were camping, having a nice time, and the next we're fighting daily for our lives."

"It's undeniably unbelievable," answered Lexa. "What a story we'll have to tell if we survive."

"You said it...if we survive."

Lexa looked at CeCe, laughed, and jokingly said, "They'll probably lock us up, thinking we're crazy, if we tell our story to anyone."

CeCe nodded in agreement. The two talked for many hours into the night. It was the first time they felt comfortable enough to talk about the strange predicament they were in and openly discuss each other's fears. Somehow the seclusion of the bluff offered them a new peace of mind, one they had not yet experienced while trapped in the world of Extinctus. It was the first time they felt they could survive if abandoned to live in this world, the world 55 million years before their own.

The night was quiet for the first time they could remember since entering Extinctus, and soon both were sound asleep high up in the canopy of the trees.

Chapter 24

Give Me Shelter

The time had come for Eric and Hope to build a permanent home on top of the bluff that overlooked the vast plain below the sandstone cliffs. From the vantage point of the bluff, they could see the roaming herds of ungulates, solitary predators, and approaching danger, both human and beast, way before they reached the cliff walls below the bluff. This early warning detection system allowed them ample time to assess the oncoming danger, deciding to stay and fight or to flee from the impending threat.

It would take weeks, even months, for the humans to fully map out the environment on top of the bluff and to be completely sure if their new home remained isolated from the valleys below. They still needed to explore the far side of the outcrop to see what type of landscape ran below the other side of their future home. They were not certain if the ends of the bluff blocked roaming creatures from accessing the bluff top sanctuary either. Did these natural barriers flow down to the lower elevations or did they drastically drop off to the valley floor?

Eric and Hope would search in all directions to see where the bluff went and ended, but first they needed to build shelter. What type of shelter would be step one?

"Should we build a stick structure or build one in a tree?" asked Hope.

The fragile white humans were a long way from the small cave, their first shelter in the Miocene Epoch, after Creo, Aves, and Arti left them alone to survive in the harsh prehistoric world—a world full of capable predators and extreme elements—15 million years ago.

"There are advantages to both," Eric replied.

Eric leaned towards a permanent structure made like a log cabin. They had Amp and Shai for protection if attacked, so a place on the ground was plausible.

They decided to build a permanent structure, one that would afford security from predators, shelter from the elements, and most importantly peace of mind. Finding the materials for construction would be the most difficult part.

Eric's backpack bore only a hand axe and a medium sized saw; the only tools available to cut and shape the poles for the structure. If they could somehow find trees already downed by a storm or micro-burst, he could strip the bark with his saw. The trees needed to be big enough in girth to deliver strength and protect them from wandering Creodonts. The huge ungulates, if left unprovoked, did not concern Eric; it was the carnivores he feared.

To this point, Eric and Hope had yet to come across any sign of an early primate species, either ape or hominid, further supporting the notion they were truly still in North America; it would be millions of years until either of these species arrived on the scene in this part of the world.

Eric knew, if they were not in North America, the probability of an encounter with early humans was inevitable, and they would have to deal with that threat eventually. Amp and Shai would be pivotal in frightening off any attack by ape or early man if that day ever arrived.

The white skinned natives left to survey their unfamiliar territory. They searched for smaller, downed trees, ones still green, recently knocked over by the wind or by random storm. They would be heavier than dried out trees, but they would offer better overall strength.

The search for the necessary materials took several days to complete. They wanted to build their new home close the edge of the bluff, so they could look down upon the vast plain below. They wanted to see below the bluff from their shelter, but they did not want the shelter visible from below—the trees needed to camouflage it.

Hope and Eric chose to build the new shelter in a small opening which ran behind a row of trees, behind the tree line, which ran across the top of the bluff. The spot was in the open more than Eric would have liked, but since it was behind the trees, it was marginally visible from down below.

Several medium sized trees, mostly maple, scattered close to the building location, made up the bulk of the building material. Maple, due to its superior hardness, would give the shelter a solid outer shell, virtually impenetrable by predators. In addition, the building spot was close to the steps Eric built weeks earlier to allow access to the vast hunting plain below.

Hope and Eric started to pull the downed trees into the meadow to prepare them to the correct length. They tied Amp and Shai up to the larger trees, using them to help drag them to the area of the new shelter. It took days to obtain the needed material to build the new shelter.

Once the Asvald clan transported the maple trees to the building location, Eric and Hope began the lengthy process of removing the branches, which they saved to later help insulate the roof.

They decided to leave the bark intact just in case the Super Extinctos arrived to rescue them from the Miocene Epoch. Stripping the logs would take a considerable amount of time and energy—energy best kept for hunting. The area seemed safe, but that could change at any moment. The Extinctos Creo, Aves, and Arti could return for them any day.

The days turned into weeks as they slowly constructed their new home. Eric and Hope dug long, narrow trenches in the shape of a square and placed the bottom of the logs into this trench. After the tall tree trunks steadfastly lined the trench, they tied the tops of the poles together with fibers to hold the logs firmly together.

Next, the white humans filled in the trench with wet mud after they finished placing the logs into the trench and tying them together. Once dried, the mud held the base of the shelter together like cement.

The task of building their new permanent home was particularly challenging, especially placing the upper logs for the roof to the needed height. Eric devised a rudimentary pulley system to raise the logs to the top of the house, but it still took great strength, and the help of the bear dogs, to pull the logs up to the needed height.

To build the roof, Eric and Hope used smaller maple logs, running them parallel across the width of the cabin. They applied heavy foliage, thatched together with vines, to form a thick, waterproof barrier, which covered the entire roof, keeping the inside of the cabin warm and dry.

It took months to finish the construction, but in the end, they had a secure and dry home. Eric built a magnificent rock fireplace which lined one of the inside walls of the cabin, running through the roof, channeling the smoke from the burning wood fire pit to the open outdoor air. It allowed them to cook in the cabin and gave warmth when needed.

Eric and Hope prepared for any type of weather. They knew they were in the Miocene Epoch which spanned from 23 million to 5.5 million years from their time. Eric guessed they were in the later part of the Miocene. This he could tell by the reduction of the forests and the emergence of grasses.

Towards the end of the Miocene, the Earth, turning arid and mountainous, transformed the environmental landscape and altered the evolutionary direction of many species. The grazing species dominated the new open landscape and with their population explosion, the predators thrived as well.

Eric and Hope, learning to adapt to their new world, studied the migration patterns of the large herds. Someday, this would pay off for them when it was time to hunt for meat.

Amp and Shai, now almost full grown, exemplified early evolutionary perfection. Amp topped the scale at around 1200 pounds with a length of 9 feet while the smaller Shai was over 1000 pounds. They were beautiful specimens of the species Amphicyon galushai.

The bear dogs spent more time away from Hope and Eric now, becoming more independent as they staked out their own territory. Protecting the bluff from unwanted intruders, a continual job, took the bear dogs away from the humans on a weekly basis but they always returned home to their loyal masters.

Amp and Shai were wild creatures but for some mysterious reason, they still thought they belonged to the Asvald pack; so, the two giants came and went on a steady, regular basis. When Eric or Hope went out to search for food or to explore the region, one of the bear dogs always arrived to protect their masters from marauding predators.

The months slowly clicked by as Eric and Hope, living alone in the cabin, continued to build on their cabin and fortify the surrounding area around the home. Now alone in Extinctus for over six months, the humans often wondered about their missing friends. They wondered if time was still moving in the real world. Would they eventually return to the modern world only hours from when they vanished, or would it be a parallel time span? They had no idea of how time worked in the world of Extinctus.

Eric and Hope went about their daily life which consisted of finding food, water, and exploration. They were both in great physical shape, brought on by the struggle to survive. They developed a close bond as they lived now as a couple. They genuinely loved each other and would gladly give their life for each other.

High up on the bluff, they overlooked the vast plain below. They studied the migration patterns of the large herds of ungulates as they moved across the plain to and from the forest. Food was very abundant in their new land.

Eric spent the long nights constructing spears which he tipped with obsidian projectile points. The humans found a small open mine pit of the highly prized material while exploring the area to the East of the cabin. From this material, Eric fashioned very sharp knives and tips for the end of his arrows. He perfected the art of bow making, spending many hours in the safety of the cabin refining the process. He made long distance bows and shorter-range bows. These allowed him to bring down varying species of grazers.

Both Eric and Hope were extremely successful in bringing down the smaller creatures like Merycodes, a small pronghorn-like animal, and the Cranioceras, a slightly larger pronghorn creature that had three tall pronged horns, two of which came back towards the creature's head and the third horn that was longer and jutted out in the opposite direction. It reminded Eric of a sling shot.

Eric found it easy to bring down these smaller creatures, but it was the larger ones that eluded him. He realized to fashion stronger weapons and insulate the cabin better, he would need the much thicker hides from the elephant-like Platybelodon or "shovel tusker" and the massive Paraceraterium, a rhinocerotidae rhino, the largest ever land mammal. Just one hide from one of these behemoths, would supply them with all the needed materials for making clothes and blankets. Killing one of these giant beasts would feed them and the bear dogs for months if stored properly. These giants were what the old-world hunter set his sights on.

The vast plain below the bluff teemed with life. The struggle for life and death waged on daily. It had been 60 million years since the dinosaurs vanished, creating an explosion in biodiversity. The Miocene was a time of evolutionary experimentation that saw the rise and fall of thousands of species.

Towards the end of the Miocene the world started to cool down causing trees to give way to grass land. The animals that adapted to the cooler climate and the grassy vegetation thrived while creatures suited for the warmer climate, soft fruits, and ambush tactics perished.

Eric continued to hone his weapon building skills, often returning to collect obsidian from the large cache of the rare mineral hidden in a secluded mine in the general vicinity. The perfection of the spear is what he needed if he wanted to bring down the larger game. The bow was good for killing smaller creatures and wounding a larger beast, but it would be the thrust of the spear that would give the death blow to the giant ungulates.

Eric knew he would need the help of Hope, Amp, and Shai to hunt the imposing larger creatures that inhabited the valley floor. The two bear dogs would distract the beast while Hope kept an eye out for intruding predators. To try such a feat just months earlier would have been out of the question. Now it seemed like a natural progression.

High up on the bluff overlooking the vast plain, life continued virtually uninterrupted for what seemed ages. The occasional roaming predator would visit the area but leave quickly once it realized it was trespassing on Amp and Shai's territory. The two, now fully-grown bear dogs, patrolled their home territory vigorously. They would disappear for sometimes up to a week, leaving Eric and Hope wondering where they went for so long a period.

The top of the bluff formed only a small part of the human's territory. Compared to below and beyond the bluff, the top of the bluff was small in overall area. Eric and Hope knew what creatures lived below the bluff close to the cabin, but they had yet to fully explore the land beyond the far side of the bluff.

Hope and Eric primarily hunted on top of the bluff or below on the plains from which they had originally journeyed from. To this point, there was no need to venture further for food. In the end, it would be curiosity more than necessity that drove the humans to explore the unknown land on the other side of the bluff.

It was a colder, rainy morning when Eric decided the group should travel to what he now referred to as the new land. He considered himself a new world explorer, now understanding how Christopher Columbus must have felt as he set out to explore the new world.

"I think we should travel to the far side of the bluff and possibly below," Eric told Hope as he dressed inside the warm cabin.

"Why? It could be dangerous and besides, we have everything we need now," Hope answered.

Hope didn't understand the need to leave the safety of the bluff and risk injury or death. What more could they need?

"We have everything we need here."

"I know, but it would be nice to see what access is possible from that side of the bluff."

Eric was interested in the security of the bluff too, but he really wanted to see what was beyond the rim of the far side of the bluff.

"If you think it's necessary, then I'll pack some food and water for the trip."

She had given up trying to sway Eric's mind. She would humor him and go along. Besides, they had Amp and Shai for protection.

It was mid-morning before they finished packing and were ready to leave the warm, dry cabin to set out on the journey to the other side of the bluff. The two bear dogs were eager to leave. They paced back and forth, waiting for their human masters to utter the words, go!

Eric and Hope put on their now tattered rain jackets to keep them dry on the journey. Soon they would need to fashion their own clothes from the various animal skins they had collected and dried out. Their human clothes were beginning to show signs of extreme wear. Fortunately, the back packs were still in decent shape. They put these on and headed outside to explore.

Amp and Shai bounced out front and soon disappeared. The bear dogs were extremely fast and could cover great distances quickly, but they always returned to check on Eric and Hope. Once assured the humans were safe, they would dash off ahead once again. They performed this over and over as the band moved closer to the far side of the bluff.

It took close to 3 hours for the group to reach the edge of the bluff, where the trees ended at the bluff's edge. Far below, on the valley floor, a large, wide river flowed horizontally across the plain. The valley teemed with life.

The rolling plain stretched for miles, populated by a massive forest of trees, one that outnumbered the trees on the plain below the cabin by two to one. This side of the bluff had its own unique climate. It was cloudy and raining when Eric and Hope left their side of the bluff, but on this side of the bluff it was sunny and warmer. It was as if each side of the land mass embodied two uniquely different worlds.

Hope and Eric peered over the edge of the bluff and spotted several large herds of ungulates. One of the hidden gems in Eric's pack was a pair of binoculars, which he readily wielded to survey the valley below.

There were herds of Merychippus, a pony-sized horse, Synthetoceras, a deer sized creature with a Y shaped horn, Miotapirus, an early ancestor to modern tapirs, and many other unique beasts of the time, all grazing in large herds in the region below the bluff.

There were other creatures too. Eric and Hope could pick out several predators. Eric spotted a pack of the hyaena-like Osteoborus, a horrific scavenging beast with bone crushing jaws. There were three of them traveling up one side of the river searching for a dead carcass or any unsuspecting victim that they could ambush and quickly dispatch.

Down on the opposite end of the valley, Eric spotted a more menacing threat. It was a large pack of Daphoenodon, the largest canid of the time. These were exceptionally large dog-like creatures, even larger than Amp and Shai. They would be a danger to not only the humans, but the bear dogs as well.

The two pack hunting carnivores, Osteoborus and Daphoenodon, were species best avoided.

"It's quite dangerous down there. This valley with the river is full of life and danger. We shouldn't venture down there yet," Eric simply said.

"I'm good with that; I feel safer up here. No need to take any unneeded chances."

Osteoborus and Daphoenodon were only two potential threats to the humans. This time span offered many other predators; like Dinictis, a lone cat-like hunter the size of a modern mountain lion, and Megalictis, a solitary creature like the wolverine but the size of a black bear. Both would be hidden threats, more likely to ambush the humans.

Eric was confident Amp and Shai would deter either of these two creatures from attacking them if they had the misfortune of running into one. These were only a few of the frightening beasts of the time and many more lurked in the darkness eager to strike. It was best for Eric and Hope to stay on top of the bluff, a secluded sanctuary from the callous world below.

"Let's turn around and head home," replied Eric, who had seen enough of the valley of the river, as he now called it.

The humans would only venture to the valley of the river out of absolute necessity. It teemed with life, life threatened by continual death, compared to the plains below the cabin. It was stunningly amazing to see the contrast.

"I think that would be best," answered Hope, who after seeing the many predators roaming the valley of the river, never wanted to venture into it.

Hope was content to stay on the bluff for as long as it took the Extinctos to return. She knew eventually they would have to return for Eric. He was the link to this whole nightmare.

Eric and Hope along with the two bear dogs turned back towards the cabin. It was nice to know what laid beyond the bluff in the other direction, but it was also very frightening. The threat of death loomed much larger in the valley of the river than on the plain below the cabin.

For now, Eric and Hope would hunt below the cabin or on the top of the bluff, which offered many smaller game species. There was Lepus the modern rabbit that evolved around this time, and Epigaulus, a two-horned gopher that populated the area. There were squirrel-like animals in trees that occasionally ventured to the ground. These offered small meals, but the humans needed the larger beasts for skins to fashion clothes and blankets from, and to supply an abundance of meat for them and the two bear dogs.

Eric and Hope were confident Amp and Shai could support themselves, but it would be nice if they could feed them to keep them closer to the cabin for protection.

"We need to kill larger prey," Eric said as they traveled back to the cabin.

"What kind of animal should we hunt next?" Hope asked.

She realized the need but worried about the dangers involved in taking down a large ungulate.

"A mid-sized ungulate will do."

Eric was not ready to take on a Platybelodon or Paraceraterium yet. These two giants posed too much a danger to all involved. An injury to himself or Hope could mean imminent death without modern medicine.

"What about one of those larger deer-like creatures we saw on the journey before we found the bluff?" Hope offered as she looked at her handsome partner.

She thought one of these would give them a good cache of meat and a larger skin to work with. From the skin she could fashion clothes to replace their worn–out clothing from the real world.

"That's a promising idea. Synthetoceras or Cranioceras will be our first choice... but we may find some other beast during our hunt to harvest."

The group returned to the cabin. Eric was relieved to know what was beyond the cabin on the far side of the bluff. It strengthened his conception that the bluff, secluded and isolated, offered a great deal of security from the beasts that dwelled in the area. He could not have hoped for a more secure environment for himself, Hope, Amp, and Shai.

The Asvald clan settled in for a comfortable night in the security of the cabin. Tomorrow they would venture down to the plain below and hunt for larger game. For now, they filled the evening with talk about the day and life in general.

The morning arrived to find Eric ready for the hunt. He woke up Hope from her deep sleep. Amp and Shai were always up early and eager to go outside. Eric let the two bear dogs out and they raced off into the forest.

"It's time to go hunting," he excitedly called out to Hope.

"You act like a little kid on the first day of snow," she laughed.

Hope got up and put on her clothes. She packed up lunch to take along on the hunt.

Eric ventured outside to get extra spears. He built a large arrow holder out of a good piece of maple, slowly burning out the inside until it was light enough to carry. It held ten arrows easily, allowing for quick and easy access. He tipped his arrows with razor sharp obsidian projectile points and used grouse feathers for the top of the arrow shafts.

He grabbed his knife and stuck it in his belt. Hope always carried the axe. It was razor sharp and she had gotten good at throwing it. If she were within range, she could kill a game bird without any trouble. Eric always carried at least two spears in case one broke while he was hunting.

Hope finally exited the cabin and grabbed two spears. She was now ready for the long climb down to the plain below.

"It's about time," Eric kidded.

He was eager to go.

Hope, not happy with Eric's smartness, replied, "There's plenty of game on the plain and I'm sure it won't all vanish before we get down there."

She did not understand the lack of patience in men.

Eric whistled for Amp and Shai, and within moments the two bear dogs appeared. They had grown into fine specimens. The group set out towards the ladder Eric built months before when they first found the bluff. They slowly climbed down to the base of the bluff. The morning air was cool, a welcome relief from the heat of the day. Earth was cooling down towards the end of the Miocene, but it was still hotter than Earth today. It would be another 6 million years before the ice age began.

Eric and Hope decided to travel along the base of the bluff for protection from detection. This would allow them to hide behind the large boulders that littered the base of the bluff. It was a good plan.

The wind, blowing directly towards them, concealed their scent from unsuspecting beasts in front of them. They could not have asked for better conditions for a hunt.

Amp and Shai stayed close to the humans. They somehow knew when the pack was hunting and waited for the signal from Eric before attacking or taking the lead. The group hunted together on many occasions, but this was the first time they would try for larger game.

They walked for at least an hour before Eric stopped and took out his binoculars. Hope and the bear dogs rested behind a large boulder. She took a long drink of water then offered some to Eric, who took a quick drink and then at once returned to surveying the area for game. Amp and Shai were eager to move forward and hunt.

"I see a large creature about a half mile from us," Eric whispered.

"Can you tell what it is?"

"No, but I think we should stay along the base of the bluff until we get closer."

Eric led the way, slowly moving from one boulder to another, trying to stay concealed from sight. Hope and the bear dogs followed quietly behind.

The clan traveled for close to an hour until they heard a faint bellowing sound, obviously coming from a distressed creature of some type. As they cautiously approached the direction of the sound, it became louder.

The hunt swung into full motion as Eric, Hope, and the two bear dogs focused on the looming prey. They were all business. The kill was close.

Eric signaled for Hope to keep Amp and Shai with her as he crouched down and slowly moved towards the last large boulder at the end of the base of the bluff. Eric, briefly exposed to the vision of the bellowing beast, as it increased its loud cries, quickly moved behind a large boulder to hide his presence.

The Norseman crept to the edge of the large boulder and peered around the corner. The scene both surprised and amazed him. A young Platybelodon calf, stuck in a thick pool of mud, struggled to free itself from the quicksand like muck. The little orphan was nearing exhaustion from the continuous exertion to free itself from the thick sludge. It kept up the bellowing sound trying to summon its mother. Eric looked in all directions with his binoculars, but he could not see the Platybelodon mother. He waved to Hope, signaling her to follow. She soon arrived with both Amp and Shai in tow. They were ready for the kill.

"What is it?" Hope asked as she crept up to Eric's side.

"It's a baby Platybelodon. It's stuck in the mud and can't get free," he whispered to Hope as he pointed to the defenseless proboscidean.

"What should we do? Help it?" asked Hope, obviously distraught over the plight of the poor creature.

"I guess we could try to pull it out with ropes tied to Amp and Shai."

"Do you think we can save it?"

Eric created a large lasso with his rope and tried to throw it over the head of the struggling beast. He missed on several tries but eventually the opening fell around the large calf's head. The worn-out calf sensed the help and stopped bellowing. Eric knew that if he could hear the cries of the calf, then other predators could as well. Time was vital. They had to get the calf free and move away from the area before bigger danger arrived.

Eric tied the end of the rope to Amp and called for the bear dog to follow him. Amp started to walk towards Eric. The rope tightened, but the weight of the trapped beast stopped the mighty bear dog in his tracks. Amp was a powerful animal, but unfortunately the young proboscidean outweighed him two to one. Amp strained as Eric continued to call him.

The young calf started to move as Eric, Hope, and Shai all grabbed onto the rope to aide in the pull. They continued to pull until finally the young Platybelodon reached the solid ground just outside the mud pit.

The intense struggle to save the trapped Platybelodon left the Asvald clan exposed.

As Eric untied the exhausted calf, Amp and Shai started growling. The coarse hair on their backside stood up, which only meant one thing; danger.

Eric and Hope spun around in the direction of the bear dogs. There was little time to run.

"We're being attacked!" shouted Eric.

Chapter 25

Domicile

The two primitive horses, known as Equus, quickly realizing their freedom was in jeopardy, turned back towards the opening in the corral and attempted to flee back through the gate to sprint back onto the open plain to join the rest of the fleeing herd.

One, a large mare, collided violently with the side of the pen, bowing the wood just short of its snapping point. The wood made a loud creaking noise as the mare rammed into the thick timbers. She let out a loud bellow as she bounced off the steadfast poles. Tak constructed the corral with wet, green timber which increased the strength of the poles. His extra diligence was paying off.

The horses ran from one side of the corral to the other, each time testing the soundness of the structure. The posts held. The mare, a beautiful, powerful specimen, used her weight to push against the top rail. She was tan in color with a long, jet black flowing mane. Her muscles, well defined from a life of running free on the open delta, strained as she tried to jump over the corral posts.

The smaller horse, the offspring of the mare, stood at least a foot shorter than the mare. He was a fine-looking young stallion, one that would grow even larger than his mother, the mare, as he aged. He too was tan in overall color, but he had a white streak that ran from his eyes to the tip of his muzzle. His long flowing mane was more of a brownish black color, depending on how the rays of sunshine alighted it. In direct sunlight, it looked brown, but in the shade, it appeared black.

Tak, quickly joined by Maka and Canowicakte at the front of the corral, struggled to secure the opening before the two horses rushed it once again. The arrival of the large Smilodon caused the horses to panic, sending them into a violent frenzy. The mare, pawed at the ground, emitting a loud ear-piercing cry. The young stallion kept close to his mother the mare.

The terrified horses were ready to defend themselves from their common foe. Under normal conditions they could out distance the predator with their superior speed in the open prairie. The Smilodon could not match the horses in speed but was capable of ambush from the hidden seclusion of the forest.

Tak, unsure how Cano would react to the fresh meat on the hoof, motioned to Maka to keep an eye on the giant cat.

"Watch Cano," he yelled.

"I'll do what I can, but if she attacks, I won't be able to stop her."

Tak yelled at Canowicakte to stay put, and surprisingly, the apprehensive cat stopped and sat down. This willingness to obey by the Smilodon gracilis, was a great sign for the humans. It meant the massive Smilodon understood their commands and was trainable. Up to this point Cano was free to come and go as she pleased. It was the first time either of the natives had tried to command the killing beast.

Both natives had deep reservations about their ability to keep the apex predator in check, often wondering if someday she would attack them. She could easily kill one of them in a flash if provoked. It was a great relief to see the Smilodon obey.

The horses, realizing the big cat posed no imminent threat, started to settle down. They huddled together in the far corner of the corral. It was a cool brisk day with just a hint of snow, causing steam from the horse's bodies to rise steadily into the air. The exertion spent while trying to escape capture caused the horses to release a considerable amount of perspiration. They were cooling down. It was the first time the horses had experienced the loss of their freedom.

Tak took a large arm load of grass over to the corner of the pen and tossed it into the corral. He did this several more times until a large pile built up just inside the corral. Tak and Maka, expecting this day to eventually arrive, spent days stocking grass for the horses. This was the first step in taming the wild perissodactyls.

Tak was an excellent horseman. Some would call him a native horse whisperer. This talent, first discovered when he was a small boy, perplexed the older members of his tribe. At an early age, he could approach a wild horse, calm it down, and be riding the beast within a couple of days. His innate ability astonished the elders in his Sioux tribe. The talented native went on to rodeo which eventually led to him going to college in Montana, where he met Eric and the others.

Takoda, Maka, and Canowicakte returned to the warmth of the cavern. Maka threw more wood on the fire. Soon the temperature in the cavern increased to a satisfying, comfortable level, as the light of the flickering flames danced off the cavern walls. They had a small meal of fish for lunch, while they patiently waited for the wild horses to calm down.

The humans needed a larger kill to provide them with a good supply of meat, especially if the snow piled up making hunting extremely challenging. It was time to plan a hunting trip. The two natives were unfamiliar with the erratic climate, a climate that could change within hours from sunshine to blizzard like conditions. They had no idea what season it was. Was this winter or summer?

It would take weeks if not months to chart out the movements of the various creatures that lived in the area; to learn their behaviors and everyday patterns would give the natives a hunting edge. It was best to prepare for the worst and stock up on both firewood and meat. Once trained, the horses would give the natives a better success rate in bringing down larger prey. The four-legged beasts would give them an unrivaled advantage over the species that inhabited their new world.

Maka set about making a meat drying rack for drying fish fillets and red meat. She made this from bamboo. She kept Cano with her inside the cavern, so the two horses could settle in without the added fear from the scent of their mortal enemy.

Tak ventured outside to check on the two new additions to the native clan. The two horses were quietly eating the grass Tak had thrown over the corral poles early that morning. He slowly walked up to them, holding out his hand. The mare gave him a stiff warning by pawing the ground and vocalizing. The smaller stallion kept his distance, his ears pricked up on alert.

To tame the wild beasts could take weeks or months, depending on the resistance level of the two prehistoric horses; that point when they would yield to the will of a human; the first humans these two horses had ever seen. Humans did exist in this time, on certain continents, but it would be thousands of years before they colonized the planet.

Tak began the training by getting the two horses used to his voice and presence. He gently talked to them while he walked around the outside of the corral. The wild creatures, through the constant socializing by the native, would hopefully become accustomed to the sound and smell of the strange human and eventually accept domestication.

Tak's deepest concern was predation at night. The horses, while left in the pen, were vulnerable to attack. The walls of the corral nullified their usual method of avoiding predation, which was speed. Tak decided to build a wood brush fence, one like the type used in Africa to keep lions and other predators from livestock, around the corral. For this he would need plenty of brush. He called for Maka to come outside of the cavern.

"What do you need?" Maka answered as she exited the cavern.

"We have to place branches or something sharp around the top of the corral to keep out predators. Can you help me gather some?"

"Sure," responded Maka, ready to get back outdoors into the cool fresh air.

The two Sioux collected all the dead brush they could find in the surrounding area. Sagebrush, a new species to the plain, grew sparsely, but they managed to find several large patches of the tough plant, which they cut off in pieces with the axe. They found large tumbleweeds, ones with very sharp pointed barbs, which would deter predators from climbing up the outside of the corral.

It took the rest of the day to build the brush fence, a solid enclosure that would protect their new investments. Tak and Maka worked tirelessly to finish the barrier before nightfall to protect the horses from roaming predators that night. Predators would see the horses as easy prey without the protection of the brushwood.

At dusk, Tak put the last piece of sagebrush onto the area by the gate and headed for the cavern. Maka was cooking dinner. The tantalizing aroma of prairie grouse filled the cavern. She grilled the grouse with some wild mushrooms, collected in the forest in the area around the natural spring.

The beautiful native cooked two of the medium sized birds and gave one raw bird to Canowicakte. The large cat sniffed at the dead bird then picked it up in her powerful jaws and took it over to the far corner of the cavern to consume it in privacy. The big cat preferred to eat in isolation.

Canowicakte, growing larger and larger every day, needed more fresh meat daily. Soon the Smilodon gracilis would reach her full growth potential becoming capable of taking down large prey by herself. The natives often wondered if she would stay with them.

Tak entered the cavern, securing the primitive door from the inside. It had been a long day.

"That grouse smells delicious! I'm starving."

"It's just about done," replied Maka, as she stirred the sizzling grouse meat and the wild mushrooms together.

"I didn't realize how hungry I was until I smelled the meat."

Maka dished out the grouse and mushrooms. It was good to have a great meal after a long hard day's work. The two new additions to the native clan were secure in the corral. They were safe from predation, had water, a food source, and human affection. Tomorrow, Tak would spend time getting closer to the beasts until they accepted his presence. This could take hours, days, or even weeks—it was up to the horses.

"We need some good names for our horses," Tak said.

Maka instantly started thinking of good Sioux names.

"How about **Kohana** for the mother?" she said.

Kohana meant "swift" in their native language.

"That's a fine name, I like it."

"What about **Ohitekah** for the young stallion?" Maka offered.

In Sioux, Ohitekah meant "brave."

"Excellent! It'll be a while before we truly know if the little one will be brave, but it is a good name."

The two horses now had strong names. From that day on, they would be known as Kohana the Swift and Ohitekah the Brave.

It was time to settle in for the night so Maka, as was now the custom, threw a large pile of wood on the fire to keep the cavern warm during the night. Each night, the natives would add wood throughout the night to keep the chilling cold from filtering into the cavern.

The nights were getting colder. The Pleistocene Epoch was a time that saw frequent glacial movements. Massive ice formations repeatedly advanced and retreated, which created deep valleys between mountain ranges. This pattern continued for over one million years.

The glacial retreats allowed warmer climate species to return, especially plants, for brief periods of time. Animals retreated south during the colder spells but returned to their normal habitats during the warmer times.

Takoda and Maka only knew it was getting colder. They were clueless to what time they were exactly in or where. They knew they were in Pleistocene times, but this pre-history stuff was Eric's specialty. The natives knew it was colder than normal, or at least what they considered normal. Most of the beasts here had thick hides or thick fur to stay warm.

If stranded here for the rest of their lives, the natives would need some of those thick furs to stay warm. Capturing the horses was the first step to getting these furs. They would return to the ways of their ancestors and harvest the meat and hides of the larger creatures for food, clothing, and shelter.

To this point, Tak and Maka doubted the existence of humans, which would give them an edge in hunting the larger beasts. Creatures like mammoths, rhinos, and bison would have no experience with early humans, thus making them more vulnerable to attack.

Humans on horseback would confuse the giant beasts even more. Both anomalies would give Tak and Maka a slight advantage although hunting these mighty giants would still be extremely dangerous. One catastrophic event could end in death for them and the horses.

The lack of humans in any form added to the native's belief that they were somehow still in North America. The mega-fauna and the oversized species coincided with this hypothesis.

First, Tak needed to tame and train the horses before trying to hunt for larger game. This undertaking would start in the morning and would put even Takoda's patience to test.

Kohana and Ohitekah, undoubtedly the first two horses ever domesticated, would allow the natives a new unmatched freedom to roam the plains in search of new species and water ways. They were the first anatomically correct horses, ones with an actual hoof and not toes.

Equus evolved two million years ago from earlier forms of perissodactyls also known as odd-toed ungulates. Now that the world climate was cooler, the Earth cooled down and this cooling caused the land to dry out. The loss of thick forests, more suitable to a warmer climate, created open, sparsely treed plains for grasses to flourish on. Ungulates thrived on the new grass species and evolved anatomically to run on the open plain. This environment was perfect for the perissodactyls, especially the horse.

The task of taming Kohana and Ohitekah would prove to be difficult even by Tak's standards. The Sioux native trained hundreds of horses in his brief time as a ranch hand, but never such a wild breed. Imagine trying to train a wild zebra—training was one thing; breaking was quite another. Breaking the will of the horses would be the biggest challenge for Tak. Completely wild in spirit, the two horses had no experience with humans. These were just obstacles to the native, obstacles he was confident he could overcome.

The next morning, Tak was up early at dawn. He stoked the fire and gathered his things in preparation to leave the cavern. Cano was ready to exit the cavern and journey into the forest.

"I'm going out to check on the horses."

"Be careful. They're still wild beasts. I'll get up and join you shortly."

Maka was up and moving within minutes. She and Tak were beginning to grow fond of each other. They were always together as they lived as a family unit. It was only a matter of time before this friendship turned into more.

Tak and Cano left the cavern. Canowicakte bolted for the forest, vanishing in the direction of the natural spring. Takoda walked over to the corral hidden behind the newly constructed brush fence. He removed the debris from around the gate and looked in. The two horses were calmly eating the grasses given to them the day before.

The mare, Kohana, stopped and turned to see what noise was coming from the opposite side of the corral. At the sight of the native, she shook her head up and down and bellowed. The young stallion, Ohitekah, followed suit as he hid behind the mare. The horses were nervous.

Tak gently spoke to the two wild animals, trying to calm their fear. He called them by the new names Maka had chosen for them, in a deliberate effort to get them familiar with his tone. He did this for several days while he kept his distance. To force himself on the wild beasts would be a catastrophic error, one that could leave him seriously injured or killed by a swift kick.

Maka followed suit as she gave water to the pair. Her voice was soft, and the young stallion was more relaxed in her presence. Tak was excited by this new development. He encouraged Maka to focus on the stallion as he would initially try to tame the mare first.

Every day, Maka traveled several times to the natural spring to gather water, filling the two water bottles up many times a day. This was fine for the humans, but the horses needed a greater supply of the liquid to survive. She needed to find or devise or a way to carry more water. The spring was too far away to build an aqueduct which left the task more challenging.

Maka decided to journey into the forest to search for a suitable vessel to transport the vital fluid in larger quantities from the spring back to the cavern.

"I'm going into the forest to look for something to haul water to the horses in."

"Do you need my help?" replied Tak, who was once again talking to the horses.

Tak performed this ritual several times a day and his patience was beginning to pay off. The horses were now familiar with his scent and presence.

"I'll be careful and get back before dark."

"Take a spear and my knife with you."

Tak handed Maka his knife. She grabbed the weapon and placed it on her belt.

Maka took the axe as well. She was ready to go in search of some type of container to haul water in. She called for Cano, but the cat did not respond. Maka assumed the Smilodon was off hunting or exploring the territory. It was entirely possible that she would run into her while she searched in the woods for a water carrying vestibule.

"I'm off," Maka shouted back to Tak once she secured her weapons.

"Scream if you need me," laughed Tak.

Maka walked towards the forest, disappearing into the thick canopy of the nearby evergreens.

Tak focused his attention on the two horses once again. He was now inside the corral with the two wild creatures. It had taken him three weeks to get to this point. He wished he had apples or oats to bribe the mare with, for he wanted to tame the mare first.

The stallion was young enough to easily coerce once the mother accepted the human. The climate was too cold for fruits and vegetables and only offered grass to motivate the mare to accept him. He threw piles of the life sustaining grass to the horses twice a day. They were getting accustomed to this behavior, behavior that gave them free meals. The horses quickly learned that if they stayed in the enclosure, food appeared every day without the fear of predation. It was the first step in domestication.

Maka quietly moved through the forest. She followed a winding pathway which crisscrossed in and out of the trees. The pathway, well defined by deep ruts made by a multitude of forest dwelling creatures, allowed for easy travel through the forest. She needed all her senses to focus on the noises of the forest. Her best weapons were her eyes and ears.

The native listened intently for any unusual sounds. If she heard any, she would move into the trees and hide. The forest was thick, but the cold climate kept the smaller forest floor plant species in check. She could see down the trail for some distance, but when the path turned, this left her vulnerable. Every sense was on high alert as she slowly moved through the forest.

The trail led Maka deeper and deeper into the forest and farther away from the cavern. She had not journeyed this deep into the forest or this far from the shelter before. She looked in all directions, searching for anything that would carry water. She approached a small clearing, an opening from the old forest growth, where she paused by the last tree before entering.

Several bird species flew from high in the trees to one area in the clearing. A giant woodpecker landed in a tree close to where Maka stood assessing the opening. Everything looked quiet and calm so Maka walked into the clearing, heading directly for the far side of the opening where the trees started once again. Instead of hastily heading for the trees, Maka, her interest sparked by the behavior of the birds, walked towards the spot where the birds continued to land.

The birds, now alerted to the human's presence, voiced warning calls, which in turn caused the remaining birds to flee from the spot. Maka slowly approached the spot, which was behind a large mass of downed trees. She was unable to see what lured the birds to the spot until she rounded the fallen trees.

Dead trees littered the area. Once she rounded the last fallen trunk, Maka realized what was attracting the birds. A large spring of water bubbled up from inside of the Earth, creating a pool of water. She could see steam rising from the surface of the pool. This piqued her curiosity, so she walked to the pool and stuck her hand in. The water was very warm; Maka had found a natural hot spring.

The warmth emitted by the hot spring, attracted the birds for both a drink and a respite from the cold. Maka decided to take her first bath in months. She undressed, placing her clothes and backpack on the branches of one of the nearby fallen trees and entered the giant bathtub.

The water felt amazing as she slowly entered the pool. The naturally filtered spring erupted from the far end of the pool, closer to the fallen trees. Maka dove under the water then swam towards the spot where the water exited the Earth. The pool's temperature increased as she neared the source. The water not only increased in degrees, but it became deeper as well.

She swam down to the opening in the ground and could see the pool ran under the large body of downed trees. The water formed a series of channels under the dead trees, an alien world oblivious to the outside ecosystem.

Maka returned to the surface of the hot spring and moved around the pool, investigating her new private sanctuary. She found a small ledge by the edge of the pool and sat down. Half submerged, she sat in the warm water. This was the first time she had been clean in months.

When abducted and brought to Extinctus, it was a stroke of luck that Megalo's helpers grabbed all the backpacks. She reached for her bar of soap. The items included in these small vestiges from the outside world were the only link that still connected the humans to the world they had left.

Maka relaxed in the warmth of the hot spring. She could hardly wait to share her find with Takoda. It would provide them with not only a place to bathe but give them a relaxing reprieve from the dangerous world they now inhabited.

Maka had a soft heart towards Tak. They seemed compatible. She let her thoughts drift as she daydreamed of her future with Takoda as she enjoyed the pleasant warm water of the natural spring.

The quiet serenity of the pool caused Maka to ease her guard. Her mind strayed to her future with Tak as she relaxed in the warm water. She unwittingly ignored the warning calls of the nearby birds as they started chattering all around her. The approaching commotion went unnoticed, until she heard the distinct sound of snapping branches, sounds that jolted her back to reality.

Maka slid from the ledge, slipping silently into the pool. She moved slowly towards the channel beneath the trees to hide, her head slightly above the surface, as she moved silently through the water. She was within a few feet of the trees when a giant beast rounded the last fallen tree and approached the hot spring. It was a prehistoric American Mastodon.

The massive beast had a long, shaggy coat and two gigantic tusks that stretched some 14 feet in length. The lone creature stopped at the edge of the pool, sniffing the air for any signs of danger before entering the warm water.

Maka, now completely submerged except for her nose and eyes, moved back under the first fallen tree and stopped. She did not want to give away her presence to the lumbering beast. She was extremely lucky the giant Mastodon had extremely poor eyesight and could not see her or smell her.

The bronze beauty moved silently into the cavern behind the source of the spring in the dead fall. The beast once again tested the air for the presence of any scent while intently listening to the sounds of the forest. Sensing all was safe, the giant entered the hot spring, lumbering into the pool which sent a large wave towards Maka at the far side of the pool. The tidal wave rolled over Maka, momentarily submerging her entire head.

The massive Mastodon continued to move deeper and deeper into the hot spring. It moved until its giant head barely broke the surface. The brute, very fond of the warm water, finally relaxed and let out a deep sigh. It reminded Maka of the bison in Yellowstone National Park in her world. Every year the bison would travel to the network of hot springs and geysers in the winter.

The giant Proboscidean stood motionless in the warmth of the spring. The Mastodon looked old to Maka. It had several large scars that ran along its long trunk, the result of some epic battle for survival in this hostile land.

She could only imagine the hardships the creature must have endured during its brutal lifetime. It was an old bull at the end of his time, visiting the hot spring to soothe its weary bones.

Maka, trapped in the hot spring by the giant Mastodon, had nowhere to go. Behind her were the channels that ran under the dead fall, to where she had no idea, and in front of her soaked the old Proboscidean. The channels were too risky and dangerous to swim into. She could easily become entangled in the network of roots and drown.

She decided to wait out the intrusion by the Mastodon. The only real concern besides detection, was darkness. The trip back to the cavern in darkness would be impossible and extremely reckless. Her only hope was for the beast to leave before dusk. It would take her at least two hours to trek back to the cavern. She needed ample time to travel back to the cavern while still light.

The massive creature seemed intent on staying in the natural warmth of the water to profit from the potential healing qualities of the spring. Maka continued to keep still, trying to avoid detection. She patiently waited for the lumbering animal to grow tired of the respite, but the old giant seemed determined to stay in the pool.

The hours clicked by as the old weary bull rested in the soothing water of the hot mineral spring. Maka stayed still just within the entrance to the channels that ran beneath the dead fall. Her only options were to wait out the tired creature or risk the dangers of navigating the deep entangled channel of roots that led away from the front of the hot spring. Maka accepted the only safe options was to wait for the behemoth to leave the pool.

Maka, isolated in the back of the hot spring, by the lingering beast, decided to move herself to a tiny shelf just past the overhanging branches of the downed trees. The shelf allowed her to lift her upper body out of the water, offering a place for her to sit.

Sitting up on the shelf, allowed her to conserve her energy. She sat patiently waiting for the old giant, who was oblivious to her presence, to leave. His massive head rested towards the front of the spring which left his backside facing the trapped native. The giant Proboscidean never looked back in her direction even once. He stayed calm and relaxed in the heat of the natural spring.

Maka, trapped by the old Mastodon, quietly waited in the natural hot spring as dusk ascended. She was in for a long, terrifying night.

Chapter 26

The Bluff

The sound of the forest creatures resonated throughout the night as CeCe and Lexa slept high up in the canopy of the giant Sequoia trees. The long journey to find the sanctuary towering up on the bluff took CeCe and Lexa many miles from their first shelter constructed of bamboo. It was a logical conclusion that the bluff was the safest place for them in the violent world of the late Paleocene Epoch.

Trapped some 55 million years ago in a land of dramatic evolutionary experimentation, the two humans stumbled upon the safest setting to survive in—the isolated bluff.

At the end of the Cretaceous Period, which resulted in the K/T boundary extinction of most large animals, the Earth began over with a clean slate. The early Paleocene was practically void of terrestrial predators. The ones that did survive were small, comparable to current day rats. Land crocodiles, snakes, and lizards were the main predators during the early Paleocene. These species somehow survived the mass extinction event.

There were two major groups of placental mammals that developed during the Paleocene; the Creodonts and much later, early true carnivores. Creodonts would rise to dominance first and become the apex predators during the Eocene which followed the Paleocene. They would rule most of the planet for millions of years, rising to power during the Eocene 55–35 million years ago, until replaced by the faster, smarter, and more efficient true carnivores.

Creodonts evolved into some of the largest land predators of all time, ranging in size from a small ferret to ones larger than a bear. Megistotherium was one of the largest land carnivores of all time, weighing up to 2000 pounds.

CeCe and Lexa, trapped in this time of Creodont expansionism, tried to avoid contact with the brutal predators whenever possible. They were no match for these fierce predators in a face to face confrontation. Their best strategy hinged on early detection which allowed them to use their intelligence to outmaneuver the slow minded carnivores.

One advantage CeCe and Lexa did have was the lack of population. The Earth was a large place without any interference or influence by the modern human, which resulted in the creation of vast territories for the creatures to roam. The probability of a confrontational encounter, like running into a grizzly while hiking in the mountains of Montana, dwindled with this lack of population. Besides, the humans had the relative seclusion of the bluff as a protective barrier.

"We're lucky we found this bluff," CeCe said. "It's pretty secluded and protected from most predators."

CeCe was superstitious, a trait engrained in him by his aunts, and he needed the notion of some semblance of safety in this world.

"I agree. It'll be a lovely home if we're abandoned by the Super Extinctos and left to fend for ourselves."

The bluff would be their next home, so CeCe and Lexa decided to stay in the safety of the trees at night. It was possible that some species of Creodonts climbed trees, but it was a risk the humans were willing to take.

They settled on expanding their current sleeping area, situated high up in the branches of the trees. Lexa, an experienced engineer, started the process of mapping out the expansion. There were three giant sequoias nestled together overlooking the entire region. The original sleeping area, hastily built as a temporary shelter to escape from the potential terrors that roamed the ground at night, afforded safety while sleeping, but it did not protect them from the elements of nature, primarily rain.

After surveying the possibility of incorporating the temporary structure into the design of the new shelter, Lexa decided to abandon the site and start entirely from scratch. They could use some of the materials from the sleeping area as bedding for the new shelter.

In their haste to reach the safety of the trees, CeCe and Lexa built the temporary sleeping area on the wrong side of the sequoia. The large tree would not align with the other two trees she wanted to connect to.

"This spot isn't going to work," she shouted down to CeCe from up in the tree.

CeCe looked up and shook his head. He did not like to waste his efforts, and completely starting over angered the big fella.

Lexa decided to build a platform that crossed from tree to tree. This large platform would create the foundation on which everything else built would rest on. She needed to construct a serious of ladders to reach the upper elevation first. Between the two of them, CeCe and Lexa had an axe, a hand saw, rope, and the drive to occupy their time. They started by collecting the materials the bluff offered. They found a small stand of pine trees which they felled to use as lumber.

CeCe and Lexa worked tirelessly for days to fell and split the pine into usable primitive boards. Once felled, they stripped the pine trees of the bark, to reduce infestation by the annoying insects that flourished during this time.

After he removed the bark, CeCe used his axe and a primitive hammer he created from a large rock, to split the trees into long usable strips. It was an arduous task that took hours to complete.

When CeCe finished splitting the trees into even strips, Lexa used sturdy, thick pieces of pine for steps that would allow access up to the new shelter. She pounded these steps into grooves she notched out in the trunk of the giant sequoia.

Once driven into the grooves, the wide strip boards, although primitive, protruded out from the tree, allowing the humans to climb up the base of the tree to the higher elevations. For added support, Lexa used smaller tree trucks around 3–4 inches in diameter to help strengthen the steps.

Lexa drove the first tree trunk into the ground and pounded it up against the base of the tree, up under the first step. She repeated this process between each step all the way up to the last step. After finishing the last step, both Lexa and CeCe climbed up the step ladder stairs to test the strength of the steps. All steps easily held the weight of the large football player.

In the days that followed, CeCe and Lexa repeated the same process on the other two trees. They needed to reach the same height in the other two trees to chop out grooves to support the platform.

After the humans finished the rudimentary steps, allowing access to all three trees, they climbed up into the canopy, Lexa in one tree and CeCe in another. They used the rope, from the backpacks, to transport the platform floor from the forest floor to their new home high up in the sequoias. This was a tedious process. The pine strips had to be the exact length to wedge one end into the slotted groove on the adjacent tree. It was easy to attach the first side, but entirely another issue to pound in the second side into the groove. They repeated the task until the platform pine strips were all locked in place.

It took weeks to finish the complete project. They used most of the rope to tie in the middle pine strips, an action they would later come to regret. Some nails would have been priceless.

Once they completed the floor of the platform, Lexa and CeCe supported the structure by running poles from the adjacent trees at angles to wedge the structure from below. This system worked surprisingly well, and before long they had a sturdy platform base to work from.

Next, they built walls from bamboo. Bamboo, which was easy to cut and bend, was easy to work with. The walls were ten feet high to allow CeCe some headroom.

The last project centered on the roof—to keep out the rain. In this humid tropical time, it rained on a weekly, if not daily basis. Lexa decided to use palm leaves, which were large and easily intertwined with the bamboo poles, to cover the roof. They installed bamboo across the roof and then covered it with palm leaves and whatever else was readily available. As an added feature, Lexa engineered a series of funnels on the corners of the structure to capture rainwater to supply them with fresh rainwater.

The shelter was complete. It was high enough, nestled in the sequoias, to give them protection from roaming predators, and strong enough to withstand any major storms the Paleocene had to offer. It was Lexa's and CeCe's new home; a home they were extremely proud of.

"Now that was a long hard job," CeCe commented as he gazed at the fine workmanship of their new home.

The big man had lost at least 20 pounds since entering Extinctus. Between fighting for daily survival and constantly searching for the next meal, CeCe's body mass dwindled to a more fit level. The African American was in the best shape of his life now.

"Yea... but look at the security and protection from the elements it'll give us. Hey, I wonder if I could use this for my senior engineering project?" replied Lexa, who was immensely proud of her primitive engineering undertaking.

The weeks went by as CeCe and Lexa explored the bluff. The bluff was extremely isolated from the land below on one side and the sea on the other side. Building the tree house had consumed their time for weeks, so much, in fact, that they had forgotten about the sea.

It was time to travel once again to the far side of the bluff and explore the sea. Seafood would be a magnificent change in diet for the two humans. They could place set lines out into the sea to catch fish or any other unsuspecting sea monster that ventured up from the depths below. Lexa would build crab pots from bamboo to trap shellfish and mollusks—all excellent in nutritious vitamins and protein.

The humans had no idea what types of creatures lived in the sea 55 million years before their time, but they were eager to find out. Lexa and CeCe needed a new food source which would help vary their diet.

Up to this point, their main staple had been a squirrel-like rodent called Paramys. This was the first known rodent that lived over 60 million years ago until vanishing during the mid-Eocene. It was a tree climber and grew to over 2 feet in length.

Months had gone by since they last tasted the flavorful salmon-like fish CeCe caught in the stream before the Dark Extinctos captured them. The Paramys were plentiful but the flesh of the rodent was tough and chewy. Even roasted, it had a foul taste, but CeCe and Lexa had to eat to survive, so they endured the distasteful rodent.

CeCe and Lexa still lacked the confidence to take on the larger ungulates. They had excellent sharp bamboo spears, ones that could easily penetrate the tough hides of the larger herbivores, but they lacked the nerve to use them. The Paramys gave them adequate meat as a necessity, and Lexa supplemented their diet with fruits, nuts and various plants, but they were confident the sea could offer a reliable source of high protein for their diet.

"In the morning, we should head for the sea. We need a new food source," commented Lexa.

CeCe nodded in approval. He was very tired of rodent meat.

"I'm ready for some fresh seafood or anything different from the rodent we've been eating," he joked.

They decided to leave for the sea early the next morning.

That night, CeCe and Lexa prepared their spears and inventoried their fishing supplies. They had plenty of fishing monofilament and a handful of hooks. Once they reached the sea, they would use rocks to weigh down the fishing line.

The plan was to leave early in the morning, allowing time to make it across the open meadow before the sun came up. CeCe and Lexa realized the bluff afforded them added safety from the roaming predators living in the area, but once they left it, they understood the danger of attack could rise.

It was a gamble they needed to take to gain a more sustainable food source. If isolated in the Paleocene for the rest of their natural lives, they had to exploit the resources it offered, which included harvesting creatures from the sea and eventually traveling back down into the thick rain forests below the other side of the bluff to kill larger game species.

One added feature Lexa engineered for the tree shelter was windows. On all four side walls, she cut out openings in the bamboo, so they could visually study the migrations habits of the creatures they shared the bluff with. They spent countless hours observing the activity on the ground and in the trees around them.

They spotted countless bird species as they flew from one tree to another to harvest insects. The insects were ruthless pests, some growing quite large. Watching the birds, as they preyed upon the relentless swarms of terrorizing insects pleased the humans—any reduction in their population helped them.

The occasional Amblypod would ramble by, entirely unaware of the human presence just feet above it. Amblypods were early hoofed mammals that flourished between 60–30 million years ago. They were slow, cumbersome herbivores; early herbivores that ranged in size from a sheep to the massive Uintatherium.

Pantolambda, the size of a sheep with short legs and canine teeth, would be the first target for CeCe and Lexa. It would supply a great amount of meat to the humans if they could kill it.

Amblypods were the main experimental mammals during the Paleocene, especially in North America. They would eventually succumb to the quicker more agile ungulates. Many lived in swampy areas, but some did roam the forests and plains.

Early Creodonts hunted Amblypods by ambushing the unsuspecting beasts from dense, overgrown foliage. The Paleocene was a new experimental world, a slate left blank by the K/T extinction event. During the same period, sub–ungulates would evolve on other continents, primarily in Africa and Asia. Amblypods developed odd horn patterns, some with up to three pairs, and most kept their canines. They were the perfect prey for the slow footed, slow thinking Creodonts.

CeCe and Lexa spent hours watching for anything that roamed below the tree shelter. Their observations helped them develop patterns of migration. The bluff, over thousands of years, evolved its own biodiversity. There were several species of Amblypods and several predators that occupied the bluff with the two humans.

The humans saw three peculiar looking predators pass by on various occasions. During the early Paleocene, large herbivores were absent from land after the widespread extinction of the dinosaurs. This left an evolutionary niche. The predators of the time were Condylarths, Creodonts and several variations of these, which evolved much later in the Paleocene Epoch.

Condylarths descended from early insectivores and were early hoofed mammals. They were the first mammals known to be omnivores or herbivores. Protungulatum, meaning before ungulate, was the earliest known Condylarth. Its teeth allowed it to crush and grind its food, which allowed it to eat plants, fruits and still some insects. Protungulatum belonged to the family known as Arctocyonid, the least herbivorous group of the Condylarths.

Another species Lexa and CeCe knew all too well, named Chriacus, was a small arctocyonid that climbed trees. It often ventured close to the tree shelter. Chriacus had a long body with short legs and an exceedingly long tail, like a raccoon or civet, and it was at home climbing in the trees.

A larger arctocyonid named Claenodon roamed the bluff as well. Claenodon, comparable to a bear in size, could still climb trees, and it is possible it was the main predator during the earlier Paleocene.

A third family of Condylarths, the Hyopsodontidae, flourished during the late Paleocene. These were small animals that resembled insectivores in appearance.

The last family of Condylarths, the Phenocodontidae, may have included the ancestors of more modern ungulates, the Perissodactyla, which included horses. It is hard to conceive that early predators belonged to the same family that evolved into ungulates and herbivores.

CeCe and Lexa spotted a large omnivore the size of a bear on a cyclical basis. They did not know it as Claenodon, but they saw it as a threat, a creature to avoid. It looked slow and awkward as it ambled by the tree shelter, roaming its secluded territory for food and encroaching competition.

The more frightening beasts were the mighty Creodonts. These larger creatures are best known from later Paleocene fossils. Creodonts went on to become the dominant carnivores of the time.

The first Creodonts were members of the family Oxyaenid, which flourished in the late Paleocene in North America, preying on small mammals, eggs, and even insects. They could climb trees, which presented a danger to Lexa and CeCe.

Early members of the Oxyaenid were cat-like and small. Creodonts during the Eocene would grow to become some of the largest carnivores that ever lived. They preyed on the exploding ungulate populations that also grew to enormous size during that same period.

Lexa and CeCe, alone towards the end of the Paleocene, a time when primitive forms were evolving at a rapid pace, had to fear the early life forms, forms nearing the end of their rein on Earth, as well as the newer evolving species which included the Creodonts. The terror birds thrived in this time and always threated the two humans.

CeCe and Lexa, barely survived the attack by the terror cranes earlier while escaping the clutches of the Dark Extinctos, but to this point the humans had not seen any sign of the hideous terror birds on the bluff. The only problem was they had no idea what kinds of creatures existed in this time. This was Eric's specialty; he was the pre-historic aficionado.

At times, Lexa and CeCe would talk about the plight of the others. Would they ever see them again? How were they surviving in their alternate times?

The night passed without incident as usual, and Lexa was the first to rise. She stood up and gazed out one of the shelter windows.

"It's time to get up," she said as she nudged CeCe.

Lexa was ready to head for the sea.

"Is it that time already?" replied CeCe, who liked to sleep—it helped him pass the time in this dreadful place.

"We better get moving. It could take us some time to find a way down to the sea," Lexa urged the sleepy football player.

Lexa scaled down the tree ladder and was soon waiting below the tree top sanctuary. CeCe put on his backpack and climbed to the forest floor. The air was warm and humid, as usual. It often rained early in the morning, but on this day, it was dry.

They grabbed their spears and headed for the plain that led to the sea, moving quietly through the forest, keeping alert for any sound or any sudden movement. When they reached the edge of the forest, they paused to survey the land in front of them. Lexa climbed up a tree and looked across the plain in all directions.

"It looks clear. I don't see anything."

Lexa climbed down the tree and returned to the forest floor. CeCe led the way as they left the protection of the forest behind them and headed out into the open. It took the two about fifteen minutes to cross the opening. This time they walked at an even pace, constantly looking for danger.

They reached the edge of the bluff and looked down upon the sea. It was a calm day as the waves slowly rolled onto the beach. The sea seemed endless as it continued as far as the human eye could see. The water was crystal blue with a tinge of green at the top of the waves as they broke on the shoreline.

They decided to go in opposite directions to search for a way down to the sea from the bluff. CeCe and Lexa were some fifty feet above the sandy beach. The bluff continued for miles in both directions. They had used most of the rope to build the tree shelter, which left them with about thirty feet or so to work with. It would have to do.

Lexa went to the left and CeCe headed to the right. The plan was to search for an hour and then return to the same spot. CeCe left his backpack as a reference point. He carried his spear, knife and water bottle with him. Lexa kept her backpack with her as she parted ways with CeCe.

"I will see you in an hour," she said, taking her spear and the axe for protection.

"If you find a way down, come back and wait for me to return," CeCe told her.

Lexa nodded as she walked off heading in the direction of the sun. Her pace was slow and deliberate as she searched for any way down the bluff to the beach below. She found several routes that showed promise, but when she climbed down to investigate them, they ended in sheer rock faces, impossible to navigate without at least fifty feet of rope.

The bronze Latino was about to head back to the meeting point when she came upon one last possibility. It was a trail that zigged along the cliff until it ended around twenty feet above the beach. It reminded Lexa of a switch back. She was confident they could use the rope to reach the beach below, so she quickly climbed back to the top of the bluff and ran back to the meeting point.

She arrived at the backpack first. CeCe had not returned yet. When they left, the big man journeyed to the right towards the taller side of the bluff. There was a slow rise in elevation in the direction he took.

To this point, CeCe and Lexa had not yet journeyed to the far edges of the bluff, deciding to stay in the forest close to the shelter. The area around the shelter gave them the added safety of the trees to hide in if attacked by a predator. This was the second time they travelled to the sea. The first time they traveled this far was months earlier when they first found the bluff.

Lexa decided to walk in the direction CeCe had taken, to search for her friend. She felt confident she would run into him at some point. She tracked his steps for just under a mile when suddenly the trail went cold. There were no more footprints in the loose soil to follow.

Lexa concentrated on where CeCe's footprints ended. She went to the edge of the bluff and peered over the side. The drop on this side of the bluff was at least twenty feet farther from the beach than the side she investigated. Lexa strained to look over the bluff's edge. Due to the erosion of the rock face, which curved in from the top, seeing the beach directly under the rock face was impossible.

She walked back in the direction she had come from, searching for any sign of CeCe. She came to a point and looked over the ledge. She spotted the rope tied to a large boulder just below the lip of the bluff. She climbed down on the ledge to inspect the rope.

The rope, securely fastened to the boulder, dropped down a sheer rock face. Lexa spread out flat on her belly and looked over the rock face. To her anguish, she spotted the big football player lying motionless on the beach below. CeCe did not move. The big man had fallen to the beach below during his descent.

Lexa quickly untied the rope from the boulder and climbed back up the cliff. She picked up CeCe's backpack as she ran back to the spot she thought might lead down to the beach. There was no time to waste as every minute was critical. CeCe's life depended on it. If he survived the fall.

Lexa secured the rope to a large rock, dropped it over the edge, and quickly climbed down to the beach below. She ran along the beach at full speed until she spotted CeCe's lifeless body sprawled out motionless on the sand.

The big man was not moving as the Latino knelt beside his still body to check his breathing. Lexa detected a faint pulse but CeCe was laboring to breathe. She checked for broken bones but did not see any protruding through his skin, so she gambled, turning him over on his back. CeCe was unconscious.

Lexa looked up the face of the bluff which ended some thirty feet above. She estimated CeCe had fallen from at least that distance. She checked for a pulse once more. She could not find one.

"You should have waited for me...big oaf," she screamed.

Lexa tried to revive the big man by performing CPR, but CeCe did not respond.

In that moment, with CeCe now gone, Lexa realized she was all alone in this hostile world.

Chapter 27

The Dark Truth

Eric, Hope, Amp, Shai, and the Platybelodon calf all simultaneously turned to meet the attacking danger. The young calf, still exhausted from its ordeal in the mud pit, did not have the energy to flee. The tiny Proboscidean emitted a low rumbling sound, a call to its mother. The little beasts struggle, to free itself from the mud, had attracted predators from the surrounding area.

Giant vultures, always on the lookout for a free meal, started to arrive on the scene. Eric and Hope grappled with two options; one, flee from the scene, or two, stay and defend the small calf.

Amp and Shai wheeled to meet a pair of cougar-sized carnivores known as Dinictis, an early primitive cat-like animal, the ancestor of the stabbing, biting cats that evolved later, evolving into many giant species, like Smilodon fatalis, referred to as the saber-toothed tiger.

The two bear dogs turned and rushed the attacking cats. The two Dinictis, eager to avoid conflict, sprinted for the forest on the other side of the plain, quickly vanishing into the trees to escape the bear dogs. The two bear dogs chased the fleeing Dinictis until they disappeared into the trees then turned around to head back to their masters.

Amp and Shai returned to Eric and Hope seeking praise for a job well done. The threat from the Dinictis only lasted a few moments, until the large cats met fierce resistance from the two bear dogs. Once again, Amp and Shai had proven themselves invaluable.

"What do we do with the calf?" asked Hope.

Hope did not have the heart to kill the little beast for food. Besides food was plentiful, it was larger skins they needed for warmer clothing.

"I don't really know what to do with it. We can't take care of it."

Eric knew Hope had a big heart, a soft spot for the lesser creatures, so he did not want to upset her gentle nature. This was a quality he found very appealing in his beautiful mate.

"Right, there's no way to get it up the bluff anyway," Hope sadly answered.

They decided to continue the hunt for bigger game. Eric led the band back towards the rock out cropping to protect them from searching eyes. The little calf followed them even though it was obviously terrified of Amp and Shai. What else could it do?

The group walked for a short distance before stopping for water. The poor calf, still in a weakened state from hours of fighting the mud, dropped to the ground. The humans decided to let the tiny beast rest for a little while before continuing the hunt.

Amp and Shai traipsed off to search for their own lunch. They were now fully experienced hunters, very capable of killing their own food. Eric and Hope no longer felt the need to supply fresh meat to the pets, who were fully self-sustaining.

Eric and Hope rested on the boulders with the little calf. It had been an eventful day to this point. The little calf suddenly perked up and let out a loud bellowing cry. Eric and Hope instantly went on the alert. Eric climbed up on one of the boulders to survey the plain. He yelled down to Hope.

"I see danger coming our way! It's a pack of Daphoenodon and they're heading straight towards us. They must have heard the calf bellowing."

Daphoenodon, the largest canids of the day, were fierce predators. They were wolf-like bear dogs that hunted in packs. It is possible they were omnivorous, but Eric and Hope knew different. They had personally seen them hunt prey, running their quarry to exhaustion before moving in for the kill, on the vast plain below the cabin.

"What should we do?" Hope asked, confident her and Eric could escape, but worried about the little calf.

"We need Amp and Shai for protection," Eric replied.

Amp and Shai were still missing. They had not yet returned since leaving earlier when the group stopped to rest. Eric and Hope would have to decide, once again, whether to leave the calf to its doom or stay and protect it.

The pack of Daphoenodon closed in, they could smell the calf, so they picked up the pace once they caught the scent of the little shovel tusker. To the pack, the calf meant an easy meal.

Eric and Hope braced for another conflict. They held their spears firmly as they stepped in front of the calf to protect it. They hoped the Daphoenodon would fear their unrecognizable scent, which had worked to their advantage several times since arriving in this time. This was their only hope to save themselves and the calf unless the two bear dogs miraculously appeared. The stoic humans braced for the attack.

There were three of the large canids in the group. The leader was much larger than the other two. They all had long slender bodies, with short limbs and long, thick tails. The Daphoenodon were brown in color with thick coarse hair.

The leader of the pack stopped around 25 yards in front of Eric and Hope. It sniffed at the air trying to recognize the strange new smell of the humans. It seemed unsure of the scent of this new prey, which caused it to be overly cautious. The two smaller creatures stayed behind the larger leader. It was clear they did not want to instigate the fight with the strange new species they found themselves confronted with. They were still juveniles.

As a stiff warning, the lead Daphoenodon bared its yellowish canines by curling its upper lip. It was trying to get the humans to abandon the calf, which it wanted for lunch. Eric and Hope assumed the canids would not leave without a fight.

Eric yelled for Amp and Shai, but to no avail. The two giant watchdogs were obviously out of earshot. It could be days before the humans saw them again. They were leaving for longer periods of time now, but to this point, when they left, they always returned to the cabin on the bluff.

The calf continued to bellow as loud as it could. It sensed the impending danger, calling out for help from the herd. The lead canid growled at the two smaller pack members, trying to encourage them, then attacked.

Eric and Hope braced for the assault. They screamed at their foes to show signs of confidence. Eric pulled back his muscular right arm, flinging one of his spears into the wind. It whizzed through the air, striking one of the smaller dogs in the shoulder, sending it to the ground in agony. The obsidian point penetrated the creatures hide with slicing severity.

Hope threw her spear at the other smaller canid, but the quick reaction of the beast caused it to miss its mark. The leader of the pack jumped on the back of the calf as the little Proboscidean continued to bellow at full lung capacity. The other remaining canid attacked the humans. Eric drew his knife to defend himself and Hope. In his haste, he forgot his long bow behind them on the rocks. The second beast lunged at the humans.

In a flash, a giant Proboscidean came from behind one of the adjacent boulders, scooped up the unsuspecting beast in its oddly shaped shovel–like mouth. In an instant, Eric and Hope heard the unmistakable sound of the canid's bones crack.

The giant Platybelodon instantly dropped the lifeless form of the canid to the ground and rushed to the defense of the calf.

The leader of the pack relinquished its hold on the calf, dropping it to the ground, and ran off. It knew when to fold. The first Daphoenodon, writhing in agony in the dirt from the spear wound, tried to stand up as the calf's mother stepped on it, crushing what little life it had left in its mortally wounded body.

The huge matriarch now turned her focus on the strange looking humans. Confused by the alien sight of Eric and Hope, the massive elephant hesitated.

The humans retreated towards the bluff face, stopping up against the base of the bluff, as the calf cried out in joy as it ran to its mother. The mother stepped towards Eric and Hope, let out a thunderous roar, which terrified the humans, then turned and led the calf back out onto the plain.

The ordeal was over. It was on that day that Hope, and Eric gained a new admiration for the giant Proboscidean, deciding they would not hunt the massive beasts while living in their time.

"Now that was a close encounter of the giant kind," laughed Eric.

Amazed by the sheer size of the Platybelodon, Eric looked at Hope and just shook his head. Instead of a trunk like modern elephants, the Platybelodon had two large, long openings with wide blade-like teeth coming out of the lower jaw. This acted like a shovel. **(Image 14: Platybelodon: page 141)**

"It was amazing and frightful," Hope answered, glad to be alive.

Hope felt relieved that the little calf escaped certain death by the Daphoenodon and reunited with its mother.

"We better head back to the cabin," Eric said as he motioned towards the bluff. "We've seen enough excitement for one day."

They walked back to the ladder to scale the cliff face. It was mid-day now and a small rainstorm was rolling in from the forest on the far side of the vast plain below. Eric and Hope climbed up the primitive series of ladders and ledges until they reached the top of the bluff. Eric stopped, pulling out his binoculars to scan the open plain below for the little calf. He spotted the little calf, as it followed its mother Platybelodon into a larger herd of the giant tuskers. He was happy to see the little orphan once again within the protection of the herd. The series of events worked out in a positive way, which is not so often the case in the wild.

Eric handed Hope the binoculars to take one last look at the little calf as it rejoined the herd.

"I'm glad we helped save the little thing," she said.

Hope had a huge heart which was full of respect and consideration for all living things. She realized the necessity to eat to survive but took taking the life of another species very seriously.

"Me too," replied Eric, proud to have held their ground against the Daphoenodon pack.

Eric and Hope reached the safety of the cabin, built a fire and cooked up a meal that consisted of Cranioceras meat. It smelled and tasted comparable to modern-day pronghorn antelope flesh. The ordeal of the day left the humans exhausted, so after eating, they quickly fell into a deep sleep.

The cabin was warm, dry and virtually impenetrable from the outside. Eric and Hope spent countless hours fortifying the shelter with strong maple logs, filling in the gaps with mud, mud that once dried, hardened like cement. If forced to live in Extinctus for the rest of their natural days, they would at least live in comfort.

Sometime during the night, the loud growls of Amp and Shai woke up Hope. The two bear dogs, having returned from the plain below late during the night, were alerting the humans to looming danger. Their growls increased in intensity.

"Wake up, Eric," whispered Hope.

She gave Eric a swift kick and he sat up at once.

"What are you doing?" he angrily asked.

Then he heard the loud growls coming from just outside the door. He walked to the door and peeked through a small hole he carved into the door to allow vision to the area directly in front of the cabin. He could barely see Amp and Shai. The two bear dogs stood with their hind quarters up against the door, protecting their human pack members hidden inside the cabin. They would not allow access into the cabin and would defend the humans with their own lives if necessary.

The early light of morning was beginning to break. Dawn during the Miocene came early, and dusk descended quite late at night. It reminded the humans of the long summer days in their time. It would start getting light at 4 AM and stayed light until 10 PM.

Eric could now see the thick hair of the bear dogs standing straight up, a certain indicator that there was a clear and present danger approaching the bear dogs. He turned to Hope and pointed to the spears. She ran to the far wall of the cabin and picked up two of the obsidian tipped killing sticks. She handed one to Eric and kept the other one for herself.

The danger, too close to open the cabin door, forced Eric to leave Amp and Shai outside to face the threat alone. There was just not enough time to open the door and bring the two-loyal bear dogs inside the cabin. Eric could see the bear dogs posturing for an attack when he heard a familiar voice bellow loudly from outside.

"Call off your hounds before we have to kill them," the voice commanded.

It was Creo. The Extinctos had returned!

Eric opened the door and stepped in front of Amp and Shai. He reassured the massive pets with his calming voice. Hope exited the cabin, placing herself between the giant protectors and the Extinctos. She put one hand on each shoulder of Amp and Shai to calm the loyal guardians. The bear dogs calmed down instantly and moved towards the trees. They did not trust the new intruders, but they followed the command of their pack leaders.

"I see you have made some friends," replied Aves, the giant eagle, as she nodded in approval.

"One can never have enough allies," interjected Arti.

The massive Extincto, with his three-foot snout, gazed over at the two beautiful specimens.

"You've finally returned for us," Eric said, the relief and elation obvious on his grinning face.

"It has been a long journey for us as well," replied Creo.

The powerful Creodont looked tired from months of traveling to recruit help for Megalo's army.

"It's great to see all of you," Hope finally said.

She walked over to Creo and gave him a big hug. The giant, obviously surprised by the overwhelming show of affection, turned red.

Hope then went to Aves and Arti and hugged them as well. It was a new experience for the Extinctos. In their world emotion was an uncommon feeling. It was a liability. They both blushed and awkwardly tried to reciprocate the foreign act.

"We've traveled to many time periods in an effort to figure out what Thylac is up to," Creo said, his demeanor and tone turning to one of urgency and seriousness.

Creo spent the next few hours explaining the situation to Hope and Eric. Thylac, obsessed with vengeance against Eric's bloodline, was the main catalyst behind kidnapping Eric and his camping party. The Extinctos needed Eric to ensure Thylac was unsuccessful in not only this goal but a much larger one.

Eric's grandfather, Asvald, mysteriously vanished years ago in Extinctus, and to this day, if he still lived, had escaped capture by Thylac. Years later, Eric's father Tolf, went missing while searching for Asvald. Creo was unsure if Tolf had ever actually entered Extinctus. Evidence to this was unsubstantiated but periodically strange, vague stories would surface about a hairless white ape traveling from one-time period to another. Each time the Extinctos went to investigate these rumors, each led to a dead end.

Creo went on to explain the deep concern Megalo had that Thylac would try to capture the grandson of Asvald and kill him out of pure spite. Megalo believed Thylac truly thought that Asvald and Tolf were dead and assumed that with the demise of Eric, the bloodline, now wiped out, would allow the species Thylacine to roam Earth as it had for millions of years prior to mankind.

Thylac, driven by this obsession, tried to capture Eric but the Light Extinctos beat him to the task. Megalo sent Creo and the others to kidnap Eric and bring him to Extinctus to hide from the evil clutches of the dark Extinctos. The Dark Extinctos would stop at nothing to complete their mission.

Megalo quickly realized, once Eric was safe in Extinctus, that Thylac was devising an even more evil plan to wipe out the link to mankind. He and his henchmen, along with hundreds of other species, were systematically trying to eradicate Homo sapiens.

The supply of species, eradicated by the hand of humans, was endless and it took little effort to persuade them to help Thylac carry out his scheme. Some species joined for vengeance, while others joined for the possibility that they would rise to fill the niche vacated by the modern human. Yet still, others joined out of fear of the Dark Extinctos.

Eric, with a look of confusion on his puzzled face, asked Creo, "What happens if Thylac is successful? If I'm still alive and safe in Extinctus, how will the loss of Homo sapiens change the Earth?"

"We are not sure, but it is possible that your world may be altered by the change in the dominant species. If we keep you alive in Extinctus, your species may have a chance," answered the massive Creodont.

Eric and Hope, both perplexed by this latest information, sat down on the ground. If Homo sapiens vanished from the world of Extinctus, it would be as if the species never existed at all. Where did that leave them? Would they vanish?

"Creo, we are confused. There are six of us humans that you brought into Extinctus. If we stay alive, then Homo sapiens would not be extinct," replied Hope.

"As we told you before, our intention was to just bring Eric to Extinctus, but all of you were together so we abducted everyone," answered the giant Creodont who was getting agitated by all the questions.

"If Thylac eradicates your early ancestor species in Extinctus, this changes the whole evolution of the species. It is like it never existed at all. In Extinctus, we call this re-extinctification. No species has tried re-extinctification of another species in Extinctus before. So, you see, we are not entirely sure what will happen. We do know that by bringing you here, it increases our chances of preventing the loss of your species. Since Eric's grandfather was Thylac's original target, it was logical that we take any of his direct blood line descendants first. You must understand that the original intent of Thylac was to eradicate the blood line of Asvald Asvaldsson to exact revenge. When your grandfather vanished somewhere in time in Extinctus, Thylac spent decades searching for him. Once we brought Eric to Extinctus, we learned that Thylac had set his sights on eradicating the entire species, which in theory would bring back millions of extinct species to current Earth. This created a much larger problem for us. We are the protectors of Extinctus and must protect our world and your world. This puts us at odds with millions of species that vanished due to the carelessness of man. We Extinctos understand most of us would have vanished without interference by humans, but Thylac has worked vigorously to persuade and intimidate other species into believing that the removal of the humans would aide them all," the giant carnivore sighed as he spoke.

"So where does that leave us?" asked Eric, now completely astonished by this new twist in the tale.

If his species vanished in Extinctus, then he and his five friends would be the last humans.

"Then Thylac would have to kill us also to complete his entire quest?" chimed in Hope.

"Yes, but without the original Homo sapiens species, who knows how your world would have evolved. You and your friends would become missing links. If you were in your world and Thylac is successful, you would disappear from existence, but because you are here in Extinctus, if Thylac is successful, you would escape extinction. It is unclear to us what would happen if you returned to your world after your species disappeared in Extinctus. As you can see, there are many questions we do not have the answers to yet," answered Creo.

"Well, that's as clear as mud," mocked Eric, his mind reeling from the complexity of Creo's story.

The thought of him and his friends being the only humans left was shocking and terrifying. Would they have to stay in Extinctus forever?

"Will we get to see our friends soon?" asked Hope, eager to find out if the rest of the group were still alive.

"Are they all still alive?" asked Eric.

"They will be coming within the next few weeks. Megalo has sent the Extinctos to search for them and bring them here, but I don't know if they all live," replied Creo.

"We won't know until they get here," spoke Aves, which to this point had been silently listening to the story told by Creo.

"They will all arrive," Hope answered in her always positive tone.

The Creodont continued, "The goal now is to save Homo sapiens from re-extinctification. Once we assemble our groups, we will travel into the Pleistocene Epoch. Homo sapiens evolved some 40,000 years ago. We will go to that time and work our way forward in time. It is logical that Thylac will begin his assault on your species in the first stages of the species' evolutionary process, when there would be fewer individuals to eradicate. If he tries later in time, the population of the species would be greater. He would have to kill many more and the task would be way more difficult."

"You two will stay here," interjected Arti, pointing to the cabin.

"It will be safer for you here," replied Aves.

"Will the others get to stay with us?" asked Hope.

"We will get that answer when Megalo arrives," responded Creo.

"Now we must go!" Creo ordered as he pointed to Aves. "Arti will stay and protect you."

The giant Artiodactyl walked into the forest and disappeared. He would keep an eye on the humans from a distance.

The story was hard to grasp. Eric and Hope had many unanswered questions. If Thylac and his horde were successful, where did that leave them? Where did it leave their Earth? Were Tak, Maka, Lexa and CeCe still alive? Could all of this be possible? Was the fate of mankind really in their hands?

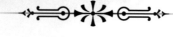

Chapter 28

Masters of the Plain

Maka Dove, trapped in the natural spring of hot water, patiently waited for the huge Mastodon to leave the sanctuary of the soothing water. Darkness fell on the forest, casting its dark spell, as the birds silently flew to their secret night sleeping spots. Recently, the nights were getting extremely frigid and snowstorms were now quite frequent. The forest birds endured the cold climate by nesting high in the trees in insulated nests, or by huddling together inside thick evergreen bushes, out of the reach of the icy wind and hidden from the predators that hunted during the darkness of night.

Maka enjoyed the heat emitted by the hot spring as it kept her warm, but she would gladly trade it for the chilly night air if she could return to the cavern. She had no other choice but to wait for the old creature to leave.

It started to snow as the temperature dropped. The snow fell, wet and heavy, covering the tired old Mastodon in a blanket of white. The warm air, rising from the spring, quickly froze around the creature's eyelids and nostrils. Ice crystals formed on any exposed hair or flesh, of either beast or human, left open to the elements. The massive old patriarch seemed impervious to the cold as it rested in the warm water. Maka wondered if the aged creature would ever leave the tranquility of the hot spring.

The snow continued to fall deep into the night. The forest floor disappeared as the frozen precipitation amassed. The temperature steadily dropped as the hours clicked by. The beast did not move. On several occasions, it broke the silence of the night with a loud agonizing moan. The agonizing sound persisted throughout the course of the night.

The notion finally dawned on Maka that the old bull might be at the end of his days. The weary old giant must have journeyed to the spring for one last moment of warmth before succumbing to age and to the elements.

Maka felt deep compassion for the tired, weary beast as the tragic last stages of life played out right in front of her eyes. To see such a majestic creature, one that lived a life of power and struggle, reach its end was heartbreaking. Maka could feel the tears run down her face. Life is precious to every living thing no matter how advanced or primitive that life form may be. Death has a sobering finality to it.

The night seemed to last forever, as the old bull clung to life while Maka huddled in the corner of the hot spring. The loud moaning became less frequent as the night wore on.

Around daybreak, when the birds came out to announce the dawn, the noise stopped all together. Maka, now weary from the long, sleepless night in the hot spring, slipped back into the warm water of the pool. The warmth of the water was a welcome relief from the frosty air, but the lengthy time in the water was hard on her physically.

She crept closer to the lumbering beast until she could almost touch the giant Mastodon as it rested close to the bank of the hot spring. The long trunk and tusks of the giant gently rested on the ground outside the spring. The rest of the Proboscideans body lay submerged in the warm water. The old bull did not move or make any sound.

Maka quietly swam through the water towards the motionless beast. She did not know if it still lived or if it had died during the night. She was certain the old creature had perished during the night, but she still approached it with extreme caution. If it were still alive, it could kill her with one blow from its mighty trunk.

The old, somnolent, creature did not move. She swam closer to it sensing, by the position of its massive head, that the poor giant had lost its battle for life sometime during the night.

Deeply moved by the passing of the old tusker, Maka slowly swam up next to the deceased behemoth. She could not explain her profound feelings. It was just an animal, one from a time long ago, but she felt an overwhelming sorrow towards the passing life of the seasoned giant.

What a life the old bull must have lived, Maka thought. It was at least 70 years old as it visited the hot spring for the last time. The old beast spent decades visiting the hot spring to bask in its rich healing mineral water, but it would not leave the prolific waters of the pool this time. The dominant old bull more than likely lived, roaming this area of the world without fear for generations; yet in the end, age, the defining factor in all life, ended its reign.

Maka gently placed her hand on the now lifeless head of the old tusker. She placed her fingers between its eyes, eyes now unable to take in the natural world, and uttered an ancient Sioux prayer. She was helping the old bull's spirit pass into the next world. It was sad to see such a majestic creature, once full of life, now reduced to a tired mass of flesh, bone and hide. Such is the way of life though. The Mastodon's life had come full circle.

The Sioux native climbed out of the hot spring and retrieved her clothes. The morning air was frigid as the snow continued to fall. Maka, certain Tak would be searching for her at first light, rushed to the game trail to head back to the shelter. She was eager to return to the cavern. She retraced her steps back towards the shelter, finding herself at times, distracted in thought by the scene that had played out the night before.

Maka could not rationalize why the passing of the old Mastodon emotionally troubled her so. Death can be a strange catalyst into the realm of feelings and emotions. It can trigger a sense of vulnerability which in turn can create feelings of lack of insignificance. These feelings often fade with time, but if these emotions stayed just below the surface, the world would be a kinder place.

Maka moved through the forest with ease and urgency. The long night trapped in the hot spring without sleep drained her physically and the snowfall soaked her clothes. She needed to reach the shelter before the first stages of hypothermia set in.

The native beauty picked up the pace once she reached the familiar pathway just a short distance from the cavern. She came around a stand of trees and saw Canowicakte, the forest hunter, in front of her. She smiled at the now full grown Smilodon gracilis. The big cat met her in stride, rubbing its huge head on her leg.

"I'm glad to see you too," laughed Maka.

It was comforting to be close to home again, close to the security of the cavern. She was freezing in the frigid cold and wet clothing.

Canowicakte turned and led the way back towards the shelter. Takoda approached from the trail towards them.

"What happened? I've been worried about you all night," the Sioux native said as he smiled and gave Maka a huge hug.

"It was an incredible night but sad."

Maka explained to Tak the series of events as they had unfolded the day before. When she got to the point in the story of the old Mastodon, she broke down into tears. Takoda could see the strange incident deeply touched Maka. He told her they would journey to the hot spring the next day and try to pull the giant from the pool and lay him to rest on solid ground. They would take his tusks in honor of his life and display them in their shelter. It was all they could do.

Tak, thankful Maka was safe, took her into the cavern to warm up and get some food. Her body was very cold from the long, wet walk back to the shelter. Tak knew he needed to raise her body temperature. He threw more wood on the fire to create a large blaze which would heat up the inside of the cavern. It took hours to warm up Maka, but between the warmth of the fire and the hot water she drank, she was soon feeling better.

The next day, Maka and Tak traveled back into the forest to the hot spring. They left early in the morning, the fog and mist still hugging the dark forest floor. The forest was exceptionally quiet. The birds were silent.

The two natives walked silently through the trees towards the hot spring. When they came to the clearing, they both stopped just within the tree line. It was wise to use caution now. The death of the giant would have lured predators for a free meal.

Tak surveyed the opening and spotted the downed trees in the distance. The hot spring was on the other side of the dead fall, which blocked his view of the dead Mastodon. He motioned Maka to follow quietly. They moved out into the clearing silently progressing towards the dead fall and the hot spring. They both stopped when they reached the back of the dead fall. The old giant's lifeless body was on the far side of the deadfall, hidden from sight.

Tak decided to go to the right of the dead fall and not follow the game trail to the left. The grass was tall and wet from the snowstorm and morning frost. In some places, the snow from the earlier storm, still hugged the ground in the shaded areas. Tak and Maka slowly walked through the grass around the right side of the downed trees. They came to the edge of the debris. Tak put up his hand to signal Maka to stop. She stopped at his side as he pointed to the hot spring. The giant Mastodon was gone!

The old tusker had vanished. Tak and Maka moved to the front of the hot spring, where the old battle-scarred beast had succumbed to the elements and age. The only thing left of the massive beast were two long ivory tusks.

Maka, a look of total disbelief on her bronze face, turned to Tak and asked, "How can this be? It's impossible the massive creature could vanish in less than one day."

"I have no idea. There's no evidence of blood or hide, or anything. This is very strange indeed."

The two natives looked for any sign of carnage but found none. It was as if the beast had just disappeared into thin air, leaving behind two incredible ivory tusks. Tak searched for predator tracks in the mud and snow but found none. The only tracks he could find were smaller Mastodon tracks leading away from the hot spring which he could not explain.

Did the giant Mastodon journey to the natural hot spring intending to die in peace in the warm water and then be re-rejuvenated, leaving the spring an energetic, young calf? Had Tak and Maka found the fountain of youth? It was a preposterous thought but how else could they rationalize it. It was impossible that thousands of pounds of flesh could just vanish in one day. This was a mystery the natives realized they could never understand.

Tak and Maka could only carry one of the huge tusks at a time. They headed back to the shelter carrying the heavy load. Each tusk weighed a few hundred pounds, hundreds of pounds of pure ivory, rich snow-white color with the occasional black grain running in long vertical lengths.

The walk back to the cavern was an arduous one, the weight of the tusk straining their limits. They reached the shelter and placed the tusk on the ground in front of the cavern. Both decided to rest for a while before heading back for the second tusk. They went into the cavern and cooked up some lunch. Canowicakte as usual, appeared for lunch. The big cat, always ready for a free meal, rubbed up against Maka. This was the Smilodon's begging ritual.

After lunch, Tak went out to check on the two horses, Kohana, meaning "swift", and Ohitekah, meaning "brave", in Sioux. The two were finally becoming familiar with the scent of the humans and acted less nervous around them. They were becoming partially domesticated.

It was Canowicakte, one of their mortal enemies that they still feared. Certainly, Kohana had some experience in the wild with the large predator, watching as other herd members fell victim to the Smilodon. Ohitekah, the young stallion, was too young to have gained experience with the large cats. In the wild, they were natural enemies.

The two horses let the two natives advance and pet them now. They no longer displayed blatant aggression towards their human domesticators. This was a great sign. Tak would begin training them the next day. He made a primitive halter from some of the rope he still had left. His next step would be to get them familiar with the rope around their head. This would take several days, but Tak was confident he would be riding the mare within a week.

It was time to return for the second tusk. Maka and Tak, once again, set out for the natural hot spring, which they now dubbed the fountain of youth. The journey to the hot spring was uneventful. The sun was out but the temperature still only hovered around 55 degrees. Since their time in Pleistocene, the temperature stayed cold compared to modern Earth. Both were familiar with cold winters, but here, the weather seemed to stay the same with very slight variation. Storms were more frequent here, they lasted longer, sometimes for days on end. The natives were fortunate to have warm coats with them, but if forced to live in this time forever, they would need warm furs and skins to replace their modern clothes once they wore out.

Tak and Maka approached the hot spring once more, keeping completely silent as they rounded the dead tree fall. They quickly hoisted the massive tusk onto their shoulders, one end on Tak's, and the other end on Maka's. The second tusk was larger and even heavier than the first one.

The trip back to the cavern was a grueling one. They strained under the immense weight of the second ivory tusk, which forced them to stop several times to rest. In the end, they made it back to the shelter and placed the second tusk on the ground by the first one.

Worn out by the strenuous task, they entered the shelter to rest. They ate a small meal consisting of dried fish. Tak went out to check on the two horses, who seemed excited to see him, then he fortified the front of the corral and returned to the shelter to sleep for the night. Canowicakte bolted out of the shelter to roam the forest. The big cat liked to hunt during the cover of darkness, which offered greater stealth for the feline menace.

The next morning, Takoda was up early and working with the horses. It was time to break them. The stringy native worked with the mare Kohana first. She would be the main mode of transport for the Sioux native. Ohitekah, still young, would need added time to develop in both size and strength.

Tak, to show a positive projection of energy, entered the corral relaxed and calm. The native treated the animals with respect, a respect needed to achieve a relationship that was based on mutual cohesiveness. This method served him well in his many years of training and breaking horses. To Takoda it was the only method that would ensure a strong bond that would last for the lifetime of the relationship.

Kohana, the mare, was still very protective of her offspring. She put herself between Tak and the young stallion. Tak gently talked to both nervous creatures as he continued to walk towards them. His tone was soft and low which calmed down the horses. He had been in the corral several times before, but to this point had not tried to place a harness on either of them.

The horses did allow the natives to pet them, but they still dictated the terms of the relationship. It was time for this to change which meant the humans would have to break the will of the wild perissodactyls. Besides, in theory, these would be the first ever domesticated horses in the history of the Earth. Early humans, to this point in time, had not yet crossed into North America, via the land bridge across the Bering Sea. This would not happen for thousands of years. That was if Tak and Maka were in North America.

Takoda approached the mare, who was beginning to calm down in response to his soft non-threatening tones and movements. He touched Kohana on the muzzle and gently stroked the horse's jet-black flowing mane. The mare relaxed her deeply defined muscles and accepted the native.

Next, Tak slipped on the harness made of rope over Kohana's snout and around her head. The horse, confused by the new object, shook her head violently. Tak continued to gently coax the mare with his subdued tone until the beast relaxed. Kohana had accepted the harness.

Maka exited the shelter, walked to the edge of the corral, climbed up on the top rail and sat to watch the lesson. She marveled at Takoda's horsemanship. This was the first time she had the opportunity to witness Tak in action. The native was a natural when it came to training horses.

Tak placed the harness in this left hand and threw his right leg over the mare. He gracefully mounted the wild horse, and the struggle was on.

Kohana, feeling the weight of the human now on her back, bucked violently. This was the first time she ever experienced an intrusion like this. Normally, in the primitive horse's history, an attack like this meant a predator was intent on killing a member of her herd.

As Kohana's instinct kicked in, she thrashed wildly trying to dislodge the foreign intruder. She jumped high in the air, twisting her body and kicking violently. Tak held tightly on the reigns, while hugging the sides of the mare with his strong legs. He would not give up until the mare relinquished control and surrendered to his authority.

Kohana continued to thrust violently. Maka sat on the sidelines and laughed as Tak continued to flop around on the unwilling beast. She watched in awe as Tak moved with fluidity, countering the wild mare's moves perfectly.

Finally, after a good half hour, Kohana was exhausted. The strong-willed mare stopped thrashing and kicking. She stopped and stood motionless. Tak gently stroked her long black mane as he pulled on the reigns and commanded her to turn left and then right. Kohana responded with grace and agility.

The wild creature, Kohana, now domesticated, slowly walked to the edge of the corral. Tak and Maka were now true plains natives, ones with horses for transportation and a giant pet Smilodon for protection from other predators. Now they could explore a much larger region on horseback. They could search for new game and bring down larger prey with the aid of the horses.

A month passed before Takoda decided to break the young stallion. Ohitekah was now as big as his mother but with more detailed muscle tone. He was strong and independent. Maka rode Kohana daily and had taken possession of the fine mare. The two would go on long rides on the plains and sometimes deep into the forest.

Ohitekah, once broke in, would belong to Tak. The young stallion displayed enormous potential and Tak looked forward to running the young horse at full speed across the open plain. Takoda was confident the stallion would be exceptionally fast. He came from good stock. Soon both he and Maka would be able to ride across the plain in search of new prey for food and other necessities. Nothing would go to waste.

Tak approached Ohitekah in the same fashion he used to tame the stallion's mother. The beautiful tan stallion, now familiar with the humans was still apprehensive—as such a wild creature should be.

Maka rode the mare up to the stallion for support. She talked very quietly to the young stallion. Ohitekah appeared calmed by this so Takoda gently slipped the rope harness around his head and muzzle. He then hopped on the back of the strong beast and the contest began.

This time it took Tak an hour to subdue the wild creature. In the end, Ohitekah relinquished his independence and obeyed the native.

Over the next several weeks, Tak and Ohitekah made incredible progress and became inseparable. The horses were now content with their role as beasts of burden and in return received food, water, shelter and more importantly human affection and protection.

Kohana and Ohitekah even formed an odd bond with Canowicakte, who sensed the horses were part of the pack. This bizarre relationship would last the rest of their lives. In fact, Cano would never kill a horse like creature again in her lifetime.

Days, weeks, and months passed without any sign of the Extinctos. Tak and Maka moved on with their lives, sometimes enjoying and even preferring the solitude of the Pleistocene Epoch. They often wondered about Eric, Hope, Lexa, and CeCe. What had become of their old friends? Would they ever see them again? Would they ever go home again? Then these feelings would pass and life in the prehistoric era would take center stage once again.

It was a struggle to survive in the brutal cold climate at times, but there was also a tranquil peace which existed by living a less stressful life. The daily grind in the modern world to succeed and make a living seemed much more difficult than deciding on where to go hunting the next day in this time. Sometimes, the two humans contemplated staying in Extinctus, to live out their days just like their ancestors had lived for thousands of years.

Both horses were completely docile now. They had traded their independence for security and affection. This was beneficial for Tak and Maka, who could now travel greater distances to explore foreign regions for new game, new waterways, and different resources.

One morning they left the shelter and moved towards the hot springs. They wanted to stop by for a warm bath before starting out on a journey through the forest. This time they decided to travel beyond the forest past the hot spring. This was new unexplored territory for them.

Canowicakte led the way through the forest always on the lookout for approaching danger. Her keen sense of smell and hearing were priceless to the natives. The big cat could sense danger much earlier than the humans.

The group approached the hot spring and took the trail to the right. They quickly dismounted and removed their clothing and entered the warm water. The two horses quietly grazed on the tall grasses while Cano stood guard.

The warm water felt wonderful to the humans. It was a rare treat to take a bath.

"This water feels so good," replied Maka.

This was her first time back in the spring since the passing of the giant Mastodon months earlier. She often still wondered how such a massive creature could just vanish in one day.

"Yeah, this is great. We should make it a habit to travel here at least once a week now that we have transportation."

"That would be nice," Maka agreed.

The two humans swam in the refreshing water for around an hour then decided it was time to travel on. They dried off and put their clothes back on. This was the first time Takoda realized the natural beauty of Maka. She had long flowing black hair, soft smooth bronze skin, and was in incredible shape. Her muscles, deeply toned, added to her beauty. Tak, smitten by Maka's lovely presence, continued to gaze at her.

"What are you gawking at?"

Tak turned bright red as he turned his head away. He put his clothes on and mounted Ohitekah.

"We better get going."

Maka finished dressing and then mounted Kohana. She was ready to go.

"I'm ready," she said with a big smile.

The two humans followed Canowicakte back into the forest. The game trail led deep into the heavily treed, perpetual forest. Tak estimated they had about 8 hours daylight left which meant they would need to move at a faster pace if they wanted to return to the shelter before dark.

He nudged the stallion, and Ohitekah answered with a great burst of speed. Maka followed suit and soon was right behind the lead horse. They moved through the forest at a swift pace. The game trail was well defined and devoid of brush, so the fear of injury due to tripping was minimal. The denizens of the forest obviously travelled this path often.

The game trail continued, as it flowed through the forest, to new unknown territory. They had no idea where the trail would take them, but the urge to explore drove them on. They were free to move through the forest or out in the open now with the aid of the horses.

Maka and Tak, exhilarated by their new ability to expeditiously travel anywhere with the aid of the horses, exuded new confidence. The horses gave them a new unbridled freedom. They were confident they could outrun predators if threatened and explore lands far from the cavern and still return to its security by nightfall.

Canowicakte lead the way, always searching for danger ahead. If early humans did exist in North America, this strange band of travelers would certainly have perplexed them. They would have considered Tak and Maka mystical gods led by a feared Smilodon. It would be unexplainable to their primitive logical understanding.

Hours passed as the two humans continued to follow the trail until they reached a large clearing, where the tree line abruptly ended, opening to grass and shrubs. Cano ventured out onto the open plain but at once froze in alarm. The large cat's muscles were tense, and her ears pointed straight up and twitched. Something was coming.

Tak and Maka stayed on horseback in case they needed to turn and flee back into the forest. Kohana and Ohitekah were nervous. Kohana wheeled around and pointed in the direction that lead back into the forest. She stomped the ground with one of her hooves in warning. Something was coming from that direction too. The natives, trapped by approaching danger from two directions, huddled together with Cano out front.

Takoda and Maka prepared for battle. Tak unsheathed his hunting knife and pulled a spear from under his leg. Maka followed suit.

"You move to the prairie side and I will take the forest side," commanded Tak.

This would allow Maka to have Cano for added protection if an attack came from her side.

The natives switched sides and waited. The animals continued to communicate danger. Canowicakte crouched in a defensive posture, signaling a defined warning that danger was impending. Tak and Maka braced for attack.

"You're not going to kill us...are you?" replied a familiar voice.

It was Arcto, the giant short-faced bear, followed by Perris, the Perissodactyl, and Arc, the gargantuan tree. The Extinctos had returned.

"Boy are we glad to see you!" yelled Maka, the excitement clear in her tone.

"It has been a long time," answered Perris the horse Extincto.

Arc, the tree, stayed silent as usual, he did not talk much.

Arcto relayed a similar story to the one Creo had communicated to Eric and Hope. His story, full of greater details, astonished Tak and Maka. It had more detail compared to the condensed version Megalo portrayed months earlier. The two natives now understood the gravity of the situation. The fate of the human species was at stake. They would help in any way they could.

It was time to leave the Pleistocene for now. Arcto pulled out the short piece of ivory tusk, spoke, and they all vanished.

Chapter 29

Loss

Lexa, devastated by the loss of CeCe, felt the heavy burden of sorrow rush over her. It swept over her like an ocean wave, a wave of despair and looming solitude. Now left alone in a hostile world where one had to kill and risk death daily, Lexa wept for the loss of her dear friend, one she had grown very fond of over the last few months. Every day, this brutal world teemed with hidden, life threatening, danger. The type of danger which usually ended as a meal for some fearsome creature.

The Latino was a species out of time. How could she cope in this brutal world without the help of the big African American? CeCe provided her with companionship, conversation, and added power to combat the daily threats that occurred on a regular basis. The big man, a natural when it came to talk, could always cheer up the Latino lass with his sharp wit or his ability to twist a true tale into something more vivid, usually a departure from the actual truth. She would miss this trait the most. CeCe made this place better.

Lexa, in the depth of her despair, decided to journey back to the tree house on the other side of the bluff. She journeyed back towards the tree house, across the open plain, filled with deep, distracting, reflections of thoughts. Tears streamed down her soft cheeks in a steady flow symbolizing her sorrowful release of grief.

She returned to the tree shelter to retrieve a shovel she had engineered from hardwood saplings and rope. She used it to dig up roots to help fortify their diet, but now it would dig the final resting place of her dear friend CeCe Davis.

Lexa, lost in thought, climbed up the tree ladder and entered the shelter. The house seemed quiet and empty now. She sat in one of the corners of the shelter, burying her head in her hands as she gently sobbed. What chance did she have surviving on her own in this ruthless place?

She drifted off into a fitful sleep brought on by the emotional drain. She slept for two hours before a high-pitched shrieking sound jolted her to alertness. The sound pierced the quiet solitude of the tree house coming from above the treetops, as something flew over the tree house above the forest. She could not see the beast, but she heard the loud flapping of massive wings. The sound became less audible as the creature flew farther away from the shelter.

Lexa ran down the ladder to the forest floor below. She rushed to the forest trail which led her to the tree line. From the edge of the forest, she spotted a beast flying in the direction of the sea; in the direction where CeCe's motionless body still rested where it had fallen. There was no time to waste, she needed to get to the beach.

The Latino watched as the avian threat sped towards the sea. She sprinted out onto the plain, heading straight for the cliff above the sea. She still had a few hours before nightfall; the glowing orange sun just beginning to relinquish its blazing hold on the landscape.

Lexa reached the edge of the cliff, quickly scaled down the rope ladder, and jumped to the sandy ground. The sand was beginning to cool down from the long sweltering day. A cool, soft breeze blew in from the sea helping to lower the temperature around the bluff.

The Latino beauty raced towards the spot where she had left the motionless body of CeCe just hours earlier. Terrible thoughts raced through her mentally weary mind. She imagined horrid scenarios as she raced up the beach. Terrible predatory beasts might have eaten her friend or carried him away to gorge themselves on his alien flesh.

CeCe could be the first human ever preyed upon in the history of the Earth, but not if Lexa had any say in it. She would not let her friend become carrion for predators without a fight.

Lexa rounded a massive boulder strewn on the beach before she could see the spot where CeCe had fallen to his end. She heard a terrible shrieking sound coming from the area where CeCe's body laid motionless. She spotted the grotesque shape of the Dark Extincto, Odon, trying to lift CeCe's body from the beach.

The monstrous beast struggled with the weight of the big man as it tried to lift its quarry off the sand. Lexa quickly dropped to the sand, hiding behind a boulder. The hideous flying monster did not see her as it continued to struggle with the heavy weight of CeCe's body.

With one final powerful flap of its skin covered wings, Odon gained lift off and flew out over the sea with the lifeless body of CeCe firmly grasped in its flesh tearing talons, disappearing on the distant horizon.

Lexa watched the beast for as long as her sight allowed. Her dear friend was gone, carried away by the mutated monstrosity Odon.

CeCe Davis, friend to Lexa, Eric, Hope, Takoda, and Maka vanished that day in the cruel world of Extinctus.

It was with a heavy heart that Lexa once again climbed up the rock cliff to the top of the bluff. She scanned the horizon one last time in search of the monster Odon, the hideous flying creature, part Dimorph**odon** part Hyaen**odon**.

Odon vanished out over the vast sea, carrying her dear friend CeCe to his unknown gruesome end.

Lexa walked back to the tree shelter in silent thought. She found herself lost in thoughts, thoughts of CeCe's life. What would she tell Eric and the others? How could she tell them he was gone?

She reached the shelter and climbed up to the security of the tree house. She ate a small dinner consisting of roots and vegetation. Darkness of night fell upon the land as she fell asleep with a heavy heart.

There were no stars that night. Clouds blocked any light from reaching the floor of the Earth. The blackness of the night was a fitting end to a miserable day. Lexa, now all alone in a world without humans, would have to make her own way in the Paleocene Epoch. She knew her chances of survival on her own were poor, but she would not give up. She would fight on, supplying her own food, forging her own weapons, and protecting herself from all predators. How long she could survive would depend on her will and resourcefulness. She still clung to the hope that the Extinctos would return to lead her out of this nightmare.

It would take several weeks for Lexa to replace her feelings of despair that come with loss with the positive thoughts associated with CeCe. Overtime, her sadness, became replaced by laughter, as she remembered the good things about her friend. She would always miss her dear friend, but when she thought of him now, a big smile lit up her face. If nothing else, humans are resilient, and the passage of time can heal all wounds—it is one of the traits of being human. How other species deal with loss is an unknown mystery.

Lexa occupied her time with engineering projects. She developed an impressive water collection system to capture the daily rainwater that drenched the land several times a day. She used bamboo, which is hollow inside, to transport rainwater from the leaves of trees to collection vestibules. These she fashioned from gourds she found on the forest floor. Once the gourds dried out, she scooped out the insides and placed them inside the shelter and along the forest floor to catch the rainwater. This system provided her with an ample supply of fresh water.

She spent long hours cutting and shaping bamboo stalks into different length spears, using the long ones for throwing during the hunt and the short ones for hand to hand close encounters. She always traveled with her axe, the knife, and at least three spears, two for throwing at prey and one short one for defense against a close ambush attack.

Lexa explored the bluff region alone now, so it was crucial she stay on the alert and ready to defend herself in all situations. She could move in and out of the forest with great stealth, like many of the more elusive creatures she shared the territory with. She engineered small bamboo traps for killing smaller mammals. She hunted larger game with her spear and knife. If she could trap it, she could kill it.

Physically, Lexa was lean and muscular. Her soft skin, kept that way from using extract from the aloe Vera plant, became deeply bronzed by the rays of the sun. She was small in stature to begin with, and adapting to the rugged terrain, developed her into peak physical condition. The Latino could run for miles now and quickly vanish from sight in an instant, blending in with the foliage or scaling a nearby tree to avoid detection.

Lexa, now fully assimilated into the Paleocene world, spent countless hours studying the habits of the creatures that lived during this time, adapting to hunt them or learning to avoid them if needed. She was exceptionally well prepared to live out her days here without fear now. The scared, unsure Lexa after the loss of CeCe was gone forever. She was the top apex predator of the bluff now. Lexa killed only what she needed to live off for food. She killed only when necessary, for protection, trying to avoid detection at all costs. She had become the ghost of the bluff.

The months passed as life continued at its constant indifferent pace. Since the loss of CeCe, Lexa had not returned to the sea, but her desire to explore the sea region to harvest food was growing. The sea, the last region in her tiny hemisphere, the only place she had yet to fully explore, beckoned her. She wanted to visit the spot where CeCe had fallen before the horrid beast Odon carried him away. She needed to pay her respects to her old friend. This would be her priority when she returned to the beach.

Lexa was extremely curious about what types of sea creatures existed during this early time in the history on Earth. She really wanted to catch an early form of sea snake, so she could harvest its poison. She would tip her spears with this highly potent substance. It could kill quickly, helping her avoid possible physical injury while moving in for the final thrust of the spear or knife. Lexa searched for frogs as well but had yet to find any brilliantly colored specimens. Many species of the amphibians secreted poison to deter predators from attacking. Either poison would do.

She decided to journey to the sea one day. She gathered her weapons, placing each of them in a pile in the corner of the shelter, and loaded the contents of CeCe's backpack into her backpack. She would take his pack to hold any fish or food she found while on the trip. Her spears, the axe and the knife were razor sharp. She spent hours honing them with sharpening stones she had collected on her various explorations of the bluff. It helped pass the time. Lexa preferred to keep busy with various projects—they preoccupied her time. Once everything was ready for the trip, she settled down for the night.

The next morning, Lexa woke up to the sound of birds singing outside her shelter. She had several frequent visitors of the avian type. She enjoyed the giant woodpeckers the most. They helped keep down the resident insect population that relentlessly pestered all living mammals. In the warm humid climate of the Paleocene, insects thrived year-round. There was no escaping them, they filled every niche in every environment.

Luckily, Lexa still had some insect repellant left to help deter the tiny torturers. In the future, she would need to find natural reoccurring chemical compounds released by plants, to keep the pests at bay. The only relief came during the rain when flying insects were momentarily grounded. Insects were one consistent consequence of living in a world with a year-round warm, humid temperature.

Lexa sprayed on a layer of insect repellant then scaled down the tree ladder to reach the forest floor. She stopped to listen to the surrounding sounds of the forest. It was the unusual sounds that Lexa keyed on, not the normal everyday noises that she was familiar with.

Once content the forest sounds were normal, she headed for the open plain, stopping as was always the practice, at the tree line to survey the open grassland that stretched to the top of the cliff above the sea.

Spotting no evidence of danger, Lexa moved out onto the plain. She headed directly for her rope ladder to scale down to the beach.

The bronze Latino dropped the last five feet to the beach below. She stepped behind a large boulder to shield her from the sight of any marauding predators. Lexa visually searched the beach in both directions, looking for any sign of predators. Satisfied that no danger was in the general area, she moved onto the sandy beach and walked to the waves, as they gently rolled onto the sand.

The water felt good. It had been sometime since she had fully bathed. The urge to jump in the water overpowered her cautious nature, so she undressed and entered the sea. It was good to finally get completely clean. She dove under the waves, their power tossing her around like an article of clothing in a washing machine.

The sea was different from the ocean she was familiar with in her world. It had less salt. It was a balanced mixture of fresh water and saltwater.

Lexa could open her eyes under water without the stinging effects brought on by the salt. The clarity of the ocean was excellent. This allowed her great vision both below her and around her as she washed her body.

The diversity in fish species was staggering. She spotted hundreds of distinct types of fish, some swimming in schools while others swam alone. The sea could provide her with an endless new food supply. She would string up set lines along the beach and check them every other day to start. Then she would dry out the flesh and store it in her tree house for later use.

The sea was shallow, seeming to never deepen as she swam out farther. It seemed unusual, but everything about this place was unusual. She decided to return to the beach to grab a bamboo spear to try her luck at spear fishing. The fish were so plentiful, she was confident spearing one would be easy.

The bronze beauty walked out of the sea towards her pile of clothes, her backpack, and her weapons. She slipped on her clothes, which needed washing as well, and walked back into the sea.

Thirty feet from shore, a small coral reef ran parallel to the beach. Lexa decided this would be the best place to spear fish, so she swam out and dove down to the reef. She spotted a large bulky fish, some type of grouper, swimming along the reef unaware of her presence as she surreptitiously approached from above.

Lexa dove towards the unsuspecting fish, swiftly waylaying the creature before it realized the threat. She drew back her long spear, thrusting the sharp point into the giant between the gills. The heavy fish struggled as the spear tip struck flesh and cartilage. Lexa held on with all her strength until the last violent spasm of life faded from the fish. It was her first kill in the sea.

She swam back to the beach and walked up on the sand carrying her prize. She filleted the fish, throwing the guts back into the sea for some other aquatic organism to consume. She washed the fillets one last time in the sea then placed them in CeCe's backpack for the trip back to the tree house. It would be the first time she would dine on something taken from the sea. She would eat her fill tonight and dry out the rest for later.

Lexa turned and walked to the spot where the body of CeCe rested before the treacherous Odon discovered the fallen human and carried his motionless corpse out over the sea. She placed a makeshift grave marker by the spot, driving it into the sand with a rock. It was all she could do. This gave her some closure to the loss of her good friend CeCe. It would be a place to visit her dear lost friend if left isolated in the Paleocene for the rest of her days.

It was time to head for the rope ladder to climb back up to the top of the bluff, so Lexa said a final farewell to CeCe and walked back to the ladder. The sun was getting low on the horizon as she scaled the cliff wall and stood upon the edge of the bluff. She looked out over the sea. The orange light of the sun lit up the horizon. It was a beautiful scene—the waves slowly rolling over the shoreline and the orange blaze of the sun changing the color of the surrounding landscape.

The sea here was quite tranquil compared to the oceans in her time. The sea in this time was very shallow with small waves. Lexa was unsure if there were larger oceans out there, but she was content with the one in her world. She now had a solid source of protein, offered by the expansive variety of fish life that flourished in the sea.

Food and water were easily accessible here in her small paradise. It was the solitude that she worried about. The loss of CeCe left her all alone in this world. It would be millions of years before any human form would evolve in the world. Lexa, now the Queen of the Paleocene, was the sole human in this time.

Lexa started back across the open plain towards the edge of the forest. Preoccupied with thoughts of her solitude, she did not notice a lone creature moving along the forest edge to her right. It was the resident roaming beast Claenodon, the bear-like arctocyonid.

The primitive brute was on course to intercept Lexa before she could reach the tree line. Her scent had reached the nostrils of the brute which now quickened its pace.

Lexa returned to her senses, at once spotting the omnivore moving towards her. The Claenodon had short thick legs which made it a clumsy animal. Lexa's only hope rested on outrunning the slow-footed beast.

The Latino turned left and broke out into a full run. The Claenodon followed suit, reaching its top speed after a few moments. Speed was in Lexa's favor. She was a perfect human specimen which allowed her to run for hours without getting winded. The Claenodon was another story. The bulky beast could only run at top speed for a few minutes.

She easily outpaced the creature then angled back towards the forest. She slid into the cover of the trees, vanishing behind a giant Sequoia.

The Claenodon, exhausted by the short chase, slowed to a walk. It sniffed the ground trying to follow the scent of the human. Lexa stopped to watch it from a safe distance. She was confident she could easily outpace the brute again if necessary.

There was a loud burst of screeching coming from the forest. Lexa glided around the giant tree to gain better vision in the direction of the sound. It was a hunting pack of terror cranes. There were three of them moving slowly in her direction.

Lexa, trapped between the Claenodon and the terror cranes, moved up against the mighty base of the giant Sequoia. A light rain started to fall which helped conceal her scent. She moved from the tree and dropped to the ground to help conceal her body. The grass, long and thick, afforded some cover for her. Her small stature helped her hide in the grass.

She could hear the terror cranes approaching by the loud squawking they made. Terror cranes were very noisy creatures and easily detected from a distance. She could not see or hear the Claenodon which concerned her.

The terror cranes stopped at the edge of the forest to survey the plain. Lexa could see them from her hiding spot in the tall grass. They were on the opposite side of the tree. Two of the flock members were looking out over the plain while the third one turned and looked back into the forest.

Lexa continued to hold her position. The third terror crane turned back towards the meadow and walked closer to the giant tree. Lexa continued to stay calm, keeping motionless. The terror crane moved towards her hiding place. She silently withdrew her knife with her right hand while switching her spear to her left hand. She prepared to fight back.

The third terror crane moved around the tree. It peered down in the grass. It had a massive killing beak. Lexa poised for the attack.

The terror crane moved in, its large eyes sensing danger. Lexa jumped up and struck the crane in the chest with her spear. The creature let out a loud cry and dropped to the ground. Lexa's spear penetrated the heart of the killing bird.

The ghost of the bluff moved into the open to await the following attack by the other two members of the bird pack. The remaining two cranes fled out onto the prairie, alarmed by the attack on the third member.

Lexa rushed from behind the tree trying to hold her ground. She knew she could not outrun these beasts. The earlier attack, months ago, on her and CeCe taught her this valuable lesson.

Lexa faced in the direction of the plain, keeping her back to the trees. The terror cranes turned to look at the assailant, but quickly turned back to the open plain. They were confronting a more serious threat: the Claenodon.

The large bear–like creature reached the edge of the forest just as Lexa attacked the crane by the tree. It focused its attention on the terror cranes now. Lexa dodged behind the tree once more to watch the prehistoric battle. The two remaining cranes spread apart to meet the advancing attacker.

The Claenodon, the thick, coarse black hair on its back standing straight up to increase its threatening size, slowly approached the two cranes. It growled in extremely low tones while exposing long pointed, blunt fangs.

The terror cranes squawked back and forth in some primitive form of communication. One crane, the leader, lunged for the Claenodon by jumping into the air and landing on the back of the clumsy Claenodon. The Claenodon violently shook itself, trying to dislodge the crane.

The second crane moved in for a side attack, while the first crane continued to batter the bear–like beast with its large, powerful beak. It pounded the back of the Claenodon's head with heavy, sledgehammer like blows. Blood started to rush out of the head wound created by the incessant bludgeoning.

Lexa quickly realized the Claenodon, outnumbered, was no match for the giant killing birds. She moved out from behind the tree and pulled her spear from the dead crane. She moved towards the battle.

The second crane dashed in at the Claenodon, striking it on the side, which rolled the beast which in turn dislodged the first crane. Lexa stepped out of the tree line and thrust her bamboo spear with all her might at the second terror crane.

The spear hit the bird from behind, penetrating the backbone which caused the terror crane to turn and rush towards her. She could see the spear tip exiting the front of the crane as the mortally wounded killing bird ran towards her in a state of unparalleled rage, blood gushing from the mortal wound, turning the entire front of the beast bright red.

Lexa withdrew a second spear and held it out in front of her. There was no time to throw the spear. The crane was too close. She braced for the final attack. The terror crane, now within feet from Lexa, suddenly stopped, falling dead to the ground.

The terror crane leader rolled off the Claenodon and landed on its back side. This was the advantage the Claenodon needed, as it jumped to its feet. It leaped on the terror crane, still trying to re-gain its senses, with a heavy thud. The Claenodon gripped the crane's neck between heavy jaws and crushed the life out of the menacing flightless bird.

As the last terror crane fell lifeless to the ground, the Claenodon let out a tremendous roar that sent a chilling tingle up Lexa's spine. She turned to meet the victorious Claenodon. The beast stopped and looked at the fragile human warrior. It was the first time the bulky brute had seen such a species, which confused the dim-witted creature's tiny brain. tiny brain.

The Claenodon looked at Lexa and then at the dead crane at her feet. The beast was obviously conflicted by the urge to kill her, which would be the normal response, or to let her go.

Lexa reached down and pulled her bamboo spear from the body of the dead terror crane. She decided to follow the action of the Claenodon and screamed at the top of her lungs.

The bear-like beast cocked its head in bewilderment. Once again it looked at Lexa, then looked at the dead birds. Lexa slowly backed up towards the trees. The Claenodon watched her in confusion, then it knelt and began devouring the lifeless crane.

The Claenodon did not attack Lexa, Queen of the Paleocene. The battle ended with three dead terror cranes, three less deadly killers habituating the bluff. The outcome had been a mutually beneficial one. The Claenodon and the human both won that day. Lexa and the Claenodon reached a mutual benefit that day. Lexa wondered what would happen if they met again someday.

The bronze Latino entered the forest with the breast meat she harvested from the first kill. She left the rest for the Claenodon. It was getting late in the day, so she picked up the pace to get back to the tree shelter before dark. The day had been bountiful giving both fish and poultry.

She arrived back at the tree house while it was still light, quickly climbing up the tree ladder and entering the shelter. She started a small fire to cook some of the fish harvested from the sea and took a long drink of refreshing water. It had been an eventful day filled with adventure. She ate and quickly fell asleep. The night was quiet except for the sound of raindrops hitting the shelter roof. The water ran into her collection system, trickling through the lines to replenish her water supply. Lexa slept all night without interruption.

The morning light was just breaking when Lexa woke up. She heard a noise coming from below. She quickly grabbed her spear and went to the ladder. She peered down from the tree shelter.

"Are you going to come down?" a familiar voice spoke.

It was Bronto the Super Extincto.

Lexa, overwhelmed, rushed down the ladder to the forest floor. She ran up to Bronto and gave him a huge hug. Tears flowed down her soft, bronze cheeks. She turned and ran to Pith and Gorgo and gave each a large hug and a kiss. The two brutes grinned from ear to ear; the awkwardness of the reunion overcome by the necessity to interact.

Lexa was not alone anymore.

Chapter 30

Together Again

The massive Brontotheres surveyed the tree house resting high above the forest floor. The brute seemed astonished by the detail, the design, and the craftsmanship of the permanent home.

"Where is CeCe?" he asked as an expression of confusion crossed his face.

The massive Bronto, the giant Extincto with massive legs to match his huge body, looked concerned by the absence of CeCe. His Y shaped horn, thick and pointed, stretched a good four feet out from his nose.

Tears of joy changed to tears of sadness as Lexa relived the story of the loss of her dear friend. Bronto, Pith, and Gorgo all felt a sense of loss that day. They still felt responsible for the death of CeCe, even though Megalo had ordered them to leave the humans behind and recruit soldiers for the coming battle to save the human species. The Extinctos realized the dangers, but somehow, they wished they could have prevented the loss of CeCe.

The giant ape Pith seemed shocked by the loss. He remembered the time when CeCe roasted some meat from the Uintatherium and laughed when he burnt his mouth. A wry smile crossed Pith's lips as he turned and walked into the forest. The loss of CeCe profoundly affected the giant ape.

"That is sad news," Bronto said, keying on one part of the story; the part when Odon, the Dark Extincto, carried off the body of CeCe. "Are you sure it was the beast Odon that carried off CeCe?"

"I'm sure Bronto. CeCe and I were captured by Odon and Therio when we first arrived here, but we later escaped in the forest."

Lexa continued to tell Bronto of the strange events that had befallen her and CeCe since the Extinctos had left them months before. The giant listened intently, nodding occasionally. The stoic Brontotheres seemed impressed by the tree house and the detail that went into its construction. Bronto considered it an engineering marvel, one that surprised him and contradicted his belief that humans were a weak, unintelligent species.

Bronto moved towards the clearing, motioning for Lexa to follow. It was time to leave the Paleocene. Bronto, Pith, Gorgo, and Lexa walked to a small opening in the trees. Bronto pulled out a small piece of ivory gotten from some old Mastodon and spoke the words; Miocene Epoch 23 M-Y-A.

The four creatures vanished, moving through time in an instant, appearing 30 million years later in time, another time completely alien to Lexa.

They were now in the Miocene Epoch, a world of great biodiversity. Evolution had been busy over the last 30 million years. There were hundreds of thousands of new species roaming the world, a world that was violent, hostile, and unforgiving for humans. Savage carnivores both large and small stalked even larger ungulate forms. Danger lurked everywhere. The population of animals, exploding in comparison to the Paleocene, had continued to diversify. Nature had been busy. The percentage of conflict, with other species, had exponentially risen. Species were now dense in population and covered every niche of the planet.

Lexa wondered how any human could survive in this environment. The new carnivorous species in this place frightened her. Bronto led the way, followed by Lexa and Gorgo while Pith took up the rear. The colossus ape protected the group from a rear attack. Pith would stop occasionally; turn towards the direction they had come from and sniff the air for the scent of a potential predator. Once he was confident it was safe, he would grunt and turn back towards the group, quickening his pace until he caught up to the motley crew once again.

They traveled for what seemed hours. The group did not talk as they moved through the thick forest. They tried to be as quiet as possible, so they did not announce their presence to other creatures. It was hot and humid which brought out vast swarms of biting insects.

The lush vegetation slowed down the pace, as Bronto continually labored to cut a trail through the forest. He constantly searched for game trails to make the way easier to navigate as they pushed on. The insects persisted relentlessly, as they whizzed by the members of the group, sporadically landing on flesh to bite or sting.

The sweltering heat caused Lexa at times become dehydrated. They stopped whenever they found water to quench their thirst and to cool down by drenching themselves with the priceless liquid.

The band finally reached the edge of the forest, where the forest gave way to a vast plain. Far in the distance, Lexa could see a large bluff, rising above the valley floor. It jutted from the plain below, stretching to the sky.

"That's where we need to go," Bronto said as he pointed to the bluff far off in the distance.

"Is that where we'll see Eric, Hope, Tak, and Maka?" Lexa questioned.

Lexa was excited to see her friends again but dreaded telling them the story of CeCe.

"If they have arrived, you will see them," replied Bronto.

A new drive to reach the bluff engulfed Lexa. Her energy, now renewed by the anticipation of human companionship again, surged. Many months had passed since all the members of the camping party were together before parting ways and journeying into different time periods within Extinctus.

Bronto led the way out onto the plain. There were several herds of odd-looking ungulates, both small and large. Some had bizarre horn patterns, as these jutted out in all directions from the skulls of the beasts. Some were gargantuan, standing over 20 feet tall. Strange carnivores followed the grazing herds looking for any opportunity to pounce on any unsuspecting, weak straggler.

The band continued for hours until they reached the base of the bluff. It was late in the day as the early shadows of dusk began to fall on the walls of the bluff. The group found a small cave at the base of the cliff that had the left-over ashes of a fire pit, obviously used by humans. Gorgo and Pith walked off to investigate the surrounding area for any sign of danger—Bronto stayed with Lexa.

"In the morning, we'll search for a way up the cliff to the top of the bluff," Bronto told Lexa.

Lexa smiled at Bronto and asked, "Is it safe to stay down here tonight?"

This time teemed with life, which put fear into the Latino's heart. The possibility of conflict seemed a probability here. The number of species skyrocketed in the Miocene compared to what the Latino was accustomed to during the Paleocene.

"It'll be as safe as anywhere."

"I hope you're right."

Lexa was eager to see her friends again. She could only imagine the hardships that had befallen the other members of the camping group over the last months. Life in the Paleocene had been brutal on her and CeCe with many trying moments, but it also had been an exciting adventure. She was eager for human companionship again and looked forward to talking with Hope and Maka the most. They all shared a common bond that made them all great friends. It would be nice to see Eric and Tak once more as well. Humans tend to be more comfortable in groups. Increase the human number, fear dwindles, and courage soars.

It was with renewed optimism, the type that springs from anticipation, that Lexa quietly laid down to sleep with that night. She would rely on Bronto, Pith, and Gorgo to keep her safe.

Bronto stayed with the human for the night. It was the first time any of the Extinctos ever used the odd ivory to keep themselves in the bi-pedal form at night. The ivory was extremely rare, only used in emergency situations. Pith and Gorgo returned to the forest for the night, to live as they normally would—in beastly form. The night came and went without incident.

Bronto, up with the first light, watched as Pith and Gorgo returned from the forest. After discussing the options to navigate the cliff, Pith went off to find a way up the cliff, while Bronto and Gorgo waited for Lexa to wake up. The Latino beauty, hearing the commotion, popped up. She was eager to see her friends.

"Are we ready to go?" she asked.

"Pith is searching for a way up the bluff," responded Gorgo.

The huge therapsid, rarely spoke.

Lexa walked along the base of the bluff, in the opposite direction taken by the giant ape. Within moments, she came to the ladder built by Eric and Hope. The ladder, now overgrown with vines, was difficult to see.

Lexa shouted to the others, "I have found a way up."

The Extinctos quickly came to the base of the cliff wall and looked up. Lexa pointed to the ladders that ran up the side of the bluff.

"How do we get to the first ladder?" questioned Bronto.

The massive Brontotheres looked up at the first the ladder, now covered in overgrown vines.

Lexa looked at the rope ladder and then at the Extinctos.

"You three are tall enough to jump to the first ladder without difficulty."

The Extinctos agreed with simple nods. Pith jumped up with ease, grabbed the bottom of the first ladder, and quickly scaled the cliff wall. Within minutes, the giant ape was standing on the top of the bluff.

Gorgo followed Pith and although he lacked the grace and fluidity of the ape, he too was soon standing on top of the bluff waiting for Bronto and the frail human.

Lexa watched as Gorgo climbed to the top of the bluff. The first ladder was 20 feet from the base of the cliff, which was out her reach. Lexa looked in both directions. She could climb on Bronto's tremendous shoulders, and the beast could carry her, or she could find another way up.

Bronto looked at the human and motioned for her to climb on his back. Lexa walked back towards Bronto. Just before she reached the big beast, she noticed a tunnel that ran up from the base of the bluff.

"I can get up here," she shouted to Bronto.

Bronto nodded then jumped to the first ladder and slowly began to scale the bluff. He was an enormous, thick creature, a creature of tremendous bulk. His actions were deliberate and slow as he scaled the cliff wall.

Lexa crawled into the tunnel, exiting just below the first rung of the rope ladder. She cautiously climbed from ledge to ledge using the rope. It took her longer to reach the top of the bluff, but she soon stood on the top with the Extinctos.

The group looked out over the immense valley. The view from on top of the bluff was staggering, as the plain stretched for miles until it reached the forest, the forest from which Lexa and the Extinctos had journeyed from. Earth, although extremely dangerous during this period, was beautifully overgrown with plants, trees, and animals. The atmosphere was rich in oxygen.

Pith now led the way into the forest on top of the bluff, followed by Lexa and the two remaining Extinctos. The band traveled a short distance until they found a cabin nestled in the trees. It was the home of Eric and Hope.

Lexa marveled at the well-designed construction and the quality workmanship of the cabin. It was sturdy and strong, solidly built to hold up against the giant beasts that lived in this time.

Lexa called out, "Is anyone home?"

She walked towards the door, enthused to see her long-lost friends. Months had passed since they last saw one another. Were they all still alive?

A series of loud growls started from within the cabin, causing Lexa to take a few steps back from the door as a precaution. The growling continued to increase in intensity until she heard a familiar voice call for the growling beasts to quiet down.

The door of the cabin flung open and two massive dog-like creatures bolted out of the cabin, stopping directly in front of Lexa and the Extinctos. Amp and Shai, now fully-grown bear dogs, over eight feet long and weighing over 1000 pounds glared at the unfamiliar trespassers.

Bronto stepped in front of Lexa and held out his huge arms to signal the beasts to stop. The bigger male bared his long canines as the hair along his muscular back stood up. He was about to lung when a voice broke the morning air.

"It's ok Amp and Shai," spoke Hope, smiling as she moved towards Lexa.

"It's you!" screamed Lexa, overjoyed to see her friend.

The time apart had given them plenty to discuss. Both had endless questions to ask.

Overwhelmed by the moment, Hope and Lexa embraced as tears of joy flowed down their tanned, weathered cheeks.

"Where's Eric?" Lexa asked.

The elated Latino looked behind Hope into the cabin but did not see her Nordic friend Eric.

"He's out with Arti surveying the valley on the other side of the bluff."

Lexa nodded and pointed at the two bear dogs with a puzzled expression. It was the first time she had seen such magnificent creatures, creatures impressive this close.

"What are those?" Lexa asked as she marveled at the two obedient bear dogs.

"This is Amp and Shai, our loyal pets."

Lexa went up the two giant bear dogs and gently introduced herself. Amp and Shai accepted her as one of their pack members, softly licking her hand in acceptance.

"The Dark Extinctos are setting up a war camp on that side of the bluff," Hope explained. "There's a great valley, a valley of forest divided by a large river on that side of the bluff. Eric and I journeyed to it on one occasion, but it was just too dangerous for us to explore. The carnivorous predators are vast and hunt in large packs, so we thought it best to avoid that area."

Hope then went up to Bronto and gave the massive Brontotherium a giant hug followed by a big kiss. The brute blushed in the awkward moment and smiled. She then followed suit with Gorgo and Pith. Pith giggled like a small child at the alien expression of affection. He then went to the edge of the forest and disappeared. Gorgo the older more ancient species just shrugged off the incident.

"Where is CeCe?" questioned Hope, not seeing the big man arrive with the group.

"CeCe is gone," replied Lexa, as she looked away from her friend.

Tears started to flow as Lexa relived that sorrowful day again. She knew the day would come when she would have to tell the others about the fate of CeCe, but this did not make the task any easier—the scar of painful loss heals slowly, just below the surface, waiting to surface through the emotions.

"What is it?" asked Hope, sensing the anguish in Lexa's voice and seeing the sorrow in her deep brown eyes.

"CeCe fell off a cliff, hitting his head on the beach below," sobbed the Latino.

Once Lexa regained her composure, she continued, "The Dark Extincto, Odon, carried him off before I returned to bury him. When he fell, I didn't feel a pulse when I checked it several times, so I tried to resuscitate him without success. I returned to the shelter to get a shovel to bury CeCe with, but when I returned, the Dark Extincto Odon was carrying him off. I am most certain CeCe died from his injuries."

"That's terrible," replied Hope as she came and hugged her friend to console her. "It must have been awful for you to experience such a horrific loss all alone."

A blank stare overcame Hope as the grave news sunk in. She cried for the loss of her friend while trying to console Lexa. The loss of his good friend CeCe would deeply affect Eric, and she dreaded telling her best friend the fateful news.

Bronto and Gorgo informed the humans they had to leave. The two behemoths needed to begin the process of assembling the army to help support Megalo in his effort to save Homo sapiens. All the Extinctos traveled for several months to recruit allies to help battle Thylac and the Dark Extinctos. It was time to bring these supporters to this time.

The conflict to save the human species loomed on the horizon. The two giants said their goodbyes, left the cabin, then vanished into thin air. Pith stayed to help Arti protect the humans.

Hope and Lexa walked into the cabin to continue sharing the experiences that had befallen them both over the last few months. Amp and Shai stayed just outside the open cabin door to protect the women and to signal any approaching danger. Both bear dogs were full grown, each capable of inflicting great injury if needed and together both formed a formidable pack, capable of taking down large prey or predator.

Hearing the boisterous growls of the bear dogs, the giant ape Pith returned. The growls brought Hope and Lexa out of the cabin again to see the newest commotion. The two women gazed into the forest directly behind Pith as the hominid approached.

Takoda, Maka, Arcto, Perris, and Arc exited the forest and walked towards the cabin. The two natives had returned.

Amp and Shai continued to growl excessively, ignoring Hope's instruction to stop. The bear dogs still sensing danger, continued to pace back and forth.

Hope saw a large Smilodon cat following Maka and behind the large carnivore followed two magnificent horses. The group continued to make its way out of the forest and into the clearing in front of the cabin.

"It is us!" yelled Tak who was excited to be in the company of other humans once again.

Hope and Lexa shouted back to the party, as they walked closer. Amp and Shai stood directly in front of Hope and Lexa, protecting them from the intrusion by the motely band of misfit creatures.

Hope reassured the overzealous pets everything was okay which calmed down the overly protective bear dogs. The group shared hugs and Maka introduced Canowicakte to Amp and Shai. Initially, the introduction was intense, but after a few moments, the big cat and the giant bear dogs reached a common ground, the humans, and tolerated each other.

The two horses, Kohana and Ohitekah, stayed nervous around the two Amphicyon galushai. It would take a considerable amount of time before they would feel safe around the huge beasts. It had taken a long time for them to except Cano months earlier.

"It seems like it's been forever!" shouted Maka.

"Always the last to show up," answered Lexa, as she had a good laugh.

"'We're together again at last," Hope chimed in.

The group shared hugs as Hope introduced the bear dogs Amp and Shai to the group. Once finished, they decided Tak and Pith would journey to find Eric and Arti, while Creo and Perris would journey to assemble the army. The giant tree Arc would stay and watch over the humans.

The Extinctos spent many months recruiting species to help stop Thylac, now it was time to assemble them. Creo and Perris said their goodbyes and returned to the plain to vanish in time. Arc planted his deep roots into the soil in front of the cabin and went silent.

Hope, Lexa, and Maka went inside the cabin to prepare food and swap tales. They would make up a splendid meal for everyone in the group. They did not know when Eric would return, but they wanted to be ready.

Lexa told Maka of the tragic loss of CeCe. The native Sioux chanted a small prayer for her friend and started to weep.

Takoda departed with Pith soon after arriving, so he stayed unaware of CeCe's demise. The distraction, while journeying to scout out the opposing army, could leave Tak preoccupied with thoughts of grief instead of focusing on the many dangers the Miocene posed.

The women decided to wait until everyone was re-united before re-living the perilous adventures each had experienced over the last few months. All had life or death situations and many hardships, hardships that included near death struggles with predator attacks, shelter building, and just getting basic food supplies.

Takoda and Pith journeyed to the far side of the bluff, stopping to survey the vast valley below when they reached the edge of the sandstone cliffs. The thick forest, intersected by a large river, grew for as far as they could see.

Tak found the trail that ran down the bluff, obviously used by Eric and Hope to access the valley floor. He surveyed the valley until he spotted a large encampment to his right which looked out of place. It had to be Thylac's army, Tak assumed.

"I think that's where we need to go," Tak said to Pith as he pointed towards the camp in the distance.

The giant ape just shrugged his broad shoulders while shaking his gigantic head in agreement.

Pith scaled down the bluff wall with ease, while it took Tak a great deal of time to navigate the face of the bluff. He climbed down cautiously to avoid injury or death from a fall. Pith waited patiently for the native to reach the floor of the valley.

The base of the bluff, scattered with fallen rocks and brushy overgrowth, offered a suitable place for Tak and Pith to hide. Tak, once he reached the valley floor, motioned for Pith to follow. The giant ape lumbered behind the human as they silently weaved their way along the base of the bluff. Trekking out into the forest could be potentially perilous. The boulders afforded them some concealment. They walked for a couple of hours before they came upon Eric and Arti huddled behind a large boulder for protection.

"We have found you," whispered Takoda.

Eric turned and saw Tak and Pith coming towards him and Arti. Arti acknowledged Pith and Eric.

"Tak," Eric replied, his tone quiet to avoid detection.

The two hugged each other. It had been some time since they had been in each other's company. Eric was glad to see his old friend once again.

"What are you looking at?" Tak asked Arti and Eric.

"We've been surveying Thylac's camp for a couple days now. There are some very unusual creatures showing up," Eric answered.

Pith and Arti spoke briefly until the ape moved out from behind the boulder and vanished into the forest. Pith was always straying off on his own—it was in his nature.

Arti pointed in the direction of the camp which spread out for 3 miles, running along the edge of the forest on one side, and the river on the other.

Eric pulled out his binoculars and pointed them in the direction where Arti was pointing. After a few moments, Eric found his range and spotted a huge, cruel looking beast moving through the area, stopping at each camp of species to briefly welcome its warriors.

The wandering brute, a large stabbing cat with stripes running down its backside, stood over 15 feet tall. The creature had an enormous head with two lengthy sabers that fell below its jaw line. The two sabers, when the beast closed its jaw, slipped into sheaths that dangled down its neck on both sides of its tremendously large head.

The beast horridly astonished Eric as he continued to gaze on in fascination. He recognized the beast at once—it was the Dark Extincto **Thylac.** The beast was part **Thylac**ine, or Tasmanian tiger, and **Thylac**osmilus, a marsupial saber-toothed cat that evolved in South America around two million years ago. Thylac displayed the stripes of the Thylacine and supported the enormous head, suited with the unmistakable sabers of the Thylacosmilus. Eric could not believe his eyes.

Eric handed the binoculars to Tak, so the native could see the menacing creature. Tak looked towards the camp and spotted Thylac, as the beast roamed from campsite to campsite.

"That's one ominous looking beast," Tak gasped as he shook his head in disbelief.

"That is Thylac," answered Eric.

Tak handed the binoculars back to Eric, who at once returned to spanning the camp again. He spotted three more of the bipedal Dark Extinctos on the far side of the encampment. One was the terrible beast Odon, the flying menace part Dimorphodon and part Hyaenodon. Odon, the reptile skinned creature, had a dog-like head filled with razor sharp incisors. CeCe and Lexa saw this visually morbid brute in person, seeing it change from an Entelodont, the massive hell pig, into the flying demon.

The second Dark Extincto was **Therio**, the **Therio**dont, a primitive mammal like reptile from millions of years earlier in time. It had a thick, tuff, grey hide spattered with infrequent patches of hair. Therio wielded a large head and jaw, a jaw filled with bone crushing teeth. He too was very cruel looking like Thylac and had the indifferent emotional tendencies associated with reptiles.

The third Dark Extincto, later to be known as **Carni**, was from the family of animals known as **Carni**vora. This beast manifested itself in the form of Osteoborus, a hyaena-like carnivore that roamed the Earth in packs during the Miocene. This beast was brownish grey in color with spots that were black. Carni had an enormous head that supported a vice like jaw filled with strong incisors.

There were several other Dark Extinctos scattered around the large camp, but Eric could not see them through the binoculars. They were too far away, out of the capable distance of his binoculars, or his vision became obstructed by some other giant creature that blocked his line of sight.

Multiple groups of species inhabited the encampment. Each had its own area, which Eric figured was an attempt to ward off conflict between rival species. Eric handed the binoculars to Tak once again, so his friend could see the bizarre army unfolding in the valley.

The group, both terrifying and impressive, continued to grow in species throughout the day as more species arrived in the valley. Thylac and his Dark Extinctos had assembled a massive brutal army of terrifying creatures, some set on revenge, others opportunity, and some out of fear of Thylac.

"I hope Megalo has a strong army to take on this motley bunch," spoke Eric, seeing the convergence of a tremendously dangerous army coming in support of Thylac.

"We have spent months recruiting our army," replied Arti.

The colossal Artiodactyl, with his long snout filled with row after row of dagger like teeth, assured the humans that Megalo would amass an equally strong army.

Tak handed the binoculars back to Eric. The group decided to move closer to the camp to log the types of species fighting for the extinction of humans. Eric, convinced the number of species wanting to wipe out mankind vastly outnumbered ones wanting to help save it, was gravely unsure of the Light Extinctos odds of succeeding.

Humans were the cause of the extinction of countless species in just the brief time span since evolving on the planet. If Thylac was successful, many of the species would return to the current time on Earth. Most, however, faded from Earth due to climate change, de-forestation, or because they did not evolve fast enough to keep up with other evolving species. It was these creatures that Megalo hedged his recruitment on.

Pith re-joined the group as they moved through the boulders to get closer to the camp. They reached the end of the bluff and stopped. Eric peered through the binoculars until he spotted a small band of humans. They were shorter than modern humans but much heavier built. They wore animal skins for clothing and carried primitive weapons.

The primitive humans had large protruding foreheads, which convinced Eric they were Neanderthals. It made sense now. If the species Homo sapiens vanished from Extinctus, it is conceivable that the Neanderthal species would have filled the niche left by the departure of the modern human. Neanderthals vanished around 35,000 years ago, about 5,000 years after Homo sapiens appeared on the scene. Thylac's evil plan was now clear.

The dark cloud of the war to save the human species, as we know it, was looming on the horizon. The loss of the modern human would alter the course of the modern world forever.

Eric and Tak both now realized the significant complexity of the battle for Earth. This war would decide the fate of the human species on Earth.

Eric handed the binoculars to Tak once again. The Sioux native took the glasses and pointed them at the primitive humans. He slowly looked at the small group of primitive humans, moving the binoculars from one human to another. He focused in on the last human in sight who was standing in center of a large circle of the early hominids. This human stood a couple of feet taller than the Neanderthals. Tak focused on the taller of the primitive humans. The early human, covered in animal skins, the skins of some unfortunate creature, walked out into the open. Tak at once dropped the binoculars in astonishment.

"It's CeCe!" the confused native shouted.

Chapter 31

Out of Journal

The journals, notes, and drawings ended as abruptly as the visit from the hairless white hominid, manifested as the blue orb. The emergence of CeCe Davis in the encampment of the sinister Thylac confirmed only that CeCe Davis, now a member of an extinct Neanderthal tribe, had betrayed his camping comrades for some reason unbeknownst to Eric and the other members of the group.

Would my brother Takoda and the other humans take part in the battle between the Light Extinctos and the Dark Extinctos? What help could they be against monstrous beasts capable of inflicting horrific, brutal savagery.

I hoped the protective bear dogs Amp and Shai alongside the stealthy Smilodon gracilis, Canowicakte would stay close to the humans and help fight off the more hideous monsters in Thylac's army like Odon and Therio. At least these three protectors gave the humans a better chance of survival in hand to claw battle.

A strange fear gripped me as I finished the journal. It was entirely possible the war was over, and the humans might already be dead. Yet I was still here.

As I closed the last page of the journal, I now had more questions than ever. What happened to CeCe to cause him to switch sides and betray his loyal friends? What was the outcome of the battle between Megalo and the Light Extinctos and Thylac and his twisted Dark Extinctos? Had the war started yet? Could I vanish at any time if Thylac completed his evil plan?

The tale, filled with adventure and peril, fascinated me. I experienced a wide range of emotions, which included both sorrow and happiness, for the humans as they each struggled to survive in the hostile yet beautiful stages of the Earth's evolution—the periods on Earth they found themselves thrust into.

The story, filled with emotional hardships, rich in adventurous expeditions throughout the vast history of Earth, left my head reeling from the expanse historical knowledge woven into the framework of its incredible narrative.

I interpreted the events from the journals and drawings contained in the weathered, leather pouch as well as I could. The records, meticulously kept by the humans, filled with descriptive detail and accuracy, reflected and recorded the fate of not only the six humans, but the Super Extinctos as well.

The fate of Eric, Hope, Takoda, Maka, Hope, and even CeCe Davis, as they learned to adapt to the hostile world of Extinctus, facing daily struggles to survive while escaping the constant threat of death, filled the pages of the journals.

The fate of the six humans in Extinctus, still unknown, ended with the last pages of the journal. I ran out of story-telling material, so I placed the journals and notes back into the weathered leather pouch as I shook my weary head. I could only wait on the delivery of more material to continue the mysterious tale.

I hoped, since I was still alive and on Earth, that both Megalo and his army were successful in defeating Thylac, or the battle had yet to occur. The fate of humans, unknown at this point, still either hung in the balance, or Thylac's bid at human re-extinctification failed. I truly hoped the latter was the case.

Without further knowledge and evidence to either of these scenarios, the burden and heavy weight of the possible inevitable erasing of humanity, allowed fear to creep into my mind, and I realized I could vanish at any moment.

The journal offered the only record to the fate of the six humans but was unfinished. Were they all still alive? Did the war for the humanity begin? Was it still raging inside of Extinctus? What happened to CeCe?

I had no idea when the blue orb would return with more journals, but I remained confident that when the time was right, the hairless, white, hominid would return to pass on the continuing saga waging inside Extinctus. I could only wait until that day arrived.

If Homo sapiens vanished inside Extinctus, none of it would matter anyway.

My name is Fire Eagle, brother to Takoda Fire Eagle and I will not rest until my brother returns to us or we all vanish from the face of the Earth forever.

The End

References

Amson, E., & Laurin, M. (2011). *"On the affinities of Tetraceratops sinsignis, and Early Permian synapsid".* Acta Palaeontologica Polonica. 56; 301–312.

BOOKS, P. F.-L. (1966). *The Land and Wildlife of North America.* New York: Time Inc.

Evolution: Change: Deep Time. (2017, 4 9). Retrieved from http://www.pbs.org/wgbh/evolution/change/deeptime/miocene.html

Evolution: Change: Deep Time. (2017, 4 9). Retrieved from Evolution: Change: Deep Time: http://www.pbs.org/wgbh/evolution/change/deeptime/pleistocene.html

Group, D. L. (1985). *The Field Guide to Prehitoric Life.* New York: Facts on File, Inc.

Macdonald, D. (n.d.). *The Velvet Claw: A Natural History f the Carnivores.* BBC Books.

Paleocene mammals of the world. (2017, 4 9). Retrieved from http://www.paleocene-mammal.de/multis.htm

Paleocene mammals of the world. (2017, 4 9). Retrieved from http://www.paleocene-mammals.de/condylarth.htm

Paleocene mammals of the world. (2017, 4 9). Retrieved from http://www.paleocene-mammals.de/predators.htm

Wikipedia. (n.d.). Retrieved from Wikipedia : https://en.wikipedia.org/w/index.php?title=Paleocene&oldid=745709499

Wikipedia. (n.d.). Retrieved from Wikipedia encyclopedia: "https://en.wikipedia.org/wiki.org/w/index.php?title=Eocene&oldid=743123255"

Wikipedia. (2017, 1 14). Retrieved from Wikipedia: https://en.wikipedia.org/wiki/Even-toed_ungulates

Wikipedia. (2017, 1 14). Retrieved from Wikipedia: https://en.wikipedia.org/wiki/Amphicyon

Wikipedia. (2017, 1 14). Retrieved from Wikipedia: https://en.wikipedia.org/wiki/Cenozoic

Wikipedia. (2017, 1 4). Retrieved from Wikipedia: https://en.wikipedia.org/wiki/Cenozoic

Wikipedia. (2017, 6 14). Retrieved from Wikipedia: https://en.wikipedia.org/wiki/Pleistocene

Wikipedia. (2017, 1 14). *Gorgonopsia.* Retrieved from Wikipedia: https://en.wikipedia.org/wik/Gorgonopsia

Printed in the United States
by Baker & Taylor Publisher Services